A
Kendell
Mountain
Reunion

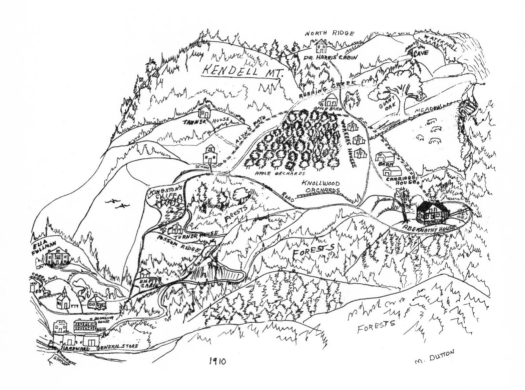

A Kendell Mountain Reunion

Final novel of the
**Kendell Mountain
Trilogy**

Marian Denman King

Hillsboro Press
PROVIDENCE PUBLISHING CORPORATION
FRANKLIN, TENNESSEE

Printed in the United States of America

06   05   04   03   02   1   2   3   4   5

Library of Congress Catalog Card Number: 2002110439

ISBN: 1-57736-275-6

Cover illustration by DORI—Betsy Dority Collins

Cover design by Gary Bozeman

HILLSBORO PRESS
an imprint of
Providence Publishing Corporation
238 Seaboard Lane • Franklin, Tennessee 37067
800-321-5692
www.providencepubcorp.com

This third Kendell Mountain book
is dedicated to all those dear readers who kept after me
to continue the story. Without their prompting, it would never
have been done. Thank you for nudging me into sitting
down and fighting with the computer again. Also, without
my son, Scott (the computer expert), the whole thing
would have gone out into oblivion!

Preface and Acknowledgments

MY HEARTFELT THANKS GO TO DARLENE CHASTAIN, who again came through for me with her expert editing. I had put dots where they should not have been and failed to use the tab, causing everything to get all jumbled up. She knew how to format everything, and I really do not know what I would have done without her assistance.

I am grateful to Martha and Royce Currie, who were fed several chapters per week to read and find the errors. This saved me a world of time.

With the assistance of my son Scott, Darlene, Martha, and Royce, my third book, *A Kendell Mountain Reunion*, is now a reality. Thanks a million! I know everyone will enjoy this light, happy story with some witty characters.

A
Kendell
Mountain
Reunion

Characters

Alyn Russell—Main Character

Dr. John Russell—Alyn's son

Teresa Russell—Alyn's daughter

Penny, Al, Peter (Pete), Susan—The Russell grandchildren

Beth Russell—Widow of Charles Russell and mother of grandchildren

Dr. Nathaniel (Nat) O'Bryan—Dentist

Raymond O'Bryan—Nat's father

Tissy Russell—Widow of Alyn's Uncle Bob and the principal of Kendell Mountain School

Ryan Ratcliffe—Student at the school

ON CENTRAL AVENUE IN AN OLD SECTION OF Pennsylvania's midtown many miles from Kendell Mountain in north Georgia, a young boy, Ryan Ratcliffe, was leaning with one foot propped up behind him against the brick wall of an empty building. His mind at the moment was busy, trying to decide just what he should do. Everyone had been pushing him, insisting that he needed to do this or that, when his mind was yet unsettled as to what actually felt right. No one seemed to understand him! His grades were not good enough for any college to accept him. His so-called friends taunted him, and his family did not have the patience to offer any help. It was always "just do this or do that," never thinking of what Ryan actually wanted. The man he met in the park today told him that he could make Ryan rich without going to college, and he would supply Ryan with joints for his personal daily use to boot. All he had to do was sell the quota the man named. "It would be easy as falling off a log," so the man told him. Ryan had never been into drugs, therefore selling them held no interest, even for the money. His conscience would not allow him to do that.

Ryan was no dummy. He did not want to be pushed into anything or bossed around. Whatever he did had to feel right. His parents, Patrick and Caroline Ratcliffe, said if he did not make it to college, then he would have to join the military forces. No son of theirs was going to slop around and be a bum or work selling burgers in a fast-food shop. These were the exact words of Patrick Ratcliffe: "And if you are ever caught doing drugs, you will go into the military for certain."

3

Since the sixth grade, Ryan had borne the brunt of taunts from his so-called friends. A boy had snatched a test paper from Ryan's desk and copied his work. And when the boy would not return the paper, Ryan reported the incident to the teacher. The cheater was given an F on the test, and he and his cohorts immediately changed Ryan's name to "Rat," which followed him even throughout high school. The students who did not know about the incident figured that the name was shortened from his last name, Ratcliffe. The nickname stuck and everyone called him Rat. Just now he felt like a rat . . . low-down and worthless.

Now, standing in front of the vacant building in downtown Philadelphia, Ryan wondered what he should do next. He noticed an empty beer bottle lying in the gutter beside the street. To him, it was not a beer bottle but an empty bottle of mystery, containing a genie who was motioning for him to pick it up and rub it, and immediately his problems would be solved. This was only a wishful, fleeting thought. The sky had just become dark when the streetlights came on. Someone walked down the sidewalk on the opposite side of the street and a car passed, but otherwise the area was deserted. A few hours before, Ryan's parents kicked him out of the house. He left without any clothes other than what was on his back, and twenty dollars in his pocket; now he was mulling over in his mind just where to go. His great-grandparents would take him in, but they were old; he would not want to be a burden on them. Also, his great-grandmother kept after him about going to church with them. When he was younger, he did. The church his great-grandparents attended was on the other side of town from where he and his parents lived, and all the kids at this church were very nice to him. No one called him Rat. Philadelphia was a large city; only the kids from his own school would call him Rat.

It was very cold during the day and now that it had become dark, it was colder. Ryan shivered even with the heavy jacket and cap he wore. He scrunched his neck down and crossed his arms in front of him, then thought of the gloves in a pocket and was retrieving them, at the same time deep in thought. Suddenly, the thoughts were shattered by the sound of an alarm splitting the air. He jumped to attention as he looked all around, then a beat-up jalopy came tearing down the street in Ryan's direction. When the driver spotted Ryan, he brought the vehicle to a screeching halt. The young man on the passenger side leaned out the window calling to Ryan and tossed out a bag to him.

"Hey, Rat! Here! Take this bag and hide it in the culvert under the Chestnut Street Bridge. Hurry! We'll cut you in. The police are on to us."

The car scratched off as Ryan stepped out to the curb, retrieved the bag in haste, and disappeared from view down an alley beside the building where he had been standing. "Oh! They've really got me in trouble now! I don't want to be involved in a bank robbery!" He was thinking this and breathing hard with his heart beating fast. "Why did I ever pick up the stupid bag? Now, what will I do with it?" He came to the end of the alley where it dumped into a little unpaved road behind the buildings. Looking both directions and seeing no one, he turned left and tossed the bag over a fence. The ground there was full of tall bushes, still dormant from the cold weather, and a pile of junk around a small tumbled-down shed. Coming to the end of the little road, he again looked both directions. A car passed with a man and woman in it, and they were not the police. When the car passed, Ryan crossed the street and went between two empty buildings until he came to another street and there felt safer among several people walking along the sidewalk. If he kept cutting across this side of town without being detected, he knew that a main highway that ran north and south would not be far away. The sky had now become darker. Two unkempt characters with long stringy hair and clothes that had evidently been slept in for weeks stepped in front of Ryan as he rounded the corner of a building. His first thought was to start running. One of the fellows stepped in front of Ryan, preventing this thought to materialize. "Hey, man," the other one said with a hand out, "'ave ya got any weed?"

"Nope. I was just looking for some myself," Ryan lied trying not to show his fear. "You guys got any contacts?" Now, he tried to sound cool.

Neither answered but one gave Ryan a swift shove causing him to stumble and fall on the sidewalk. "Nah, you're a worthless jerk!" one of the two said with disgust, and then he let out some foul language as they walked away, leaving Ryan scrambling to his feet, dusting himself off. He blew out his breath in a sigh of relief, trotting swiftly on. There were more of these hippie characters along the way. Since Ryan's hair was long also, hanging beneath his cap, they most likely thought he was one of them. On a corner where two streets crossed at a traffic light, a girl was propped against a telephone pole strumming a guitar. She was bent over the instrument, crying her mournful tune to it as if it were her lover. She looked Ryan in the face when he stopped for the light to change. "Hi, handsome. What's your name?" she asked giving a sad little smile. The light changed and Ryan only answered, "Name's 'Rat,'" and he took off across the street. "Hey, Rat, wait up! I'll go with you." Then Ryan broke into a run. When he was far enough away, he slowed for fear a policeman would come by and stop him for questioning.

The town now became more presentable with tall buildings and traffic. He saw a bus stop where people were boarding, the bus belching black fumes. Ryan reached in his pocket to see if he had any change. Yes, he was in luck. He glanced at the sign on the front of the bus. It would be better to ride for a few miles. This bus would get him closer to the highway. "What do I have to lose," he asked himself, "except the fare?"

Later, while walking along the highway, Ryan's mind was busy with many thoughts. They all were confusing thoughts and each produced an empty feeling. He was thinking how lonely he felt with no one to turn to, nowhere to go. He did not even have to go to school, or even . . . even what? Anything he did now would be his own decision. "Maybe I should have taken Dad's advice and joined the army. If not, then . . . I'll have to find a job. But not in Pennsylvania; maybe I should have gone to New York and stayed with Grandpa and Mawmaw for a while . . . they'd just call Dad and Mom, and I'd get another railing out." All these broken thoughts brought on more questions for which he had no answers. He kicked a can that was lying on the shoulder of the road. Cars whizzed by; some blasted their horns. One car slowed as if to offer the boy a ride but upon seeing his long hair and unkempt clothes, they resumed their speed. Ryan could not help feeling a flicker of fear. A blank void crouched in the back of his mind. Where was he going? And what would he do? The twenty dollars in his pocket would not hold out for very long.

In high school Ryan had given no thought that his carefree school days would not go on forever; therefore, he was totally caught by surprise to be out on his own. The fear of what lay ahead was now taking possession of both mind and body as he gloomily pondered on what the future may have to offer. Since seventh grade, he'd had a secret ambition that stayed with him throughout the rest of school. Now, he thought of this no more. What would be the use?

The more he walked, the more despondent he became. If G. G. could whisper in his ear right now, she'd say: "Sweetheart, you are young, be brave and above all have faith in yourself, but most of all, in God." When he was small, Great-Grandmother was too much to say and she had shortened it for him to merely "G. G." He loved her very much and thinking of her now, he felt remorse that he had not phoned her or Great-Granddad, whom he merely called "Grandpappy" or sometimes just "Pappy." The name started off as a joke but it stuck just like "G. G." had stuck on his beloved Great-Grandmother. They would have insisted that he come to their apartment before he decided on anything. They must be terribly worried by now, and he knew that G. G. would be praying for him. She prayed about every-thing and always told him to never do anything without praying about it first. With this in mind, he took heart and pressed on.

The stories that G. G., Pappy, and their son, Grandpa, told Ryan when he was younger seemed almost impossible to believe, but they both had said they were the absolute truth, so he believed them. Maybe he could now go and check this all out. "Possibly, I could get a job somewhere in one of the towns along the way." These little questions and ideas kept popping into his mind. Then, he wondered if the police might still be looking for him. If so, he could be stopped at any minute by the state patrol. Just as this thought worried him, a car came to a screeching halt a few feet in front of him. "Uh oh! This may be it! Could be an unmarked patrol car." Ryan stopped and waited to see who would get out of the vehicle but when the door opened and the inside lights shone out on the ground, someone put a dog out and then took off. He let out a sigh of relief, then squatted, snapped his fingers, and called the dog to him. The shaggy, brown animal crouched, obviously afraid, and whined. It looked to him like a young Labrador retriever. "Come on doggy; don't be afraid. I won't hurt you." Ryan sucked his lips, then whistled. He recognized that this was no vicious animal but possibly an abused one. The dog started toward Ryan, inching itself forward on its belly, whining as it came. "That's it, buddy, come on. Let's be friends. Come on now." He whistled again and the dog came up to its newfound friend. It sat up as Ryan reached out, rubbing its head and long ears. "Yes sir! You're a nice doggy. What's your name? Let me look on your collar." He turned the collar around to search for any identification. With only the moonlight, he could see none. "Well, now; every dog has to have a name so I'll just have to give you one." The dog wiggled and squirmed with delight. His tongue hung out and now his whole body was wagging. There was happiness in its eyes. Ryan rubbed a hand over the animal's body, separating the hair to look as best as was possible in the dim light for any skin disease or problem. Seeing none, he turned him on his back and examined the stomach. "Well, pup, you look okay to me. So . . . why did you get dumped? Well, I got dumped too, so we're both in the same boat. I'll bet you are hungry. I could use a meal myself." He was still rubbing his new friend as cars whizzed past the two beside the busy highway. "I'll just call you 'Jethro,' how's that? Okay?" The dog bounded around Ryan and then placed his front paws up on his stomach. "All right then, if that suits you, Jethro it is. Come on, boy. We'll find a roadside stop somewhere and get us something to eat. How's that?"

Now, there were two outcasts trudging along together, both much happier than before. With all the walking, Ryan did not feel the cold; his coat felt warm and Jethro lifted his spirits. "Most folks wouldn't give a ride to someone walking along with a dog," he said out loud. "Maybe a pickup will stop and someone will offer for you to ride in the back." This must have pleased Jethro for he jumped up with his front paws on Ryan's side. The boy felt warm with the dog close at his side, but he was sure if the wind had been blowing, it would make the going tough.

Chapter Two

BETH RUSSELL SAT RELAXED AND ALONE ON THE porch enjoying the smell of the woods and the delicious clean night air with crickets twanging their monotonous tunes. How wonderfully different from the city's hateful exhaust fumes! Looking up, she noticed a star millions of miles away brightly shining between the trees, and remembered the chant from her childhood that she had also taught to her children. "Star light, star bright," she whispered without finishing the sentence, but secretly wishing the family would be happy here on the mountain—dear Kendell Mountain, so remote and different from the hurly-burly city life. She had always longed for it; never in her wildest dreams thinking it would ever become a reality and without Charles here in this place that time forgot.

It was past ten o'clock, the children asleep in their beds, the little terrier, Sally, softly snored in Beth's lap as she stroked its back. Far away up over the mountain an airplane droned northward. She thought of Charles, seeing him in her mind's eye lying on the plane's floor, dead of a heart attack. Poor Charles. He wanted so much out of life, more and still more. No matter how much he made, it was never enough. Was he trying to have so much for the family, or was it to prove to himself that he was the best? Their high school annual had predicted that he would be the most likely to succeed.

"Oh, well, Sally," Beth said to the little dog, placing it on her shoulder and rising from the chair, leaving it rocking. "We did the best we could, didn't we? It's bedtime for you and for me."

10

They went inside just as the phone began ringing. She caught it on the second ring, knowing who it would be.

Dawn looked like a fragile, thin robin's-egg blue coming up over Kendell Mountain when Beth Russell's feet hit the cold floor. She sat for a few moments on the edge of the bed, yawned and stretched, then wondered if John had slept any at all. The phone call last night had been him, letting her know that he would be staying the night at Mountain General because the Edwards child was still in danger and may not make it through the night. He would catch catnaps in the doctors' lounge, he'd told her. How terrible it would be to lose a child, Beth thought, her mind darting back to the time when her two youngest children had been lost on the mountain. What a heart-wrenching time that was! This morning after she dropped the kids off at school she'd go over to the hospital and sit with the little girl's parents, Clinton and Sue Edwards. Surely John would phone again before time for them to leave for school. It would be useless for her to go over to the hospital if she were not needed.

Beth stood before a mirror and stretched, then running fingers through the long shiny brown hair, thought she should not be standing there wasting precious time, but that the children needed to be up, having breakfast, and getting dressed for school.

It had been fourteen months since Charles's death and at that time, Beth and Connie Roland, wife of Charles's business partner, had serious decisions to make about the firm. There was one thing of which Beth was adamantly certain—she did not have any desire to run the construction business. Look at what it got both their husbands. Gregg Roland was robbed and murdered in his office, and the hassle and problems had caused Charles to have a fatal heart attack. Connie also made her doubts known. It was a wishy-washy situation. If Connie kept her half of the business, she would need a partner and she did not want to buy Beth out, yet she wanted to put her okay on the person who might buy from Beth.

The two women, who had been friends for a long time, now began to be at odds with one another over the sticky situation. Connie decided it would be best if they just let the laborers go and close the business down. Definitely against this, Beth irritably replied: "We cannot put so many people out of work! And think of all the hard work and long hours Charles and Gregg poured into the firm to make it a success that it had at last become. The workers are depending on us, Connie. Can't you imagine what they must be thinking right now? They have families to feed!"

"Oh, for heaven's sake, Beth, they can get jobs anywhere with all the building that's going on. Besides, what about us?" Connie snapped back. "We'll have to make a living, too, and it won't be so easy for us."

"That's just my point," Beth pleaded. "We both need to sell. I need to pay off my house and my other debts that Charles has left."

"Well, I'm sure you will not have to worry about that! Surely your father-in-law is well heeled and Charles's brother, too. They'll certainly be right here to do whatever you ask of them. I've seen how John looks at you. That man is ready to move in on Charles's territory!"

Beth gave Connie an irritating look but thought before she answered, then smiled and said: "You're completely right, my dear. He has asked me to marry him, and I've accepted."

Connie stood and with wide eyes and a flutter of her hands, exclaimed: "So! I was right! I thought something was going on. What are you going to do, leave me holding the bag?"

Beth was sitting in a chair facing the couch where Connie had been sitting before she stood and lit a cigarette. Beth fanned the air. "Do you have to foul up the house with that thing?" Connie hastily mashed it into a nice dish—that was not meant to be an ashtray—on an end table beside the couch. "Connie, I am not leaving you holding the bag, but I do have something in mind, that is, John suggested this," and to that Connie said under her breath, "I might have known." Beth carried on as though she had not heard the uncalled-for remark. "John said that after Charles's funeral, Moses Jackson approached him about buying the business. Of course, John told him that he'd have to talk with us about it. He also said that Moses claimed his mother would back him."

Connie looked interested but thought a few seconds before asking: "Do you think the men would work for a black man?"

"If they want a job they would, and I wondered if Brad Lyles might go in with him for that very reason. Brad could handle the business end and Moe could handle the laborers. They all liked him, and Charles had made him a supervisor."

And that's the way the problem at hand was settled. The new owners were go-getters and hard workers. Yes, the two men would carry on and do well. Belle Jackson was very proud of her son. She had known when Moses was born forty years ago down in Mississippi that he would grow up some day and amount to something. It was not meant for him to stay at Kendell Mountain orchards to labor his life away for a pittance.

Beth's house in Atlanta must be sold and the furniture that would not be needed on Kendell Mountain sold as well. The children's schooling must not be changed in the middle of a school year, she informed John, and that was fine with him. In fact, hè said it would give him time to have some remodeling done on his house to make room for Beth and the children. She had a slight uneasy feeling that the bachelor doctor at age forty may not be able to cope with taking on a wife and three rambunctious children and a teenager. When consulting with Papa Russell about this, he quickly set her mind at ease by saying that it was the best thing that could ever happen to John, and he'd still have Beth as a daughter-in-law to boot!

So, the young widow's mind was put at ease and on February 15, 1972, the Knollwood Orchards house had a wedding and a reception out back under the oak that was planted on the day John had been born. In the reception line, Pete announced to Papa Russell, "Papa, we all just got married, didn't we?" With an arm around the boy, Papa Russell answered with a big grin, "We sure did, son. Yessir! We certainly did."

Since the day when he stood beside Beth and the family at Charles's funeral, John knew he would marry Beth, the only woman he'd ever loved, and bring her and the children to live in his house, the old Doctor David Harris's house. The nieces and nephews had always been dear to his heart; they were already family. Since they called their grandfather "Papa," they decided to now call their Uncle John just plain "Pop," and he liked it.

Loving John came natural and easy for Beth. Deep down she had never stopped loving him since the time they dated during their school days. He was everything she had wanted Charles to be. When John went away to college and then medical school, Charles stepped in and won Beth's affection by his winning, pushy, out-going personality. But now she realized it had only been infatuation. With John, she had everything she'd dreamed of—a loving, attentive husband and a happy home.

As Beth was zipping up her robe, the phone rang. It was John. "Hi honey; the little girl is much better, and I insisted that the parents go home and sleep. They were completely exhausted."

His voice sounded tired. "What about the child's doctor?" she asked. "Doesn't he need to come home and catch a few winks also?"

"Depends upon the doctor's wife," he answered. "Be home shortly," he smiled though she couldn't see it, and he returned the receiver to its cradle.

Chapter Three

JOHN LEFT THE HOSPITAL, ARRIVING BACK AT HIS office to check his appointment book. "I didn't schedule anyone," Emily told him. "I had no idea you would make it in this morning at all. How's the little Edwards girl?"

"She's out of the woods. Holding her own now. She'll be okay, but wow! What a night!"

"Her doctor doesn't look so good though. I'm sure you are going home and getting some uninterrupted sleep," she said in way of a question.

"Yep, but I saw Dad's truck out there. He'll be somewhere around, so I'll just talk with him a few minutes first." He turned toward the door and rubbed one hand around the back of his neck as he turned the knob with the other.

"It's funny," Emily told him, "you always rub your neck when you're overly tired. Get out of here and go on home." John nodded and went out, closing the door behind him.

Emily scurried to catch him and handed him his black bag. "I know you are tired if you leave this thing behind! I have to look after you like a mother," she exclaimed. John's office was located on the main street, which was named "Main Street," squeezed between the only pharmacy in town on the north side and Becker's Clothing Store on the opposite. Where the doctor's office sat there had been an alley, used only for deliveries to the other businesses. John bought the property three years previous to his brother's death and had the office built. It completed a row of businesses on that side of the street. Union Gap had grown somewhat over the years with the opening of a

15

hosiery factory and a livestock feed mill. John's office had a second story, now leased out to a dentist, Doctor Nathaniel O'Bryan. To the old residents, Doctor John Russell was just plain "John," therefore the dentist was stuck with "Nat," and he immediately felt accepted by the town folk.

Outside, John saw his dad talking with Nat and the Baptist preacher, Reverend Jesse Adair—Jesse to his close friends, Brother Jesse to the rest. The little Baptist church was located at the end of Main Street with the Presbyterian church directly across the street. Nat O'Bryan threw up a hand when he saw John coming toward the group swinging his medical bag as he walked.

"Hello, fellows. Hi, Dad. Looks like we have a convention here. Have you got everything all settled?"

Alyn Russell placed an arm around his son's shoulders. "Hello, son. Are you coming or going? We were just discussing having a sausage biscuit and a cup of coffee over at the Skillet. Care to join us?"

"Okay by me." They all turned toward the café situated across the road from John's building. The café was owned and operated by Mack Faber and his wife, Thelma. They started the business shortly after the feed mill and the hosiery factory opened ten years ago, and it did a bustling business with two waitresses and themselves. Alyn went by the café daily, if only for a cup of coffee and good conversation. There was always some of his friends in there to "shoot the breeze" as they called it. John felt that he should have gone on home this time because Beth would be wondering if he'd been detained with another patient.

"Have you got any Tums in that bag, Doc?" Reverend Jesse teased, as they were going inside the café.

"No I don't, but we may need something stronger than Tums after we leave here."

Behind the counter Mack looked up from what he was doing and said, "Hey, I heard that remark!" He was wiping his hands on his soiled apron and turned toward the opening into the kitchen calling, "Thelma, here are the four stooges. Bring out the set-ups and the coffee pot."

The group slid into a booth as Mack pulled up a chair from another table and threw a leg across the chair that he had turned backward. "Ya'll know when to come, don't cha? This is the first break we've had all morning. Whoowee! We've had a morning. I called Mama to come over 'n hep out for 'ah hour. She's been laying out on us lately."

"You're not complaining about your bulging cash register, are you, Mack?" Alyn asked.

"Aw, heck no; but actually it's them waitresses, Cookie and Annie, that rakes in th' dough. Look at them bulging pockets on their aprons." Annie was at the cash register with a customer, and Cookie was walking to the table with a tray of cups and a steaming pot of coffee.

"Well, Johnny," Cookie said, "we don't see much of you lately." She sat the tray down and passed their cups around.

"Ah, he just can't take that married life, Cookie," Brother Jesse said with a belly laugh.

"Son, you do look kinda haggard. Reckon Teresa and I had better look after the younguns for a while." Alyn was serious when he said that, thinking perhaps John had not yet become accustomed to having children around every day. They used to be around him mostly on a weekend. However, he failed to catch the joke the reverend had made.

"It ain't them younguns, Alyn, it's their mama," Mack guffawed while John's face turned scarlet.

"Come on, guys, cut it out. I've been at the hospital all night," John said, hoping to change the subject, "and I'm beat to a pulp!"

"Say," Mack said, "we had a weirdo in here a whilest ago."

Cookie came back in time to hear what he was saying. She leaned over the table with napkins and handed them to each place and then set a jar of grape jelly down. "I'll say he was weird alright. One of them hippie-type . . . long stringy hair an' a beard and all." She left to get the plate of sausage biscuits.

Nat spoke for the first time since they sat down; "I thought I left them all down in the city when I moved up here. They don't like small mountain towns: not enough action, I guess." He was stirring milk into his coffee.

"Maybe he's heading up north to a larger city," another one of the men added.

"Wait just a second!" Mack said spreading out his hands for silence. "Just hold the phone! Then, why do you reckon he asked me which one of these mountains around here would be Kendell Mountain?"

Alyn and John both looked at each other. "What?" is all John said and his dad answered that it was probably someone looking for the Thompson's horse farm. "I sure hope so," John said. "We don't need anyone like that up on the mountain, especially at the school," and he added that he wouldn't even be allowed to go to school there, that was for doggoned sure.

Mack looked at John and refuted his statement. "Awww, now! If he had th' money, you know he wouldn't be turned down. Maybe they'd insist on a haircut and change of clothes. And besides that, just maybe they could make somethin' outta him. Might even git 'im to wash 'is hair."

"Mack's right," Brother Jesse added. "Wouldn't be legal for the school to refuse him if he had the money."

Alyn pursed his lips thoughtfully, setting his coffee cup down. "Yep. There've been a lot of kids who got turned around up there at that school." After a moment of silence Alyn changed the subject by saying: "Gentlemen, do you realize that this group here at this table represents four wars our country was engaged in?" They all looked at one another to figure this out, but Alyn continued. "I was in World War I briefly, Mack in World War II, John in Korea, and both Nat and Jesse in Vietnam. After each war, the boys came home as men, with different lessons learned and a new outlook on life." One of them started to say something but Alyn held up a silencing hand and continued. "But . . . this Vietnam group came home vastly different than the others. A lot of them learned to be rebellious."

Cookie interrupted what Alyn had been saying by bringing out the orders and pouring more coffee. She teasingly tousled Jesse's hair commenting: "Preacher, I reckon your congregation needs to take up a collection to get you a haircut. You nearly look like a hippie yoursef." They all laughed, dispelling Alyn's serious comments, and the subject of the stranger was dropped.

After he'd eaten the last of his sausage biscuit and had the last sip of coffee, Alyn announced, "Oh, yes, Teresa asked me to invite you all up to the house on Saturday night around eight o'clock for cake and ice cream. She never gets down to town much any more with school and all, and I've been telling her about our fine new and only dentist, so we decided this would give him a chance to do a little socializing. What about it, Nat?"

"That's real nice of her to go to that trouble, but it sure sounds good to me! Just tell her to be sure to invite a lot of folks with bad teeth . . . or no teeth at all. I'm an expert at making new ones." There were comments and pokes at him for doing all the bragging. John stood to leave and reached back to leave a tip beside his plate for Cookie. Brother Jesse yelled out jokingly to John as he left the table and walked away toward the cash register. Mack followed behind him asking, "Hey, Doc, you mean to leave this here nickel on the table?" John just turned toward him and did a wave of the hand. Mack told John that Thelma would be glad for a chance to get out. "You know, she cleans up pretty nice," he grinned.

"Going home, Papa?" John asked.

"Nope. Have several other things to do first and s'pect I should go by the feed mill and get some things Joe said we needed."

"Can't Joe do that?"

"Ah, I was already down here so may as well do it myself."

Mack closed the cash drawer after the last one paid and commented to John that he should know by now that Alyn and the feed mill crew had to shoot the breeze and solve all the world's problems. This was a daily thing. His son smiled knowingly and retrieved his medical bag from beside the table where he'd left it reminding the others not to forget Teresa's invitation.

Going home, John felt peaceful and contented even though tired. Feeling fulfilled, he now had someone to go home to, and he knew Beth would be waiting. It had been a terrible mistake to lose her to Charles in the first place, but it was his own fault. There should have been a showdown back then, but he'd gone off to school and then quit to enlist in the air force. But John came home determined to pick up where he left off with medical school. The urging of Doctor David Harris was really not even necessary. However, as yet, John had not been able to shake off the guilt he was feeling for being so happy with Charles's widow and children. He had not broken down and talked with his father about this guilt. Just how could a person feel contented, yet still possess the undercurrent of guilt? He had it all: peace, contentment, and guilt.

John turned off on to the road that led up the mountain to Knollwood Road and home. He was about to pass by the school when he saw Al coming from the school driveway on his bicycle.

"Where do you think you're going, young man?" he called out the window to the boy. "Kinda chilly to be out joy riding, isn't it?"

Al stopped his bicycle beside John's car. "Hi, Pop. Miss Gibbs said I could have an hour off since I'm exempt from taking the math test. Uh, she may have meant for me to go to the library, I guess, but I sorta thought I'd ride around a little bit and stretch the legs."

"I see," is all John could think to say. "Well then, sling your bike in the trunk and drive me on home. Then you can ride the bike back down to the school library." He pulled over to the roadside, handed Al the key so he could open the trunk, and then slid over into the passenger seat.

"All right! Yes, sir!" The boy was ecstatic to get to drive. John had let him drive before on the back roads. The happy boy wasted no time disposing of his bike in the trunk and jumped into the driver's seat. He drove off easily, for John had been a good teacher. Al's face beamed with delight, but then it usually did, for being happy was inborn in him. He found delight in most everything.

"Say, have you seen a hippie-looking guy walking along here?" John asked.

"Huh? Did you lose one?"

"Don't be a smarty, I'm serious."

"Nope. Sure haven't seen any lately and don't care to."

"Just checking. On your way back, if you do see one, keep your distance and go on by, okay?"

"Sure, if you say so. You s'pectin' one to visit us?"

"Perhaps," was all John answered and closed his eyes and bowed his head in sleep leaving Al to think he'd been dreaming when he asked the perplexing question.

Chapter Four

CARS BEGAN ARRIVING BY SEVEN EVEN THOUGH THE get-together time had been set for seven-thirty. Joe's teenage son, Comer, directed them around to the back of the house, where there was plenty of room. Every time a small gathering of any kind had been planned at Knollwood, it easily got out of hand when some of the Russells would invite more than intended, thinking perhaps of someone who may receive hurt feelings for being left out. Such was the case for tonight. Teresa asked Buela Mae (Joe's wife) to help her prepare more cakes and cookies. It would be easy enough to pour more apple cider in the electric pot, and coffee, too, would be no problem. Clara said there was a good supply of cokes on hand for the kids and she would make some punch also.

Teresa had not planned on inviting those with children, but somehow it happened and this pleased the younger Russell grandchildren. The real reason for the party was because of Papa Russell's birthday. He would never agree to calling attention to the day by anyone making a fuss over him, so the adult family members were passing it off by appearing to ignore the coming date. Beth made a large sheet cake at home on the day before, while the children were in school.

"You'd think a bunch of dirty bums lived here," Alyn told his daughter on Saturday morning, "by the way you and Buela Mae have been cleaning like your shirttails are on fire."

"The dust has to be swept out every now and then, Papa. Why don't you just go somewhere today and stay out of our way," she answered with a twinkle in her eyes. She had not even told him happy birthday at all.

"Okay, if you feel like that then. I'll just go down to the feed and seed mill 'n set around with Clyde and th' boys . . . or, I could even run away," he teased.

"Good! Just be home by suppertime. I don't like to have to warm things over. John, Beth, and the kids may come down later, and don't forget that you have asked your old cronies from the Skillet to come up."

He turned to go, wearing the same battered felt hat he'd worn for years and a light weight jacket that looked just as old.

"You could get home in time to clean yourself up a bit," his daughter called after him. His grin as he turned away made Teresa suspicious that he knew something was going on besides just the Skillet gang coming. She shook her head and said: "That man just won't do! No one can keep a single thing from him."

So the invited guests had not been told of Papa Russell's birthday. Only Beth's children knew when they saw the beautiful cake being placed in the car's trunk. "But there has to be presents at a birthday party!" Susan exclaimed.

"Not for adults, Sweetheart," John replied, closing the trunk lid. "Papa would never hear of it. He says he has everything he could possibly need."

"Well, shoot! It's not a birthday party then without presents," Peter frowned and pursed his lips.

"Come on. Get in the car you two and when we go in then we'll all holler, 'Happy Birthday, Papa!' and give him a great big bear hug." John handed the keys to Al and then got in the back seat with the two little ones and Penny. Beth was in the front beside Al.

"All right!" Al exclaimed. "No back-seat driving now!"

"You just stay to the right son, and watch what you're doing," Beth told him.

Susan held her tablet with a pencil clipped to it. Everywhere she went she was equipped thus. "Why have you got that stupid tablet, Susan?" Peter emphasized the word "stupid."

"It is not stupid and stop punching me, Pete!"

"Okay, kids, that's enough. Leave her alone, Peter."

"Aww, Mom it's plain dumb! And she embarrasses me."

"Pay her no attention, Pete. If she wants to write down everything, it's perfectly alright."

"At least I made all A's on my report card," Susan whispered in her brother's ear.

"Stop spitting in my ear," he demanded irritably, rubbing the ear.

"Knock it off, kids. Enough is enough." John's words were final.

"Who all is coming, Mom?" Penny asked, hoping Preston would not be along with his parents. "I hope I don't have to listen to a lot of old folks talk all evening."

"I have no idea who your Aunt Teresa has invited but I hope each of you will use your manners and not butt in when the 'old folks,' as you call them, are talking. Just listen and maybe you will actually learn something."

"Ole Susan will tell 'im to talk slower so she can write it all down," Pete snickered, jabbing her.

"Shut up, Pete," the little girl again whispered in his ear with him again rubbing the ear. Beth and John both tried to cover their smiles at Peter's statement.

Cars were already parked behind the house when Al drove into the driveway and pulled around to the back. "Hi, Comer," Al said to him as he approached the car.

"Hey, man . . . whatcha doin' drivin'?" Comer exclaimed. Al gave him a very pleased, proud grin and stepped out. The back doors were flung open with the younger children scrambling out hoping to be the first to run inside and holler happy birthday to their grandfather. John was holding the door for Beth to get out and said: "Here comes Nat O'Bryan in behind us, Sweetheart. Go ahead in. I'll wait for him."

"Okay, just get the cake out of the trunk, please as you come in." Beth and Penny walked together around the walkway and under the arch toward the front door.

"I feel silly going in the front, Mama. We always go in the back door," Penny said. Al was already lifting the cake from the trunk when John turned from speaking to Nat. "Okay, buddy, hand over the keys," he said to the boy as he saw him drop them in his pocket, and turning to Nat, said: "So, the bachelor comes to a party without a date."

"Yep. No one would have me and I figured it wouldn't matter with just the Iron Skillet gang coming. But with all these cars here, it must be more of a party than I expected."

John closed the trunk and warned Al: "Drop that cake and you've had it, boy!" Then he looked all around and added that he was glad the rooster went to bed with the chickens! There was no sign of Ole Charlie.

"Hey! Whose birthday is it? I thought it was only the gang coming."

"Oh, my sister wanted to surprise Papa and as usual, she always goes overboard. Let's go in and we'll see who all is here." When they reached the archway, he called out to Al to hold up and let him get the door or there'd be cake splattered asunder.

All the windows were ablaze with lights. It was a perfect March evening; cool and clear with no breeze stirring, perfect for friends to gather with the holiday events now long in the past. Nat had been up to John's house at the time they had completed the deal of his leasing the space above the doctor's office; however, he had never been inside the Knollwood house.

Atlanta was always Nat's home since his birth in 1936. Growing up in the city, he never dreamed he would ever be living in a small obscure town in the north Georgia mountains . . . now, here he was and loving every minute of it. No longer than he had lived and worked in this town, these people were all like relatives to him. They took him in with open arms. He had been warned that small-town residents were clannish and that he should be on guard. On the evening that he had gone up to talk with John and sign the lease on his office space, he had thought as he passed by Knollwood that it was certainly a homey looking place. He tried to picture how wonderful it would be for a child to grow up in such an environment. He had not yet heard of the heartaches that had taken place there. Whenever he got the chance, he decided, he would ask John about the history of the grand old house. John's father should be the one to ask about the house that was there before the fire; however, as yet Nat did not know there had been a fire.

Al was the center of attention—or was it the cake?—as he came through the doorway shouting, "Happy birthday, Papa!" Everyone followed suit, except some said Alyn instead of Papa. Then they broke into the birthday song, totally embarrassing the recipient, who had not been in the least bit suspicious until so many people started coming in. "At least it was a good excuse for a party," he said. "But I was hoping it would go unnoticed so I'd not have to add another year." His eyes crinkled with laughter.

"Wouldn't make a mite o' difference," Mack said. "Why, you don't look a day over eighty-five!"

"Thanks, friend," Alyn mumbled. Never being one to take the butt end of a joke, he added in his slow drawl: "Well, I'll just tell you what to look forward to, and I'm sure some of you will understand. It's like this. Ya see . . . life is like a roll of toilet paper. Th' closer it gets to th' end, th' faster it rolls!" This brought on some laughs and some folks agreeing.

Teresa had been sitting on the couch beside Mack's wife, Thelma, when Al came in with the cake. They were all standing now after the song when John came over and introduced Nat to his sister. She had a surprised look on her face when their eyes locked. All she said was, "Oh."

"Oh?" John questioned and her face flushed. Nat waited to see how she would get out of this for she now looked embarrassed.

"What I meant was . . . well, that is . . . when I heard about our new dentist I thought you would be much older and fat perhaps."

Nat was smiling. "It is nice to meet you, Miss Russell." He held out his hand to her and she shook it limply, still into the blunder deeper. "You two can fight this out and I'll just go over there and talk with Michael and Bess," John said and then left the two to fend for themselves.

"Well, Doctor O'Bryan, do you like our little town? Are there enough people here to support your office?"

"Yes, to both questions, and please call me Nat like everyone else, " Nat answered. "So far I haven't missed a meal, however I could use some new patients." He left the subject open in order for her to give the reason why she had not made an appointment in the year since he had opened the dental office. When she smiled, he noticed her pretty teeth and felt like a farmer examining a horse's mouth.

"I will be happy to make an appointment with you the next time I need any work done. It certainly would be a pleasure to not be compelled to go out of town to get it done. I just had my teeth cleaned recently."

"Fine. You just give my secretary a call. Why haven't I seen you in town before?"

"While school is in session I very seldom get down to town and maybe on the few occasions that I have, you must have been busy in your office. There doesn't seem to be time for anything but work, you know."

"Yes, I do know but all work makes . . ."

Teresa interrupted with: "And I've heard that many times from my dad."

Just then Jed Thompson and his wife, Edna, came in the door and Teresa excused herself to welcome them. The Reverend Jesse Adair and his wife, Lucy, were coming in behind them. Then Nat turned to Emily Arnold, whom he knew well, as she was John's secretary. He also knew her husband, Mark, standing next to her.

"Hi, folks. It's good to see you tonight," Nat extended his hand to Mark.

"Hello. Same here," Mark answered as they shook hands.

Then Nat said to Mark's wife: "You're looking very pretty, Emily . . . not that you don't any other time. I've never seen you when you didn't look pretty."

"Now, Nat. You're buttering me up for something, I'll bet."

"Oh, he's just making conversation, Hon, but you told me yourself that you hated that old rag you put on." Mark gave a wink to Nat, who stated they were on dangerous territory and had better change the subject pretty fast.

"By the way, John told me one day recently that you two own that wonderful old house up on the hill behind our office."

"Yes," Mark quickly answered, "But you mean that wonderful old ram-shackled, run-down tax drain!"

"I have to agree with my husband," Emily smiled. "It is quite a monstrosity but in its day it was a beautiful mansion. It was built by Senator Fullman's father sometime before the turn of the century. The senator was Ella Fullman's husband, who came from a very wealthy family. Did John tell you that I was born in that house?"

"No, but tell me how that came about." She had more than increased his interest by now.

"Miss Ella willed it to my mother, Carlotta, who worked for her for a number of years; my father worked for her also. We lived there with her, and as long as my folks lived, they kept the place up."

John could not let the subject go without asking what they intended to do with the place and saying that it would be a shame to let it just fall down from neglect.

Mark had a quick answer. "Could you even begin to estimate the cost of putting it in living condition now days? It certainly would be more than we could ever scrape up."

Emily could not help but put in her two cents worth. "Yes, and I don't think I would care to try to wash all those windows and vacuum the floors, either," she chuckled. "But seriously, the old house depresses me. Every time I go in it, I think I hear whispers. Maybe it's because we used to have such fun there and now it's all gone."

Mark wanted to get back to the subject at hand. "We're always open for suggestions, Nat." He was curious as to the dentist's interest.

"Oh, I've always admired old mansions. Wish someone would will one to me."

The couple possibly were both thinking the same thing and seeing dollar marks before their eyes at the same time. They glanced at each other. Then Mark rubbed his chin and said, "Humm . . . now, we'd be happy to let you have it for a very reasonable sum," and his wife added, "In fact, we'd let you have it at a downright steal."

Nat waited a few seconds, shifted his feet and then said, "Sounds interesting—if your 'downright steal' is in my bracket."

"Are you really serious, Nat? What in the world would you do with it?" Emily was curious but Mark had an arm around her and he punched her on the back with a finger. He didn't care what the man wanted with it as long as he'd come up with the price they would decide upon.

Nat answered anyway, not knowing Mark didn't care one iota. "I've always been good with a hammer and a few nails," Nat grinned. "My father was an architect before he retired. He'd love the challenge, and I feel certain the two of us could come up with something to do with it. I'd welcome the opportunity to get him up here away from Atlanta anyway."

Mark and Emily looked at each other with fluttering hearts and Mark said: "Looks like the worm has turned for us, Em." He used the nickname that he called his wife. Then to Nat he said, "Let us think on this, that is, if you really meant what you said . . . and we'll give you our price." Emily added that maybe Nat could have his father come up and take a look.

"I'll do that for sure. He's the one with the money, only . . . he squeezes it sorta tight."

Pete and Susan had taken Mack and Thelma's two youngest grandchildren, Mary Nell and Josh, into the hallway to decide what they wanted to get into that would be fun. Anything other than standing around talking like old folks are prone to do.

"Come on," Pete said with authority. "Let's go upstairs and slide down the railing. It curves, and man, you can go so fast!" Then he asked Susan where her "ole" tablet was, hoping she would get the other girl busy listening to her read.

"Oh, phooie! I left it in the car and I could have read my story to you."

"Don't wanta hear no story!" the little girl answered, "but wait, guys, I know what will be fun!"

"We don't wanna do no sissy girl stuff!" her brother demanded.

"Well, just listen to this! Let's have a race up and down the hallway and on up the stairs and slide down the railing."

"Yeah, that sounds exciting!" Pete said joyfully, and Susan said that if anyone pushed and shoved they would be out of the race.

"Okay, we'll go start at the back door, all the way down the hall, up the stairs, down the railing, and back to the starting place. We'll start on the count of ten." So they decided to choose who would do the counting by doing "one potato, two potato, three potato, four" to make it all fair.

Penny and the older granddaughter of the Fabers, Gwendolyn, went to the kitchen to help Beth set out plates and silverware and do whatever they were asked to do. "Thank you, girls. I'm glad you came in to help. Everyone will be talked out soon and ready for some refreshments. Please put these things here," she pointed to the items she'd just put out, "on the buffet in the dining room and then come back for the glasses and cups . . . and, after you take these in, go out in the hall and quiet those kids down. There is no sense in them making so much noise! It must be disturbing to everyone." As the girls were going through the dining room doorway, Beth told Penny to tell them to just sit on the steps and talk or tell stories until they were called. "Now I wonder where the coffee pot is," she said to herself and opened cabinet doors, peering inside.

Gwen came back into the kitchen for the tray of glasses. To make conversation to the girl, Beth told her that she had certainly blossomed into a pretty young lady. "Thank you, Mrs. Russell," the girl said feeling quite grown for her seventeen years.

"Are you in any of Penny's classes?" Beth continued opening and closing cabinet doors still looking for the large coffee urn. There was a small one on the stove.

"No'm. I'm a grade behind Penny. All the boys think Penny is a doll."

"Oh, here it is . . . finally. Now I'll just get the coffee on and everything else is ready . . . well, then, that means you are in the same grade as Al."

"Yessum. We are in the same home room and then we have the same world history class."

"I do hope he behaves himself and makes as good grades as his sister does."

"He behaves, except . . . well, I think he is sort of the class clown." The girl smiled.

"Maybe I'd better have a talk with that young man!" Beth worried that perhaps he disturbed the class.

"Oh, please, Mrs. Russell, I wouldn't for the whole world have Al know I said that. He does behave. I didn't mean that he does anything bad. Everyone likes him a lot." Penny came through the door just then and was asked to go and ask Teresa if she would be ready to serve the guests just as soon as the coffee finished perking.

"Sure will, Mama, but I've about had it with those kids! Just listen to them. I'm going back out there and jerk a knot in their ..." the door swung closed before she got the sentence finished. A few seconds later Beth decided she had better go intervene and opening the kitchen door leading into the hallway, she saw Penny separating Peter and Josh who were rolling on the floor and the little girls jumping up and down yelling.

"Stop it, I said! Now!" Penny jerked Peter off the top of Josh and marched him toward their mother. His shirt was torn and his bottom lip bleeding. The other boy looked even worse.

"Penny, get a wet cloth for your brother's lip. What's the meaning of this ruckus, Peter? Can't you behave for just a few minutes; just look at your clothes!"

"It was all ole Josh's fault, Mama. He jerked my snake outta my hand and let 'im get away!"

"Peter Russell! You didn't bring that snake along! How did you get it in without my seeing it?" She had her son by the shoulders shaking him.

Pete dusted his clothes off and looked up at his mother. "He was in my pocket asleep and not bothering nobody, that is until ole Josh tried to get him out of my pocket. And now he's gone!" the little boy wailed with tears running down his face.

"And I wonder what your Aunt Teresa will have to say about a snake being loose in the house ... maybe crawling in the bed with her."

"He wouldn't hurt her none," Peter mumbled softly as he wiped tears from his cheeks.

By now, Penny had returned and Thelma Faber was right behind her. She grabbed her grandson by the arm and marched him to the bathroom at the end of the hall, to the tune of his laments that it was Pete's fault. "'Cause he was showing the snake off and running the girls up the hallway shaking the varmit at them, and it made Mary Nell wet all over herself and make a puddle on the floor, too!"

All the men seemed to think the episode was hilariously funny, although they tried to muffle smiles while the women kept examining the floor around their feet. They hurried through the birthday cake and coffee, then suggested to their husbands that it was getting rather late and they'd better be leaving. Thelma had gathered her brood of grandchildren and was going out the door apologizing to Teresa about the ruckus the children made. Mack followed behind her, speaking to Alyn, who was standing at the door beside his daughter. "Well," Mack said, still smiling, "I'm sure much obliged for the invite. Wouldn't have missed it for the world, old man."

"Now, wait just a minute. Who're you calling old man?" Alyn questioned, his eyes crinkling with laughter. His once blond hair had now turned gray and wrinkle lines took the place of smile lines that furrowed his brow over the years. The gray hair and wrinkles did not take away the sparkle in his brown eyes or his laughter and sense of humor. "I can still beat you at a game of horse shoes any day!"

"We'll hafta see about that! Right now I s'pect we'd best be gittin' these younguns on t' bed."

"Glad you all could come, Mack and Thelma." Alyn and Mack shook hands. "But you could've given me a hint, you know."

"And ruin th' surprise! Ya'll come down t' see us at home sometime."

"I think you see us enough at the Skillet, Mack. You don't have a cash register at home, do you?" Alyn laughed loudly and his friend poked him on the shoulder and told his wife that they'd better "be gittin' on home." The reverend and Lucy followed behind them with, "See ya'll in th' morning at church."

As John, Beth, and the children were on the way home, Pete sat in the backseat sulking, with his arms crossed and his lips poked out while Susan wrote furiously in her tablet by the light of the moon.

"I suppose, John," Beth was whispering softly to him, "that by now you are ready to send us back to Atlanta."

He whispered back: "Maybe the kids . . . but I think I'll keep their mother."

Later, after they had turned off the lights and crawled into bed, Beth told John that she thought Nat O'Bryan was rather smitten by his sister. "Hum, s'pose so," he yawned. "'Bout time somebody is. In several more years, nobody would want her."

Chapter Five

AFTER SCHOOL, BETH USUALLY HELPED THE TWO younger children with their homework before she started preparing supper. She had finished with Peter's assignments, and he left out the back door with the dog when Susan came in with an unhappy look on her face, nearly to the point of tears. She sat down at the kitchen table beside her mother. "Now, now, my sweet . . . it can't be all that bad, can it?"

"I just can't do this homework, Mama. It's too hard! Today, Miss Roberson was telling us about poems and she read a nice one to us that she learned when she was my age."

"How nice, Susie. What was it about?"

"It was about a little girl in a swing, and she could go so high that she could see over the countryside far, far away. I like my swing, too, but I can't see far away because of all the trees."

Beth smiled. "I remember that poem." She started saying the first line. "'Oh, how I like to go up so high, up in the air so blue.' But, dear me, I can't seem to recall any more of it."

"Miss Roberson says we have to learn it, and then I'll say it for you."

"That will be nice. I'd like to hear it again, but now, let's see here, what is your assignment for tonight's homework?"

"That's what I meant, Mama. What we have to do is just so hard that I can't think of a single thing; nothing at all! What am I going to do?" Susan said blankly, crossing her arms in complete disgust. "We have to make up a poem of our very own. But even worser . . ."

"'Worse,' Susan."

"Even worse, then. We will have to read them out loud, but even worser, I mean worse, than that, the one who writes the best poem will be asked to read it up on the stage in the auditorium!" She crossed her arms again and drew in and out a big breath.

"But, Susie, you are very good at writing stories so you should not have any problem at all." Her mother was trying to encourage her.

"Oh, Mama, poems are different though than stories. Poems have to rhyme. Do you know what that means?"

"Yes, I do . . . like in the swing poem."

"Yessum, she told us all about it and about rhythm, like each line has to match in syl, syl . . ."

"Syllables," Beth filled in the word that was new to her daughter.

"Oh, Mama! You do understand! Then you can help me, except . . ."

"Except what, Sweetheart?"

"It's just that, uh . . . well . . . let's don't win, okay?" Susan was worried that she may have to read her poem on the stage of the auditorium.

"Now, Susie, you have to do your very best in everything you do. You do understand that, don't you? You need to have the best grades you can make, and I don't mean just so you can be better than anyone else, but always try to do your very best. When you do that it really doesn't matter whether you win or not. Just simply aim for the best you can do, and then I will always be so proud of you!"

Susan had been resting her chin in a hand, with the elbow on the table, taking in all her mother had said. "Okay then, I promise to do my best."

"All right. What would you like to write about? You can't copy what someone else has written."

"I know. That's what our teacher said." Then the little girl gave the pitiful worried look again. "I just do not have any ideas," she shrugged. "The boy who sits in front of me said he would write a poem about his dog, and Betsy across the aisle said she would write one about her doll that she got for Christmas."

Beth thought for a few seconds and then said: "Humm . . . it is now March and the pretty flowers, dogwoods, and rhododendrons will soon be blooming. Do you remember the Heidi books that we read last summer and how she loved springtime on the mountain?" Susan nodded her head and gave a half-smile. "What about using springtime as your subject?"

Susan's chin quivered and tears appeared in her big blue eyes. "It sounds fine to me, but I still don't know how to start it off. You know how I love springtime, too, Mama because I can play outside and have lots of fun. I love our house here in the woods and I'm sure there are fairies and elves living all around us. They will come out when warm weather is here for good. Mama, could we stay up late some night so we can see them?"

Beth was amused and it showed in her face. "If there are any fairies and elves they would run and hide when people come around. Let's not get off the subject, ladybug. Don't start worrying before we even get going here. Maybe I can start off a line and you can finish it. Would that be all right?"

"It certainly would be all right with me!" The little girl's face brightened.

"Let's pretend that spring is a lady." Susan giggled as though she now anticipated this to be fun. "Get your paper and pencil and I'll help with words you can't spell." Beth put her thinking cap on. "Last night as I was . . . what, Susan? What did you do in your bed last night?"

"I was sleeping!" she yelled out joyfully.

"Yes, that is good. Okay, now write that line down." With Beth's spelling help, Susan printed the first line and said, "Last night as I was sleeping . . . That's good, now what?" she asked smiling broadly.

"Miss Spring came," Beth pointed to her daughter to finish the line. "What was she doing when she came down the path? Was she running, skipping, jogging, what?"

"Oh! I know! When you are sorta doing it all and dancing along, you are 'tripping.'"

"Very good! That fits just nicely."

"She came tripping through our yard."

"Yes, except all of that will not fit. Just use two words."

"Then I'll just put down, 'Miss Spring came tripping through.'"

"Very, very good, Susie! You are catching on. I knew you would. Now, we have to think real hard. She's going to work on the flower's colors."

"I know! I know! I even know the whole line, Mama! Like you do when you paint pictures. 'She held a palette in her hand.'"

"Oh, Susie, I'm so proud of you! That's wonderful. Now you have three lines so write it all down." Susan had to ask how to spell palette. "Tell me, what is on the palette?"

"Colors of paint," Susan answered.

"That's right but there is a better word for colors than 'paint' to use in poems. It is called 'hue,' h-u-e."

"Then I'll just say, 'With colors of every hue.'"

"Okay . . . now read all four lines back to me and let's see how it sounds."

Happily, Susan read them back and then breathed deeply, feeling intensely satisfied, like a heavy weight had been lifted from her heart.

"Did Miss Roberson say how long the poem should be?"

"She said it should be at least three paragraphs long. Do you know what a paragraph is, Mama?"

"I certainly do and right now you have one paragraph so let's get busy again." The two put their heads together and in the end, came up with four even paragraphs. "If you do win, baby doll, you should be proud to stand up on that stage and read this poem. But, it would get you an even better grade if you could say it from memory! We will work on that also. You should learn one paragraph each day until you know it well. Say that day's paragraph over and over."

Susan listened attentively and then pursed her lips as if thinking: "Here we go again. More work!"

Beth took the tablet that her daughter was writing on and read the whole poem out loud. They had decided what the title would be and Susan cleared her voice, repeated the title and the name of the author.

"Spring's Touch"
By Susan Russell

Last night as I was sleeping
Miss Spring came tripping through.
She held a palette in her hand,
With colors of every hue.

She danced along the woodland
Down the mossy trails,
Painting lovely dogwoods
White like ocean sails.

She woke the little violets
With taps of breath so sweet,
And smiled upon the crocus
Gathered 'round her feet.

This morning I went out to greet her;
To thank her for such beauty,
But, Mama said that she had left
And only did her duty.

Beth hugged the happy child and again praised her good work. "Now, please go out and tell your brother to come in and get the trash out like he was suppose to do." She rose from the chair to stir something on the stove. "Bring Sally in, too, Sweetheart," she called. "And put some food in her dish." Susan went out, leaving the screen door banging closed. In a few minutes, Beth heard the little dog barking wildly as both children came running in like a whirlwind exclaiming: "Mama, Mama, come quick! Look at Al coming up the road! He's got a billy goat tied behind his bicycle!"

"Sakes alive! Not a goat! What in the name of common sense?" Beth dried her hands on a towel after rinsing a pan and leaving it in the sink. She hurried out the door, saying to herself out loud, "We certainly do not need a goat!"

The trio came into the back yard where Al propped his bike against a tree and untied the bleating goat from the bicycle and secured him to the clothesline. "Watch out, now," he told the children and their mother, "He will butt you if you get too close." Pete and Susan danced around clapping their hands, laughing, and shouting, "What's his name, What's his name?"

"His name is 'Casey' and he's a mean ole cuss!"

"You can just march right back where you got him and tell the owner 'Thanks' but 'No thanks,'" Beth demanded. "Who does it belong to, Al?"

"I can't do that, Mom. You see, he belongs to the school and he's our softball team mascot."

She had her hands on her hips with dissatisfaction written all over her face. "If he belongs to the school then why did you bring him to our house?"

"It's like this, since I'm the newest member of the team I have to look after him over the weekend. Our first game is next Friday night and this weekend there isn't anyone to look after him. They said I'd have to or else I couldn't play on the team."

"That is a senseless reason, Alyn Russell! You know he will simply chew that rope to pieces and run away. Figure it out . . . do something with him! Besides, there's no grass in this yard, so what is he to eat?"

"He won't chew the rope as long as Sally is standing here barking and worrying him so I'll just leave him tied here until Pop gets home, and he will help me work out what I should do with him. Oh, and Mom, Penny told me to tell you that she went home with Gwen. She said Gwen told her that her father would bring her home around six o'clock."

They all went inside to get homework and let the dog, Sally, handle the goat for a short while longer until John returned home. Beth couldn't help but laugh, not in front of Al, however. Her life seemed like one big circus with never a dull moment. Maybe someday she and John could dump the kids on Teresa and Papa and go on a cruise vacation. What a pleasure that would be! No doubt, she thought; John has never taken any time off at all. She would remember to speak with him about it.

John was late getting home. It was after dark when he pulled his car into the garage beside Beth's and wearily got out. It had been a busy day at the hospital and then a full schedule of patients to see in the office. On the way home he stopped off to visit with an elderly homebound patient. He had gone without lunch and was not in a jolly mood. With the children's homework all finished, the television was now blaring and up in Penny and Susan's room, music blared. When the front door opened, John was pounced upon by the two younger children who were talking excitedly and both at the same time. When the front door opened and closed, Al came down from upstairs taking the steps two at a time, exclaiming loudly, "Guess what, Pop! I brought the ball team's goat home with me and he has now disappeared! I had 'im tied up and he got away. Man! Am I in trouble now!"

"Why in the world did you bring him home in the first place?" John asked just as Beth came into the front room.

"My dear husband," she said softly as she walked over to him and gave him a peck on the cheek, "this is part of being a parent."

"And Sally is gone, too!" Pete wailed. "She won't know the way back home like Susan and I did one time, remember?"

"Both gone, huh? How fortunate can we be?" John said softly only for Beth's ear. "Oh, I'm sure Sally will be back by morning. She won't go far out of sight of the house. She'll come back when she gets hungry. Dogs are much smarter than goats." Then he looked at Al and said, "And boys are supposed to be much smarter than goats! I'd wager that you tied him up with a rope?"

Al's eyes looked to the floor as he answered, "Yes, sir, I did."

"Then I suppose you had better be calling your coach or your Aunt Teresa. Get ready for an ear full from the coach."

"Uh . . . I think I'll call Aunt Teresa first."

"Just because she's your aunt, don't expect any favors. She is the vice principal, you know, and right now you are only a mere student."

Chapter Six

RAYMOND O'BRYAN, FATHER OF DR. NAT O'BRYAN, stood in front of the old Fullman mansion, hands in pockets and feet planted wide apart for balance, as he gazed up to the top of the awesome old structure. In all his years of designing office buildings and houses, he had never undertaken restoring such a marvel as this. He shaded his eyes with a hand, perusing the façade from portico to the Grecian columns and up to the sagging roof. He shook his gray head and turning to his son said, "Nat this is a magnificent old place indeed! It has spirit . . . aristocratic grace!"

Nat had his hands in his trouser pockets. He shrugged his shoulders and said, "It may have spirit, Dad, but I hope there are no spirits residing here." He chuckled, happy that his father at once seemed to be as awe struck with this old mansion as he was. His father's face lit up with delight and Nat thought when he turned toward him that he looked much younger than his sixty-eight years and in fact was a very handsome man for his age. Raymond was tall and trim and carried himself with dignity. Even before today, Nat had wondered why his dad had managed to escape the clutches of some designing woman. It had been ten years since his mother's death.

Weeds and vines had nearly engulfed the structure, poison ivy clutched a chimney on the front side, visible from where the men were standing. The two chimneys on each side of the house looked intact. Nat's father walked up the brick steps between two mammoth Doric columns and on to a wide veranda. Columns also graced each corner of the veranda. "Ahh, can't you picture this porch lined with rocking chairs," he mused out loud. "It's a wonder that those heavy wisteria vines hanging over the porch roof had not rotted it down by now."

"Is the porch safe to step on?" Nat asked, following behind his father.

"Seems sturdy enough so far. A house of this type architecture would have been built of only the best materials and back when this one was built the carpenters took pride in their work. It should still be sturdy after all these years."

Nat still stepped carefully, following after his dad as Raymond took a pen from his shirt pocket and stopped to make notations on a legal pad. It was his intentions to check the place over from portal to postern. Raymond O'Bryan took hold of the brass knob of one of the heavy oak double front doors and found that it was not locked. When Nat told Emily Arnold that they would look at the house today she evidently went there and unlocked the door. Inside the foyer, they marveled at the heavy paneled walls, still in perfect condition underneath a thick cover of dust. At the end of the hallway was a staircase in the middle where one could walk around the stairs either to the left or the right. In the well above the stairs hung a magnificent chandelier from a brass chain. Light from the open door flashed against the prisms causing them to sparkle like diamonds. The two men stood there transfixed, gazing in amazement. Raymond spoke first: "I cannot understand how that beauty escaped the hands of mischief seekers! It would be worth a fortune." Then, turning to his son, he said that the Arnolds would double their asking price if they only knew the cost of the chandelier alone. "When cleaned, those prisms will knock your eyes out." Before he moved from this spot Raymond turned and looked all about. "Son, Senator Fullman's father really had an eye for architectural beauty." Nat answered by saying that most old southern gentlemen did. Then he glanced through a doorway to the right of the entrance and noted the heavy tattered drapes that had a musty smell, which tickled his nose even from that distance.

"Why did they not put this place up for sale?"

"I don't know anything about it other than what I've already told you," Nat answered. "I wonder if we'd have any trouble obtaining a deed?" He thought out loud. Raymond did not answer since he had walked on up the stairs, gazing transfixed at the chandelier as he went. He poked around the upstairs rooms making notes on the pad and comments that were meant more for himself than his son. Nat followed, recognizing his father's escalating excitement. He commented on the high-ceilinged rooms and rubbed his hands over walls noting the type of wood used. He mentioned the limitless possibilities of the house when brought to a restored state.

Then Nat said that Emily had told him they sold off the elaborate furniture and paintings and purchased the house they live in with the money. "Paid cash for the house." One room upstairs must have been an office. It was lined with bookcases and the walls were paneled with walnut. "But look at that," Nat said. "Here's a painting they didn't sell! No one wanted that old austere looking gentleman. I certainly would not have him staring down at me every time I sat down at my desk."

"The artist must have liked black," Raymond commented.

After examining all the rooms on both floors, the men were now walking around toward the back of the house where they discovered a large oak had fallen over against the roof of the kitchen area. "What was up there over the kitchen?" Nat asked.

"It was the office. I failed to look for a way up to the attic. Well, I'll have to come back and bring a contractor to go over the whole thing anyway and a plumbing contractor, too. No need to go to all this expense without making it turn a profit. So, are you thinking the same thing I am, Nat?"

"An inn, of course."

"Yep. Kendell Mountain Inn. People would flock here by the droves just to sit in rocking chairs on that porch and gaze at the mountains and breathe the fresh air. I may have to build on an extra room for myself. Oh, I meant to say that we certainly should add on a wing because there are only five bedrooms upstairs . . . not enough for guests. The excursion train that only blows its whistle as it passes through would be loaded with customers!"

"Some of the older residents who don't care much for change might not be too keen on this."

"No matter how set in their ways they are, they will eventually have to accept change," Raymond said as he stopped walking when they reached the front and he looked down upon the town. "Change is inevitable. A town will die if it doesn't keep up with the times and this old house with an enigmatic personality will be part of the change."

"I certainly understand, Dad. They tell me that the feed and seed mill and the hosiery mill have brought in a lot of new people to work in them."

"Son, I think this is a great opportunity, not only for the town of Union Gap, but for you, too. I'm willing to draw up the restoration, figure the materials, and hire the people to do the work. After we get the figures of the contractors then we'll see what it will take to put the old lady back in order." Raymond had an arm across his son's shoulder. "I'm so certain it will be a great success that I am willing to go to the bank with you."

Nat grinned. He knew his father would come through. "Then we're partners, Dad." And they shook hands on the deal.

As they were walking down the tall steps at the end of the walkway, Raymond stopped and pointed to an area where he commented would be the place to grade for a parking lot. "We'll have to have room for tour buses, too. From a circular drive on up to the front, people could be let out there and then vehicles come there to park. Old folks can't manage all these steps."

"How would you know about that, Dad?"

"Can't you hear me puffing? And, by the way . . . I've got a toothache, too. Reckon you could work on it this afternoon?"

"You'd better believe it, partner! But let's go down to the Skillet now because it is about time for some folks to come in there that I'd like you to meet . . . especially Alyn Russell. You two will get along just great, and I do want you to see his place up on the mountain."

Raymond turned for another look at the grand old lady, whom he felt was now smiling at him with great satisfaction. If she could, she would even wink. Yes! Raymond O'Neal would restore her to health and happiness.

Chapter Seven

ALYN RUSSELL LOVED HIS QUIET SATURDAY MORNINGS alone on the porch where he could indulge himself in the morning newspaper and a large mug of coffee. Up with the birds, he made an early trip down the mountain each Saturday to get a paper from the box outside Becker's store. This early in the morning no one was stirring about, so his trips were just there and right back to his porch. This morning was no exception. Teresa had gone off for the weekend somewhere for a teacher's conference and Alyn decided earlier that it would be a good day to take the grandsons fishing down to Everitt Lake. Yes, that would be a great thing to do today, but not before the newspaper was read. No doubt Beth would be happy to have them out of the way while she cleaned house and perhaps John would go along with them. Being a doctor certainly had its disadvantages. He worked too much, but at least he was home every night and on weekends and Beth was happy.

Taking his glasses from a shirt pocket Alyn began to scan the pages of the sports section but before he had settled on one particular item to read, he was distracted by the sound of an automobile coming up the road. When the car got closer into view, he laid the paper on the floor beside his chair and said, "Well, I do believe that is Tiss's Chevy. She must be going up to see Beth." He took the last swallow of coffee and stood to call out to her as she went by. But . . . no, she had not kept on going. The car turned in to Knollwood's driveway. Alyn went to greet her at the front door on the other side of the house. There was a porch entrance on the driveway side, which the residents called "the front" but was really the side. Alyn had always preferred to sit on the porch facing the road.

"How do I rate such an honor as a visit from the beautiful school principal so early this morning?" he asked as the door was held open for Tissy to enter. "It's a good thing you didn't come in from the back like you always do. Ole Charlie has already attacked me this morning when I came in from getting the morning paper. That dang rooster is nothing but a nuisance."

"I didn't give him a chance this time," she smiled as he held the screen door open for her. "I hope an early visit is not an inconvenience." She stepped gingerly inside, wearing an attractive but simple navy blue pants outfit. She liked to wear what she pleased and felt comfortable in during her leisure times. Her smile showed her deep dimples that lent a youthful look to her sixty-one years. Alyn led the way down the hallway, past the parlor to the porch where he had been sitting.

"It's such a nice morning so I was out enjoying the porch. Sounds like the birds out there are having a concert just for me. Would you care for some coffee, Tiss?"

"Thanks but no, I had some a while ago. It always gets me going."

He pointed to the chair across from where he had been sitting, enjoying the newspaper, and was glad to see her although curious as to the nature of her visit. "What is my favorite aunt up to today?" he teased. She had married his uncle Bob but Alyn was about six years older than she, and he liked to tease her about being his aunt. Even so, they had always been close friends. She and Cynthia were both pregnant at the same time with Bess and John. His Uncle Bob came to Kendell Mountain as a young man of twenty-two, a preacher who had only come to check up on his young nephew, living with Joyce Abernathy, and there Bob stayed. He became a member of the Kendell Mountain School Board, as well as school principal and preacher. Their daughter, married to Mark Arnold, had two children. Bob Russell died five years ago.

"Must I have an ulterior motive to visit? And, I'm your aunt! I well remember when we all visited one another and sat on porches or in parlors, talked and laughed and ate cobbler with hand-cranked ice cream."

Alyn's brown eyes flashed with glee and his face softened when he briefly thought about those olden times when things were gentle and simple. "Come to think of it, we had one of those old time get-togethers just recently and your presence was sorely missed."

"I'm sure Teresa knew I was out of town, but I was rather glad that I missed it when word of the lost snake got back to me. By the way, was the thing ever found?"

Alyn looked down with a solemn face and then jumped from the chair as he pointed toward her feet while loudly exclaiming, "Watch out! There it is!"

Blood drained from the frightened woman's face as she scrambled from the chair, rushing to stand behind the laughing man and then discovered at once that he was only teasing. "Oh, you!" She scolded and swung her purse, hitting him on the shoulder.

He threw his hands up covering his face. "Help! Help! I give up, ma'm. Please don't hit me again."

"Alyn Russell! You act like a twelve year old. You scared the wits out of me." She sat back down and reaching for a section of his newspaper began fanning herself. Then they both broke out into hysterical laughter.

He tried to look serious, saying in a whisper, "But we never did find the blamed thing." Tissy promptly propped her feet into a chair across from where she sat.

"Now you made me forget just why I came this morning. Let's see . . . oh, one thing is about Susan's poem. Has she read it to you?"

"Yep, she sure did. Smart kid, huh? Takes it after her grandfather, you know."

"No, I don't know so much about that but I'll tell you what, if her poem is not voted the best, then something will be terribly wrong with the panel of judges. I hope the poem was not any of Beth's doing. Tell me that it wasn't."

"Beth told me she only suggested and steered her toward the words and Susie came out with them on her own."

"Okay then. That is acceptable. And . . . oh, yes . . . I am going to suggest to the next board meeting that Beth be hired to paint a portrait of Miss Ella to hang in the school's clinic. After all, she did donate the funds to build the clinic. I understand that before then the school was on shaky grounds financially. She certainly deserves this recognition, don't you think?"

"Certainly. I only wish it could have been done while she was still living." We have all been so proud of the paintings she did of Aunt Joyce and Uncle Anson as the founders. That lobby would not look right without them. That would be a very wonderful suggestion that no one would object to. In fact, I think there needs to be a special program in the auditorium that will make the students realize just how much work, sweat, and tears all three of them put into the founding of Kendell Mountain School. If only Aunt Joyce and Uncle Anson could see it now! My goodness! They would be so happy. And Tiss, I think you will be making a suggestion that is needed, in fact, long overdue."

"Yes, it is way overdue, and I only wish I had thought of it before now, or anyone else for that matter. Miss Ella was a wonderful person. Everyone loved her and her jolly, happy personality. She was actually funny and brightened, or livened up, I should say, any gathering. She put me through college, you know, and even bought my clothes. Remember, she did the same for Cynthia."

"How right you are and couldn't Miss Ella bang on that piano with her comical little ditties?" They both laughed when they thought of how Miss Ella had always played the piano at their town gatherings when they were small.

"Yes, we will have a program for this occasion and you will have to attend and, of course, the artist also will be honored. Beth does have a God-given talent for painting portraits."

"Okay then, that's that. But, is this a meeting we are having here ourselves, or what?" Alyn joked and wondered if that was all she had come up this morning to tell him. "I think it would take three to call for a vote. We're just deciding though, aren't we?" he answered.

"You bet, but this next thing I wanted to talk with you about, I hope you will heartily agree that we may do."

"If you need my input on whatever it is, then let's have it. What's next?"

A number of years ago Alyn had been president of the board and he had held very informal meetings. That was after the fire that took the lives of Joyce and Anson. At that time Anson was president and because he had formal meetings with the employees of the railroad that he owned, he had been a very good leader in forming the school.

"Okay, here it is. Would you agree to let the tenth and eleventh grade history classes go up in the cave as a group?" She did not wait for his answer but continued. "It would be a very educational field trip for them. If you agree, I'd like for you to be the guide . . . oh, but of course, there would be several teachers along. You would be the perfect one to give them the history of the cave and tell all about Chief Little Bear and his parents and also about you and Luther finding that bag of money in the cave. The class has been studying about the Cherokee Nation and the Trail of Tears." Tissy paused to look at him and read his face and then said, "Come on, Alyn . . . will you do it, please, for me but mainly for the children?"

He had been bent over with his arms on his knees listening intently and Tissy thought perhaps he was interested. This place was dear to his heart because his friend Little Bear was buried there and also the old Indian's parents, Running Wolf and Red Bud, and his siblings who had died in infancy. Alyn's thoughts quickly flashed back across the years to the time when his dog, Beans, had gone into the cave when he and Luther were frantically searching for him. They had not known about the cave being there until they started searching for Beans and found him inside. "Tiss, you know I wouldn't mind and I'd be glad to go along, but we have to lay down some strict rules to the kids. They are not to go off up there again. They could become lost in the cave completely. And then, there's the lake where they could fall in or be pushed in."

She clapped her hands together and felt a leap of heart. "Oh, Alyn, of course there would be rules. Every time there is a field trip they are drilled on the rules."

"And they would need flashlights, too," Alyn added.

"All right. It would not be until May near the end of school that we'd take them so they would have plenty of time to write home either for money to buy them down in town or their folks to mail them. Would you tell the hardware store to stock up?"

"Sure will," he smiled already looking forward to the coming event. "Maybe that darned goat has taken up residence in there," he mumbled.

"Then you'd better take a collar and chain along, I suppose." There was a moment of silence before Tissy said, "Thank you, Alyn. I knew you would come through for the kids."

"Actually, it will be rather fun. And now, is there anything else for our two-person board?" He grinned a silly grin but it quickly disappeared when he noticed a definite frown on her face.

She cleared her throat, pressed her lips into a straight line, looked down to the floor for a few seconds and then looked him in the eyes, saying, "Now I will tell you some news that you may argue with me about."

"You know I never argue, my dear, especially with someone much smarter than myself."

"I may have to remind you about that, the part about no arguing with me," she said solemnly.

Alyn straightened up and laced his fingers together across his stomach with a feeling that Tiss was actually serious about what she had said. He hoped he would not dread to hear this news that she was so reluctant to tell him about. She sat gazing at her folded hands in her lap, feeling a mixture of emotions. It seemed like an eternity before she raised her head to speak. He saw that tears had welled up in her eyes. One spilled over, sliding down a cheek when she raised a hand to wipe it away.

Alyn pulled his chair closer until their knees nearly met. He took her hands in his. "What is it Tiss? Don't tell me you are sick or something like that. You don't have something bad wrong?" It was a question instead of a statement.

Tissy shook her head from side to side. "No. No, Alyn. I'm certainly not sick." Again, she hesitated. "I just . . . well, in one way I have a heavy heart and in another way it should be a happy time."

"Then just tell me, Tiss. You know if I can help in any way, I'll do whatever I can."

She looked her perplexed friend straight in the face and said with a sad, small smile, "There will be another item on the agenda of the next school board meeting. I'm turning in my resignation, Alyn. This will be my last year at the school." She watched him anxiously for his reactions.

His eyes widened. "But for heaven's sake why, Tiss? What do you plan on doing with yourself? You're too active and on the ball! That would be like putting a good horse out to pasture before its time!"

"I'm an old lady, Alyn," she said softly, hating to admit it.

"Old? I disagree with you on that! You're a dang sight younger'n I am!"

"Now, didn't you tell me just recently that you would like to stop the apple growing business? Huh?"

"Don't change the subject woman!"

Upon hearing these words, her face, which had been set and tense, fell into a smile . . . not her usual wide smile showing the cute dimples, but one with a bit of sadness. She had been wrestling with this problem for quite a while. Alyn took her hands in both of his. "Remember when Cynthee, Luther, 'n I and sometimes your ma would let you come along, the little brat that you were, and we would sit for hours watching the school being built. Never in our wildest dreams would I have ever thought the little brat would one day be principal of that school."

Tissy removed her hand making as if to pat a wisp of hair in place but the hand wound up wiping another tear. Alyn knew she was emphatic that this would be her last term at Kendell Mountain School. "Well, you don't seem particularly happy about my decision," she said smiling weakly.

"I was just thinking that with your leaving, the school will be in a new era with the younger folks at the helm. It's rather sad." Then his eyes met her's in a long searching look. "Tiss, if this is what you want, then go for it. You have put in a lot of years there. You have worked hard and long and always placed others first. Yes, it is time for you to think of yourself for a change. You need to sit back now and enjoy life. You know, life is very precious and I fully believe the good Lord meant for us to enjoy it to the fullest. That's just what I meant when I said what I did about the orchard. It's about time somebody else did that, too." Then he drew her up and rocked her in his arms. They stood there in each other's arms for a few minutes and if anyone had seen them just then they would have sworn they were lovers.

Tissy broke the spell by pulling away from him and asking Alyn to see if he could get in touch with David and Kate Harris and invite them to come to the program, if they were able to travel at their advanced age. Alyn said he'd be happy to. He had not phoned them since Christmas and he'd not seen the couple for years. Kate was his adopted sister, since she was the daughter of Anson Kelly, and Anson and Aunt Joyce had legally adopted him. He realized they were old but if their health was still good, then just maybe they would come. He'd be happy to meet them in Atlanta at the airport.

Chapter Eight

ALYN SLID INTO THE BOOTH BESIDE REV. JESSE AND Nat early on a beautiful Thursday in April, steaming cups of coffee already in front of them. "Hi, Alyn," the preacher said as he moved over to make room beside him. Annie saw him when he came in the door and was already on her way to the table with the coffee. "Good morning, Mr. Alyn," she said with a cheery smile. "You're a little bit late this morning."

"Yeah, I got to talking to some of the fellows over at the mill." Annie placed the cup and saucer in front of him and poured his coffee. The creamers and sugar were already on the table. Nat pushed the basket of them over to Alyn.

"Well, you haven't missed anything, Mr. Alyn," she said in her slow drawl. "It's been sorta slow in here this morning. You want anything else?"

"No, thanks, Annie. I ate with Teresa this morning." Then turning to the two friends, he asked: "What's new with you fellows?"

"Same ole, same ole with me," Nat answered. "All work, ya know," and Alyn answered with sarcasm that right now it looked like he was working real hard. Brother Jesse grinned and said that about the hardest work he'd heard of Nat doing was handing out candy to all the kids in town to make their teeth rot.

"Now preacher, I think you'd better open up a confession booth in that Baptist church with you the first in line," Nat joked and they all laughed.

"Anybody seen my boy this morning?" Alyn asked between sips.

"Nope but there's several cars over there in front of his place," Jesse said and added that some of them might be waiting for the dentist to finish his coffee break. Nat said they wouldn't be his patients because he'd kept this morning open since his dad was coming up and due to be there any minute, so the cars were all for John's office.

"I invited your dad to come up to our place the next time he came, and he said he would," Alyn said as he sat his cup down. "Said he likes to fish so we might just drown a few worms."

"He's a fisherman alright but we've got some work to do at the Fullman place today."

"Well, you've got to feed him so how about the two of you coming on up to the house for supper tonight. You, too, Brother Jesse, if you are free."

"Th' reverend is too smart for that," Mack said as he heard what was said just as he walked up to the table and stood there looking down at the group. "He knows that there snake in yore house has done had babies by now!"

Brother Jesse grinned at what Mack had said. "Thanks Alyn, but I have a deacon's meeting at the church tonight, and I believe you are supposed to be there also," Brother Jesse answered.

"Aww, I forgot about that. You can do without me this once, can't you? We don't have any real important items on the agenda, do we? Nat's dad may not get back up for several weeks."

"I suppose we could let you off this once; just as long as it doesn't get to be a habit . . . only kidding, you know. I know you are always faithful to be at the meetings."

Mack had pulled up a stool and sat beside the table. Several people came in and he threw up a hand. The waitresses took care of them.

Back when the Kendell Mountain School enlarged, church services for only the students were held in the auditorium and the mountain residents moved their memberships to the Baptist church in Union Gap. That little church had now been enlarged since it was bursting at the seams with all the new members. The old building that was built in 1905 stood right against the new one because of a lack of space, and for a while this old building was being used as Sunday school rooms. Now that the new church had even been enlarged, the old building stood abandoned. Some of the new members were entirely new residents who had retired and decided to move from Atlanta to a more secluded area. They found Union Gap to be a haven of rest. At first, the older residents resented any newcomers. When they got to know each new person, they found that they were just as nice as any Union Gap resident, and it did not take long for the new neighbors to become one of them. This was particularly true after sermons in both the Baptist church and the Presbyterian church were given on loving your neighbor and being told that God loved his children in the cities as well as the small towns.

Among these new people was a couple who had recently retired from their professions who offered their services on a part-time basis to the Kendell Mountain School. Dudley Landress had been a professor at Georgia Tech and his wife, Paula, had been a high school English teacher for twenty-eight years. They were more than welcome at the mountain school.

Also among the new people in town was a retired electrician, Carlton Andrews. Nat phoned his dad to check him out before he hired someone from Atlanta. That would save having to pay room and board for one less person. Alyn had already told Nat about Abe Dodd, the town plumber, who was honest as the day was long, and for that reason everyone called him "Honest Abe." So, before Raymond O'Bryan arrived, Nat had already spoken to an electrician and a plumber. Carlton Andrews really did not need to work as he'd prepared for retirement and it was now just his wife and himself at home. He'd work for reasonable pay, but "Honest Abe" was much younger and still had teenagers at home. He would be reasonable, Alyn told Nat, but he'd ask for more pay than Dodd. Nat told the two men that he would have his dad get back with them.

When the "Skillet Gang" got around to discussing retired folks finding more to do when they retired, Nat mentioned that it seemed some folks just did not know when to quit working and enjoy life. "Seems like that's the only perk that comes with old age," he said punching Alyn.

"I don't know so much about that, son. I haven't slowed down very much yet, myself. Besides! Just who're you calling old?"

"I guess I got myself into a mess maybe. Come on, Mack, help me out a little here."

"Don't get me into it, buddy. I don't know what you're talking about. I ain't retired 'n I ain't old neither."

Nat looked around nonchalantly, rolling his eyes and then said, "My, my, it does look like we're going to get some rain, doesn't it?"

"Ah, forget it, Nat. We'll let you off free this time," Alyn said and then Mack said, "Yeah, but you better watch it, buddy." Then he turned to the preacher saying, "Have you heard the one about the three preachers telling each other jokes?"

"Can't say as I have but I do believe I'm about to hear it," Brother Jesse said, looking up to the ceiling as though he were asking for perseverance.

Mack cleared his throat and began. "Well, they were confessing their shortcomings to one another. One preacher said that his had always been that he couldn't help but gamble on the sly. The other two just said, 'tisk, tisk,' and shook their heads. The second preacher said that he just had the terrible habit of stretching the truth like it was a second nature. Then these two who had confessed turned and looked at the third one who seemed sorta hesitant to tell his bad habit. 'Come on,' one of the others said, 'We've told our little secrets so you come across, too.' Then the third preacher said, 'Fellows, I'm just real, real sorry to tell you that I just can't help but gossip . . . and you're in real big trouble now!'"

Alyn and Nat got a real bang out of that but Reverend Jesse only grinned and shook his head. "So, what's your short-coming, Brother Jesse? We won't tell a soul," Alyn whispered.

"Mine's too many to single one out," the preacher answered still smiling from the joke. "And I think this is a good time to make my exit." He laid a tip on the table and slid out of the booth with Mack getting up and removing the stool.

"Oh, I nearly forgot," Alyn told Mack. "Teresa asked me to see if you'd part with your recipe for that jim-dandy egg custard she loves so much. Said she can't order any of your other pies because she can't get past that one."

"Sure thing. That's quite a compliment. Tell her I'll give it to her but just don't go into the pie business with it or she'll have me going broke." Mack leaned over the table to retrieve a napkin and said, "Here, Al, I'll call it off and you just write it down." Alyn retrieved a pen from his shirt pocket and wrote as Mack called it off.

"It's more simple than falling off a log. Let's see now . . . four eggs, one-fourth cup of sugar, one tablespoon butter or margarine, one-and-a-half cups milk . . . tell 'er to get the milk hot . . . then one-half teaspoon of salt . . ."

Alyn broke in, "No! You don't use salt in a pie!"

"Oh, be quiet, now, who's pie recipe is this anyhow? Write it down, just like I said . . . and then one teaspoon vanilla, one tablespoon of cornstarch. Now that there's all you put in it and tell 'er to mix it all up good and pour it in a pie shell . . . not one of them cracker crumb kind you know, but made up with dough and, oh, tell 'er t' brush around the sides with melted butter. That will make the crust nice and golden." He said the last sentence with a whisper and kissed his fingers like a French chef.

"Thanks, Mack," Alyn said putting a hand on his shoulder. "I know she will be real tickled to get this."

"Well, she don't have t' broadcast it, ya know."

"I'm sure she won't put it in the newspaper." As the men went out the door, Nat's dad was coming in. Alyn shook hands with him, saying that they had just solved everything so he had nothing to worry about and they could get down to business.

Chapter Nine

LATE THAT SAME DAY, AL SCRATCHED HIS BICYCLE into the Knollwood driveway stirring up dust from his quick turn, rode on to the back, and took the steps two at a time. He had not noticed the car parked beside Teresa's in the back and let the door bang closed as he rushed inside calling loudly, "Papa, Papa, guess what?"

Teresa came from the kitchen carrying a bowl of something steaming on her way to the dining room. "Calm down, Al! What is all this racket about?"

The boy followed his aunt toward the dining room, and Al noticed voices and then laughter. "Uh, oh. I didn't know you all had company."

"Yes, we do and you may stay and eat with us if you like. Push that door open for me, please, dear." She went on in the dining room with Al following.

"Hi, Papa. Hello Doctor O'Bryan." He nodded to the other gentleman and then said to his grandfather. "I'm sorry that I came rushing in making all that noise. I didn't know you had company."

"Well, you may join us, son," Alyn told him. "Mr. O'Bryan, this is my grandson, another Alyn Russell, but we just call him Al."

"Hello, young man. By that uniform you have on, I'd guess you have just come from a ball game," Raymond O'Bryan smiled and held out his hand. Al walked around the table to where he sat and shook hands with Nathaniel O'Bryan's father.

"Nice to meetcha, sir. It was just a practice that I've been to." Then turning to his grandfather, he said, "Thanks for the invite but I am real dirty, and I'll have to get on home for a bath. But, I just wanted to stop by to tell you that I'm in the lineup to play in the game tomorrow night. My first game! And, you've just gotta come, Papa!"

"Well, now, I certainly wouldn't want to miss that for anything. Who are you playing?"

"We're playing Hayesville, and the coach says that I'm a great hitter! I knocked a home run this afternoon at practice!" The boy beamed, expecting each of them to be as excited as he was.

The four adults congratulated Al and Raymond O'Bryan said that maybe he would be headed for the big league. This made Al feel like he was seven feet tall. Teresa commented that she didn't see how they could play without Casey. When Raymond looked rather perplexed, Nat explained to him that the lost mascot was named Casey. "That goat thinks he's one of the players. It's all they can do to keep him out of the game!" Teresa laughed. "He's worth the whole admission price."

"So, your mascot is lost?" Raymond said, expecting an explanation. Teresa told him that he decided to find another home and has not been seen for a while.

Al was very pleased that his aunt did not go into the unfortunate details of Casey's disappearance. Backing out, Al said he'd better get on home, do his afternoon jobs, and get his homework done. He would stay on real good terms with his mother and not take any chances of having to sit this game out. He also said that his uniform had to be washed. After he had gone out, Alyn smiled proudly proclaiming that he'd not miss this game for anything.

The dinner plates had been served when Teresa went to the kitchen to bring in a bowl that she had forgotten in the refrigerator. She handed it to her father at the end to pass to Nat. "The game will be at seven o'clock tomorrow. Surely you will not be working in that house at night?" she looked at Nat and said in way of a question. "If not, you, and of course, you also, Mr. O'Bryan, may like to come to the game. Since it is the first of the season, the band will put on a big show and I think it will be a nice event. I would be honored for you to be my guests."

The men looked at one another, both agreeing that they would have to see her nephew's first game. Nat looked at Teresa and asked if six-thirty would be okay.

"Make it six o'clock and I'll show you around the school," she answered. Nat had previously told his dad about the school, and this afternoon Alyn filled him in on how it came to be built.

The more Raymond O'Bryan heard about Kendell Mountain, the more he longed to relocate there. He no longer needed his large house in Atlanta to look after, so what's to keep him from selling out and moving? He was serious about living at the inn. By the time it would be completed, he would be more than ready to move in. He would just bunk in with Nat while the work on the old house was going on. It would save him a lot of trips back and forth on that winding road. Frances would have loved it here. He sensed that she was nudging him to go forth on the work with all force. It would have been wonderful if she could have lived to share in this project.

Chapter Ten

TISSY RUSSELL WAS SO CERTAIN THAT THE SCHOOL'S board of directors would pass the motion that Beth be commissioned to paint a portrait of Ella Fullman to be hung in the clinic lobby that she had already told her about it. She realized that the job would take time. Beth would have to work on the project all summer to have it completed for the next school session. Beth told Tissy that it would be wonderful if she had known about it before now and could have had it ready for homecoming. "Why do we have to have homecoming at the end of this school season?" she asked. "Why can't we have it in the fall?"

"I don't know," Tissy answered, knitting her brows together. "That is a thought, you know. I will run this by the board and see what they say." She did not mention to Beth that she would be leaving; maybe not leaving the area, however. She did not know as yet just what she wanted to do. The others would argue with her that if she had not as yet made other plans, then why did she have to leave?

That day after Tissy Russell left from visiting, Beth set up her easel and equipment in the dining room. The family always had their meals at the kitchen table anyway. She was studying the photograph of Miss Ella that Tissy had left with her. The lady smiling at her was quite a character, so she had been told. "If one looking at the photo was not acquainted with her in person, could they actually capture her personality in a painting?" Beth wondered. She had heard about her from her father-in-law and from Tissy. She would also get the opinion and comments from John's secretary, Emily Arnold, who grew up in Miss Ella's elaborate home. A child's view of the woman would be a lot of help to her.

Penny came downstairs complaining that Al had his music blaring and woke her up. "Who was the visitor so early this morning? I saw a car just go out the driveway."

"It was your school principal, and it isn't so early, my dear. All of you overslept this morning except Pop, and he's out and about somewhere. You don't seem too chipper, Pen. What's the problem?"

"No problem, Mom. I just feel kind of sad, I guess. I thought I heard Sally barking last night. Must have been dreaming, perhaps. Looks like she would have come home by now. It's so sad without her bouncing around."

"I know, Sweetheart. We all miss her and maybe she will show up before long. How do you think your old mother is going to feel when her little girl leaves to go away for college in the fall?" Beth gave a sad little smile as she reached out to enfold her daughter in her arms. "Wouldn't you like to take some course that Kendell Mountain College offers instead of going away to nursing school?"

"It all seems so blank, Mom. One minute I am sure about what we had decided, and then in the next minute I get to feeling so doubtful. Really, I am quite confused. But . . ." the girl shrugged her shoulders, "we have already applied and I've been accepted." Then she spread her hands out and sighed. "If I feel any different later, say . . . perhaps after I've had a year there, couldn't I make a change then?"

"Certainly, Sweetheart, but I was thinking that since Kendell Mountain College is only a two-year school, you could go to the nursing school after that. But, we will help you any way we can. You know that, don't you?"

"Of course, Mom. I love you."

Tears came to Beth's eyes as they embraced, then Beth said, "And I love you very much. You know that will never change."

"Thanks, Mom. I feel better already. I'm hungry! What is there to eat?"

"You're on your own there! The kitchen is that-a-way. But you'd better watch out, here comes the storm down the steps."

"I think I'll just have a banana and get outta here!"

Chapter Eleven

"THIS IS CERTAINLY A WELL-BUILT BUILDING," Raymond O'Bryan commented as he and Nat went up the stone steps of the Kendell Mountain School. "I wonder who the builder was?"

"Of course I don't know," Nat said, "but I understand that this building was built not too long ago, as well as some of the dormitories. They were about to pop out at the seams and had to enlarge. Teresa will have to fill you in on the construction." They reached the top step where Nat tried the knob of the massive door, only to find it locked. He cupped his hands and peered through the glass and noticed the principal's office lit up. Teresa must be in there, he thought, and rapped on the door. He saw a lady come out from the office and she walked over to the front door with a question on her face, asking if she could be of assistance.

"Ma'm, I'm Nathaniel O'Bryan and this is my father, Raymond O'Bryan," Nat said, realizing that this lady was the high school principal whom he had not met. "We were looking for Miss Teresa Russell. She asked us to meet her here before the game."

"Yes, of course, Mr. O'Bryan, she asked me to tell you that she would be a few minutes late. I believe she offered to show you around the school. I was just about to leave, but I will be glad to show you myself if you don't mind. My name is Patricia Russell, the principal."

"I'm Doctor O'Bryan but folks around here just call me Nat, and we wouldn't want to put you to any trouble, Ma'm. We could just wait outside," Nat answered.

"It would be no trouble at all. I'm always proud to show visitors around. Just let me get my keys from my desk." She turned to go back inside the office and Raymond spied two paintings hanging in the hallway and walked over to inspect them with Nat following behind.

The gold plates at the bottom of the paintings told them that the two people were Anson Kelly and Joyce Abernathy Kelly, founders of the Kendell Mountain School.

"Two very nice looking people," Raymond commented and looked to see who the artist was.

"Yes, Beth Russell, Alyn Russell's daughter-in-law. John's wife. Have you met her? I've heard she is a fine artist."

"No. I have not had the pleasure," his dad answered. "It does look like these Russells have things rather sewed up around here, don't they? And how does this Patricia Russell fit in?"

"The family and close friends just call her Tissy. She was the wife of Alyn's uncle, the Reverend Robert Russell, who died a few years ago."

"You know, son, when we get that inn operating, it would be a good idea to have this local artist display her paintings there. She could put prices on them. I'm sure they would sell." Just at that time, Tissy walked up behind them.

"They were two of the most wonderful people in the world!" she said with sincerity as the two men turned to her. "They raised Alyn Russell. He was their adopted son."

"Oh, I had not heard that," Nat mused. "Well, I learn more about this place every day it seems. Alyn has told me a lot down at the Iron Skillet over our morning coffee, but he hadn't mention that."

"Well, it is no secret. Joyce took him in when he was five and Anson came on the scene about six or seven years later. They loved him like he was kin by blood. I knew them when I was a child and I'll tell you the truth, Beth certainly captured them as if she knew them."

"The painting looks very life-like. She is a talented artist," Raymond said as he backed away to look at the paintings from a distance. Then, there was a loud knock on the front door and the three standing there could see that it was Teresa.

"She has a key," Tissy Russell said but went to let her in.

"Oh, I did a silly thing and left my keys in my desk drawer," Teresa said making a disgusted motion with her hands. "I'm glad you had not left yet," she said as they walked back to the men. "Hello, gentlemen. I'm so sorry to be late, and I'm glad you could come early, but you've had a good guide, I see." And turning to Tissy, she said, "Thanks for coming to their rescue. Will you join us on our tour?"

"No. But, thanks. I have to dash home before the game. I'll grab a quick bite and change these uncomfortable shoes. Ball game hot dogs don't set too well with me, but I wouldn't announce that. Folks might think I would be knocking the team's funds."

"I'm sure there are others who feel the same way," Raymond said, smiling as if he understood. "It was very nice to meet you, Mrs. Russell," Raymond put out his hand to her and she returned the gesture. "I'm sure we will see you at the game. I met a very excited young man yesterday who is looking forward to playing."

"I would not have to guess who that was. The coach says he is a good player, and I hope he will make us proud tonight. We lost the last two games. I'll see you folks later." She went out the door leaving Teresa to give them a tour of the building and a commentary of the school's beginning.

"Has my father told you about the lady who owned the house that you have bought?" Teresa asked as they were going into the chapel auditorium.

"No, he hasn't," Nat answered, "but I'd like to know whatever you could tell us about her."

"Oh, she was a funny lady, I understand. I don't mean funny, like someone 'turned funny,' you know. What I meant is that I've been told she was very jovial and enjoyed a good time. Get Papa to tell you about how she got so much in funds donated toward the school's construction. He could tell you better than I could. And, she was always ready to help out someone . . . like, for instance, she paid for Tissy Russell's college and her clothes, also. Tissy's mother had died and her father was a no-account. She taught music here at the school up until a short time before she died. They say that she was a cut-up at any gathering and amused everyone by singing and playing little ditties on the piano."

"She sounds like someone who would have been a pleasure to be around all the time," Nat said.

"This is a very nice auditorium," Raymond observed out loud as he looked all around and up to the light fixtures that hung down along the aisles. Being observant had been instilled in him with his job over the years. He appreciated the nice construction work here.

"We've had some wonderful programs here as well as the Sunday church services. Only the boarding students attend the Sunday services now but for years the mountain residents attended also. As the school grew in number, the locals started going down in the gap to church." She turned to Nat and said, "Right before school is out for the summer, we will have a nice program and I would like to invite you both to attend. It will be interesting, nothing boring, I assure you."

"Thank you for the invitation, just be sure to remind us," Nat answered, knowing he would like to come whether his father would or not.

"I will tell you that you will learn more about Mrs. Fullman at this program, but I am not at liberty to say more at this time."

"Now you really do have my curiosity going!" Nat grinned. "We'll be here for certain, won't we Dad?" And Raymond agreed.

The men were shown the parts of the school that Teresa felt would be of the most interest as well as the outside of the other buildings and ended their tour fifteen minutes before game time. "I hear the band playing," she said as they were going down some steps from the second floor. "We need to get on over to the field before the best seats are all taken. I hope Papa will save three seats for us." They followed a sidewalk around the main building to the rear and across a grassy field. "We've missed the main gate so we're sneaking in," Teresa laughed. "We would ground kids for doing this."

Cars were filling the parking lot and people were streaming through the gate toward the bleachers. In front of the Kendell Mountain School bleachers, cheerleaders were performing. On the other side of the field, the same was going on with the Hayesville School people. The bleachers on that side were filling rapidly as well. It looked like before long this game would have packed onlookers with standing room only in the back.

Tissy was talking to a group of parents who were seated on the front row when Teresa and the men with her walked over to where she saw them. As Tissy spied them she excused herself from the people she had been talking with. "Hello again," she smiled. "So you got the fifty-cent tour instead of the twenty-five-cent one, and she nearly made you miss the opening pitch."

"Yes, Mrs. Russell," Raymond began. "You have a very good tour guide here," he returned the smile with Tissy thinking what an infectious smile he had.

"Call me Tissy, everyone does, except the students, of course. Come with me. I saw Alyn and his crew on up there toward the middle. Let's see if we can persuade the folks beside him to tighten up a bit and let us squeeze in."

They moved on up several rows and over toward where they saw Alyn waving to them. Tissy said, "Excuse us, please," as they were passing by people and trying not to step on toes. Of course, everyone knew the principal and the assistant principal and spoke to them as they scrounged closer to let them pass. Raised eyebrows turned to one another and cupped hands went to mouths. Before this game could be finished, everyone in the bleachers would be talking about the double date.

After being seated, Raymond leaned behind Tissy and tapped Alyn on the shoulder. "Hope our boy is in good form tonight. What position will he play?"

"Hi, Raymond. Glad you and Nat could make it. I don't know where he'll be. He said he'd been on first at the practice games."

John and Beth also leaned over speaking to the new arrivals. "Thought my sister had taken ya'll down to the dungeons," John said.

"Oh, John . . . don't pay him any mind . . . however, I'll admit they could probably use a dungeon at times," Beth said.

"Where's that pretty daughter of yours?" Nat asked. He had told his dad what a beauty the girl is and that she looked just like her Aunt Teresa.

Beth answered that she was somewhere among the students sitting with a date. "She's bringing a group of them home for refreshments afterwards." Pete and Susan were directly in front of their mother and John, also with some of their school chums, chattering away. Even the younger children felt the electricity in the air. This would be an exciting evening, a perfect evening for a game, no clouds anywhere but cool after the sun had gone down.

Kendell Mountain High School had been archrivals with Hayesville High for years. Away from the campus, there had been fights. After some had been expelled, the fights were now prearranged in a cornfield or some out-of-the-way place. Tonight may be no exception.

Every game drew a crowd, but tonight the crowd exceeded expectations. Yes, the concessions stand would rake in the money, which Teresa had told Raymond and Nat when they passed by the booth would go to buy new uniforms and equipment. Al's uniform fit rather snug, causing him to tug at the sleeves every now and then. Even so, he felt very proud of the number twenty-five emblazoned on his back in bright red and "Russell" in capitals above the numbers.

Kendell Mountain would be in the field since they were the home team. Their pitcher, Red Kennedy, and catcher, Duke Mason, were warming up on the sidelines, and the umpire and managers from both teams were in a huddle. At the edge of the field in front of the Kendell Mountain bleachers, the cheerleaders were revving up the crowd. They had begged the principal to let them cheer at the game. "But we only have cheerleaders at a football game," Mrs. Patricia Russell had told them. "But we really want to, Mrs. Russell, and it will give us so much practice before the football season." Mrs. Russell relented, much to their delight, but only if they would stay along the first row of benches behind the net backdrop. She said that before the game started they would be allowed to perform on the edge of the playing field. Cheerleaders or not, the players of each team were fidgeting on their benches like birds on a power line.

At exactly seven o'clock, a speaker from up in the announcers stand crackled and a loud voice blared out the words, "Let's play ball!" Players on both sides took their places raring to go. Then the announcer came back on to give the starting line-up. The Hayesville coach and manager were both issuing orders and pointing. Duke Mason, catcher, came out putting on his mask, took his place and the first batter up, Craig Lessinger, their pitcher, took his place at the plate, with Mason crouching behind him, punching his mitt. For Kendell Mountain, Red Kennedy was on the mound. It had been said that the moment he received his graduation diploma, he would be snatched up by the major leagues. He was known for his fast ball. The umpire raised a hand and loudly hollered "play ball!" Kennedy stood on the mound eyeing the batter, who was slinging the bat, anticipating one of Red's famous fast balls. Kennedy straightened his cap, which was already straight, dug his left foot into the dirt, then raised a leg, stretched the pitching arm back and let go with all his force. Lessinger struck at the ball, fouling it back right into the catcher's mitt.

"Out!" the umpire hollered. Lessinger slung the bat in disgust, trotting back to the Hayesville bench.

Next batter up was James Jordon, Hayesville's first baseman, who had not struck out once during the previous season. He felt confident and was ready for anything Kennedy might throw. Red Kennedy looked toward Al Russell on first base and then to Jason Appleby on second. Then quickly he gave the stretch and the throw, catching Jordon off guard who swung and missed the ball by a mile.

"Ste-rike!" called the umpire and the Kendell Mountain crowed cheered.

Kennedy caught the ball from Mason, again straightened his cap, dug his left foot in, as though stalling, and then quickly threw a curve that was high and outside.

"Ball one!" The count was now one and one on Jordon. He hit the base and was now poised for the throw. It was delivered, hit, and fouled into the bleachers, making the count one and two.

It was Kennedy's battle. His teammates stood like statues waiting to spring into action. Al Russell was hoping Jordon would make a hit and the ball would come sailing right toward him. He was ready for action! There were calls from the crowd and the cheerleaders were jumping up and down.

Another ball was thrown in to Kennedy who quickly threw a screwball that frightened the wits out of Jordan. He stood there frozen while the umpire called "Ste-rike!" making the count two and two.

Red threw a breaking ball right across the plate that only caught the tip of the bat and rolled right to the pitcher's mound. All the players came in closer hoping for a piece of the action, but the pitcher grabbed the ball and tossed it to Al Russell on first base. "Out!" called the umpire, which retired the side. Kendell Mountain players went to the bench.

The first batter up was right fielder Darrell Ledbetter with Hayesville's pitcher, Craig Lessinger, taking the mound. Lessinger strutted around like a peacock. He spat on the ground, looked right, looked left.

Al, sitting on the bench with the rest of the team, said to Skipper Wilson to the right of him, "Looks pretty darn sure of himself, doesn't he?"

"Yeah, he's a smart aleck if I ever saw one. I'd like to knock 'is block off. He'd better not mess with me."

"I just want to get to bat and knock him down with the ball and then have it keep sailing clear over to their bleachers," Al replied. "Man! That would make me feel like a million!"

"What's the batting line-up?" Scott Meadows on Al's right leaned over and asked. Al answered that all he knew was that his own name was number five batter.

Ledbetter swung at the first ball, which came right across the plate, and strike one was called. Lessinger went into his peacock dance again before the next pitch which was low and outside for ball one. His dance didn't help any. Someone in the bleachers yelled, "Hey, get 'em over the plate!" The next time, he wound up his arm like it had come unscrewed and was about to fall off. There came a fast freight train ball that caused Ledbetter to jump aside. "Ste-rike!" was the call. A fan on the other side yelled, "If you can't hit 'em then get off the track!" The batter stepped back to the plate, the ball was delivered, contact was made, and it rolled through the pitcher's legs on out to second base while Ledbetter ran to first. No outs, one man on, with Hank Soseby stepping up to bat for Kendell Mountain.

Soseby was a fair hitter. He'd never knocked a homerun but he usually managed to get on base. He was a good left fielder with a powerful arm and could catch what was thrown to him without hesitation. He was also a great bluffer and fast runner. If he got a chance to steal a base, he was gone!

The pitch was delivered . . . high and outside for ball one. On the second throw, Soseby hit a line drive straight toward second base, caught by Tip Crosby, second baseman for Hayesville, for out number one and then quickly thrown to first base, but not in time. Ledbetter had slid back on first just in the nick of time, with the umpire giving the safe signal, his voice hollering "safe" drowned out by the roar of the crowd. The count was now no runs, one out for Kendell Mountain. Craig Lessinger was still pitching for Hayesville.

Alyn held his little battery-powered radio in his hand. Those around him could hear the play-by-play account by the announcer in the booth located high over the concession stand. At this point the announcer could hardly be heard from the radio because of the noise from the crowd. As the crowd was settling down, listeners close around Alyn could hear the announcer say that next up to bat would be Thomas Adkins, the count still no runs, one out for Kendell Mountain, and Craig Lessinger pitching.

Thomas Adkins, third baseman, trying out the bat before stepping up to plate, found a small crack that he didn't like and called for another. The batboy ran out with a new one and took the damaged bat away. Thomas was ready; he felt confident. The first ball pitched made contact with his bat and he ran to first, Ledbetter to second as the third baseman threw the ball to first . . . too late. Now the count was no runs and two hits with two men on base; the pitcher was worried. Hayesville's manager came out to the mound to talk with his number one pitcher; possibly to find out if his arm was tired and to give him some advice. He patted Lessinger's back for reassurance.

Alyn Russell's radio sounded excited with Kendell Mountain having two men on bases. While the game was momentarily halted, Alyn leaned across Tissy asking Raymond how the transaction of the Fullman house was progressing. "About ready to get the construction started. We close out the sale next Friday. I haven't been this excited in years though everything is all down hill for me from now on. But here I go again. Hope we haven't bit off more than we can chew."

"Oh, no," Tissy broke in. "I think it is a lovely idea. It will enhance visitors to our little town and help our economy as well. It is just what we have needed, and I'm sure Emily and Mark Arnold are overjoyed to have it off their hands!"

"I'm glad to hear that, and I hope the rest of the town will be in agreement," Raymond answered. Then he said to Alyn, but intending for Beth on the other side of her father-in-law to also hear his next statement, "I also would like to hire John's wife to paint a portrait of Mrs. Ella Fullman to hang in our lobby."

Beth drew in her breath, thinking to herself, "Wow! One for the school's clinic and now this one!" She leaned over and said to Raymond, "I think you should talk with Papa's daughter-in-law about this! She just could be very interested."

"I'll do just that and also our gift shop could use some Kendell Mountain and Union Gap paintings by a very talented artist."

Now, Beth's heart did flip-flops. What an opportunity! She never dreamed that her art might actually come to this. Possibly her hobby could turn out to be more than only a hobby.

The crowd settled down when Bryan Alverson stepped up to bat for Kendell Mountain. Hayesville's manager again patted the pitcher Craig Lessinger on the back and walked away. The umpire cried, "play ball." The peacock did his dance, looked at the two runners at first and second, as if warning them that thou shalt not steal, then he quickly turned and threw a slow curveball outside for ball one. "Walk 'im," someone yelled. Ledbetter slipped off of second base. When Lessinger turned toward him, he returned to base until the pitcher turned back to the batter, and then Ledbetter walked off again, anticipating a long hard drive that would at least carry him to third. Lessinger looked toward first, then made the stretch, the leg lift, the wind-up, and tossed one outside for ball two on Alverson. The next pitch was fouled up against the fence behind the player's bench for strike one. The drum started beating as excited spectators chanted "Go, Bryan, go, Bryan, go, Bryan!" This may have been the charm that he needed. His next swing sent the ball out to left field where Kimmerman scooped up the rolling ball, dropped it, grabbed it again, and tossed it to third where Ledbetter stopped before the ball arrived for the safe call. Now Alverson was on first, Adkins on second, and Ledbetter on third; the fifth batter coming up would be Al Russell.

Al's family was yelling with all the breath they could gather. They were standing, as was everyone else, because the bases were now loaded. The cheerleaders were working down on the front row behind the screened backdrop and someone in the audience had a loud horn blasting.

"Yes!" Al shouted when his name was called; he jumped to his feet, grabbed a bat that was handed to him, and trotted to the base. Al said to the catcher as he pulled the mask over his face, "Ya'll 'er gonna get murdered right now, boy, and I'm gonna grind you into the ground." The catcher stood up face to face with Al and pulled his mask off. "You and who else, you skinny runt?" The umpire took two steps over and gave them a warning. That was okay with Al. He got his two cents in, turned and tagged up, tapped his bat on the base, and stepped back, waiting for the pitch.

Nothing would please Lessinger more than to strike this one out! He had heard that he was a pretty good batter. He wound his arm up to make sure the ball left his hand with the momentum needed for great speed. It sailed through the air heading directly to Russell's bat, made contact as he swung with all the force he could gather, sending the ball over the pitcher's head, over the short stop's head, on out beyond center field, with the bat cracking in two! Al was running fast as his legs would carry him, one run came in, the runner at second was moving to third, first was moving to second, and just as Al

Russell reached first base—with the crowd going wild—there seemed to be some kind of commotion at the gate. Al did not know this; he was too busy running.

The excitement at the gate was none other than old Casey, the goat. Mr. Jed Thompson had found him among his cattle and, knowing that the school was missing their mascot, decided to return him while the game was going on. The rope that he had tied to his collar was jerked out of Jed Thompson's hand by the lunging goat, who heard all the excitement and noise of the game and wanted to be a part of it all. He took off with great speed toward the field, spied the runners, and decided to fall in behind Al Russell who was now leaving second base heading for third. The crowd was on their feet on both the Kendell Mountain side and the Hayesville side. The Kendell Mountain folks were yelling, "Go, Al! Go, Casey! Go, go, go!" The band struck up, adding to the noise. Both the *Hayesville Times* reporter and the *Kendell Mountain News* reporter were running along the sidelines with their cameras flashing. This would reach the Atlanta papers within the hour!

In the bleachers, John slapped his dad on the back and then hugged his jubilant wife. Nat became so excited that he hugged Teresa, who looked up into his face amazed and shocked. Tissy, on one side of Alyn, was in a fit of laughter. She could not contain herself.

The first two runners crossed home plate, then came Al and Casey. After crossing home plate, Al turned and grabbed Casey around the neck, with the umpire there to assist, his long straight-laced face actually breaking into smiles. Casey would soon put an end to his smiles. He had other aims in mind. He shook loose from Al, danced around behind the umpire, and butted him to the ground. This would make a wonderful newspaper photo! The fans on both sides exploded with laughter.

The game finally resumed and ended with Kendell Mountain winning five to four, but the newspaper item said that Casey's run should have counted also.

Filing out of the bleachers, Raymond O'Bryan said he'd not had that much fun in years. Teresa invited the group up to Knollwood for coffee and cake where they would laugh through a replay of the game. "But, I thought Penny was having a group up to our house?" John turned to Beth and asked.

"Oh, she is . . . well, we can take in both parties," she answered.

Al and his teammates were invited to the coach's house for hot dogs and hamburgers, but mainly to keep them out of trouble.

"I feel sorry for the coach's wife," Teresa said, and Tissy answered that they would have a gathering in their barn and the band would be invited, too. "I'll have to make an appearance there, myself."

Alyn announced that all should go there instead of his house; it would be senseless for Al to have them up to John and Beth's also, so they would need to head him off now. The coach would expect them all to come to his barn. John agreed and speeded up his pace to go find Al. "Beth, you find the little ones and meet me at the car. We'll go on home with them."

Chapter Twelve

IT HAD BEEN FOUR MONTHS SINCE RYAN AND JETHRO began their journey southward. Ryan had never been any farther south than the next county from where he lived. His sojourn along the way found him doing several jobs to earn money. The jobs fed him and the dog sufficiently and provided a place to sleep and have an occasional bath. Ryan learned much with each job but most of the people he worked for were nosey. They all said he was too young to be off by himself. "Heck!" Ryan mumbled to himself on one occasion, "I'm not too young to join the army!" He actually looked younger than his eighteen years.

There was one job where he had been offered a permanent position. This was in Kentucky at a horse farm where racing horses were stabled and raised. His job was cleaning the stables and brushing down the horses. This was too tempting to pass up. He could stand the shoveling without liking it, just to be working near the wonderful horses; they were beauties! As the days turned into weeks, he was offered more money if he would stay on. The owner liked him and said he was a natural with the animals. Ryan told Mr. Tyler, the owner, that if his original plan did not work out, then he would be back for sure. Mrs. Tyler fed him well, and he had a place to sleep.

One morning, Mr. Tyler came out to the barn where Ryan was hard at work and said that he was going down to Tennessee, about thirty miles south of Nashville, to get some horses from a horse farm there. He offered for Ryan to ride with him that far on his journey if he still insisted on going away.

"Yes, sir, I guess I'd better move on, even though I certainly do like it here. Maybe I won't stay but I just have to go on for a while at least. If you will still have me later, then I'll be back."

Mr. Tyler placed an arm on Ryan's shoulder and shook hands with the other. "Boy, I know my wife will be sorry to see you go, too. You just go on up to the house and tell her goodbye. I'd bet a dollar she'll whip up a sack of food for you to take along. And, with the money you've made here, I'd like to suggest that you get yourself a motel room instead of sleeping outside in that sleeping bag. Just take your time in getting ready, have a bath, and put on a clean shirt. I'll be ready in about an hour."

"Thank you, Mr. Tyler. I appreciate you and Mrs. Tyler being so nice to me and Jethro," Ryan answered with a feeling of sadness in leaving. He still held an anxious curiosity for Kendell Mountain and must press on. Jethro followed right at his heels. He must have sensed they would be leaving shortly and waited on the back steps after Ryan went inside.

Ryan and the dog got out of the truck in Tennessee where the weather was much warmer and hanging on to the coat was cumbersome. He took the advice that Mr. Tyler gave him that night. The motel had a kennel out back where Jethro slept. Ryan did not want to spend any more of his money on food or bus fare. Mrs. Tyler had generously placed plenty to eat in the bag she had handed him with her well wishes.

"Young man, you get your business done down there, whatever it may be, and hurry on back up here. I declare, in the short time you've been here I feel like you belong with us," Mrs. Tyler had told Ryan, making him feel that someone cared about him.

Chapter Thirteen

FOR SOME STRANGE REASON THAT WAS BEYOND HIS grasp, Alyn Russell felt a pang of lonesomeness this bright April morning. Everyone on the place was busy at their own jobs but there was nothing right now that suited his fancy. He had thought about going fishing, then decided that he did not want to go alone. If it had been Saturday, the boys would have jumped at the idea of going along. Then he thought about how he should catch up on some much-needed bookkeeping. His desk was rather piled up, but that would always be right there waiting and could be done at night. So that was out of the question for today.

He was sitting on the porch with the newspaper scattered on the floor beside the chair where he sat with his thoughts turned to long ago. He had always heard that when a person gets old they usually live in the past, but recalling old times was a joy. Some memories were not pleasant so he pushed them aside. He loved thinking about growing up on the place, watching the school being built, and walking Cynthia home from school. In Alyn's mind, he could almost smell the spring-time fragrance of the mountain bursting forth with blooms. Little did he realize that the heady fragrance was right beside the porch now where a wisteria in full bloom was clinging to an oak tree. Along the other side of the road from the house were rhododendrons vying for supremacy. They made his memories even more realistic.

Alyn Russell loved this house, where he liked to think that it was where he grew up. But it was only a replica of the old house.

Now, it was where his children grew up and his grandchildren felt that it was a very old house that held many secrets. They all loved it as well. For these reasons, Alyn could not leave it. The orchards had become a headache and his heart was not in that part any more, other than gazing upon the beautiful orchards at the season when they were in bloom. He remembered the times when the place bustled with workers at apple-picking time, crating and shipping them out. There was always a dinner on the grounds and a lot of pickin'-and-grinnin' afterwards. Now, the large grocery chains were buying only from the huge orchards, which they were told to buy from, and shipped to warehouses where they were distributed out.

Alyn was toying with the idea of growing only enough to furnish the school for their projects and what he could sell to the local stores in town. A good many old trees needed replacing but he would not fool with that for certain. He had assessed enough funds for himself to live on for the rest of his life, so why should he work so hard at it any more? If Tad and Joe and the boys wanted to handle them, then they would be welcome to them. Maybe they would want to truck them down to the state Farmers Market below Atlanta.

Then his thoughts turned to Teresa, his beautiful daughter, the spitting image of her mother, Cynthia. He knew she would want to remain at Knollwood, the only home she'd ever known. She had always been very economical with her earnings as a teacher and now would earn even more as principal. She had been a frugal person. So, she would be all right and he'd not worry about her one bit.

Now that this was settled in his mind, he'd talk with John about it and see if he had any suggestions. "The coming crop in the fall just may be the last I'll ever handle," Alyn thought and, "I kinda think I'll enjoy watching others do the work."

Chapter Fourteen

THE FOLLOWING SATURDAY MORNING, BETH AND Penny were house cleaning when the two younger children came racing up the front steps yelling, "Mama, Mama! Come quick!" They dashed across the porch and stormed inside, leaving the screen door to bang closed on its own. Beth turned off the vacuum sweeper and said, "For crying out loud!" as she put her hands out to take the little dog, Sally, from Peter's arms. The dog turned its head up and licked Beth's face, its tail wagging wildly. Penny, who had been cleaning a bathroom, emerged when she heard the commotion and then a bark from the little dog. "It's Sally!" Penny exclaimed. They each tried to have a hand on the dog, rubbing her back. "What's wrong with her leg?" Penny exclaimed.

"Yeah, and who put this splint on it?" Peter asked. No one knew so no one answered his question.

Beth hugged Sally and headed for the kitchen to retrieve the dog's water bowl from beneath the sink. "Here, Penny, get her some water."

Penny filled the bowl and sat it on the floor. "You, know, Mom, she doesn't look like she's been starving. You can tell she's been taken care of by someone who put the splint on her leg."

Peter was opening a can of dog food and placed it beside the water bowl. He got down on all fours along with Susan; they rubbed Sally as she lapped some water and sniffed at the food, turning as if to say thank you but her wagging tail said it instead.

Peter took off running out the back door to give the good news to Pop and Al, who were tinkering around in the garage. "A splint?" John questioned, rubbing his hands on a shop cloth. "Now, who do you suppose has been taking care of the little dog?"

"Come on and see, Pop. It's really Sally!"

"Where did you find her, son?"

"She was sitting by the front steps and couldn't climb up them."

After examining Sally and finding that she was in good condition, he removed the makeshift splint and discovered that the leg was broken and someone had graciously bound it up. He bound up the leg with gauze and tape, placed the sticks back on with more tape, cotton, and gauze and declared that he had never doctored on an animal before, but supposed this is about all a veterinarian would do for a broken bone, other than an X ray. He handed the dog to Peter and told him to get his wagon, put an old blanket in it, and pull her around to keep her off the leg. "You'll have to take her outside to do her business every now and then."

"Okay, Pop. Thanks. Me and Susan will take real good care of her."

Susan was already on the telephone calling Papa Russell to tell him the good news. John commented to Beth that a compassionate person had taken care of the dog.

"But, it does look like that person would have returned her to us."

"That person did not know who the dog's owner was."

And Beth only answered, "Oh, you're right. Then we don't know who to thank."

"Here, Pete," Penny said with her hands outstretched, "let me hold her for a minute." She took Sally from his arms and stroked the dog's back and held her close to her cheek, with Sally licking the girl's cheek. "We have certainly missed you, young lady, yes we have. I dreamed I heard you barking too, but now I think that I actually did hear you. Just where have you been? That mean ole goat took you off up the mountain, didn't he?" Sally gave some pleasant sounds as she wiggled happily in the girl's arms.

"Let me have her, Pen." Al took Sally from her arms and started out the door. "Come on, kids. Get the wagon. Pete and Susan, you go get a blanket of some kind." Sally barked with pleasure at all the attention she was getting.

As they were going out the kitchen door across the back porch John told them that they should let the dog alone for a while for she must be very tired. He said they should make her a comfortable bed somewhere inside and let her be.

"Well, half another mystery solved," Beth said to John as the four scattered to their own jobs. "We may never know just who it was that took care of her." She put some apples from the refrigerator into a pan in the sink, retrieved a paring knife from a drawer, and started peeling an apple.

"Nope, but the object is that someone did it and probably didn't want any thanks for it," John answered, kissing the back of Beth's neck, her head bent over the apples she was peeling. He turned her around to him, with the paring knife clinking to the sink, and kissed her again, this time a more affectionate one. "I love you more every day, beautiful lady."

"I don't know why, with all you've had to put up with since we came into your life," she smiled up at him.

"You've been in my life from the first day I met you. The first time I laid eyes on you, I was a gonner."

"Why was I so blind back then?"

"You just didn't know how wonderful I was?" he joked with his eyes crinkling at the corners. "I'll tell you what, let's go upstairs right now and start adding to our family."

"John! What a ridiculous thing to say! I'm too old to think of such a thing. Look at Penny . . . she's ready for college and think how embarrassed she would be."

"She'd get over it. How old was your mother when you were born?"

Beth thought for a few seconds while she calculated the answer. "John, she was about five years younger than I am now!"

"That wouldn't hurt a thing. You're in perfectly good health and you have the best doctor in the world who adores you and would take the best care of you and wouldn't even charge you one red cent!"

"Oh, you! Get out of here and let me get my work done."

"Women! Well, if I'm getting the cold shoulder, then I'll just go down and check on old Mama Cowart. She's always happy to see me drive up, and I can hardly get away from her."

"Is Mama Cowart sick, John? I haven't heard anything about it if she is."

"Ah, not really, but I do know it makes her feel so good to have visitors and someone to dote on her and drink her awful herb tea. Say, why don't you come along?" He pulled the apron strings untied and watched the apron fall to the floor as he kissed her again. "Your choice . . . Mama Cowart or John Alyn Russell III?"

"For now, Mama Cowart. There's too many kids milling around to knock on doors and yell, 'Mama, Mama.'"

Chapter Fifteen

"WELL, IF THAT DON'T BEAT ALL!" ALYN RUSSELL SAID as he replaced the telephone receiver after talking with Susan.

"If what doesn't beat all?" Teresa asked when she entered the kitchen and heard what her father had said. He had been sitting at the table with a cup of coffee in front of him when the telephone rang. He had just hung up and returned to his place at the table. She walked passed him to an overhead cabinet and retrieved a mug for herself, then across to the stove and lifted the coffee pot.

"Who was that on the phone?"

"It was Susan. She said their little dog has appeared in the yard with a broken leg. It had a splint on its leg and couldn't get up the porch steps. Now what do you make of that?"

Teresa pulled out a chair across from Alyn. "There's always something going on up there. John has really received an extension of his education since he and Beth married."

"Yep." Alyn took a sip of coffee. He leaned back in his chair and ran a hand across his mouth as if to wipe away a grin that had suddenly formed. "But, he's happy, you know."

"I've noticed, Papa, that he acts like a teenager."

"That's what I meant, but what about my beautiful daughter? Is she happy?"

"Of course I'm happy. What makes you think I'm not?"

"Are you going to be satisfied being a spinster school principal?" Alyn was always blunt and to the point. He had said before that there was no reason to beat around the bush and added that he knew a lot of folks who wouldn't be so long winded if they'd just come right to the point. Tissy had informed Teresa that she would be stepping down as principal and she could rest assured that the job would fall in her lap after the next board meeting.

"And, my dear father, does being school principal require that I am to always be a spinster?"

He took another sip of coffee and eyed the woman before him who looked the spitting image of her mother. "Weel, you know . . . a father can be inquisitive about his younguns, and you will always be my little girl in my old eyes. You might say, I was just checking." He got up and placed the coffee cup into the sink. "I think I'll just go down to town and pick up my morning paper and see what's going on. Might check in on the progress of the inn."

"Surely they won't be working on Saturday, Papa. After all, the men do need the weekend off."

"True, true. Maybe Raymond will be around though and he'll let me poke around. I saw a truckload of lumber heading up to the house yesterday. They may need my expert advice, you know."

"Now, Papa, you just stay out of the way and keep your nose out of it. I think they can manage very well without your help."

Alyn reached for his hat that always hung on the wall behind the kitchen door—when it was not on his head—and turning to Teresa, said, "Catch you later, kiddo."

When he took a paper out of the box and closed the door, he heard someone calling his name and glancing around spied Gloria Spearman walking toward him. "Oh, rats!" he said under his breath with disgust and wished someone would suddenly appear to distract the busybody. But no one was in sight and he had to stand there waiting while she crossed the street toward him wobbling on her high-heeled shoes. He despised her shrill "yoo-hoo" and the silly wave of her hand when she always said it. She was such a busybody and could ask a million and one questions in rapid fire order. Did she think those high-heels and all that makeup made her look sexy, he wondered, not looking straight at her again but down at the newspaper. Her features jumped out at anyone with only one glance. Standing there just now, he hoped she was not going to invite him again to her house for cake and coffee. He'd made the mistake once of accepting. That was a few months ago and since then she'd seemed to appear out of thin air every time he came to town.

"Oh, thank the Lord," he said to himself, "here comes John." He threw up a beckoning hand to him. John was coming from the direction of his office. Alyn, standing by the paper box, was two buildings away and in the other direction. Gloria was walking fast as though she was in a foot race with John. They met at the paper box at the same time.

"'Lo, Papa. Good morning, Miss Gloria," John greeted both. "I hope you are feeling fit as a fiddle after your bout with the chiggers, Miss Gloria," John made the mistake of asking and Alyn broke out with a whooping laugh.

"Chiggers!" he exclaimed. "You been rolling in the grass, Gloria?"

"Alyn Russell! How could you think such a thing! I'll have you know I was checking on the blackberry blooms to see if they would produce a good crop this summer. And just for that smart remark I'll not ask you over for blackberry cobbler and ice cream. I still have some in the freezer from last year." She raised her nose up in the air and hurried on down the sidewalk in the opposite direction, leaving the two men standing there unable to contain their laughter.

"Now, Son . . . have your forgotten your professional manners? Do you go around discussing folk's ailments with everybody?"

John had an arm around his dad's shoulder as they walked along. "Only to my dad. Did I have good timing, or what? I didn't mean to break up any prospects for a hot date."

"You did and for that I am thankful. That woman is making a nuisance of herself. Hey, look at this." He unfolded the newspaper that he had been looking at when Gloria called to him. "Look what's on the front page! Just look at that, would you? Nat and his dad really have the ball rolling now, don't they?"

It was a picture of the proposed Kendell Mountain Inn, as it would look when completed, sitting up on the hill in all its restored glory. And there was a picture of a truckload of lumber and behind it, another truck loaded with shower stalls and commodes. "Whew! They must be shelling out a lot of dough for all that!" Alyn exclaimed.

"There's no doubt about that. Nat told me this morning that the workmen will be arriving tomorrow sometime in order to begin work. Did you come down yesterday, Papa?"

"No. I had a meeting with Tad and Selma about the orchard, and we had to go over a lot of paper work. Thanks to all your good advice, I'm going to start enjoying life as long as I can. May do a little traveling."

"I'm proud to hear that, Dad." He had not called his father dad since the grandchildren came along and started the "Papa."

The men walked automatically to the Skillet, which had now extended its Saturday hours until two o'clock to catch the lunchtime business of the growing town. Now, there would be even more folks to feed with the workmen coming to Union Gap to work on the inn. Some may even be bringing their wives. The Skillet looked nearly full already. As they went inside Alyn made the comment that it looked like nobody cooked at home anymore. Three waitresses were scurrying about. "Looks like Mack has put on some new help," John said.

"Good morning, you two," Thelma said as she passed John and Alyn with plates lined on her arms. "There's a booth over there in the back," she told them dipping her head as a way of pointing toward the direction of an empty booth. "Be with you in a minute or two."

They greeted people at tables along the way and stopped at one where Jed and Edna Thompson were seated. Jed made quips to Alyn, which brought on more conversation and by the time they turned around to go to the empty booth, it had been taken. "Oh, just sit here with us," Edna offered. They had already received their orders and it looked like they were nearly finished with the meal. "We'll be finished here shortly but you are welcome to join us."

"Thanks, we'll take you up on that," John said. The Thompsons slid over, moving their plates and cups to make room. "Whatcha been up to lately, Alyn?" Jed asked.

"Not too much really. How 'bout you all? Got them horses groomed and ready for that big race up yonder in Kentucky?" Alyn asked his old friend.

"Nope. Our only hopeful bruised a foot on a rock and he's hobbling around. We'll sit this one out. We've taken in a few new ones to board. Some folks down in Atlanta just wanted theirs looked after so's they could come up and ride on weekends."

"How's that pretty daughter of your's, Alyn? I haven't seen much of her in a while, except just to speak to her at church." Edna inquired.

"She's fine, just doesn't like to cook breakfast . . . no time to do that anyway, and I'm just plain not going to cook. All those teachers are trying to finish up with this last quarter. Won't be long 'til school will be out."

"My, how time does fly!" Edna exclaimed.

Jed wiped his mouth on a napkin and grinned. "I'm still chuckling over your boy and that goat, John. That sure was some game. I reckon everybody will remember that one for a long time to come. I sure was surprised to find ole Casey in my pasture."

"Al will never live down that episode. I wouldn't be surprised if they don't have a picture of that in the school annual. Al strutted around so he nearly got the big head. We had to cool him down and get his head into the books. Even threatened not to let 'im drive any more." John was looking at the menu even though he knew it by heart.

"Well, folks. We hate to leave good company but we've gotta be going," Edna said. John and Alyn stood up to let them out of the booth. "Ya'll come over to see us sometime. We just don't get together much anymore like we used to. That birthday party Teresa pulled on you was a lot of fun. Found any more snakes in your house?" Jed grinned.

"No. And not even the one that Pete brought in. Say, you're gonna have to have another bar-b-que, it looks like," Alyn told them. They had not had another one since the children got lost on the mountain and their little granddaughter was killed when she fell into a ravine.

"We just haven't had the heart to," Jed said. "Afraid it would bring back unpleasant memories, but maybe sometime we will."

"It might be the best thing for you," John said as he shook hands with Jed and then reminded them that tomorrow would be homecoming at church.

When the Thompsons left, Brother Jesse came in, spied John and his dad, and came toward them. "I figured one of you would be here," he said and sat down. "Hope you don't mind if I join you?" He did not wait for an answer but sat down when John moved over.

"Have you ever asked before?" Alyn said. "You are a member of this club, aren't you? Doesn't your wife cook on Saturdays?"

"Not if she can in any way get out of it. I suppose Nat and Raymond are too busy these days to eat."

"We may not get to eat either. Looks like they are behind in the kitchen," John told him just as Annie came to the table with two cups of coffee.

"Well, hello, Preacher, I didn't see you come in. I'll be right back with another cup. You guys ready to order?" She took out her pad and wrote down what Alyn and John ordered. "Mr. O'Bryan and Nat haven't been in yet this morning."

"Annie, you may as well pull up another chair because they can't go much longer without eating. In fact, here they come now," Alyn said turning his head around to see the door.

"Gentlemen, that big round table is emptying out right now. Do you want to move over there?" Annie said. "You won't be so crowded."

"Sure, Annie, we'll get our cups and you just keep th' coffee coming." Brother Jesse said as they all got up; the other two coming in saw them and headed their direction.

"Here are the celebrities," Alyn said, slapping Raymond on the back.

"Celebrities? What celebrities?" Raymond asked and Alyn handed him the morning newspaper. "Hey! Look at this, Nat!

We are celebrities." They passed the newspaper around. Other people around them turned to make comments and give congratulations.

"Dad, I guess we'd better go get the men on the ball," Nat grinned then added, "but not before we get some fuel for the tummy."

Alyn said that the both of them were going to have to hunker down, too, and how did he expect to keep all the folks' teeth from rottin' out with all his time away from the dentist chair?

"Put an ad in th' paper, I suppose, for an assistant," Bro. Jesse suggested and then added, "maybe Miss Gloria might like a job." This brought on laughter with Raymond asking just what was that funny. No one answered. John only said that he was thinking of someone much younger.

"Well, the church needs a good man to fill the job of teacher for the boy's class ages ten through twelve, since Emily's husband resigned. They say they're going on a cruise. Here are four good prospects right here to fill the position. Now, don't be bashful men. Each of you are very capable for this job."

"Not me," Raymond said. "That's something I could never do. It would scare the wits out of me!"

After the orders were placed, Brother Jesse commented that surely they would not be working on Sunday; he would expect to see their smiling faces in church, and they could expect a grand spread of food since it would be homecoming day. "Yes," Alyn reached over and lowered his voice to Raymond, "we want to introduce you to a ravishing red head who makes the most delicious cobblers you'll ever eat." John elbowed his dad in the ribs. Then Alyn added, "If she don't light your fire then the wood is all wet."

"Why haven't you set your cap for this one yourself?" Raymond shot back.

"Oh, I was afraid she'd get me fat with all her good cookin'; besides, she's more your type."

"You know," Alyn said after he found his cup empty and held it up for the waitress to see, "speaking about needing someone to teach a class, I remember the time when my Uncle Bob was our preacher up on the mountain. He was trying to find somebody to teach a boy's class and everyone was turning him down. Finally he cornered old Leonard Jenkins and asked him about doing it. Said he explained to 'im that he'd have to find something to interest the boys and promise them to do whatever it was he could think up and he reckoned they'd come. As it was, there weren't but a few boys in the class and they weren't very regular either. He expected Leonard to back down like everybody else, but he didn't think for only a minute and said he'd take the job and knew just what he'd promise them to do right off."

Annie stopped by the table and replenished the coffee cups. "Any of you guys need anything else? Sounds like I hear the makings of a long tale."

They waved their hands, declining, so the tickets were left on the corner of the table and Alyn continued his tale.

"Said he'd take 'em coon hunting."

"Coon hunting!" Raymond grinned. Being from the city, he could not understand how a boy would like that kind of a promise.

Reverend Jesse laughed. "I could just see what would happen if they were offered that kind of enticement now days."

"Well, wait just a minute. Bob said th' boys were excited and tickled to go on a coon hunt. Everyone showed up just raring to go. So old Leonard and his boys went traipsing off into th' woods with the hound dogs baying. Leonard had two prize dogs that loved to coon hunt. They took off way ahead of th' boys just a-baying up th' mountain and those little guys was trying their best to catch up with 'em. Old Leonard, he just let 'em go and he waited for the dogs to do their job. They'd tree a coon and wear 'im down 'til th' hunters would come with their guns. Those little boys came home with three coons. Every last one of 'em showed up th' next day for Sunday school and never missed a Sunday because that old teacher had something different each month for them to do, but he'd give a good lesson, too."

"Now, that's what I call a gifted teacher," Brother Jesse said. "Yes sir, I'll just tell our Sunday school superintendent about that, and he could suggest his teachers doing the same."

"Well, gentlemen, come Monday we're going to be plenty busy up at the Kendell Mountain Inn so you may have to come on up to catch me by the coattail, perhaps," Raymond said changing the subject.

"Dad, you can get the men to working and not have to look over their shoulders all the time, you know. You will still need your morning coffee and sausage biscuit," Nat told him.

"Maybe we'll have to set us up a table up there," Alyn answered.

"Nat's going to need to make a lot of false teeth to pay for that place so he'll have to stay on the job," John laughed. "And, speaking of work, I've got to be off right now myself."

"Hey, buddy! It's Saturday, don't you know?" Alyn exclaimed.

"Yeah, but this is not the kind of work where you make money. I promised Beth I'd . . ."

"Okay, okay," Alyn interrupted. "We know you've been sucked in with all those 'honey-dos.'"

Mack came to the table before anyone else could make a remark, saying to Alyn that Benny over at the hardware store wanted to see him before he left town this morning. "Somethin' 'bout some flashlights."

"Oh, I'd forgotten all about that. Thanks Mack. Tissy wanted me to place an order for the school. I guess they're in."

"What's up now?" Mack questioned. "They goin' on a power bill saving thing up there?"

"Ah, she's wanting the kids from one of the classes to make a tour of that cave up yonder before school's out. I don't rightly like the idea, but you know women. They get these notions, you know, and their mind's all set."

"Yeah! Don't we know." John said as he got up, reaching for his ticket. "Beth's painting up a storm. When she finishes with this order from the school, then she'll start on some more for the inn. Raymond, you've got her thinking she'll get rich from what she sells there. Well, I'll be off. Catch you guys later

. . . oh, Papa, tell 'em about Uncle Bob getting stuck in Mr. Nelson's pond." John grinned, playing this one back in his mind as he reached in a pocket to get some change. He laid it on the table before he walked away, knowing his father would draw the tale out in detail.

"How could anyone get stuck in a pond?" Nat questioned.

"Couldn't he just swim out?" Nat's father asked.

"Could have if he hadn't got stuck," Alyn said and leaned back from the table to give the others time to wonder what had happened. He always relished a tale that kept his listeners in suspense.

"Weel . . . you see, it was like this," Alyn began. "It was back when our little church didn't have a baptistery and the baptizin' always had to be done in th' creek. But at this time, it hadn't rained in a spell and th' deeper part in th' creek had become too shallow. Some of 'em wanted to go down to th' river but it was too much of a trip. At that time we just had wagons and on this here particular day we was going to have a dinner on the church grounds so it would take too long to go to th' river. Then, some wanted to go to Everitt's Lake up on th' mountain, but that wouldn't do either 'cause it stepped off too deep. Old Uncle Asa Jones was to be baptized; he weighed about two hundred pounds and said he couldn't swim so Everitt's Lake was out. Uncle Asa was a real cantankerous old soul . . . Bob had been working on getting him saved for years and he finally gave in. Well, th' closest cow pond was down there next to Jed Thompson's place, so everybody decided that this would be best."

"Oh, come on, Alyn, get to the point," Brother Jesse said.

"Now, that's what I think about some of your sermons, Brother, just give me time . . . now who's tellin' this anyhow?"

People at several tables around the group were listening in on this tale, straining to catch every word. They too were wishing he would get on with it.

"Well, let's see now, where was I?"

"Oh, you're just stretching it out on purpose now," the preacher said.

Alyn rubbed the grin from his face and continued. "We just loaded up in th' wagons and buggies and went on down to

Nelson's cow pasture. It was a real pretty day and everybody said their stomachs were growling from the long-winded sermon, but we all knew that the most important thing was for Uncle Asa to get baptized. Anyhow, it had rained for several days before and th' sides around th' pond were all slippery. It's a wonder that Uncle Bob and old Asa didn't just slide right on into th' pond. There was two men who said they had boots in their wagons and the preacher and Asa could use 'em, so they did, they put 'em on and went slippin' and slidin' on into th' pond. Asa got baptized all right. There was plenty of amens and clappin' goin' on and Uncle Bob just dropped 'im one time but he got up okay. Somebody on the side helped get 'im out but the funny thing was that Uncle Bob couldn't manage to get out cause his feet was stuck in mud where the cows had been stomping around in there. Uncle Anson, he was Aunt Joyce's husband, got a rope outta th' trunk of his T-model and throwed it out to Bob and several men held on to th' other end and they had an awful time pullin' Bob out of there. Seemed like the harder they pulled, the more his feet sank down. But they rescued 'im, only thing was that the rubber boots stayed in th' bottom of that pond. I never knew just who it was that lost 'is boots."

Of course, by the time this tale had ended, everyone in the Skillet was laughing and Mack said because of the entertainment, the breakfast was on him. Several of the older customers came over to Alyn saying that they were there that day and remembered this event.

Chapter Sixteen

SUSAN HAD DIALED HER AUNT TERESA BEFORE bedtime and was now talking ninety miles a minute into the receiver. "And Miss Roberson said that I had won the poem contest, she really did, Aunt Resa! I just couldn't believe it when she announced that today. I went by your office to tell you but you weren't there, and I just had to call and tell you. Isn't that great!"

"Yes, it is, Honey! That is wonderful news. After I read your poem I felt like there would not be another one any better than your's."

"But, Aunt Resa, do I hafta read it in assembly? Mama says that I will hafta say it by heart, and I do know it by heart but when I get up there on that stage I just know I'll forget it all."

Teresa smiled into the phone imagining just how frightening that could be for a child. "Tell you what, Baby Doll, you may hold your paper behind your back and if you forget, then you can read it from there on, but I'm sure you will be just fine after you get started. You will just need to forget there are people in the auditorium and pretend you are saying it to your mom."

"Well, I will keep practicing on it."

"Yes, that's the thing to do. You will be just fine."

"Oh, and guess what else, Aunt Resa?" Before Teresa had a chance to say anything more, Susan kept going. "Miss Roberson also said all the poems that were turned in will be put in a book and mine will be on the first page."

"You will be a celebrity, Susan! Just think of that! My niece, a celebrity!"

Susan hesitated for a moment and then asked, "Just what is one of those, Aunt Resa? I don't know if I will like that or not."

Teresa laughed and explained what the word meant. "Here, talk with your grandfather and tell him all about it. Here he comes."

When Papa took the phone and said hello she blurted out happily, "Papa, guess what? I'm going to be a celebrity!"

"Oh, you are? Well, that's just fine, Sweetheart. We needed one of those in our family. I can't for the life of me think of another one in our family who has ever been a celebrity. Will you give me your autograph?"

"Of, course, Papa, if I've got one. What is that?"

"I'll let your mother explain that one. Now, is this all about you winning the poem contest? I'll bet it is."

"Yes, that's what it is but I dread having to say the poem up on the stage in front of all those people."

"Ah, that's nothing to worry about, Sweetie Pie. You've got a whole month to study over it and by that time you could say it for the president of the United States without missing a beat."

"Really!" Susan giggled. "Do you think I could?" And when Papa said sure, she answered, "I think I will just mail him a copy of my poem," and she slammed the receiver back on the phone and ran to tell her mother.

Papa hung up the wall telephone there in the kitchen where Teresa was just as he had come through the swinging door and she had handed him the phone. He turned to her saying, "Teresa, I've got that case of flashlights. I put 'em in the trunk of your car so you can give 'em to Tissy." She nodded an okay.

They were warming up leftovers for supper and placing the little bowls of odds and ends on the table. "Whew! That bowl was hot! Burned the fool out of my hand."

"Looks like you would know by now to use a hot pad, Papa." Teresa took down two plates from the cabinet and tore off two paper towels from the roll beside the sink, placing them on the table while Alyn looked in a drawer for forks and spoons.

"I hope there's some of that good egg custard left. You outdid yourself with that one." Teresa opened the refrigerator and took out what was left of the pie. "I'm glad there's two pieces or you would be out of luck, my dear," he told his daughter. After they'd sat down he told her, "I reckon we'd better ask the Lord's blessings on this leftover stuff. Just how long has it all been in the refrigerator anyhow?"

"Just for that smart remark, Papa, you get to ask the blessing tonight."

He did and then Teresa remarked that he had a way with words and never ceased to amaze her.

"I hope you remembered that tomorrow is homecoming. What are we taking?"

"What! I'd completely forgotten all about it. Now I'll have to stay up and cook half the night."

"Just make a bunch of those egg custards and that will get you off the hook. Might even catch you a man."

"And who wants a man! I have no such notion. I have no time for one, in fact, the man who lives in this house is enough trouble." His brown eyes twinkled merrily, and he grinned knowing she was teasing him.

Chapter Seventeen

WHEN THE FIRST RAY OF SUN BROKE THROUGH THE window beside Nat O'Bryan's bed, he awoke immediately. "Who could sleep anyway with that blasted bird making such a fuss!" he told himself. He had thought before about chopping that tree down. If anybody wanted to sleep late they certainly could not. He sat on the side of the bed yawning and running his fingers through the head of thick black hair and wondering why he had failed to get a haircut the day before. Then, standing and pushing a curtain aside, he noticed little puddles of water here and there and realized it had rained sometime during the night. Usually, Nat was a sound sleeper, as was the case last night except for the agitating dream, which escaped his mind and now could not be recalled. He believed it was something to do with Teresa Russell. "Humm," he thought, again rubbing his head, "She'd be a nice subject to dream about."

Nat's father was still asleep in the back bedroom on the opposite side from the tree with the singing bird. The little rented bungalow was plenty large enough for Nat, a meticulous housekeeper. But Raymond had been spoiled for years by Nat's mother, then by a maid, and now he left a trail of newspapers, magazines, house drawings, clothes, or whatever strewn all about.

Nat slid his feet into the slippers beside his bed and trudged to the kitchen to put on a pot of coffee. He'd brush his teeth and shave while the coffee perked, then Raymond could have the bathroom to belt out his off-key singing in the shower. If the next door neighbors were not early risers before Nat's dad came to live with him, they certainly must be by now. It would either be the bird or Raymond, whichever side of the house their bedroom was on next door. Nat had promised Brother Jesse they would be at church this morning and the preacher had insisted that they were not to worry about bringing any food, as there would be a gracious plenty. The Union Gap and Kendell Mountain women always tried to outdo one another when it came to "eatin' meetins" and especially a homecoming. Now in the kitchen he turned the radio on loud to rouse his dad.

Nat had been to church several times since moving here but as yet had not joined. His dad most likely had not been since his wife died a few years ago, and he may put up a fuss about it this morning,

Over a simple breakfast of cereal and toast and jelly, Raymond complained that he had a lot of bookwork to do regarding the reconstruction project. "Dad, you really need to go," Nat told him. "Most of the town people will attend on this special day and you need to get to know folks. We may find some opposition before we have this thing completed. Some may not like having a trainload of people dumped on the town, as well as tour buses bringing folks here for the day. Of course, that's not the main reason you should go."

"The business owners should welcome the money coming in with open arms," Raymond answered simply.

"Yeah, I know that, but there's always a few who'd oppose anything that created change and you know our project is bound to make changes in the town." Nat took his last sip of coffee and stood to reach the coffeepot from the stove and refill their cups. "But, there's another reason as far as I can see it."

"Okay, let's have it. Just don't throw any monkey wrenches at me."

Nat leaned across the little kitchen table and said in a whispery voice, "Haven't you noticed that Tissy Russell has given you an undue amount of attention every time we've encountered her? I tell you, Dad, that woman's got her eyes on you."

"What? You've got to be kidding me. Why, I've just been cordial to her and haven't given her any reason to . . ."

"I know. I know. But you just mark my word, Dad, I know it's true. Just watch her today."

By church time, the parking lot had overflowed and cars were now parked along both sides of the street, leaving the Presbyterians to grumble but so far, their parking spaces had not even filled. Sunday school was over and the bell across at the Presbyterian church could be heard tolling loud and clear calling their members to church. The bell also served the Baptist to come to their own church. At the Town Hall meeting building in the park right off the square, a few women had been assigned to accept the dishes of food, cakes, and pies and to get everything all set up. It was cool inside and cloths had already been placed on round tables where people would sit. Coolers were sitting along the wall containing ice and drinks.

The rain during the night would have not only dampened the ground but the children's high spirits, who were looking forward to playing outside and wading in the shallow brook that ambled through the park. However, the sun was out now, and it was going to be a beautiful day.

Nat and Raymond found seats about half way back in the middle section just as the choir was coming through the door of the choir loft. Raymond counted nine men and twelve women. As the leader motioned for them to be seated, he noticed Tissy Russell in the middle of the front row. Nat elbowed his dad and whispered in his ear that she had smiled directly at him. Raymond covered his mouth with a hand so she would not think he was smiling back at her. In the audience, Teresa sat with John and Beth's family. Her father served as an usher. Later, he would probably sit in the balcony with the others who were ushers.

Brother Jesse welcomed the visitors and old members who had returned while the ushers handed out visitor's cards to be filled out. Some of the old members who had moved away had not returned since the new building had been added in front of the old one. The church was sparkling with new chandeliers and new stained glass windows. Red carpet down the aisles and on the platform brought out the reds in the windows. The visitors and old members could easily be picked out of the crowd by their gazing up and all around the auditorium in admiration. When Beth first came to church here after she and John had married, she fell in love with the beautiful painting above the baptistery. It never ceased to amaze her.

"Why did they leave the old building out back?" Raymond whispered to Nat.

"Alyn said that it would have cost a fortune to tear it down, and they thought it might be used for other purposes if need be," he whispered back.

People were milling around now welcoming each other as Preacher Mitch asked them to do, which seemed very uncalled for, Raymond was thinking. The place sounded like a hive of bees buzzing. Was this going to be church or a social gathering? But people were shaking his hand and saying they hoped he would come back again and some were saying they were looking forward to seeing the old mansion completed before long; so even though it seemed unusual, Raymond rather enjoyed the attention he was getting.

After they were seated, announcements were made, then a prayer was given by old Thomas Clark that went on and on. No Baptist church service would be complete without a collection taken and several songs sung. Then the choir sang a beautiful piece with Tissy Russell taking the solo part and when she began singing, Nat elbowed his dad. He turned his head toward Nat and raised his eyebrows in surprise. When they sat down he whispered behind a hand, "Beautiful job."

Just before the preacher got started on his sermon, Al Russell turned to his mother beside him and whispered that he felt sick and needed to get some air because he felt like he would throw up. She softly told him that he would miss all the good food later, but he said he'd feel much better if he could just go out for a little while and walk around. Beth nodded okay and he quietly went out, careful not to let the door close noisily. Beth turned to John and raised her shoulders in a question.

Al walked around through the parking lot to the back where he leaned up against a shade tree for a while. "That was pretty good," he thought but knew that it could not be pulled on his mother again so he'd better make the most of this time. Percy Tyner rode by in his patrol car, slowing nearly to a dead stop when he spied Al, who raised a hand in sort of a wave. Percy put one finger up to his cap in recognition and rolled slowly on by.

After a few minutes and now feeling bored, the boy looked around to see what he could do and hoped that his mother or Pop would not come out to check up on him. He looked around at the old church building behind the new one, wondering about it. It certainly was an old building and rather an eye sore. It sure looks like they could have torn it down. It looked like an old haunted place but he knew better than to believe in ghosts. Still, it looked like a building that might be used as such in a movie. He thought about a movie that he saw a couple of years ago where a hatchet murderer hid in an old church building. He hoped this one was locked up. The more he gazed at the structure, the more intrigued he became and decided to investigate, if he could find that they had not secured the place. So he walked over to the stone steps that led up to the side of the building. "May be dark in there, but then . . . the light through the windows will be enough for me to poke around a little." Yes, the door was unlocked and he went in. "Strange," Al thought. "Somebody up to no good could hide out in here, I bet." He had not heard of any unsolved murders lately, nor anyone missing either.

The door creaked as he opened and closed it softly, stepping inside. "Whew! It smells musty in here." Al stood there looking around and saw that this was a side room with another door which should lead into the foyer so he turned that knob and it, too, creaked from years of not being used. "That could use some WD-40," he said out loud. As he suspected, this led into a small foyer where there were double swinging doors that would lead into the auditorium, so he went inside. Soon he was behind the pastor's rostrum pretending to be giving a sermon, pounding the stand and walking from side to side, silently in case he might be heard through to the new church. Then, spying an old songbook on the rostrum, the boy picked it up, turned a few pages and pretended to lead the invisible congregation in singing, swinging his right hand as he held the book with the left. "All right, now you may be seated," he said and then told himself that he'd done it backwards. He'd done the sermon before the song. "Oh, well, we'll just turn the program around a little this morning. And just to be very different, we'll not take up a collection, how 'bout that?"

Tiring of this, Al moved on poking through rooms and marveling at how old everything looked. "It's a wonder this place hasn't fallen down by now. I wonder just what year it was built." Behind the auditorium, he found some stairs and decided to look on the second floor. The steps squeaked as he mounted each. At the top he followed a hallway with rooms on each side that were most likely Sunday school classrooms. That hall ended where another hall ended on the right side at a door. "Now, what could be behind that door?" he asked himself and, being the curious person that he was, went to investigate. Upon opening the door, Al saw some narrow steps leading down and another set of steps just like these on the other side. There was darkness except at the very bottom where a little light shown. This mystery stirred his curiosity to the point that he decided to go down and check it out. Creeping softly down the steps as though something might jump out at him at the bottom, he soon came into a concrete bottom and as he turned toward where the light was coming in, discovered the whole homecoming congregation quietly listening to Reverend Jesse loudly expounding on his sermon. This was the baptistery and the curtains were open!

There Al Russell stood facing the congregation with a very surprised look on his face . . . only not as surprised as the people gazing at him. When Brother Jesse saw some people break out in smiles during a most serious part of his sermon, he turned to look behind him. Al raised one jaw and did a click, click with his teeth, pointed a forefinger with the thumb raised and loudly said, "Catch you later, folks," as he walked on across the baptistery and up the steps on the other side.

At first there was dead silence but when the preacher could contain his laughter no longer, the whole congregation also broke out in laughter. The laughter died down into smiles, although some had a hand across their mouths trying to hide their giggles, but the shoulders convulsing up and down could not be hidden. When Reverend Jesse's laughter started again and having no one to hide behind, he just let it all out, causing the congregation to erupt in laughter as well. The rest of the sermon could not be given. They tried to get through a song and then went out. Beth wanted to crawl underneath a pew. Her face turned as crimson as the rosebuds on her dress; the rest of the family took it lightly as did everyone else. When John and Beth came to the door where folks were shaking hands with the pastor, he merely put his arms around the couple and the three of them wept tears of laughter. "A merry heart doeth the soul good," he finally said and commented that this day at church would be forever remembered whereas his sermon might not have.

The clubhouse was filled to capacity, spilling outside under the great oaks. People had come from near and far today to renew old friendships or visit with relatives. Younger couples had moved away to cities to seek their fortunes and raise their families. It was always good to come home again. Alyn Russell had called Doc and Kate Harris, hoping they would come down for the church homecoming and stay at Knollwood until Kendell Mountain School's big day at the end of May. But they decided to skip the church affair. Doc told them that they had a problem at the moment and felt they should not come right now.

"What kind of problem did Doc have?" John asked, balancing his dish of cake and ice cream on one hand while he took a sip of drink with the other.

"Well, he didn't rightly come right out with it," Alyn answered. "Seemed to me like he didn't feel free to discuss it so I didn't ask. But he did promise that they would come down in May, and I told him to let us know about their flight and some of us would meet them at Hartsfield."

John and Alyn were standing with several other men in a little cluster discussing town affairs, the coming Kendell Mountain Inn, and whatever anyone threw in, when Nat walked up with his dad. John started introductions for the benefit of several who had not as yet met Raymond.

"John, it looks like your boy struck again!" Raymond said with a twinkle in his eye. "He's quite a character. Yesser, I like that one!"

"I'm afraid he's going to be grounded for quite a while," John answered.

"Here comes another star of this morning," Lew Hendrix, the hardware store's owner, said as Tissy walked nearby with a lady friend. The lady was talking a mile-a-minute, making motions with her hands as well. "Miss Tissy, come over here," Lew beckoned, holding a hand out to draw her into the group. "You did a beautiful job this morning. You just never cease to amaze me with your pretty singing." The others in the group made nice comments as well.

"Yes, ma'm," Raymond piped up. "I had no idea you were so talented."

"Oh, you flatter me, gentlemen," Tissy said with a wave of a hand, "but I do thank you . . . and, oh, Mr. O'Bryan, where is your plate? Come right along with me and let's find you something delicious and loaded with calories." She held her hand out to Raymond and drew him away with her. He looked back at Nat with a smug look on his face.

"How do you like that, now! She didn't invite me to go for something delicious," Nat grinned. "I must not make much of an impression on the ladies."

"Not the older ones, anyway," Alyn said, "and maybe not the younger ones as well but, ahhhh, that's life; some are winners and some are losers."

"Out back of the building is our horseshoe spot. How about a game, anyone?" another of the men said and they turned to get a hot game going, except for Nat as he had more interest in another matter.

Penny and her friend Gwen were sitting beside the creek that meandered through the park, talking and watching the younger children splashing one another. Pete tossed his shoes up to his sister who grasped them by the strings and flung them on a picnic table nearby. "Let's move up there, Gwen, before they decide to include us in their mischief."

"That suits the life out of me. I don't care to have my new dress all messed up." When they stood up and turned around, the two Hanson cousins were walking their way and joined them at the table. Jimmy had a bottled coke in his hand and offered to go get the girls drinks. Both declined. Jimmy was in the same grade as Gwen and Penny's brother, and Archie was in several of Penny's classes. They both made comments about Al's escapade this morning at church, laughing and saying he must be hiding out somewhere.

"Nope. Not my brother. He doesn't care what anyone thinks. That is, except our mom and pop, and I know he'll catch it when we get home. He may even get grounded for the rest of his life."

"Ohhh, I'd hate to be in his shoes," one of the boys commented.

"What are you guys going to do this summer?" Gwen asked. "Anything interesting, or just get jobs somewhere?"

"We're going to our grandparents place in Savannah for a month," Archie said with a broad grin. "The beach, girls in bikinis, you know."

"Yeah, the whole bit. Boy! That will be the life. Are you girls going to be stuck here in this hick town all summer?" the other boy added.

"Haven't made any plans yet; I may go to New York and get myself an acting job. Who knows?" Penny said smugly, tossing her head and brushing blonde tresses aside, acutely aware that she had the boy's undivided attention.

"Yeah, I'll bet!"

"Sure, I was talking with an agent just the other day." Penny demurely lowered her dark lashed eyelids and examined her nails. She was making the tale up to have something more interesting to tell the boys than their trip to Savannah Beach, not expecting them to believe her.

Then Gwen piped up that she had taken a job with a modeling agency in New York and she and Penny were going to room together. The boy's eyes widened. "Wow! You two may be famous some day and here we are sitting at the table with celebrities."

"Speaking of celebrities," Penny added, "have you heard that my little sister has won a poem writing contest and her poem will be included in a book?"

"No! You don't mean it! That little squirt?"

"Yes, you are sitting at the table now with famous people. Come along, Gwendolyn, let's leave these peons." The girls lifted their noses in the air and walked away.

The horseshoes could be heard clanking as they hit the poles and others had gathered around to watch. Out front of the building inside the gazebo, Nat had cornered Teresa where they were now sitting in a swing. "I wouldn't have missed this day for anything," Nat told her, and meaning every word of it. "I've never been to nice country affairs like this. It's so . . ." He was groping for the right words to say. "Well, it's so relaxing and enjoyable. I guess I was born in the wrong place and perhaps a wrong time even. Have you ever felt that you belonged in another time?" He looked at Teresa, hoping that he had not said something absolutely stupid. It was how he felt and how could he explain it?

She saw that he was embarrassed and might be feeling that he wished he had not made that remark. "No. I suppose I've never actually felt that I was born into a wrong era, but I have wondered a lot of times how it would feel to be living in another era. Maybe everyone feels that way at one time or another. I even pass by houses on the roadsides and wonder how I would feel living in this house or that one and what the people who live there do for a living. We all have our personal whims and thoughts."

"Have you ever wondered about your ancestors and how they came to be in the place they were and about all their hardships? I think about how people must have suffered years ago with bad teeth and all the pain they endured with having them yanked out. Of course, any operation would have been very difficult, too. But, have you noticed the actors in the cowboy movies . . . how beautiful their teeth always are?"

They both laughed at this. "I'd like to know more about the people here in this town, not from being nosy but just how they came to be here."

"My, you do have a lot of wonderings, don't you?"

"See, I knew you'd think I'm some kind of an old kook. But really, it would be a neat idea if every family would write their own family history about where they came from, and I'm not just talking about their genealogy, but give information about the people themselves."

"I think I know what you mean, Nat, and that's real sweet of you. Most men don't give a hoot about where their grandma and grandpa came from and some folks may not even appreciate all the hard labor that they did."

"I've been wondering about Miss Tissy. I've met her daughter, Bess, but I've not heard anything about any other family except her husband, Reverend Bob Russell, who died. She is such a nice lady and my, what a beautiful singing voice for someone her age."

"Some singers lose it and some don't. I guess if you don't use your talent you lose it. Tissy had a very sad life when she was growing up. The old house where she, her parents, and grandmother lived is up on the mountain beyond John and Beth's place. Her father was a no-good-so-and-so. Please don't speak of this to Tiss. I'm sure she's had a long hard pull in dealing with it." Nat nodded his head and she continued. "Her father, as deputy sheriff, had my mother's father hanged unjustly. My grandfather was innocent of the charges he made against him. Tissy's brother was shot and killed when he and his father were being arrested. Alonzo, her father, was sent to the penitentiary and he died there. After Tissy's mother died, Tissy was taken in by Mrs. Ella Fullman, the owner of your mansion. So . . ." Teresa, pressed her lips together, "you see, some families would not like to have some things revealed. Her story would be very heartbreaking. She was a lot younger than Bob Russell but had been in love with him since she was a teenager, before Miss Ella took her in. She lived in the house alone for a while like a hermit." Teresa gave a long sigh and held both hands out. "But she turned out to be one fine person. There's not anyone anywhere who could hold a candle to her, in fact I see her as a paragon of perfection."

"I'd say she deserves a gold star in her crown! I do hope you don't think I was in any way prying into the lady's life. I was just struck by her . . . her dignity, her voice, and her command of the school. Wow!"

Nat turned toward Teresa in the swing and said, "And now . . . tell me about Miss Teresa Russell."

"Oh, no you don't! There's nothing at all to tell. She is just a country girl and wants to remain that way. Oh, I see Beth coming toward us; could you scoot over and make room for her, Nat?" Then she threw up her hand beckoning her sister-in-law to come sit with them.

"Hi, you two. Is she giving you all the low-down, Nat? I hope I wasn't one of your subjects. My son didn't learn all his shenanigans from me. Talk with his granddad." She backed up to the swing that had been squeaking on a rusty chain and when she sat down, the swing promptly broke leaving the trio sitting on the ground laughing. They stood up, brushing themselves off just as John found them and said the singing at the church was about to begin. The kids would stay for story-hour and playtime inside the clubhouse with some ladies in charge.

Full of fried chicken, potato salad, pies, cakes, watermelon cold from the creek, and anything else anyone could name, folks trudged across the street for another hour of music and singing. Penny, Al, and some of their friends opted to stay in the park and have their own singing since one of the boys brought his own guitar.

Chapter Eighteen

ACROSS THE CREEK FROM WHERE THE YOUNG PEOPLE were gathered around a concrete table and benches was an oak tree with spreading branches, shading a bench where Ryan Ratcliffe was sitting, eyeing the young people, his dog curled up on the bench beside him. This was the first time he had ventured out from his hiding place and the only reason now for his doing this was because of hunger. Behind the civic center he had discovered a garbage barrel loaded with wasted food from the day's picnic. He and the dog were more than satisfied, and he'd even found a bag that now held a good supply of things he would take back to his hiding place.

Ryan's mission was now completed. He had reached his destination and again found himself trying to make up his mind what to do. He was staring into the water that made little tinkling sounds as it fell over rocks. Some careless person had dropped a styrofoam cup into the creek and it floated by his gaze like a little boat. He watched it until it was out of sight. Many things were floating through his mind. Should he get a job and stay here or go back to the horse farm in Tennessee? This looked like a peaceful, wonderful place to live. The residents that he had encountered were very congenial. The school he saw up on the mountain may need some help perhaps. He could certainly sweep and mop floors; another possibility Ryan thought about was that the feed and seed mill at the edge of town may need someone to load trucks or something, anything. Decisions, decisions! The adult world seemed to be made up of nothing but decisions. But he would not want to be a small

113

child and have to go through with all the family arguments again. No. Not ever.

Whatever he decided to do, he'd contact his great-grandparents when he got himself settled in to a job of some kind. That little yapping dog had taken off with the splint on its leg and he hoped it found its way back home again. That's exactly the way Ryan felt, wounded and alone. Right now there was nothing about him that could be helped by a splint. Would he ever find his way? What he had always thought he would like to do is be a veterinarian, because he loved animals and wished now that he had some of his books on the care of animals. Since he was small he had taken in every stray that came into their yard—cat, dog, crippled birds, whatever. He couldn't understand why his parents made so much fuss because he hated world history and English. Those were the subjects he had failed that caused him not to graduate. His grades in math and chemistry were excellent, and he certainly would not need any history or any knowledge of conjunctions and dangling participles to be an animal doctor.

Ryan knew his parents just wanted him out of the house . . . period. They were hippies from the word go and he knew they smoked pot and went to wild parties. If his other grandparents had been living closer by, they would have seen what was going on and helped Ryan all they could, but they were way out in California. His two cousins both were brains, so this was thrown into his face daily by his parents.

This brought on thoughts of the little deer he had been taking care of up on the mountain. Evidently someone had shot the doe and left the little one to wander on its own. He'd have to go back up there and see about him. Ryan had clapped his hands and frightened the little deer back into the woods just as he'd reached the road. Patches, he had been named, stopped after a few feet, looking back at the boy and dog heading on down the road.

"Okay, Jethro," he made a clicking sound with his teeth, "let's be going, boy." And he stood, with the dog happily jumping up against his side. The group of teenagers glanced across the creek to the motley-looking boy and his dog walking in the opposite direction from them.

"Who in the world is that?" Gwen questioned, pointing emphatically.

It was Al who answered. "I dono, but Pop asked me one time if I had seen a hippie around here. That's as rare around here as seeing an elephant walking down th' street."

Chapter Nineteen

RAYMOND O'BRYAN TACKLED MONDAY MORNING LIKE his coattail was on fire and he expected everyone else in his employ to do the same. "There that old house sits, squatting up on that hill like it has for over a hundred years," Alyn Russell told him just that very morning over breakfast, "so, it sure is not going anywhere. There's not any need to kill yourself over getting it fixed up in such an all-fired hurry either." But Raymond was in a hurry. The more work that was done on the place, the more excited he became. Over breakfast, he really did not know just how excited he would become when he left the Skillet. Each time when he parked and walked up the hill and looked up at the "grand ole lady"—as he called the house—he felt a leap of heart and an urgency to put a fire under his men.

This morning, he rechecked what had been done the day before and again felt proud of the progress. Then checking his clipboard for notes he'd made at home last night, he heard Joseph Simmons, one of the carpenters, call for Mr. O'Bryan to come take a look. Joseph was back in the kitchen area, where the walls had been taken out to connect with the adjoining room, the dining area, in order to enlarge the kitchen. When Raymond walked in where Joseph was, he heard his excited voice saying, "Mr. O'Bryan, come lookie in here! What'er you make of this?"

Raymond came anxiously to where Joseph was standing next to where the wall between the kitchen and dining room had been torn out and saw him peering down into a gaping hole in the floor. "I seen th' way these boards were shorter than th' floor boards and were nailed down with extra nails so I ripped 'em up, and this here looks like a cellar may be underneath th' floor."

"That's odd, Joseph. Go get us a flashlight and let's take a look." While Joseph was gone, Raymond got down on all fours squinting down into the blackness trying to see if he could see anything. Joseph came right back with the light and handed it to Raymond as he dropped to his knees, head-to-head with his boss. "Can't see a carnsarned thing, Joe. Let me have your tape measure." He held his hand up, taking it without looking up and ran it down into the hole with the tape stopping on nine feet. He whistled and then struggled to his feet with Joseph giving him a hand. "Wow! I wonder what could be down there! Boy-oh-boy, we've got us a mystery here." Then he asked Joseph to go for a ten-foot ladder and when another workman appeared upon hearing Raymond's exclamations, he was told to go down to Nat's office and tell him to come up just as quick as he could get away. Before the man got out of the room, Raymond flashed a grin and said, "Tell 'im not to leave a patient with false teeth plaster in his mouth."

Being the impatient person that he was, Raymond walked around anxious for his son to get there and discover with him what was down in the hole. He walked to a water cooler and poured himself a cool drink, thinking at the same time that he had never heard anyone say that the house had a basement in it. "Could have been a wine cellar. If any wine was down there, no telling how old it would be. Could be some old trunks with Miss Ella's old clothes in them. If that be the case, then we can donate them to the school's drama department, but they may be rotted into shreds by now."

Then Raymond walked to the front of the house, inspecting things along the way and talking with another workman about the windows in the parlor. The glass in them was wavy and distorted on the outside, as glass of this age would be from the process used in making it back in the era when the house was built. Usually one side came out rough. "No! By no means will we replace the glass. That's part of the charm of the house. We'll plaster the room and paint the window frames, but the window glass remains the same."

Joseph came through the door with the long ladder, heading toward the kitchen with Raymond falling in behind him. "Mr. O'Bryan, if we hadn't have got that wall between th' rooms out, th' wall would've been in th' way and th' ladder wouldn't go in th' hole."

Nat came rushing in with excitement showing in his eyes. "Have you been down there yet, Dad?"

"Nope. I was waiting for you. Wanna be th' first one down?"

"You go ahead and scare out all th' ghosts, Dad, and I'll hold the light 'til you get down."

"Hump," Raymond grunted. "You always were afraid of th' dark." And he started slowly down the ladder rungs with Nat shining the light for him. Nat told Joseph to send somebody to get another light while he plugged up a cord for an electric light to drop down to them. Others had gathered in the kitchen area to wait for news about what was found beneath the house. The men were all like little boys on Christmas morning, anxiously awaiting the wonderful surprise that Santa Claus had left.

Chapter Twenty

"YOU STAY RIGHT HERE, JETHRO," RYAN COMMANDED the dog. He reached into the bag and gave Jethro a bite of something to eat. The shaggy dog wagged its whole body and made two complete turns before settling on the top step with head down between its paws. Then Ryan entered the building and looked around. There was no one milling around for him to ask questions so he walked over to what looked like an office with a sign on the door that read: Principal Patricia Russell. That's what he was looking for and knocked softly on the glass, almost apologetically. A young boy opened the door and said, "This here is the principal's office. You must be in trouble, too. That's her office behind that door. Miss Sullivan, the secretary, said for me to tell anyone that comes in to sit down and wait. I s'pose she went to the john." The boy sat down in a chair where he must have been sitting before.

"So," the boy continued after Ryan sat down, "what did you do to get sent to the principal's office?"

Ryan smiled at the boy who must be about eight or nine. "I didn't get sent. I just want to talk with her. I don't go to school."

"Wow! Neat! How'd you manage that? My name's Justin."

"I'm already out of school, Justin. I'm eighteen."

"Oh, you're already growed up. Well, when I grow up I won't come back inside a school and ask to see no principal, I betcha."

"What did you do to get sent to the office," Ryan inquired.

"I didn't really do nothing bad or anything. I just told the boy behind me something funny and we got to laughing and couldn't stop. The teacher made him stand in the corner, and she sent me to the office. I don't really think that was fair, do you? What is your name?"

"It's Ryan, and well . . . maybe she did that because you were the one who started it, and I guess you weren't even supposed to be talking. What was so funny, anyway?"

"Well, you see, when I was on the way down the hall to class I ran smack dab into old Mr. Foster; he's our janitor, you see. He had a long push broom holding it up over his shoulder and coming around the corner of another hallway and when we bumped into one another, he just looked down at me and crossed his eyes and stuck his tongue out from underneath his bottom teeth." His teacher would no doubt have given him a failing grade on his speech for using so many "ands." "It was so funny I just couldn't stop laughing and kept on laughing when I came in the room. But, what I want to know is, how did Mr. Foster do that, you reckon? I tried but it won't work for me."

Ryan grinned from ear to ear but before he could answer Justin the secretary came back in and asked Ryan what he wanted. "I'd like to speak with the principal, ma'm," he told her very mannerly as he stood.

"I'll see if she is available to see anyone. Wait just a minute please." The secretary turned toward another closed door and disappeared inside.

Ryan sat back down beside Justin and reached over whispering in his ear that the janitor has false teeth and he could lift them up with his tongue. The boy clapped his hands over his mouth when the giggles started again and he bent over his knees laughing, trying to muffle the sound so he would not have more time added to his office stay. Tissy Russell came to the door with the tall austere-looking secretary who must have alerted her that a strange, straggly young man wanted to see her. Instead of inviting him in at once, she walked to the outer office and inquired as to the nature of his visit.

Ryan placed his sack of food in the empty chair opposite from where he was sitting, stood, gave his name, and asked if the school might have some kind of job available as he needed work.

"No, young man. I'm afraid we don't at the time," Tissy told him and noticed how his face fell into a disappointed look.

"Oh, Mrs. Russell, there may be something," Miss Sullivan said. "Mr. Hartwell in the ag department wants to see you. He asked me while you were on the phone just a while ago to tell you that he desperately needs an assistant with the livestock. Maybe this young man would like to have this job."

"Oh, ma'm!" Ryan said with excitement, "I have experience working with horses and cows, and I would like to give the job a try. I will work hard and never be absent. I'm very dependable and honest."

"What about references, son?" Tissy asked.

"I can't give you any references from right around here, but I could call the man I worked for in Tennessee on a horse farm, and I'm sure he will be glad to tell you I'm a hard worker. He didn't want me to leave but I wanted to come to north Georgia because I had heard it is such a nice area."

"Alright. Just come on in my office, fill out an application, and I'll phone this man for you."

Ryan's hope rose with excitement building. It felt as though a gigantic weight had been lifted off his shoulders and he would have liked to hug this lady's neck. As Tissy went into her office, Ryan followed but turned his head back to the boy in the chair and gave him a grin and a wink. He knew this job was cut out for him.

Tissy pointed to a chair beside her desk. "Have a seat Ryan, and I'll just get a little information from you. We must keep records, you understand, and get you on the payroll."

"Payroll!" He was thinking. "What a wonderful word!" She looked every bit like an angel. What a nice lady, not anything like any principal he'd ever known. This was just simply incredible! First, he had found some wonderful people on a horse farm and now this.

Tissy sat before her desk, opened a drawer, pulled out a form and reaching over, took a pen from a cup. When her eyes met his, she saw that his relief was clearly visible for there was a slight smile on his young face. She would have loved to have had a decoder for the thoughts going on in his head at this moment.

"Alright, let's get down to business. What is your full name Ryan?"

"Ryan Alyn Ratcliffe."

Her pen stopped in mid-air. "How do you spell your middle name?"

"A-l-y-n"

"That's strange. I know someone with that name, and I had never known anyone else to spell it that way."

"My great-grandmother named me. She said she also knew someone who spelled his name the same way. Since my mother said she didn't have any idea what to name me, G. G. suggested my name, and it suited my mother and father."

"I'll have to tell the Alyn I know about that, and by the way, his grandson is also named 'Alyn' but he is just called 'Al.' He is about three years younger than you." After thinking for a moment she added, "So, it looks like we will be blessed with another Alyn. But, then it doesn't matter since you are called Ryan." And she wrote his full name down on the form. "Now, where do you live Ryan?" Tissy looked up from the form awaiting his reply and saw that he was struggling for an answer.

"Uh, well, uh, Mrs. Russell, you see . . . well, frankly, I don't have a place to live, and I've just been hanging out until I could get a job."

"Where have you been sleeping, Ryan?" Her question was direct and to the point.

He bit his bottom lip and shrugged his shoulders. "Frankly, ma'm, I've been staying up on the mountain in that cave."

"What! In the cave? How did you know there was a cave up there?"

"I, well . . ." he was trying to think but not coming up with anything that would sound feasible. "I just heard somebody talking about it one time and wanted to see it for myself so that's why I came here. Now I've seen it, and I have to get a job and settle down."

Tissy was wondering what she had gotten herself into. "Now you must have a place to stay if you work here." She held the pen with one hand and with the other she kept taking the pen's cap off and putting it on again. Click, click. "Did you know that this cave you were speaking of actually belongs to the Alyn that I just mentioned?"

"No ma'm. I did not know who it belongs to. I never saw anybody around it. It certainly is an interesting place. I have a flashlight, and I looked around in there. Man! I never dreamed I'd see a place like that with a waterfall and all those things hanging down from the top. But, you know, I saw some graves in there and that was sorta spooky, so I just stayed up close to the front of the cave. I have a dog, too. His name is Jethro."

She studied his face. He seemed to have an honest face and she believed his story, but the boy must have a place to stay. "We'll skip that question for right now, Ryan. How old are you?" He told her his age and then she asked about his schooling. He went through his story about failing to graduate and how his parents had tossed him out.

"I didn't want to join the army, Mrs. Russell. I wanted to get a job but nobody wants you if you don't have that diploma."

The poor kid, Tissy was thinking. He does need help. "Ryan, what would you like to do for your life's work? Have you ever thought about it? Is there something you would like better than anything else in the world?"

"Oh, I know what I want but I can't do it now because of my failing school. All I've ever wanted to be is an animal doctor."

"You do have an ambition and don't think for a minute that it has all been flung out the window. You still have a chance if you will work real hard."

"I don't see how I could have much of a chance now but I'm more than willing to work hard, and I told you I would."

"Yes, I know you did but you meant only on the job. If you do work hard on the job, then you will have another chance to do what you have always dreamed of doing."

Her statement really caught his utmost attention and he leaned forward in the chair, hoping she would come out with it and tell him what she was talking about.

"I'll tell you what, son. If you will go to school here, study hard, and finish your grade, we'll get your records from your old school. You can work in the agriculture department every afternoon for your board and a small salary. There is a room in the basement of the old building that you can call your own and take your meals in the dining room. I will work up a schedule for you and give you an advance on your wages. With some of that money, you will be expected to buy some personal items to groom yourself as we will not allow our students to look like bums. You will be expected to be in class on time and to keep your grades up. If you need any help with any subjects, you are to tell your teachers and they will arrange for extra help. You will be expected to attend church services each Sunday morning and Sunday nights. No student is to be allowed to leave the campus without permission."

Ryan sat there with his mouth open. How did he ever fall into such a chance as this? He could hardly believe his ears! Never before had he been touched to tears and tried to hide them as he wiped tears from his cheeks. Tissy saw the tears and was touched that the boy's gratefulness showed. Through her years of living with Bob Russell and sharing all the kindness he had given to people in need, she had learned many lessons from him. This she felt was the best thing she could do for the boy instead of merely giving him a job and seeing how he would have to struggle through life without an education. She had the inborn sense of discerning when people were honest with her and this boy did not have a dishonest bone in him.

"Now, about your friend, Jethro," she smiled. "We used to have a dog here. The man that he belonged to left, but the doghouse is still out in the barn area. He can stay there and you may feed him scraps but he is not to come inside the school building."

"Yes ma'm! Thank you so much. How will I ever be able to thank you for all this?" She had stood up so Ryan got to his feet and reached out his hand to her. Instead of shaking hands, she held his hand in both of her's and said finally after holding his hands and looking him straight in the face, "I know you will not disappoint me, Ryan, and you will not disappoint yourself. I will be the one to sign your report cards so when you receive one, bring it here to me."

"May I please hug your neck, Mrs. Russell?" And he did, with Tissy glancing up toward heaven, wondering how long it had been since he'd had a bath. Then she took him to his room, introduced him to the showers, saying she'd get him some towels and washcloths. Then she took him to meet the man who would oversee his job, Mr. Thomas Hartwell.

"I'm mighty pleased to meet you, son, mighty pleased." He pumped the boy's hand and added, "I sure need some help around here."

Chapter Twenty-One

"TERESA!" ALYN CALLED AS HE STOMPED DISGUSTEDLY up the five back steps and onto the porch. She heard her father at once and knew by the tone of his voice that he was not in the least bit happy. She appeared behind the screen door that she held ajar for him.

"What in the world is it, Papa? What were you yelling about? I thought something terrible had happened to you."

He stopped on the top step, holding on to the banister and turned, pointing to the culprit out in the yard, then stepped on up the last step and rubbed the back of his left leg just above the ankle. "He really got me this time, and I do believe he drew blood. Here," he pulled up the pant leg, "take a look."

Teresa came out to where Papa Russell was standing holding the pant leg up. She took a quick look at just a small red spot on the leg and, seeing no blood, said if he would stop kicking at the old rooster he wouldn't attack him every time he got out of his truck.

"I tell you, that carnsarned rooster has got to go!" he said emphatically, meaning every word of his oath. "I'm sick and tired of having to run to the house every time I get out of the truck. We're gonna have him for Sunday dinner, I swear." He stooped over and tried to see the spot for himself.

"Papa! Stop swearing!"

"Okay, okay . . . but I mean it. It's a funny thing to me that he doesn't bother anybody else."

"That's because they don't kick at him." She followed her dad into the house where he had stopped to hang up his old battered hat. "You know he was the kid's Easter chicken several years ago, and we certainly can't eat him."

"Well, they can just take him on home with them the next time they come. Call Beth and tell her to get 'im, or I eat 'im."

Teresa smiled. Her dad saw the smile and that did not please him at all. "And you can just wipe that silly smile off your face, young lady. You don't think I'm serious evidently."

"Oh, it's not that, Papa. I just hate to imagine you out there running all over the place trying to catch Ole Charlie. What would you do if you could catch him?" Then she answered her own question. "You'd probably be full of bites and scratches worse than you are now."

He followed her into the kitchen where she had been sitting at the table reading over some school material that she had brought home with her. "Well, that would be the last bite of me Ole Charlie would get."

"Oh, sit down and cool off," Teresa joked with an exaggerated frown. "I just made a pitcher of lemonade. It's in the frige." Papa Russell peered inside the refrigerator and took out the pitcher, filled a glass with ice, poured the lemonade, and sat down across from his daughter. "We have a new worker down at the school, and a new student," she told him.

"Who are they?" he asked, looking over his glass as he took a sip of the drink.

"It's not a 'they' but a 'he,' and he's a senior student."

"Senior, meaning like an 'old' person or in the senior class?"

"Certainly not an old student. He's eighteen. Tissy said he's from up north. He came walking in looking for work, and she talked him into finishing school."

"Oh, another freebee, huh? That sounds just like Tiss. There're so many mountain kids this term, the school will soon go broke! It would be cheaper to bus 'em for free down to the public school in town. Actually, what you need is a class for the parents to teach 'em what . . ."

"Papa! Your mind is in the gutter!" She saw that he was trying to suppress a grin. "Haven't you forgotten the reason the school was built in the first place? I think Colonel

Abernathy had the destitute kids in mind when he came up with the idea of the school."

"Ah, yeah. S'pose you are right, daughter." He leaned back in his chair, intending to get the last word and said, "But that durned ole rooster has got to go!"

"Did you go down to town today?" Teresa asked, changing the subject.

"Nope. Had to clear up a few more things with Joe and Tad. They've worked the orchard for years and think they know it all, but they still have a lot to learn. Folks seem to think all there is to it is putting a tree in a hole and watching the apples grow and then pocketing the money. They know about putting in new trees, cutting off diseased or damaged roots, soaking them in water, and about taking out real old ones, but they didn't understand about the soil's pH and about adding lime and what would happen if there was not sufficient drainage . . ."

Teresa interrupted him here, "You don't have to go into all that with me, Papa. I've heard you talking about all this for years. The important thing is telling the guys all they will need to know."

"I'm sure they'll come running to me with lots more questions from time to time. But they are tickled with their new business and frankly, I'm tickled that they are tickled because I'm sure ready to retire. I think I'll do like the hippies do and just go away somewhere and find myself, as they call it."

"Papa, I didn't know you were lost. What you need is a vacation; a nice, long vacation. Where would you like to go? Now, really . . . if you had your druthers, where in the world would you like to spend a vacation of doing nothing but having a good time?"

Papa Russell rared back in the chair with his arms crossed behind his head and looked up to the ceiling, thinking for a few seconds, his eyes already in another place far away. "Well, I s'pose if I were to go anywhere, I'd rather go to that place where my aunt and uncle took me to when I was just thirteen. There were a lot of sailboats on lakes and inlets and the houses all had colorful flowers in their yards. It was a pretty place, but at that time all I wanted was to be back here on Kendell Mountain."

"You told us when we were kids about their whisking you away to New Zealand. I guess that's where you were talking about. I never thought you would really like to go back there. But, as long as you are daydreaming, you can go anywhere you like." She spread her arms out to emphasize her statement.

Chapter Twenty-Two

THE LIGHT BULB MADE GHOSTLY SHADOWS ON THE rock walls as the two men cautiously descended down the ladder into the unknown. Each carried a flashlight in the event the light the carpenter had rigged up on a drop cord would not fan out far enough. Their expectations may have been too great as to what they would find, but what a disappointment if the basement was found to be empty.

"Look. There over in that corner. There's a pile of stuff, Nat."

"And would you look at all the old furniture would you!" Nat answered.

Raymond shot his flashlight up to the ceiling and all around the basement. "I wish you'd look at these boards! They are extra wide. I'd say they are every bit twenty inches wide, and that's yellow pine."

Nat was more interested in the other items and headed toward what they had noticed when the light first caught them. What Raymond had seen over against a far wall were several trunks—a large one and two smaller ones. The larger was a steamer trunk and the other two were barrel-stave, each had locks on them. "Oh rats! Wouldn't you know it. Now where do we get a key to fit them?"

"We'll have to get a locksmith, and I'd bet there will not be one in this town." Both men stood looking at the trunks as though they could just wish them to open. "Let's see how heavy this one is," Nat suggested. He held one end of the larger one and Raymond took hold of the leather strap on the other end. They gave a hefty tug and discovered that this one was indeed heavy. "You know, Son, there just maybe will be an antique dealer around somewhere who will have some old trunk keys. I'll ask Alyn if he knows of any antique shops."

Chapter Twenty-Three

ON SATURDAY MORNING, THE SUN THAT BEAMED golden rays through the window beside Teresa Russell's bed awoke her. If it had not been the sun that woke her, then it would have been Ole Charlie, for he had just hopped up on a fence post, flapped his wings, and let out with his morning greeting, loud and clear. Teresa felt lazy but from a habit of rising early, she could not give in to the luxury of staying in bed. She stretched, yawned, and forced herself to sit on the bed's edge, letting her toes search for the slippers that had to be somewhere nearby. A decision was quickly made that this would be the day she would do absolutely nothing of any consequence, other than what pleased her. Joe's wife had cleaned the house on Friday, washed clothes, and ironed, leaving Teresa the freedom to gad about at her own free will. Beulah Mae was happy doing the one-day job for which Teresa paid her well for the good work she did.

Teresa reached for a robe that was hanging across a chair beside the bed, and decided it would be a great day to go rambling through the woods with Penny and the kids. Knowing the school schedule, she realized Al would be practicing with the ball team and no doubt John and Beth would appreciate having a quiet house alone on this Saturday morning. Papa might like to come along, too, she was thinking, and then decided that he could not drag himself away from Raymond's project. But the workers most likely would not want to work on Saturday and the house would be locked up. Papa probably had already left the house anyway or she would have heard him rambling around. As she passed by the dresser, Teresa glanced in the mirror and said, "Ugh! Is that Teresa Russell or some old hag?" She tousled her shoulder length hair worse than it was and trudged through the door toward the kitchen to put on the coffeepot. The clock on the wall showed that it was already nine o'clock. "Heavens to Betsy! How could I sleep so late?" She took the phone receiver from its hook under the clock, dialed Beth, and yawned at the same time. The phone rang four times before Beth answered.

"Hi, Beth. I hope I didn't wake your crew so early on a Saturday morning."

"Oh, hello, Teresa. No. You didn't wake anyone. Al has left already and Penny spent the night with Gwen Faber. What's up with you?"

"Not anything yet. I suppose Papa has gone for his newspaper and, of course, he'll go by the Skillet. I was thinking perhaps the kids would like to poke around on up the hill with me this morning."

"Well, I'm sure they would have earlier but they're out back with John. He promised to build them a tree house this morning. I'm glad they're out of my way for a while because I've got to work on those portraits today."

"Humm," Teresa said into the phone. "Seems like everyone is all tied up. Oh, well . . . another time perhaps. How are you coming with the paintings?"

"Slow. Too slow, but I'm getting there. It shouldn't take much longer, I hope."

"That's good, Beth. I'm very excited about having them for our program." There was a short pause, then she said, "Okay, that's all so you go back to your paintings, and I'll catch you later."

Teresa was not used to having nothing at all to do and being alone in the quiet house. She sighed as she hung up the phone and turned to go out on the back porch to retrieve her favorite jeans that she had hung there last night on a line to dry. Papa's old rattletrap truck was not in the shed and she knew he would be sitting down at the Skillet "chewing the fat" with some of his friends.

Before the jeans were unpinned from the line, there came sounds of a vehicle coming around the house crunching gravel on the driveway. "No rattles, so it will not be Papa's truck," Teresa thought. She was placing the clothespins into a holder that was pinned to the line and saw Nat O'Bryan's Jeep stop in front of the shed. It was pulling a rowboat. "Oh, no! Not him! Not the way I look." She thought about making a quick escape but it was already too late, for he saw her. Nat threw his hand up to her and a wide grin was on his face when he saw how she looked.

He pulled up right in the spot where the surly Rhode Island red rooster had been scratching and pecking the bare ground. He opened the door and got out, side-stepping Ole Charlie, who was now strutting around with his chest thrown out and making unhappy clucking sounds. The only thing Teresa could do was to wait on the back porch in her embarrassment until Nat reached the steps. He stopped, with one hand on the rail post, looked up into her face that was void of any makeup and the hair that looked like something he might see on Halloween night.

"Good morning. I see you put on your finest this morning. You must have known I was coming," he grinned in amusement and rested one foot on the bottom step.

"Well, you could have called, you know. Serves you right to be greeted in my present state," she murmured, noting his amusement at catching her looking her worst. Her face felt warm. She knew she was blushing and the color deepened when she noted the male ego thing that he was enjoying when he made a valiant effort to act as though he hadn't noticed her ratty appearance. Her amethyst eyes were still beautiful even when they shot fire, the tight-lipped mouth showing her displeasure at being seen without the usual pink lipstick and turned up corners.

After an embarrassing silence, Nat cleared his throat and asked a question at the same time Teresa asked her question.

"What brings you here so early in the morning?"

"Is Alyn here, Teresa?"

The embarrassed mood was broken when they both laughed. "I'll go first," Nat said. "I came because your father and I were to go fishing this morning but I see his truck is not in the shed so I suppose he isn't here. Maybe he forgot about our plans."

"That isn't like Papa to forget about a fishing date, Nat. I really don't know where he went since he was gone before I got up. It is rather puzzling. Did you go by the Skillet? He could be there?"

"No, we agreed to meet here so I just had coffee and toast at home."

"Then maybe he went to look in on Raymond's progress at the inn."

"Well, neither Dad's car nor Alyn's truck was parked up there as I came by, so that must tell us that they went somewhere together."

"Older folks do strange things sometimes, don't they? We have to let them know where we're going but they just take off into the wild blue yonder without as much as a word to us." There was a moment of silence, then Teresa said, "I didn't know you had a boat."

"It isn't mine, I borrowed it from one of the carpenters." He looked down at his feet contemplating as to whether or not it would be an insult to ask such a refined lady as Teresa Russell if she would care to go along with him. Before he could ask, she suggested that she might like to take her dad's place and go fishing with him.

The shock showed in his face as he gave a smile of relief. He didn't have to ask and risk being turned down and made to feel silly for asking. "Frankly, I'd much rather have you go with me than your dad. He told me he'd show me a great fishing place. You wouldn't happen to know the place, would you?"

"Well, I do know the streams up here are too shallow for a boat. No doubt he had in mind going down to Everitt's Lake. Have you been there?"

"No, I haven't."

"He says that's a good place to catch some big ones. I'll tell you what, Nat, if you will give me just a jiffy to get dressed . . . but, just come on in and you can put us some sandwiches together while I get ready." He came on up the steps and held the screen door open as she went ahead of him. "There are some canned drinks in the frige and a little cooler under the sink. There's some mayonnaise and lunch meat and the bread is in that bread box." She pointed toward the cabinet where it sat. "I'll only be a minute or two," she said, hurrying out the kitchen door.

Nat was thinking as he opened a drawer looking for a knife to spread the mayonaise with. "Hummm, this is getting better all the time. I'd much rather have her go than her dad." He wondered if she had ever been fishing before. Surely Alyn had taken the three kids fishing while they were younger. Yessir! This fishing trip was working out just dandy. He made three sandwiches, assuming she'd only eat one, and found some cookies in a jar on the cabinet. They would be a nice addition. He looked under the cabinet and got out the cooler, filled it with ice, and added the soft drinks. Just as he finished, Teresa came back in, looking like an entirely different person from head to toe. Her hair was all in place, swinging around her shoulders as she walked, and she had on makeup. The jeans fit like she had been born in them! He was thinking that women must keep a fairy godmother in their dressing rooms. "Do you like to fish, Teresa?" And then thought, "What a stupid question that was!"

She was looking for a little basket to put their lunch in and was bending over peering into a cabinet. "Oh, it beats watching paint dry," she answered.

"I can say that I've never watched paint dry. Then the reason you offered to go must be because of my appealing person-ality," he teased.

"Think what you like. I offered to go, didn't I?" He figured he had better leave well enough alone, picked up the basket and cooler, and followed her out the door and down the steps.

She directed him down the road past the school, on past the cemetery to a little narrow wagon trail that wound around curves, and descended into the woods. "Say! I never would have thought a lake would be up here," Nat said in amazement.

"That's what most folks say," she answered.

"Oh? Do you usually take your men friends fishing here?" He thought his question would make her squirm. On the contrary, she shot right back that she usually took them horse-back riding. He didn't know whether to believe her or not and gave her a quizzical glance. Either she was being smug or felt that this was none of his business.

Nat steered the Jeep down the rough road with the little fishing boat bouncing behind. He looked back to see if he could make the next curve without hitting the boat against a tree that grew right next to the road. "Do you do much riding?" he asked as he turned back around.

"Actually, not much in the past couple of years. Just been too busy with school work but Papa and I have done a lot in the past. When Beth visited here from Atlanta, she and John rode a lot. Sometimes I wonder why Papa keeps the horses. He has two, a smaller one named Dolly and then Prince, Papa's pride and joy. Way back when I was a little girl, this old man who lived and worked on the farm used to plow a garden with the horses . . . not the same horses, mind you. Come to think of it, he used a mule, but we did have horses then, too."

They rounded several more curves and came to a spot where the lake could be seen down below, shimmering where bright sunrays shone on the water. "Now this is what I like," Nat said with feeling. "This is a beautiful place and I really don't care whether we catch a single fish or not. Just being here is enough." He actually meant what he said. "Look at all the dogwoods in bloom! What a sight!" The area was bordered by tall pines and rhododendrons and dotted with dogwood that gave a snow effect. The foliage still sparkled with morning dew, each leaf bathed in sunbeams that streamed through branches, lending a sparkling diamond effect. "This is really postcard pretty." Then Nat suddenly remembered his camera under the seat and reached to retrieve it. "Here," he said handing the camera to Teresa. "Hang onto this. I'd like to have some snapshots of this place," and then added that hopefully it would not be too shady for snapshots to show up what he beheld with his eyes.

"I'm rather surprised that you would like this kind of thing . . . with your having lived in the city all your life I mean. That's why it seemed strange to me that you would care for fishing at all." When Teresa turned to him, their eyes met, the Jeep hit a large rock, causing the boat to bounce and he exclaimed, "Whoa!" as he jammed on the brakes. The subject about whether or not Nat cared for fishing was forgotten as he let the vehicle roll slowly to where the road ended. "Is the way clear so I can back the boat up to the bank?" Nat questioned as the Jeep came to a stop at the bottom of the road.

"Yes, there's a place to put the boat in. Just pull in here," she motioned to the right. "You can back on out to the lake."

"If you would hop out please, Teresa, guide me as I back in close enough so we can slide the boat into the water." She answered sure and gingerly stepped out. They had placed the cooler and basket of food inside the boat before leaving the house. She also thought to place a blanket in the boat in case they decided to picnic on the ground instead of eating while they were fishing. "And thank goodness I didn't forget a roll of paper towels," she thought. The food would not taste very good if held with hands smelly from handling bait.

It had been a very long time since Teresa had actually been out on a date, if this occasion could be called a "date." She really only thought of it as going fishing with a friend. Even so, she had twisted and turned before her bathroom mirror and felt satisfied with her hair and the fit of the jeans. She was now glad that she had bought the short-sleeved sweater down in town at Doris's Dress Shop only yesterday afternoon after school. Nat had noticed, with approval, how nice she looked. Even at the church homecoming, he hardly took his eyes off her. Usually her dates were school affairs with one of the teachers. There were several male teachers and the only one she really enjoyed being with had gone to another school this term.

Nat had dated several young women in Atlanta before he came to Union Gap and opened the dental practice. There had not been much of an opportunity for a personal life while he was getting the dental office established, except for the times when he went back home to visit his father over a weekend. He found Teresa to be a refreshing change from the city girls who loved only the nightlife, while he was more of the outdoors type.

Nat backed the boat to the water's edge like an expert and came to a stop, jumping out of the vehicle. Together, they slid the boat into the water and Nat stood holding on to it with one hand, assisting Teresa with the other, then he scrambled aboard.

"Can you swim?" Nat asked.

"Of course. Why? Were you planning on getting me out in the middle and pushing me overboard?"

"Wouldn't think of it. I'd have your dad to answer to," he chuckled. "Not any crocodiles in this lake, are there?" he humorously asked.

"Nope. Only a lot of water moccasins," she answered matter-of-factly, trying not to smile. To her knowledge no one had ever reported seeing any of those snakes in the lake. "Just row very gently and they won't bother us . . . maybe." Nat did not know whether or not to believe her. He looked her in the face to see if he could see any trace of mirth. For a few seconds she did a good job of keeping a straight face, then to his relief, she laughed gleefully like a child.

Nat was gently rowing toward the center of the lake. "You didn't have me fooled for a single minute."

Teresa sat on the blanket she had placed on the floor at the bow of the boat, allowing a hand to trail along through the water. "Ahh, this is the height of relaxation. I certainly need a day like this, Nat, and I'm glad you asked me along . . . even if I was a second choice."

He looked at once after she made this remark, in an effort to detect if she had been serious. Had he known Alyn's lovely daughter better, he would have realized that her cheerful and teasing demeanor had been inherited from her father. "Miss Russell, I would have gotten down on my knees to ask you to go fishing with me if I hadn't been so afraid of a rejection. Most highly educated ladies of your caliber would have laughed at such a gesture."

Teresa gave a giggle when she answered that a person in his profession must have had more than a high school education as well. "But I still can't understand where Papa and Raymond went off to this morning."

Nat stopped rowing when he decided that this would be a good spot to throw the anchor over; he then placed the oars inside, bent over retrieving the anchor, and dropped it over the side of the boat. "Oh, I'll bet they went somewhere to see about getting a key to fit in the locks on the old trunks. Dad mentioned to me that Alyn had suggested they try an antique dealer."

Teresa sat up, drying the wet hand across her jeans. "Well! You've got to be correct! I would guess they went to some antique shops down in Blue Ridge. Yep. That's it. But they are in for a rude awakening if they come across a dealer who will let any keys out of the shop without their buying them."

"That's true and if they buy them, then they may not fit the locks either," Nat answered.

"And they may come across some dealers with greedy intentions, wanting to also see what's inside the trunks. Some may want to come with keys and not turn any loose to anyone else unless they bring them themselves."

Nat thought for a few seconds and then answered that if there were things of value inside the trunks his dad would not let anyone get their grubby hands on whatever was there. "He'll probably take up residence in that house and personally be on guard."

"Oh, how I love a mystery!" Teresa exclaimed.

Nat handed Teresa a rod commenting that she'd have to bait her own hook.

"I would if I had some bait," she said and looked around for any sign of a bait can.

Their eyes met at the same time. Both Nat and Teresa realized at once that neither of them had placed a bait can in the boat. Nat laughed, but his fishing partner only looked disgusted. "Now, wait a minute!" he held both hands up. "Don't blame me. It was Alyn's fault because he said he would have the bait so I didn't even think of it." Then they both laughed.

"Who ever heard of anyone going fishing without any bait?" she giggled. "We'll never live this down. In fact, maybe we'd better not even mention that we came here, and certainly without any bait." After a few minutes of just sitting there, Teresa said, "Well, just row around a bit . . . but wait," her voice lowered to a whisper. "Look over yonder." She pointed to the far end of the lake where a doe and her twin fawns were drinking at the water's edge. The doe jerked her head up when she discovered the visitors out in the boat and then they were gone into the bushes as quick as a wink.

"Where's the camera?" Nat asked looking around.

"If it's not in the boat, then that's your fault. I handed it to you."

"Never mind. It's underneath the seat where you're sitting," she said.

He glanced under the seat and saw the camera but left it there. "Too late now. We're striking out all around, aren't we?" He picked up the oars and started rowing toward the far end where they had seen the deer, ripples gently rocking the boat.

"Oh, it's not really a washout, Nat. It is a beautiful morning, isn't it? We can just enjoy a boat ride and some sandwiches. Maybe another time we can have a nice trip up to the falls on horseback, that is, unless you're game to attempt another fishing trip."

Nat looked quickly at her to see if he could detect a serious look on her face or a teasing one. "Is that an offer, ma'm, about the horseback riding?"

"I guess so. That is, if you care to. I'm going to be plenty busy for the rest of this month but perhaps we could do that on a Sunday afternoon, if you'd like."

Would he ever like! Nat had decided he would set his cap for this intriguing young woman with an irresistible grin. She may not want to be caught though. Surely she'd had plenty of chances. No guy in his right mind would pass up the opportunity of the offer she had just made, even if he had never been on a horse in his whole life . . . which he hadn't. He had been thinking these thoughts and was so long about answering that she may change her mind. "Uh, . . . oh, sure . . . of course, I'd love to do that. Sounds great to me so you just name the day."

"First, Nat, let me ask you an important question," Teresa said half-humorously, covering her mouth to conceal a big smile. Nat stopped rowing and looked her in the face wondering, "What now?"

"What I was going to ask is . . . do your feet feel slightly wet?"

"My what?" Then he looked down and saw water circling around his shoes and trickling on across the floor toward where Teresa was sitting.

"Oh, drat the luck!" Nat said looking behind him. The back end was fast filling with water. "What in the world! I'll lose dad's favorite rod and reel. Let's take our shoes off, Resa." He thought he had just made up a nickname for her without even thinking. She didn't take time to think about it since she was used to the nieces and nephews calling her Resa. Nat started rowing as fast as he could but the water was coming in so fast that it was to no avail. Teresa looked around for something to bail with and finding nothing, suggested that they jump in with the copperheads.

"You are only kidding aren't you . . . about the copperheads. Tell me you are," Nat pleaded.

"Oh, there's no time for joking. Of course I was only teasing but here I go. Come on Nat." She stood up and dived over the side with Nat quickly behind. They swam to the closest bank. Nat got there first and stood, reaching for her hand as she came in right behind him. He pulled her to her feet and hugged her close to him with water dripping from both. They stood there laughing and shivering from the cold water.

"Man! That's the coldest swim I've ever had," he said. At once they realized they were embraced and each let go at the same time, their eyes still locked. "I'd offer you my shirt, but it's slightly wet."

Teresa giggled, adding that she'd lost a brand new pair of shoes. She pulled a strand of hair out of her face and patted it in place. "Well, the fish are probably having a nice picnic." They both laughed so hard that it took a while to get over it.

Nat offered her his hand as they walked up a beaten path toward where the Jeep was parked. "All we need now is for the Jeep not to start!" Nat said.

Teresa stopped beside a tree, dropped his hand, and reached down to pick a lone violet. She held it up by the stem and said, "Look, Nat, all is not in vain." She placed it in her wet jean pocket to take it home and press it.

Later, and at Teresa's insistence, Nat was standing in the living room in front of the mantel waiting for her to finish changing clothes. His shirt had dried enough not to be uncomfortable, and the jeans were still very damp but would be okay until he got home. He would have insisted on letting her out at the back of the house, but she wanted him to come in for coffee and a quick snack. Surely she could come up with something from the refrigerator that could be popped into the microwave. She brought him some of her dad's house shoes, slides that she knew he could wear until he got home. He had put on the coffee pot and, not wanting to sit on any chair without Teresa furnishing a towel, went to the living room to look around and wait for her.

At once, he noticed the antique furniture that he had not noticed at all when he was here before for Alyn's birthday party on March fourth. It probably went unnoticed because of the crowd of people in the room. It all looked as though he had stepped back into time before the turn of the century.

Nat stood before the walnut mantel, noticing a framed photo of Alyn Russell and his three children, taken when they were small. Sweet little Teresa sat on her father's lap, the boys standing on each side of the chair where they sat. He had not noticed this photograph when he was here before nor did he know that Alyn had another son. "Alyn was a handsome young man then," Nat thought. Then he moved over to stand in front of another photograph in an ornate gold frame. It was beautiful Teresa in a stunning green dress that brought out the color of her eyes and her shoulder length hair. He lifted the frame from the mantle, studying her warm and compassionate expression just as she entered the room.

Nat turned when she entered the room and commented on her different appearance. "Well, you look like you just stepped out of a picture," he smiled, placing the photo back on the mantel. "Like you looked in this picture. I'd wager a guess that you were about twenty to twenty-five here. Am I right?" Then, fearing she may think he thought her to look much older at the present time, added, "However, you don't look any older right now though. This is a beautiful photo of you, Resa."

"Thank you for your kind remarks, Nat, but you are wrong. That is a photograph of my mother, Cynthia." Teresa had gazed sadly at that picture many times during her childhood, wishing she could just snap her fingers or say some magical word and her mother would step down out of that frame and throw her arms around the little girl. She looked up at Nat with a sad face.

"Oh, really." Is all he could think of at the moment to say. When she said nothing further, he added, "I would have sworn it was you. You are the spitting image of her."

"That's what Papa has always told me." They were standing right next to each other, so that when Nat turned, he was looking down into her face and could not help but lower his head, and lightly kiss her on the lips. Shocked, Teresa stepped back, not knowing what to say.

He saw the shock on her face and said softly, almost in a whisper, "I couldn't help but do that, Resa. Who wouldn't? You were just looking up at me so beautiful-like and yet so much like the little girl on her daddy's lap."

"Did I say I didn't want you to, Nat? Did my look say that?"

He placed a finger under her chin, tilting it upwards, gazing into her eyes, whispering a reply. "No, the look you gave me said this." Then he kissed her again, only this time a long and tender kiss.

Chapter Twenty-Four

THE IRON SKILLET WAS A BEEHIVE OF ACTIVITY WHEN Nat walked in the door at two o'clock. The place was usually closed at this time of day on Saturday. When he entered, a jukebox was blaring a loud "you done me wrong" song, two waitresses were up on ladders hanging curtains with chickens all over them, and another one was setting vases of artificial flowers on each table with salt and pepper shakers. There were ceramic statues of roosters and hens on shelves along the wall and on top of the cash register. A teenaged boy was washing windows ahead of the waitresses who were hanging curtains.

Nat stopped when he discovered the new music contraption all lit up with flashing lights. Mack and his wife, Thelma, were standing in front of it admiring their new attraction.

"Well! What have we here?" Nat said loudly in order to be heard above blasting music. Mack turned when he called out to them.

"Hi, buddy. Ain't this a duzzie! Boy! Just think of th' dimes this thang'll rake in." He placed an arm on Nat's shoulder.

"Yep. You and Thelma will probably get rich quick. The young folks will pile in by the droves."

Thelma looked at her husband. "Did you hear that, Mack? I told you we didn't need this thing. We don't need this place to turn into a hang out. Why, we'd have to hire a policeman to keep them in hand!" She walked away shaking her head.

"Women!" Mack mumbled. "You're smart, boy. Stay single. She was all for it when I suggested gittin' a jukebox.

It's bound tuh hep out." Then shrugging his shoulders, he said "Oh, well . . . time'll tell, Nat. Whatcha up to, boy?"

"Just wondering if you've seen my dad and Alyn today? They must be off together somewhere."

"Yeah, sure did, earlier this morning. They come in together and I heard 'em discussing about going down tuh Blairsville and Blue Ridge."

"Okay. That solves that then. Teresa said she hadn't seen her dad either. Thanks for the information . . . say, what's with all this sprucing up?"

"Just thought we'd better sorta keep up with the inn, ya know, lest ya'll take all th' business," Mack joked.

"I tell you what . . .we just won't have breakfast up there, so you can have all that trade. I'd miss coming in here before going to work anyway. Need my daily news and advice. Can't say so much about the cholesterol though."

"Then I guess we didn't have tuh put up all them new curtains and table cloths and stuff," Mack laughed.

"Bet I can guess why you put up all those signs all over the place," Nat said as he looked around and read the little framed signs hanging all around. One read, "Welcome Y'all," another, "We speak Red Neck here," and "Fresh road kill, what's yore choice?" There were signs above each table along the walls. He laughed when he read another sign that said, "If you don't like what we have, then go on down yonder to Mama's house. She'll cook anything." Then he told Mack that customers of the inn would come in here wanting to buy their signs. "Good!" he answered, "I can get more where them come from. Just come on out with it, Nat, what'er you think? Folks will have something to read while they are waiting for their food and won't complain about the slow waitresses. Ain't that smart business sense?"

Chuckling, Mack gave John a punch on the shoulder. "Wanna cup of coffee, Nat? Have leaded and unleaded for you health nuts."

"No, but thanks. I just had some. Guess I'll be going. See you later, Mack." He had walked toward the door but turned back and added, "Tell Thelma when I come in next time I'll probably see kids dancing in the aisles."

Mack grinned and answered that maybe he'd better not tell her that. John had hold of the doorknob and turned saying, "Just one more suggestion, Mack. I think you and Thelma should change the name of this place to 'The Chicken Coop.'"

After Nat left the Skillet, he decided there was nothing else to do except go on back home and watch the Braves game on TV, a pre-season game being played in Florida. He knew Raymond would be anxious to get back to the inn and try out the keys that perhaps he and Alyn had rounded up. He would go on up there in about an hour and see if they had returned. He had much rather have stayed with Teresa but did not want to push it with her. He figured leaving her wanting would be the best tactic. He would watch her for signs that she was more than interested in a relationship with him. They seemed like a pretty good match to him and he knew that the kiss would put her to thinking. He wondered why she had never married. Surely she'd had plenty of chances.

The house that he rented was only two streets off the main street from the Skillet, so he'd parked in the driveway and walk there. Now, walking back home along the sidewalk with hands in pockets, he was thinking all these thoughts. His heart was light; in fact, if he had been a kid, he would be turning cart-wheels. "I know she'll be in church tomorrow. Wonder if she will sit with me? If she gets there before I do, should I squeeze in the pew? I know she will sit with Beth, John, and the kids. Alyn will be at the door with the ushers. Maybe I'll move my membership tomorrow. Hope Dad will also."

Nat was deep in thought when he popped to his senses by hearing his name called from behind. Al rolled up beside him on his bicycle. "Hi, Nat. Oh, my mom said I should call you Dr. O'Bryan but do you care if I just do that when I am at your office?"

"Well, here's our baseball champion." Al braked, jumped off the bike, and walked along beside Nat. "Now, everyone else calls me Nat so I don't see why you must do otherwise but if your mom insists, maybe in her presence you could do what she says. Where're you headed?"

"Oh, just trying to find somebody to hang around with."

"Then how about doing me a favor, would you?"

"Sure thing. Just tell me what it is. I'm at your service." Al gave his usual mischievous grin as he looked up at Nat.

"Okay . . . here we are at my house. Just pull your bike off the sidewalk up in front of the steps and come on in." The two went up on the porch with Al following Nat inside. "Want a softdrink, Al?"

"Sure. I am pretty thirsty after riding around town. Coming down the hill off the mountain is a cinch but I was kinda dreading the pull back up. Mostly, I have to push the bike. I had ball practice this morning and that got me pretty tired so a cold softdrink would be just great."

Nat had walked toward the kitchen while Al was rambling on. He opened the refrigerator, took out two canned softdrinks and handed one to the boy, who thanked him and took it gratefully. They popped them open and took sips. "Ahhh, that does hit the spot, Al. Tell you what I'd like for you to do please. Oh, just have a seat at the table while I go get them."

Nat disappeared into the next room and then reappeared with a pair of slippers in his hand. "Here ya go." He held them out and asked Al if he'd just drop them by to Teresa on his way home.

"Huh? These don't look like any she would wear, and I believe her feet are much smaller than these, don'tcha think?" The boy looked totally confused as to why he should give these to his Aunt Teresa.

"She'll understand, Al. Just give them to her please."

"Well, sure. I'll be glad to, but I think she'd much rather have a dozen roses," he answered, anxious to please even if he was left totally in the dark. "You know how women are," he added, spreading his hands out with expression, leaving Nat to wonder just how Al happened to know how women are.

Chapter Twenty-Five

SUSAN WAS SITTING ON THE FLOOR OF THE TREE house, her legs crossed with a tablet resting across them and a stubby pencil poised, ready for action should something suddenly come to mind. She was thinking hard when Pete came stomping up from the ladder onto the floor and let little Sally jump from his arms.

"Pete! For goodness sake! Don't you know Sally shouldn't be jumping!" she scolded her brother. "Certainly not until that cast comes off her leg!" The dog ran over to Susan with its tail wagging and licked her on the face as it jumped on the tablet, giving her more licks and causing giggles. Her blonde curls bounced when she twisted her neck from side to side to escape more slobbering licks. "Get off my tablet, Sally! Stop! You're ruining my story!" Pete mumbled that it was already "ruint." Susan grabbed the tablet and jumped to her feet. "Bad dog, Sally!" The little animal dropped its head and whined when it heard the tone of her voice and saw her sweet, pixie face turn sour.

"Now you've hurt Sally's feelings, Susan!" Pete said gruffly, "and all because of that silly story. When are you going to grow up?" He'd heard his mother use that question on his brother, Al.

Susan wrinkled her brow in a frown. "My story is not silly, and I'll grow up when I get good and ready. Just go on and leave me alone, Pete Russell! And take Sally down with you." The little girl sat down in a huff, crossing her legs and taking up the pencil and tablet again, determined to end the conversation once and for all.

Pete had intended to go down by the rope but since he had to take the dog in one arm decided to go down the slide, and away they went, with laughter and barking. Sally immediately raced around the house when she heard voices and then footsteps on the gravel road. It was Al and Ryan Ratcliffe. Al was pushing his bike. As they came nearer, Sally took off running toward Ryan and jumped up into his arms. She wiggled every inch of her body and licked the boy's face and then his arms, while making grunting sounds. Pete ran on to where they had stopped. "Well, I never saw her take on like that over a stranger before. I've seen you down at school but Sally hasn't."

"Oh, I've seen this little dog many times," Ryan smiled. He rubbed her head and hugged her close. "You haven't forgotten me, have you, girl?"

Al was dumfounded and as confused as Pete seemed to be over their dog's affection toward Ryan. Then he realized the truth. "Oh, I get it now. She was lost for a while, and I'll bet you saw her then. Where was she, Ryan?"

"In the woods," he answered. "I found her limping along with a broken leg so I fixed it with a stick and some cloth that I tore from my shirttail." He looked at her leg now and saw that it was bandaged up properly. "How is the hurt leg, little one? The broken bone must be healing up good by now. I saw you holding it up to run though." He handed Sally to Pete who was standing there with outstretched arms. "I have a dog, too, but he is a big one and they let me keep him down at the school."

"What's his name?" Pete asked.

"His name is Jethro," Ryan said and Pete giggled saying that was a very funny name. "Maybe, but he likes it and comes when I call the name." Then turning to Al, Ryan said he guess he'd better be getting back. "I was just walking around a bit. I'd wondered who lived up here. This is a nice place back here at the end of nowhere. It sure would be nice to live in the woods." He turned to go and then turned back saying, "So Penny is your sister, huh? She is in my history class. She has been helpful to me and seems like a real nice person."

"Yeah, she's my sister. This is her last year and she's going off to nursing school down in Atlanta at Georgia Baptist

Hospital except I get the feeling that she wants to stay another year at Kendell Mountain School."

"I want to be a veterinarian. And your dad is a doctor, you said. What kind of a doctor is he?"

"A medical doctor. He has an office down in town. Actually, he's my stepfather. Say . . . why don't you come on in and meet my folks. I'm sure my mom wouldn't mind, and we can have some cookies and a softdrink."

"Yeah, Ryan," Pete chimed in, "come on and I'll show you my new tree house."

"Okay, if you're sure it will be all right."

While Ryan waited for Al to park his bicycle inside the garage, Pete bounced up the steps, where Sally stood waiting on the porch. They both exploded through the doorway, loudly announcing that the Russell household had a visitor. Beth came from her painting, wiping her hands with turpentine on a paper towel. John was in his office with the door closed. He had been on the telephone checking on patients in the hospital, as well as some students in the clinic at school. Now retrieving his bag from a chair, he was about to go look in on two new patients at the clinic, when he heard the boys' loud talking and Sally's barking. John came down the hall and into the living room, his bag in hand just as Beth entered, noticing the young man standing there with Al.

"Pop, Mom, this is the guy I was telling you about that has just come to our school. He's from up north."

Beth spoke. "Al, at least you could introduce him to us by name."

"Oh, yeah, I'm sorry. This is Ryan Ratcliffe and this is my mom and pop. I told him we could come in and have a soft-drink and something to go with it."

John reached his hand out to welcome Ryan, who was only an inch or so shorter than himself. "Well, Ryan, it is a pleasure to meet you and I do hope you like going to school here." Then Beth offered her hand and gave some kind words also.

"Ryan said he wants to be an animal doctor," Pete piped up. "And guess what? He's the one that fixed Sally's leg! How about that! It was him."

"Oh?" Beth questioned. "That was before you started to school then."

"Yes ma'm, I suppose so."

"Well, son, you certainly did a fine job and I'm sure you will make a good veterinarian," John complimented.

Ryan had felt reluctant to come inside but now his pride swelled with what he had done for the little dog. It felt good to be complimented by a doctor. His spirits brightened.

Then John asked how he happened to be on the mountain and found Sally. "This is private property. Did someone give you permission to be around here?"

"No, sir. I just started walking around and didn't ask. I didn't bother anything. I didn't see anything to bother. After I passed the big house down the road I cut across through the woods because I've always loved to walk in the woods and hoped I'd find a creek, too." He did not tell them that he had discovered the cave and had been living there.

Beth changed the subject by telling them to go ahead and get their softdrinks. She had made teacakes that morning and they were in a cookie jar, and she would get back to her painting. "Ryan, you come up any time and visit with us."

"Thank you very much Mrs. Russell. I would like that, and oh, I know your daughter, Penny. We have a history class together. She told me that our assistant principal, Teresa Russell, is her aunt." John interrupted to say that she is his sister. "Oh, but how does the principal, Mrs. Patricia Russell, fit in?" Ryan was not being nosey but it was rather confusing.

"That Mrs. Russell is a great aunt to Penny and an aunt to Miss Teresa Russell."

Ryan blew out a soft whistle and said there were a lot of Russells around here.

Beth laughed and said there was another little Russell out back in the tree house.

All of a sudden, Al remembered the slippers he had promised to deliver to Aunt Teresa. "Oh, Ryan, I forgot to stop by and leave those house slippers with Aunt Resa. As you go back down the hill would you please drop them by there for me? I left them in the basket on the bike." Ryan said he'd be glad to do that for him.

Beth and John looked at one another with big question marks in their eyes. "Slippers?" Beth questioned. "Where did you get them?"

"Oh, Nat . . . I mean Doctor O'Bryan asked me to take them to her. And they are not even ladies slippers but great big men's. Why do you wonder he would want her to have them, Mom?"

Beth looked at John with curiosity on her face, and then back to her son. "I wouldn't know, son, but it isn't any of our business, now is it?"

"I reckon not." Al shrugged his shoulders. "Just seems sorta odd to me."

The three boys went into the kitchen for their treats and John put his free arm around his wife saying that she was the most special Russell in the world and pecked her on the lips.

"He's the mystery boy, John, that Tissy was telling me about. He didn't want her to contact the school where he had been attending in Pennsylvania. Do you think he might have been in trouble there? It could have been the reason he left home."

"Sure. That could have been the reason but he doesn't seem to me to be a bad person and not the hippie we thought either. Wouldn't the school have to get his records before he would be accepted?"

"Normally, yes, they would. But exceptions can be made. Tissy seemed to think that if there would be any helping him, that he would have to have her trust first. I suppose she will ease into getting his approval later. He will have to go all of next year to earn a diploma."

John still had his arms around his wife and he bent down, kissing her again. "I do love you, my sweet. Have I told you that today?"

"Only twice and this makes three times, but I will never tire of hearing you say that, my handsome husband."

"Remind me to tell you again when I get back." He gave her a squeeze, taking his bag from the table beside her painting paraphernalia. With a silly smirk on his face and wrinkle of the nose as he went through the kitchen door, John said that on his way home he'd buy her a nice bottle of perfume that did not smell like turpentine.

Chapter Twenty-Six

TERESA WAS GLAD SHE HAD BROUGHT HOME SOME papers to grade from her two English classes, for the house was extremely lonely today without Papa around and, too, she was worried about him. Her worry was not necessary for he certainly was old enough to take care of himself, and Nat had phoned to inform her of the information he had gotten from Mack Faber that they had gone looking for keys. She could not seem to stretch her imagination enough to decide what must be inside those old trunks and she was as anxious to have the mystery solved as anyone. Nat seemed rather nonchalant, telling her that it most likely was only old tattered clothes. "What could be so exciting about someone's old worn-out, musty clothes?" he asked her. He said that at first he was excited but after thinking more about what could be in the trunks, he'd come to the conclusion that their running around hunting keys to open them was like kids trying to find their hidden presents at Christmas time.

The English test papers were scattered over the dining room table with Teresa engrossed in checking for errors. She was very proud to see that Penny had turned in a neat paper with no incorrect answers. That was a relief! But when she came to Ryan Ratcliffe's test paper, she noticed several incorrect answers, although not enough for a failing grade. "I would like to go over this with him to show him where he went wrong," she was thinking just as there came a knock on the front door. "Who in the world could that be? No one ever comes to the front."

Walking down the hallway, she could see through the lace curtain on the front that it was the person she was just thinking about. "Of all things!" Teresa said out loud. "It is Ryan. What would he be doing here?" Unlocking the door and opening it to greet the boy, she noticed that he was holding a bag. Was it something for her?

"Hello, Ryan. What in the world are you doing up here on a beautiful Saturday afternoon? You could have gone on the bus down to town, you know. Students are allowed Saturday off to go to town to shop or to gather in the ice cream store or the park. Didn't anyone tell you?" The students who lived in the dormitories would be given passes but Tissy Russell would have given Ryan a pass. Maybe she forgot to tell him.

"Good afternoon, Miss Russell. Yes, ma'm. I know I could have. Penny told me about it but since it is such a beautiful day, I decided to walk up the road a way. I love the woods and enjoy the wild flowers and birds. I was hoping to see a deer." Then he looked down at the sack and said as he held it out to her, "This here is for you, Miss Russell. Doctor O'Brian asked Al to give it to you, but Al gave it to me to give it to you."

He held the sack with the slippers in it out to her. She saw what was inside and smiled, all the time hoping that no one else had asked him what was inside or it would start tongues to wagging. That was very easy to do in a small town, especially for someone like Gloria Spearman, for instance. She'd take someone one of her delicious pies to hear a bit of gossip like this and she would stretch it a mile further when she retold it.

"That seems like going around the mountain . . . no pun intended. Why didn't Al bring it to me himself?"

"He said he forgot and since I was up there at his house just now he asked if I'd drop it by on my way back down to the school."

"That sounds like my nephew alright. Either he doesn't concentrate or he is very forgetful. I thank you for bringing the bag to me, Ryan and, in fact, I am very glad you came by. It seems very odd that I was just grading your English test paper, and here you are."

Ryan looked expectantly at Teresa, feeling a rush of anxiety. He was afraid to ask whether he had passed the test or not. Then a thought quickly entered his mind that the result of this test may determine his entire future. He could see it passing before his eyes. He may wind up a complete failure and be walking the streets poking in garbage cans for sustenance. With a weak voice he managed to ask if she would be allowed to tell him now if he had passed the test.

Teresa recognized his fear and would not keep him in suspense until Monday when she would return the papers to the students. "Ryan, I am very pleased to tell you that you did pass the test . . . but barely." She smiled when she saw the relief on his young handsome face. "I would appreciate it, however, if you would not reveal to anyone that I gave you the results of your test in advance. We are not supposed to do that but I wanted to set you at ease and also tell you that I would like for you to stay after school for the rest of this term for some added help."

"Whew! I certainly will, Miss Russell. I'd be happy to, that is, if you would get an okay for me from the principal to be late going to my job after school."

"Oh, I will, and I feel certain that she will agree with me. After all, your education comes first. And I thank you again for stopping by, Ryan."

"Yes, ma'm! I'm so glad I did. So, I'll see you Monday." He turned to go with a much lighter heart than he had when he stepped up on the porch. He felt sure of the other classes except for history and that test was not until next Wednesday. Penny had told him that she would get with him before then and help him study for that test. Maybe she would invite him back up to her house. "That would be great! Wow! Is my luck ever changing!" He walked down the road with a lighter step, for a load had been lifted from his shoulders.

Now, there was another load that still remained which he would have to deal with sometime. That was the worry about the money he had tossed into the bushes . . . and G. G. and Pappy. He'd have to face them sometime, too. What if they were to get sick and even die before he could contact them. "But I do not want to contact them until I can prove to them that I am not the failure that my parents made me out to be. G. G. had told me that God would look after me, so she was completely correct on that score and I know God is looking after them, too."

Teresa closed the door, feeling good that the young man was so happy and because she was a part of it. She really wanted to help him all she could, mainly because it was evident that he wanted all the help he could get and was a willing student, eager to learn. If only all of them were as eager.

She gathered up the test papers and returned them to the leather satchel, wondering what she would do next. "Surely Papa and Raymond will be back before long. If they were successful in obtaining some keys they would want to try them out at once." Then she felt sure that Raymond would want Nat present to look in the trunks with them, so maybe Nat would call her even if Papa did not use the phone there when they stopped by Nat and Raymond's house . . . "I think I'll go start some Sunday dinner. When one of them phones, I'll invite them to come up to the house to have dinner with us." Sometimes Papa Russell and Teresa went up to John and Beth's after church on Sundays and sometimes John, Beth, and the kids stopped by Knollwood. "Maybe I will also invite Tissy to have dinner with us since her daughter, Bess, and her husband are away on a trip. Yes, that would be nice. I think Raymond seems rather smitten with her. I hope it won't seem like I am throwing them together. Humm . . . maybe I am, so what?"

As Teresa busied herself in the kitchen, she decided not to include John's family this time because the kids would dominate the conversation and demand so much attention. "Yes . . . it will be just Papa, Raymond, Tissy, Nat, and myself. Too bad there was no one that Papa was not interested in." Then Teresa laughed at the thought that she could invite Gloria Spearman! "Wouldn't that take the cake! I'm sure Papa would be mad with me for at least a month if I did that. No. I wouldn't do that to him, bless his dear old sweet heart."

Teresa's heart was still all a-flutter over the kiss in the living room after the fishing trip . . . or, the so-called fishing trip. Never had she felt this way before from a light goodnight kiss at the end of an evening out on a date. Somehow, this was different. Nat was different. If she ever wanted to settle down, he would be the one. But right now, she was married to the school and about to become principal of the high school department. It would require so much extra time and to a husband, it would be like another man in her life.

The shrill ringing of the telephone quickly brought her out of the trance. She sat a pot that she had just taken from beneath a cabinet on top of the stove and reached up, taking the receiver from its cradle. "Hello," she said in a cheery voice. "Oh, hi, Nat. I was hoping you'd call with some news from our run-aways. Have you heard from them?"

"Yes, Dad called a while ago. Sorry I did not let you know at once but I have a visitor."

Her heart fluttered again at the sound of his voice. "Well, where in the world are they, Kalamazoo?"

"Just about," he laughed. "They had no luck in the places they went to so Dad suggested they go on down to Atlanta. He knows a dealer on Piedmont Road who belongs to the rotary club with him. He's been in the business for years and felt sure he would be of some help to them."

"I certainly hope so. Well, then. No doubt they'll be back before nightfall. Say, Nat, I'm cooking dinner tomorrow and would like to invite you and your dad and also Tissy to come up and eat with us."

"Uh, I know Dad would love to accept, but . . . well, you see, this company that is here is a friend from Atlanta and . . ."

"Oh, fuddy-duddy, Nat. Just bring your friend along. We'd love to have you all, that is, unless you've already made plans otherwise."

"No. We haven't as yet made any other plans, so if you're sure it won't be an imposition, Resa, we'd be glad to come."

"Of course it will not be an imposition. So, we'll look for you after church. With your company you may not go to church, but we will and will come right home afterwards."

"I don't know yet about church but we'll see you then about one o'clock and thanks for the invite. I'm sure you are a good cook and I for one will be looking forward to it."

After they hung up, she said, "Well now! I'd better come up with something extra special. Oh, first, I need to call Tissy." She made that call and the invitation was graciously accepted. She told Tissy about Nat's visitor. "Who's Nat's friend," Tissy asked. "Someone from Atlanta?"

"I don't know as he didn't say, but I'm assuming it's the dentist he shared an office with before he came here. He had told me that his friend has been wanting to come up and do some fishing. I hope he wants to do some fly-fishing for trout instead of fishing from a boat," Teresa grinned into the telephone.

"Why should you care what kind of fishing they do?" Tissy questioned, thinking her statement sounded rather odd.

"Oh . . . no reason. Just thought it would be a lot more trouble from a boat. He'd have to pull a boat all the way up here from Atlanta you know. I love a good fish dinner, but I think I'll leave the fishing to the men. See you tomorrow, Tiss."

Chapter Twenty-Seven

AFTER BATHING AND DRESSING, TERESA TWISTED AND turned before the dresser mirror, deciding that this was all she could do, so she'd go now and prepare the dining room table for her company. She did not like being alone in this big house. It felt as though she must whisper or just say nothing at all for only the walls to hear. Last night she heard every creak of the house, the eerie sound that woke her every time the refrigerator came on, and the brushing of the tree limb against her bedroom window during the light breeze. If anything were to happen to Papa, heaven forbid, she'd not live alone for one minute. Maybe she would rent out the upstairs to a teacher from the school. Then she shook her head, trying to rid herself of such morbid thoughts and threw up her hands with disgust for thinking them.

Nat phoned Teresa again last night around eight-thirty, saying that Raymond and Alyn were staying the night in Atlanta. They would spend the night at his father's house and leave out early this morning to go to Asheville, North Carolina. The friend in the antique business in Atlanta did not have any keys, his antiques being mostly very expensive furniture, but he did know a fellow who had a shop in Asheville also had keys galore. He felt this would be where they needed to go, and he was very happy to learn that Raymond had not broken the locks on the trunks. "Be sure to remember me," he told Raymond, "if you decide to sell whatever you may find inside. With them being securely locked, surely there would be something in them other than old clothes; however, some dealers want old turn of the century clothes, or some of the costume shops would be interested."

So, the men would be off bright and early Sunday morning for Asheville. What a roundabout trip they had been making. "We're going on a wild goose chase," Alyn told Raymond. "Or, maybe a scavenger hunt."

"Yeah," Raymond answered. "I remember seeing a movie once about some people going on a wild chase to round up clues about finding a treasure. It got to be rather hilarious."

"It could be that our chase may wind up to be very profitable for you, my friend. Let's look at it that way," Alyn said, giving Raymond a ray of hope.

They were pulling into the driveway of Raymond's Atlanta property. The big house was a dark stone two-story building with an attractive manicured lawn. The house was surrounded with neatly trimmed shrubs, and when Alyn commented about the neatness of the place, Raymond told him that he had hired a lawn and grounds service to tend to it all, even before he had come to stay with Nat in north Georgia. The driveway led around back to a two-car garage where he now parked the car and they got out.

"I suppose our kids are wondering what has become of us," Alyn said.

"Yep, I know they are. I'll give Nat a call and he can phone Teresa or you may call her if you like."

Later, they were sitting in the den watching TV, but not paying it much attention as they talked. "Ray," Alyn had been calling him lately, "why don't you just put this place on the market and stay up yonder with us old country folks? What's the use of your living here by yourself? This is a beautiful place, but haven't you felt rather lonely since Nat has moved away?"

"I certainly have!" he exclaimed. "I've tried to keep busy in the Rotary Club and also at the country club playing golf, but after a while, all that gets boring." His chair was facing Alyn on the couch. He switched positions in the chair. Talking about his personal life was uncomfortable, but he decided to talk further. "After Nat's mother died five years ago, it was extremely hard. Nat had returned from Vietnam and had gone into practice with a dentist friend of his. He was seldom at home . . . you know how the guys are when they come back, restless and not wanting to stay around home, so it really was just the same as when I was alone."

"I know the feeling, other than the fact that I had been left with two boys and a newborn baby girl . . . and man, that was extremely hard! I did have the women there on the farm to help take care of the kids. The boys were forever fighting and getting into scrapes. But life goes on, no matter what state we are in."

"I know what you mean. My wife was very active in the church and when she died, the members were a big help to me, except . . ." The sentence was left hanging in mid air when Raymond smiled and looked rather embarrassed.

"Except what, Ray . . . out with it. We're telling our secrets here." Alyn returned the smile, expecting an answer.

"Well, I sort of had several widow women running after me, so frankly, I just stopped going to church altogether. I didn't realize how much I missed it until Nat and I started going up there at your church. So far, the women have left me alone." He wiped a hand across his mouth as though to wipe away another smile coming on. "However, there is one there that rather attracts me. I don't know whether or not she feels the same way toward me, and don't ask . . . I'm not ready to say any more."

"Okay, Ray, and I didn't mean to be prying into your personal life. It's just that I had started out to suggest that you sell this place and come on up for good. I also wanted to suggest, if I may, that you build yourself a little apartment on the back of the inn. There's plenty of room out back that could be cleared off."

"Yes, I've noticed there is more space back there that could be cleared off and have been thinking about having a nice garden for folks to walk along a stone walkway through arches adorned with wisteria, a sun dial, statues, and so on. There's lots of possibilities, and what you said about living space for myself has already crossed my mind."

"Actually, if you have enough room, you could add on a couple of rooms for myself," Alyn added and his words shocked even himself after he had said them. What would he do with himself other than sit on the long veranda in one of the rocking chairs and read his newspaper? That could get boring. What does one do with one's self at his age? All he ever knew was to work on the place, other than an occasional time out for fishing. He never would want to be a burden for his children to bear.

"Oh?" Raymond leaned forward in his chair. "What's this? You don't plan on leaving Knollwood!"

"Well, not right now, but I was thinking that if ever Teresa should marry, I'd like a little place of my own. That monster up on the mountain is too much for me now and yet if my daughter were to ever start a family, they would need the place to themselves."

Raymond thought for a minute before replying that Alyn's daughter seemed to be married to the school. "And, didn't you tell me that she will be the principal next term? Won't she be more tied down than ever?"

Alyn had an elbow on the arm of the couch, his head propped in the hand. "Yes, she'll be the high school principal, but that shouldn't keep her from having a family if that's what she wants. She could take a leave of absence if it became necessary."

The two men talked on for a while, then watched the news program and went to bed. While Alyn was dozing, he was thinking about how much he liked his new friend, Raymond O'Bryan. They seemed alike in many ways, yet they were so different.

Chapter Twenty-Eight

THERE HAD NOT BEEN A GOOD HARD RAIN IN SEVERAL weeks and the farmers and cattlemen were grumbling to this effect. Even the pastors had been including this need in their prayers and asking members also to pray for rain. These prayers were answered on Sunday morning as people woke up to a drenching rain with rumbling thunder. The foyer of the Union Gap Baptist Church displayed an array of umbrellas propped in corners and stuck behind pots containing plants, where some members tried to hide theirs from those who just might go away with the wrong umbrella. The rain did not deter many, maybe only the elderly, who preferred to stay in their robes and slippers and watch a service on their televisions.

Teresa hurried around setting the dining table and doing final touches for her dinner guests. She dashed out of the house with only a few minutes to spare until church time. John drove by honking the horn when he saw her car in the driveway and her with her umbrella, running toward the car. With her purse and Bible in one hand and the umbrella in the other, she could not acknowledge the horn honk with a wave. She was disgruntled because Nat had told her about their fathers being further detained on their scavenger hunt. "And here I've gone to the trouble to have them all for dinner," she had grumbled to herself. Then she thought resignedly that Nat's friend would make up for one of them being absent. She also wondered if this dentist friend would be wanting to go in with Nat at his office . . . but, no . . . Union Gap is not large enough for another dentist. She guessed that he probably would only have come for a visit with his long-time friend.

Teresa had asked Beula Mae if she would come in at noon and warm up the food for her, and she would pay her extra along with her weekly salary for cleaning. Then she would not have to rush home so hurriedly. Beula Mae said she would be happy to oblige. She was always happy to oblige when money was involved. Her hands were usually out with avarice.

When Teresa talked with Beula Mae, she also learned that Moses was coming up today from Atlanta for a visit with his grandparents, Tad and Selma. He had not been back since he had gone to work for Charles Russell and now had taken over the business with a partner, Brad Lyles. Teresa mentioned that she would like to talk with Moses, and wished that his mother, Sassy, would come with him also.

Ryan asked Mr. Hartwell for signed permission to go off campus today for church at the Union Gap Baptist, which was approved. The students were allowed to go to the church of their choice and Ryan rode the bus down with the others, some of whom chose to go to the Presbyterian church and some to the Lutheren church. Some said the Lutherens got out earlier than the rest and that would give them time to go to the ice cream shop before the bus loaded up. Ryan had purchased a new pair of trousers and shirt the week before with his earnings and yesterday got a haircut. This morning a spiffy young man looked back at him from the mirror when he took one last look before going out the door with Bible under arm.

He'd attended services in the school auditorium but Penny was nice enough to invite him to attend her church in town and then come home with her family for dinner. He felt proud to be included and would not pass up an opportunity like this. He loved the house in the woods where they lived, and her parents seemed very nice . . . so different from his own parents. No one had as yet been nosy enough to pry into his personal affairs, and hopefully they would not today either. Of course Mrs. Russell had to dutifully ask a few questions in filling out his school enrollment. She had not even as much raised an eyebrow when he slightly touched on his home situation.

By the time the bus rolled into the church parking lot, the much needed rain had come to a stop. Some of the farmers would be complaining that it would take a longer rain than this to water the fields and gardens. Before the bus had come to a stop, Ryan noticed both Penny and Al waiting out front for him. Penny saw him sitting about midway on the bus and threw up her hand to him. He returned the greeting, noting that they were walking to where the bus would park. They greeted students that they knew as they came off the bus until Ryan appeared, who walked away with them. They told him that the school bunch usually sat in the balcony and he could either do that or sit with their family on the first floor.

"Of course, I'd like to sit with your folks since you invited me, and I've told the bus driver that I'd be returning with you to your house. Do you think there would be enough room for me in the car?"

"Certainly," Penny said.

"Yeah," Al added, "we're used to making room. My little sister can sit in between Mom and Pop up front."

They were walking up the front steps with the group from the bus when Penny told Ryan that he looked very nice today. "Not that you don't during the week, I mean . . . but you look extra nice today."

Ryan's face flushed with embarrassment even though he appreciated the compliment coming from the pretty girl, which gave a boost to his confidence. Inside the double doors, the group turned to go up the steps to the balcony and when Ryan followed beside Penny, one of the boys said, "Hey, Ryan, we go up the steps here, buddy." Ryan only gave him a wink and shook his head, grinning. So, the word quickly spread among the group that it looked like Ratcliffe had taken a fancy to Penny Russell. "Nah," one boy told those around him that it was Al who invited him to sit with his family. "Penny's stuck-up and she's a brain. She wouldn't give him a second glance," someone else was heard to say. The bus driver and a teacher went to the balcony with the school group to insure there would be no misbehaving.

Ryan noted after they had sat down that the inside of the church was very nice, with beautiful stained glass windows and sparkling hanging chandeliers. The painting up over the baptistery could capture a person's attention even during a sermon. And the red carpet down the aisles matched the padded pews. Before the service even started, Ryan felt a peace and was happy that he came. When the choir marched in from each side, he noticed Mrs. Russell, the school principal, and he thought that she was a very attractive woman for her age. He wondered about her family.

Al leaned over and whispered to Ryan that his pop had a surprise for him today; however, he was not to let on that he had said anything about what he had just told him.

"Mom, here comes Aunt Resa. Please tell Pop to slide on down so we can let her sit at this end." That put Teresa on one side of Ryan, who smiled and spoke softly to him as someone was already making announcements. She looked around to see if she could spot Nat and his friend, all the time feeling that he would use his visitor as an excuse not to attend this morning. There was no sign of him from her point of view. Surely they would show up at her house after church for dinner. "If he doesn't show up, his name will be mud!" she thought. Just as the speaker left the platform, he came walking down the aisle beside where she sat, holding the arm of a beautiful young woman whose perfume reeked behind her. Teresa's mouth opened slightly and her eyes widened. Anyone who might be looking toward her at the moment would have noticed the astonishment on her face. She was fuming, not a Christian-like character and very unlike Teresa Russell. Nat stood aside for the peroxide blonde to sit after the people on that pew had moved to make room for them. None of the family members knew of Teresa's feelings toward Nat. They all noticed them come in but only Penny looked around Ryan to make a comment to Teresa. "It looks like Doctor Nat has a girlfriend." Teresa did not answer; in fact, she did not even hear much of what the pastor's sermon was about.

Alyn made the comment to Raymond that he felt very strange about missing church. He had not missed a Sunday in years; not since a big snow that closed everything down, especially the road down the mountain. They were backing out of the driveway, stopping at the street to let some cars go past. They had decided to start out early and get on up the road before much traffic began to fill the highways; it was now barely daylight. Raymond looked down at the gas gage, saying that they would have to stop to fill up. "I'll wait until we get to Northside Drive," he said and kept going. "There's a Seven-Eleven there that we can dash in and out of and not waste much time."

"Man! I'd hate to live around here where the streets are like a maze. You'd have to get an early start every day to get across town. How do you ever get to an appointment on time?"

"Ah, you soon get used to it."

They rode in silence for a few blocks, then talked about how this trip may turn out to be a waste of time. Alyn said that at any rate he'd enjoy just being away, as he had not been out of their little town for a while.

"Sometimes, I get to feeling rather stale and useless."

"I suppose most everyone does after they retire. Do you think it is a good idea to turn your orchard over to Tad and Joe?" Raymond inquired.

"I really wouldn't know unless I just haul off and do it, and that's what I've just done, so we'll see. I hope they won't make a mess of things."

In a few more minutes they came to the station where Raymond said he usually traded, and seeing only one car there, felt lucky to get to park at the pump closest the door. The car was parked off to the side and probably belonged to an employee. "Al, how about you putting the gas in and I'll go on in to pay," Raymond told Alyn and they both got out. He walked to the door and just pushed on it, when a rough-looking character pushed on it from the inside, nearly knocking Raymond off his feet. He was brandishing a wicked looking switchblade. Then another tough guy bumped backwards from the other door, waving a gun in one hand and a bag that surely contained money with the other hand.

The one with the knife grabbed Raymond by a wrist and jerked him out the door with him. "We're gonna need yore car, mister! Git on out there and gimme yore keys," his partner with the bag of money said. Raymond whispered through clinched teeth that the keys were in the ignition. "Looks like he has a friend, Blade. We'd better take 'im along with us! Throw this 'un in th' back and th' other'n in front, and be quick about it. Th' clerk has already called the cops by now."

The robber with the money shoved Raymond along to the car, jumped into the driver's seat, and held the gun pointed at Alyn while the one called Blade tossed Raymond in the back, then ordered Alyn to get back in the passenger seat. He shoved the bag of money underneath the seat. "You hold th' gun on 'em, Blade," he said handing him the gun, then turned on the switch and the Lincoln started up immediately.

"This is some fancy car we've got here, Blade. Man! It's got power!" The driver exclaimed, with wheels squealing as they took off in a cloud of dust.

Alyn had screwed the gas cap back on and then took a paper towel and a brush from the water bucket and was washing the windshield when he had been taken by surprise. He had not looked up to take notice of what had happened. This peaceful Sunday drive had taken a very different change in plans.

"What now?" Alyn was thinking as he sat in the passenger seat with a gun to the back of his head. If Ray were to make one move toward taking the gun, it would go off and blow his head to smitherines in the ruckus. This was some situation . . . like none he'd ever encountered! He was contemplating what he should do, if anything, when his army training came to mind. He would wait for an opportunity and hoped that Ray would not do anything foolish. Maybe they could learn something if he could only get them to talk, or he'd just play like a dumb old man.

The driver turned a number of times, going down streets that even Raymond did not recognize. Evidently, he was making an effort to throw the police off their trail. It seemed to Alyn that they were heading south. The sun had not as yet come up and most likely would not, as the weather report had predicted rain for Sunday morning. The driver was staying off main roads. It seemed that he knew exactly where he was heading. Neither Alyn nor Raymond could read any street signs due to the car's speed and also there was not enough light. Alyn said with a slow, matter-of-fact, drawl, "Son, if you wreck this car, then they'll find you for sure 'cause you'd be on foot." The two thugs looked no more than boys to him, but, even so, he wondered why they could not think that far ahead. It took many years of living to be able to discern right from wrong, if it had not been pumped into a kid from the beginning. It couldn't be the kid's fault every time, for some of them had never had a chance from the start.

"Shut up you old fool! Just keep your trap shut! I know what I'm doin'," the driver yelled. And the one with the gun nudged Alyn on the back with it as a warning. "The man in th' back is a lot smarter than you. He keeps quiet and you'd better do th' same."

The Lincoln squealed around a curve so fast that it slid, barely missing a telephone pole. Ray had not uttered a word, but was cautiously watching first one man and then the other, with wheels turning inside his head. He was wishing he had pried the locks off the trunks with a screwdriver and was now sitting in church listening to Tissy Russell sing in the choir.

Chapter Twenty-Nine

BY THE TIME CHURCH WAS OVER, THE RAIN SETTLED down to a mist and the sun peeped through, promising a clear day later on. Pastor Jesse Adair made his usual appearance at the double doors, only this time right inside to stay out of the dampness as he shook hands with the congregation. Teresa Russell wanted to get away before Nat and his visitor caught up with her. She told Penny to tell Beth that she had to leave in a hurry to prepare for company and she slipped out of the pew and on up the aisle, making her way without the usual jovial banter. She hurried past the preacher, made a comment about the nice service, and went on down the steps and out to her Chevrolet at the curb. Reverend Adair commented to John that his sister seemed to be in a big hurry when she came by him and then asked about their absent father.

Teresa was driving in a hurry up the mountain road when the thought hit her that she had nothing to be so upset about. After all, she had no strings on Nat O'Bryan and surely he kissed most of the girls he dated. "But not like the way he kissed me in our living room!" It had unsettled her and caused her to act like a schoolgirl. "I'll not let my resentment show this afternoon. It would serve him right to let him think I don't care how many women there are on his string . . . I'll show him." Having made that decision, she lifted her chin to finalize her statement. She would serve her dinner with the grace of an English countess.

She had just returned home as Beulah Mae was going down the back steps. "Everything's warmed up and the coffee pot is plugged in, Miss Teresa, and the table sure do look pretty. I hope you didn't mind iffen I pulled some flowers from your garden, and I used the best china and silverware."

"Oh, thank you so much, Beulah Mae," she told the woman with earnest, standing at the bottom step until she came on down. "You are a dear."

"T'weren't nuthin'. I wuz plum tickled to do it," she replied, her white teeth the most prevalent thing about her dark face. "Anything else you wanted me to do?" She shooed Ole Charlie away with her apron. "Git! Shoo!"

"No Buelah Mae, it sounds as though you've covered everything. You just go on to your own dinner fixings. I thank you so much." Before Teresa got in the door, John's car pulled into the driveway and John tooted the horn to get her attention before she went inside. She waved a hand to the car's occupants as she went back down the steps and out to the car. John had lowered his window. Teresa poked her head in, speaking to everyone and noted that Ryan Ratcliffe was with them. "Hi, Ryan," she said to the boy and heard a soft, "Hello, Miss Russell," in reply.

John spoke first. "Sis, have you heard anything from Papa and Raymond? I didn't see them at church and figured they didn't make it back last night."

"Yes, Nat called and said they were spending the night at Raymond's house and were planning on going up to North Carolina this morning to see an antique dealer there who specializes in old keys."

"Of all things!" Beth exclaimed before John said anything. "Looks like they are being given the run-around from everyone."

"Frankly, I think they are rather enjoying themselves with this venture." Teresa answered.

"Well, they must be old enough to take care of themselves, so we'll see them when we see them, I suppose," John put in.

"Aunt Resa, guess what?" Susan asked excitedly. "Ryan is going home with us and guess what else? He's the one who tied up Sally's hurt leg."

"Oh, he did? We were wondering who did that, weren't we?" Then to Ryan she said, "You did a good job, Ryan." In his embarrassment for the recognition he did not reply, only gave a slight nod and smiled.

Teresa all of a sudden had a bright idea. "Why don't all of you just get out right now and have dinner with me? I'd love nothing better and there is plenty already cooked and Beulah Mae has come in and warmed things up and set the table. Please say yes, in fact, I'll not take no for an answer." With that, she opened the back door of the car, and Al was the first one out.

"Sounds good to me," he grinned, hugging his aunt. "Come on folks, it sounded like she meant it and besides, we can eat what we've got ready for supper."

So they all piled out. Pete ran toward Ole Charlie, who was happily pecking at the ground, and scooped him up into his arms. The rooster obliged as though he was used to the children's affection. Susan came to where they were and rubbed his back, laying her head over against him. "Let me have him, Pete," she demanded.

"No! I will not. I got him first so just go away."

"Children, put the rooster down and come on in. Dinner's ready so you both need to go wash your hands," Teresa told them.

Everyone went inside to the good aroma of coffee brewing and other nice smells in the air of warming food.

In the kitchen, Beth told her sister-in-law that it looked as though she must have been cooking all day on Saturday. She lifted lids, peering inside to see what the offering would be.

"I did kind of keep busy cooking because I was expecting Papa and had invited Nat and his dad also, and Tissy as well."

Just as she got the name out of her mouth, Tissy called out a "yoo-hoo" and poked her head inside the kitchen. "Oh, you didn't forget, Tiss. I'm so glad you could come," Teresa told her.

"What made you think I would forget, my dear? I've never forgotten a meal here, of all things!" Her dimples showed. She placed her purse on the cabinet and asked what she could do to help out. "And where is Alyn? And Raymond, too? I didn't see either of them in church, and you know from the choir I can see everyone who is there." Teresa explained the situation and then said that Nat would also be coming and his friend with him.

"Yes!" Tissy said, "I did see a woman sitting with him. She is quite a looker. In fact, I figured she must be a model."

The women placed bowls of food on the table and ice in the tea glasses while Penny and Al showed Ryan around the house. John had gone to Papa's room to take off his tie and coat, placing them on the bed when he heard Nat coming in the back door. The woman with him sounded excited.

"I tell you, Nat, it hurts! Look at the red place it made!"

John met them in the hallway. "Hi, Nat, what's the problem?"

"Ole Charlie attacked her," he replied with a big smile. It looked as though he was trying to hold back laughter.

"It isn't funny, Nat," John said when he saw that the pretty woman had tears in her eyes, and to suffice, suggested that he would get some cotton and rubbing alcohol. Hearing the loud talking, Teresa came into the hallway. When Nat explained the situation, Teresa could not help but laugh. Her actions brought daggers shot at her from Nat's friend.

"Nat, I'm sure the lady has a name." She introduced herself without a reply from the visitor. Nat mumbled, "Excuse me, Resa, this is Lila Pelfry."

"Come with me, Lila, and we'll get something on this." She took the young woman by the arm and led her toward her bedroom.

Lila did not make a comment as she followed Teresa and did not notice Nat holding his hand over his mouth and his shoulders rising and falling. John was just coming out of a bathroom with the cotton and bottle, following them to Teresa's bedroom. When she sat on the dressing stool holding a shapely leg up for him to examine, he saw that the redness had already disappeared and the only real damage was to her stocking and her pride. The stocking sported a large tear that caused a run on to the ankle.

With the dabbing on of the alcohol done, John and Tissy took the two into the living room until Teresa and Beth would call everyone in to the dining room. Lila's eyes darted around the room disclosing her disapproval of the old furnishings. She made a comment about how out of date the furniture was and that her own apartment was strictly ultra modern, in a tone that Tissy deciphered as "hers was much more superior."

"Everyone to their own tastes," Tissy said. "Alyn Russell worked very hard to duplicate the way things were before an unfortunate fire."

"Fire? Oh, how simply terrible." She waved a hand in the air and then placed it across her chest. "Yes, I thought I smelled where wood had burned." John told her that she couldn't have smelled it because it had been years ago and the house had been completely rebuilt.

"Oh, then it must be dinner burning." Before anyone else could reply, Lila walked to the mantle where the framed photographs sat and took the one of Teresa's mother in her hands. "This is a beautiful photograph of Miss Russell, Nat . . . Resa, I believe you called her. Have you seen it? It really flatters her, don't you think?"

"Yes, I've seen it, Lila, only it isn't Resa, but her mother." His statement left her wondering if he had come here to see the Russell woman before. She may have felt very intimidated if she had known that right in the spot where she stood, Nat and Teresa had been in a steamy kiss.

John said that the photograph was made even before he was born.

"I knew her quite well," Tissy told them. "She was just as beautiful a person as that photograph shows, not only in looks but a beautiful soul. And she loved Alyn Russell with all her heart. It is such a shame that Teresa never got to know her wonderful mother."

Teresa poked her head in the door announcing that dinner was on the table. "John, would you please call the kids?"

John, at the head of the table where his dad always sat, asked the blessing and started passing bowls of food. They all made the usual jovial dinner talk and explained to Lila just who each person was. She over-exaggerated her comments about the younger children and made over Penny. Then she dominated the conversation by telling about herself and how she had known Nat for years and years and how close they had always been. Both of their parents had decided they would marry, but the Vietnam War started and took poor Nat away. She turned toward Teresa, and with honey dripping from her red lips asked, "And, what do you do Miss Russell?"

"She's my English teacher," Ryan spoke up. "And a very good one, too. She'd have to be good to get me to understand adverbs and adjectives."

"Yes, an old maid school teacher," Teresa said as she shook the ice in her glass of tea.

"You're not old, Aunt Resa," Susan said. "And I hope I grow up to be just like you," and turning toward Lila, sitting next to her, the little girl said that she is also the school assistant principal. Lila, who probably had a rusty brain in her attractive blonde head, simply raised her eyebrows, feeling sorry she had asked the question.

"Thank you, dear, about the 'you're not old' part." Nat thought he had been the one who came up with the name Resa, until he heard the children calling her this today.

The table talk turned to other topics. Tissy talking about the upcoming field trip up to the cave raised slight interest from Lila and great interest from Nat, who asked many questions. When Tissy told about the Cherokee Indian, who had lived all his life in the cave, Ryan was all ears. To himself, the mystery of the graves inside the cave was answered. They were the graves of the Indian's family.

"I don't think I will tell any more about this now as it would spoil Alyn's talk that he will make," Tissy said mainly to Ryan and for his sake. "Maybe I should have waited to let him tell about the Indian. You children just keep that to yourselves." She was looking at Pete, who then chimed in excitedly that he wanted to go to see the cave, too. The children had been demanded by Papa and also John to keep away from the cave area for fear they would venture off up there alone. Deliberately, Papa Russell had frightened the children into having no desire to go in the cave because a bear may be living in there. Tissy told Pete he would have to talk with his Papa Russell about taking him along. She knew Alyn would lecture the two little ones about never going there alone.

Ryan had a secret about the cave that no one else knew, and now he was anxious to tell Al about it. Ryan did not know Al's grandfather and was dubious about whether or not he should speak to him when he returned from his trip. If he told Al the secret, he felt that Al would be anxious to tell his Papa Russell. He decided that if he told Al, he would tell him that he wanted to be the one to tell his grandfather about the secret.

Lila changed the subject to the reason she had suddenly appeared on the scene. "Isn't Nat's new venture simply brilliant!" She was looking at Teresa when she said that, causing Teresa to conclude she was speaking to her. Without any reason, Lila felt that this Russell woman, school teacher, assistant principal, very attractive and single, was a direct threat to her ulterior motives. "It is such a beautiful old mansion!" Then she looked across at Nat, giving him her most charming smile. "Nat, you are absolutely the most brilliant man I've ever known." Teresa used her napkin to conceal the amusement. She could see right through this conniving feline, whose claws were digging in. She took a drink of her tea, feeling that she would choke if she could not laugh and, excusing herself, went to get the tea pitcher to refill glasses.

She brought the pitcher in from the kitchen and replenished the glasses. As Susan sat her glass back down it accidentally touched the end of a spoon and tipped over, spilling the whole glass of tea and ice into Lila's lap, who was sitting to her left. She jumped up screaming and in the process, turned her own glass over as well. The whole front of her dress was soaked. She ran from the room with Teresa in hot pursuit and Nat following close behind, leaving poor little Susan in tears. John had stood to sooth the child and rub his napkin across the front of her dress. He had seen the regrettable accident and later told Beth that it served Lila right for all her rude remarks. The only scolding Susan got was to tell her to be more careful where she placed a full glass and to apologize to Miss Lila for causing the mishap.

"Nat, just go back to the table," Teresa said. "I'll get her something to put on." As the two women went down the hallway to the bedroom, Lila exclaimed in a loud voice, "First I was attacked by that . . . that chicken and now this! I think you people are out to get me!" They looked through the clothes closet and finding nothing that would suit, Lila told Teresa just to go throw her dress and slip in the clothes dryer, and she'd wait there in the borrowed robe. Teresa obliged, all the time hoping that the dress would draw up to Susan's size.

Penny and Susan cleared the table while the women cleaned up the kitchen, and Nat and John waited out back, laughing about poor Lila's predicament and talking about things in general. They were sitting in the swing under the oak tree when Moses' car pulled up at the shed and parked. Moses discovered John and wondered who the man with him was. He ambled over to where they were. John stood and the two men shook hands like very old friends.

"Well, Mo! It's about time you came for a visit. Where's the family and your Mama?"

"It's good to see you, Johnny. Oh, they had other plans today."

John turned to Nat and introduced the two. "This is my old buddy I told you about, Moses Jackson."

"Oh, yes, the one who bought Charles's business. It's a pleasure to meet you Moses. John has told me how well you are doing in the business."

"This is the dentist who rents part of my building, Mo."

"Nice to meet you. I'm sure you've got everyone in Union Gap walking around with sparkling teeth and wide smiles now days."

"Pull up that chair over there, Mo, and sit with us for a while." John pointed to the chair to the side of the tree trunk. It had been a long time since Moses had come to visit his grandparents. "Have you heard about your grandpa and Joe taking over the orchard?" Then he thought that he should not have said that in case Tad was hoping to tell Moses about the good news himself. "I hope I haven't spilled the beans."

"Well, I didn't know, but I won't let on to him that I have heard about it. Why in the world would Mister Alyn throw in the towel?"

"Oh, I think he just wants to retire and enjoy doing nothing. There comes a time, you know?"

"I wouldn't know yet, Johnny, but our time's coming, don't you know? Our business is booming, and I suppose after I've put in all the years like your dad has, then I'd be ready to slow down, too."

John turned to Nat telling him that Moses' mother, Miss Belle, or "Sassy" as the family always called her, is with Brown University in Atlanta. "She grew up right here on Kendell Mountain, and man, could she ever sing!"

"And she still does. S'pose she'll be singing her way through those pearly gates!" Moses said.

"Uh, oh," Nat said, turning his head toward the back porch. "Here comes Lila so I know that means we are leaving. Guess I'd better go protect her from Ole Charlie." He grinned, got up, and shook hands with Moses, wishing him continued success with the business and then hurried to protect Lila. Moses continued on out to his grandparents' house down behind the barn. He turned his head toward the back porch in time to see Lila as she sauntered down the steps with languid grace, her head held high.

After they drove away, Tissy came out with Beth and the children, Teresa following them off the porch out to where John was waiting in the swing. Tissy told Ryan to check in before five o'clock at school, then said her good-bye's to everyone. Teresa followed John's crew out to the car. Before John got in, he reached over and whispered in his sister's ear, "Sis, I've been wondering why Nat sent you a pair of slippers instead of a box of candy?" Then he grinned from ear to ear as he got in and closed the door, leaving his sister standing there with a scarlet red face.

Chapter Thirty

THE SEVEN-ELEVEN HOLD-UP MADE THE TELEVISION late night news. The clerk had told police that the two men took a customer at gunpoint out of the store and left in the customer's black Lincoln. They took another man, who had been waiting in the car. The customer in the store had paid with a credit card, so the police had his name and also the credit card, which had not been returned to the customer's hand. The clerk dropped it to the floor as he found himself all of a sudden staring down the barrel of a gun. When the newscaster gave the name of the Lincoln's owner as Raymond T. O'Bryan, a resident of Atlanta, Nat jumped to his feet and grabbed the telephone. John had done the same thing giving both telephones busy signals. Then Nat dialed Teresa. When she heard Nat's voice saying her name, even though her heart quickened, she decided to give him the cold shoulder routine.

"Resa! Did you have your television on? Have you heard the terrible news?" His voice sounded urgent.

"No, Nat. I wasn't in much of a mood to watch TV. What news?" For a split second she hoped that Lila Pelfry had been kidnapped.

"Resa . . ." the pause was so long, she noticed his heavy breathing and asked the question again, her smile of satisfaction quickly fading.

He only asked if she had just talked with John. "No, Nat. I haven't. Wait, there is a car turning in, do you want to hold on a second?"

Nat felt that it would be John, for when his line was busy John probably had tried to call him and then decided to go down to tell his sister the bad news in person. "Yes, Resa, go see who it is. I'll hold on." His voice was solemn to the point of being grave. In the midst of her thoughts while hurrying to the door, she decided that dear Miss Lila must have told him where to head in.

John fumbled with the key in the lock and let himself in, opened the door, and loudly called out his sister's name. She had heard him come in as she laid the telephone on the table beside her bed. He met her coming out of the bedroom. "What is it, John? What's happened?"

"It's Papa and Raymond, Sis, they've been kidnapped! It was just on the news. Nat's line is busy . . ."

"He's holding on for me now." John hurried to the phone in her bedroom.

"Nat! Let's call the police. If they have Raymond's charge card it only shows the Atlanta address. You call, and I'll go down and get Tissy to come stay with Resa."

"Right," Nat agreed and hung up.

"Oh, John, what will they do with Papa and Raymond!" Her tears came. She covered her face with shaking hands as John enfolded his sister in his arms. When her cry subsided, he told her to come with him to tell Tissy, but first they would go down to Nat's. He could phone Tissy from there and then pick her up on the way back.

Down the curvy mountain road, John tried the best he could to console his sister, all the time thinking it would be best to just let her cry it out. He felt like crying himself. If the thugs harmed the two, he'd go after them personally. Papa . . . who had never harmed a soul . . . kind, gentle, funny. Why did something like this have to happen to someone like him? They would all, especially the grandkids, be devastated. Life would never be the same without him.

"The police know what automobile to look for, Sis, and they know there will be two older men along. Surely, they won't get far. I'm just thankful to know they weren't harmed when it happened. Maybe the rascals will have enough sense to realize that if they killed them they would get the death sentence if caught." John talked on and on but Teresa could not say a word. She just listened, still not believing this thing had happened. It all seemed like a movie show, and this movie had to have a good ending.

Nat was standing on the front porch waiting for John and Teresa. He stood for a while, propped against the banister, then sat in a rocker, not caring whether he stood or sat. It had been only a few hours ago, two-thirty to be exact, that Lila had come storming out his door and down the porch steps. Nat had gone out behind her, carrying a little overnight bag, and on out to her bright, yellow Corvette, where he opened a door and deposited the bag, then went around to assist her into the car. She squirmed into position, pulling the drawn-up dress from underneath her and pulled away with wheels squealing. Nat stood there in the street scratching his head with a feeling of great relief. Lila had not been invited; she just appeared as though in a puff of smoke, and he was happy to see her leave that way. Her Corvette was last seen racing out of town and up Coleman Mountain on the south side of Union Gap.

Now it was late, and his whole being felt empty. He had not possessed this kind of feeling since his mother passed away. Where had they taken his father and Alyn Russell? Had they killed them? To top it all, would Resa be upset because of Lila? She certainly had every right to be, even though they had not made any commitments to one another. Surely she had felt the sparks, the same as he, with that kiss in her living room the day of the so-called fishing trip.

He saw them coming when the car's headlights flashed around the curve and the car pulled to a stop in front of his house. He walked out to meet them, opening the passenger side door helping Resa out. They stood there in each other's arms while John was getting out, coming around the car. Teresa's tears started again as Nat held her tight, his lips against her forehead while she cried into his chest.

"Just what are you fellows planning on doing with us?" Raymond chanced to ask. He'd sat still and silent long enough.

If they could get the two talking they might spill some information that would shed some light on their plans.

"Haven't decided yet," the head directly in front of him said. "I'll let you know soon enough, and you may not want to know." This was Sunday morning and the Lincoln was speeding along heading south. Like an expert taxi driver, the thug who was doing the driving had dodged the main roads that led out of Atlanta.

"I don't mean to impose on your well-thought-out plans," Raymond continued, "but just wanted to suggest that you have my car already and it is full of gas, so you could just let us out here and we'd be obliged to walk back home."

"You don't think too well, man! No better'n my two-year-old, in fact. Now, say we need some hostages, for instance . . . well . . .? Can you figger th' rest of that out?"

"A two-year old," Raymond thought miserably, "what a shame . . . and that means a little young wife, too."

"Now, Thatch, I don't aim to give you a sermon, because you are already smart enough to figure things out for yourself . . ."

The sentence was cut short with his captor breaking in with, "You'd better believe it! So, just button your lip."

They were coming to a small town that looked quiet; nothing stirring this early. A traffic light, probably the only one in town, could be seen way ahead with no cars stopped there waiting for the color to change. Thatch slowed the car in case a policeman was anywhere around watching for someone to run a red light. With small anxious eyes, he glanced around and seeing none, speeded up slightly until they could get through the town.

Alyn decided he'd chance saying something and clearing his throat said he sure could use a cup of coffee. "This far out of Atlanta there wouldn't be any police looking for you. They'll just hit the main highway, don't you think, Thatch?" He put it in the form of a question in order not to antagonize the young man who seemed so sure of himself.

"I reckon so. Ain't seen none so far."

Blade shifted in his seat uncomfortably with the arm holding the gun aimed at Alyn's head becoming tired; he changed it to the left hand. Stealing a sideways glance, Raymond wondered if he'd ever shot anyone before with the left hand. He was keeping anxious eyes on his every move, as best as he could without becoming conspicuous.

"I'll bet you are proud of that two year old, Thatch." Alyn continued.

"Yep."

"Boy or girl?"

"Boy . . . jest like 'is old man."

"I was wondering, when he grows up if he will be proud of his old man then?"

"Sure, I'll teach 'im th' ropes. We can hold up every bank around." He gave a cackle with Blade imitating it.

"The boy and his mother may be visiting you in prison before you can teach him the ropes, Thatch. It only takes one slip, you know, and they always have an available room there, with free rent."

"Aw . . . shut up, man. I'm sick of your blabber. You're just like all the other old men, especially my old man. All he does is preach, preach, preach. I've had enough of it. Just keep quiet. I know where we're a-goin'. We should've gagged the both of you!"

Then Raymond ignored the order by saying, "Just one more question, Thatch? Will this place we're going to have a rest-room? And I hope it's not far away."

Blade piped up that this was a good suggestion because he was about to bust a gut. "And, I'm hongry, Thatch." Almost in the same breath he said he wondered how much money they got in that heist. He wished all of them were that easy. Raymond answered his question by saying that their take was probably not much more than what his breakfast would cost, unless you plan on holding up the restaurant, too, because the station's cash for the previous night would have been locked up in a safe. The cash drawer usually held no more than enough to make change. He used to go to church with the manager there, who told him this is the precaution they always took. Raymond had questioned his friend about their robbery procedures.

"Oh, shoot, Thatch! You mean we done all this for nothing? Now look what you got us into!" Blade uttered feebly.

"You shut up too, Blade!" Thatch retorted, pounding on the steering wheel. "They're just trying to get us all stirred up. That bag's full of money! It was heavy when I grabbed it. And these two will be our safe passage out of this state. We'll keep 'em 'til we are finished with 'em." Both Raymond and Alyn thought at once, without making any comment to antagonize Thatch further, that if the bag was heavy, it must mostly contain coins.

Just what Thatch meant by the statement he had just made, neither Raymond nor Alyn could quite figure out. "Finished with them" could mean one of two alternatives: either kill them or tie them up somewhere to rot before they were found. The statement left the two captives feeling unsettled. Both of them were silently straining their brains to figure out what could be done, if anything at all.

The Lincoln passed through the small town, where not one person was in sight, the highway devoid of any traffic. Unlike a large place like Atlanta where it took a lot of time to cross town, in small towns the Sunday morning traffic with cars or people walking to church did not appear until nearly church time. Fifty miles on down the road the lay of land became flatter. Farmland came into view with newly plowed fields and tractors sitting idle on the Lord's day. Farmers had probably hoped for rain today; a clearing sky proved otherwise.

Chapter Thirty-One

MONDAY, RYAN'S CLASSES DID NOT BEGIN UNTIL TEN o'clock. At this time he was to work at the jobs he had been allotted, but on this particular Monday morning, he was allowed to go down to town with Mr. Hartwell who had to order some items for the livestock. When his truck pulled to a stop in front of the feed and seed mill, Ryan asked if he could use the telephone in the booth that was in front of the general store. Since the men who worked at the mill would do the loading of his truck, Mr. Hartwell obliged Ryan's request to use the phone. "I suppose you know who will do the unloading," he cheerfully reminded Ryan.

Ryan had made certain that he had enough change in his pocket to call Mr. Tyner at the horse farm in Tennessee, therefore he came with a loaded pocket. Mrs. Tyner was overjoyed to hear Ryan's voice. "Oh, yes, Ryan, I'd know that Yankee voice anywhere! It is so good to hear from you. I cried all day when you left and would have called if we had known just where you had gone. Now, don't say anything further until I get my husband in here on the other phone. I'll just go to the door and yell for him out back."

Ryan hoped Mr. Tyner would get there in a hurry before the telephone ate up all his money. After she loudly called her husband from the back porch yelling who was on the phone, Mr. Tyner came rushing in the back door. "Hey, boy!" he said into the phone with excitement. Anyone would have thought a long-lost relative had called. "We were talking about you just yesterday and wondering how you made out wherever it was you landed up. Now tell us what you are doing."

"I'll have to talk in a hurry folks because I'm on a pay phone and don't know just how much the call will cost."

Mrs. Tyner interrupted, "First off, Ryan, give me your address so we can keep in touch." She was standing at the kitchen cabinet where a pad and pencil lay right in front of the phone and wrote down what he was telling her about the school's address.

"Sakes alive! You mean you made it in a school. I knew you were there because the principal called me for a reference, though she just mentioned something about a job. They must be very generous folks or else you got a scholarship or something," Herbert Tyner said excitedly into the phone.

Ryan explained his job and then how the principal had got him in school without his having to pay one red cent. He told about his good grades, the people up on the mountain that he'd made friends with, and about living in the cave for a while. He talked so fast and with his brogue, they asked him to slow down.

"There's going to be a special program at the end of May at the school, and I wish you two would come down here. Let me write down your address and I will send you all the details and other news, too. Oh, and I met a man down the road, a Mr. Thompson, who has a horse farm. He's a real nice guy. He used to raise horses but now, at his age, he mostly boards them. I've got lots of stuff to tell you but I'd better just write it in a letter."

Even though the Tyners would like to have talked longer, they agreed, knowing he would have to pay for the call, and said they would be anxiously waiting for his letter.

Ryan hung up with a good feeling that he had called to let that nice couple know of his whereabouts. He should have called before. Like Tissy Russell, the Tyners too had rescued him in his time of need. "Yes!" the young man was thinking, "there still are good people in this old world."

"Oh!" He said out loud as he replaced the receiver, "rats! I forgot to tell them about Doctor Russell and what he gave me," and then walking away to the feed and seed mill, thought that this would be something exciting for him to write in his letter.

After the Sunday dinner on the day before, Ryan had gone home with John, Beth, and the family, staying until four thirty. They wanted him to stay for supper; however, he explained that he needed to check back in by five o'clock. He would very much rather stay than go back for an uninteresting supper at school. He did not know that John wanted to give him the gift after supper, so now as he was about to leave, he was asked to sit for a minute while John went to his study to retrieve what it was he had for him. He came back with a thick, heavy book that veterinarians use as a reference guide. Ryan's eyes lit up like a Christmas tree. "Oh, Dr. Russell, how can I ever thank you enough for this!" he exclaimed. Then he looked up at John, who was still standing in front of the boy with excitement written all over his face. "I've wished for a long time for one of these! I certainly never expected to get one as a gift." Ryan stood, offering a hand. Instead of shaking his hand, John put an arm around the boy's shoulders, noting that there were tears forming in his eyes.

"You are so welcome, Ryan. I hope you will study it. Only after your lessons are all done, however."

Ryan agreed wholeheartedly, the book held close to his chest as he backed out the door, thanking everyone for such a wonderful day—this book was the icing on the cake. He could hardly contain himself and wished he was already in his room at school to flop across the bed and read. He would forget about supper tonight.

"Hey, Pop," Al piped up, "couldn't I just drive him down the hill to the school? I promise I won't go anywhere else and will come right back." John reached in a pocket, retrieved his car keys and handed them to Al, asking for another promise . . . that he would drive very carefully. "If you run into someone's car down there, I'd have my license taken away, you know . . . you understand, don't you? Nowhere else . . . just there and right back."

"You bet!" Al replied as he grabbed the keys, following Ryan out the door.

"Man! What a day!" John heard Ryan say while going off the porch. He turned to Beth, telling her that it was really quite a day and not even knowing as yet what had happed to his father.

Chapter Thirty-Two

ON MONDAY MORNING AT PRECISELY NINE O'CLOCK, the ringing of the telephone startled Teresa awake. She reached over quickly to the bedside table for the receiver, her heart quickening. Had Papa and Raymond been found, she fervently hoped? Then quickly a chill of fear flashed through her that something drastic had happened to them.

"Hi, Resa," Nat said softly, thinking perhaps he had wakened her. "Miss Tissy said that you would not be working today, neither am I." Before any kind of greeting was given she asked if he'd had any word from the missing two. "No, nothing. I've called the police department even though they have my telephone number, and yours too, but I just couldn't help but call. Did you get any sleep?"

"Very little, how about you?"

"Not much and what little I did get was fitful. In fact, I was really afraid to go to sleep . . . like perhaps I may not hear the phone if it rang. I suppose you could say that I felt guilty about going to sleep if maybe they were lying in a ditch somewhere." There was a short silence as they both were picturing this terrible possibility.

"Nat," Teresa said with a deep sigh, "I can't understand why they don't just let them out somewhere and take on off with the car to wherever they're going. They should know that they would not only be arrested for robbery, but kidnapping, also."

"They'll let them go, Resa, when they feel they are safely far enough away . . . I called John and Beth's and she told me that John had someone in the hospital and had to go see about them."

"Well, I'd not like to be his patient today with the state his nerves must be in," she answered simply.

"I was just wondering, Resa, since we both are twiddling our thumbs and both miserable, could we be miserable together? Could I come up this morning and sit with you a while? I called my secretary and told her to cancel my appointments. No one would expect me to come in under the circumstances, wouldn't you think? I couldn't do it anyway."

"I suppose it would be okay, Nat. We could watch the news together. You'd have to give me time to look a little more presentable. There's no doubt you haven't forgotten how I looked when you came up to go fishing with Papa!"

"How could I ever forget?" Then, trying to make his statement sound better, said, "That is, after you got fixed up, you looked like a model to me." Then before she could have a chance to change her mind, he added, "Oh, I'll go by the bakery for some donuts, if you wouldn't mind putting on a pot of coffee to go with them."

"Sounds good to me, Nat," she answered, swinging her feet over the side of the bed.

"Okay, then. I'm also going up to the inn and talk with the men for a little while. Dad would want them to get on with the work. I went to the office before the appointments were due and checked to see if there were any emergency calls. The others can be put on hold."

"Do you mean the carpenters are willing to work on an off day?" she inquired curiously.

"They're like all the rest, after that almighty dollar, you know."

As an afterthought before he hung up, Teresa asked without expecting an answer: "Oh, Nat, you're not bringing Lila with you, are you?" She heard him chuckle into the phone as he hung up. "We needed a good laugh," she smiled to herself, replacing the receiver. "Maybe it will be good for him to come up for a while. We can cry on each other's shoulder." She stood there in deep thought before moving about the day he held her in his arms and how utterly perfect it felt. Surely Lila had pushed herself on him . . . certainly he had not held her like this and looked deep into her eyes captivating her whole being.

It was around ten-thirty that morning before Teresa heard Nat's Jeep pull into the driveway. She was sitting on the back porch steps nursing a cup of coffee between both hands. A little portable radio sat on the top step blaring the song, "Country Roads Take Me Home." She had thought just as the song started that she wished Papa could be driving up their country road right this minute. The captivating tune kept swirling around in her head. Nat was walking toward where she sat. He kicked at Ole Charlie, fanning the air in front of him with his foot as a warning. The rooster spread his wings and shot across the yard with a cackle. Before he got within speaking distance, Nat noticed that Teresa had on the well-fitting jeans and her hair hung to her shoulders like a teenager, straight and turned up on the ends. Other than her haggard-worried look, she looked ten years younger than her real age. The short-sleeved pink sweater suited her well.

As he approached, Teresa sat her coffee cup on the step beside the radio and walked off the steps to the ground where Nat enfolded her in his arms, the sack of donuts in his hand behind her. His lips brushed her forehead, then a finger drew her face up and he kissed her softly on the lips.

"Oh, Nat, what are we going to do?" A tear ran down her cheek.

"That's the hard part, Resa, we can't do a single thing. I feel like my hands are tied. I've talked with the Atlanta Police Department this morning, and they say there is nothing more as yet to go on." He held the screen door open for her to enter.

"Oh, I forgot my coffee cup." He turned to go back for it but she told him to leave it. She'd get it when he left. "I just had to have a cup in my hands, not that I really wanted anything." They headed for the kitchen when the telephone rang and Teresa sprang for it. "Hello, Beth"—a pause while Beth was asking her to come up for a while. "Thanks, Beth, but Nat just came in and we were about to have a donut and coffee . . . No, there's no further news. Keep your radio or TV on. Nat says he talked with the Atlanta Police and they have no further news for us . . . Okay, I sure will and thanks for calling."

"Everyone's on pins and needles," Nat said. "The whole town's simply baffled and very disturbed," he told her, reaching inside a cabinet for the cups while Teresa sat out the milk. "Sugar, Nat?" And he answered, no, not that kind, and she looked at him with a blush and slight smile.

They sat at the table talking about the terrible event. Finally, Teresa sighed and said she'd have to think about what all was to take place in two more weeks. "How in the world can we carry on with our plans without Papa. He is a big part of this school reunion and the program. I don't think I will be able to concentrate on anything. And also, he's to take some of the classes on a tour of the cave."

"And no one expects anything of you for right now," Nat reminded her. "I talked with Tissy this morning. She called when she could not get John and said she would not disturb you, that you'd call her when you felt like talking. She told me she didn't want you coming in to work until the guys are found. She said she knew you needed to keep busy but you shouldn't try to work for a few days."

"Oh, then did she suggest that you come up to keep me company?"

"No, not at all. She didn't have to tell me that. I told her that I had already phoned you and asked if I could come up for a while and she thought that was a very good idea. In fact, I thought the sound of that waterfall you were telling me about would have a calming effect. We could take the radio with us. What about that horse ride, Resa?"

She was holding both hands around the coffee cup, took a sip, and slowly sat the cup back in its saucer. "I don't know," she answered slowly. "Do you think it would be rather strange for us to do that . . . like we were enjoying an outing when they . . ." her sentence died on her lips with Nat answering that they needed the calm and peace it would bring.

Teresa relented and said she'd call Beth back and tell her so someone would know where they were. They finished with their snack and coffee and then she went to fetch a sweater and her riding boots and to call Beth. Nat commented that he'd never been on a horse before in his life and hoped their horse liked him better than their rooster. Teresa knew how to handle a horse and how to saddle up. She noticed that he wore jeans and a polo shirt with running shoes. He said he would get his jacket from the Jeep.

"Tell me this won't be like the fishing trip," Nat teased giving his cunning smile as they went out the door.

"You'll have to admit it was rather exciting."

"Oh, I'd say the part I liked best was later in the living room." He turned in time to see Teresa's face flush. He had undoubtedly hooked a different kind of fish that day, and when he noticed the haughtiness that she had tried to conceal with the appearance of Lila Pelfrey, he felt that she cared.

Tad obligingly brought up the two horses when Teresa hailed him as he came from the barn. While he was gone toward the pasture, Teresa and Nat waited in the swing. If the situation about their dads had been different, this would be a very happy excursion. Teresa mentioned that she felt more like mourning instead of being happy, even though she felt the outcome would be a joyful one. Nat replied that it would all come to a head very soon and they really needed this outing to help their own feelings. The swing was moving gently. He wanted to take her hand, or put his arms around her and hold her close, knowing that she was hurting inside.

"When it's all over, Resa, we'll all relax and breathe a sign of relief but until then, well . . . the only thing we can do is pray and hope." She turned and smiled into his face, thankful for his faith, ashamed that her own had not seemed as deep as his.

Tad came with the horses; he had already saddled them and now was amused when he saw that Doctor O'Bryan did not know how to mount the animal. Teresa held the reins while Tad showed him the art of mounting a horse. It looked so simple when he gave the example by hopping up himself. Nat was thinking that if an old man like Tad could do it with such agility then it would be a synch for himself. He was wrong, for it took several tries and several disgruntled looks from the horse before Nat made it into the saddle. "I'll lead, and you just let the horse do the work," Teresa instructed. She clicked her teeth and they were off.

They headed off behind the house out through the vegetable garden that Tad, Joe, and the boys had recently cleared and planted, located above the apple barn. That was in the agreement of Tad's family staying on the land and at harvest time, they would share the vegetables with the Russells—Teresa was explaining this as they rode past the garden with the path edging the beginning of the apple orchard. Here, Nat could not believe the beauty of the pink-tinged white blossoms stretching for acres like a sea of color. "I wish you could have seen it in April," Teresa told him. "They are about bloomed out now." She pulled on the reins to stop the horse and they sat for a few minutes, drinking in the sight. Tiny purple and yellow spring butterflies happily fluttered and honey bees hummed. "Papa said that when he was a boy, old Adam kept honey bees and taught Tad, so we still have wonderful honey."

She went on to explain to Nat how her father hired workers to do the picking in the autumn, cull them, and pack them in barrels for shipping.

"How did they ship them out?" Nat queried, interested because, although he had eaten apples all his life, he had never known just where they came from.

"By train, and Papa's adoptive father, Anson Kelly, owned the railroad. They had to take the barrels down the mountain by mule and wagon to the train station."

"Wow!" Nat exclaimed. "We are not thankful enough for all our modern conveniences."

"You said it," she murmured, ordering the horse to lead on, carrying them on up a pathway that climbed gradually. "If you think this was a beautiful spot, just you wait."

Completely intrigued, Nat felt exhilarated with the fresh mountain air, being away from the stuffy office of patients complaining with tooth ailments. "This is certainly different from looking down people's mouths," he said. "I may not ever go back."

Teresa turned in the saddle, smiling back at him for his statement. "Oh, now. It's all been like this for ages and will be for ages to come so you can come back any time you like."

"I'd like, yes, I would like, but only with a beautiful lady I know."

"The lady wouldn't be . . ."

He cut her sentence off in midair. "No. Not whom you are thinking."

Teresa was smugly silent, and the two rode on in silence, the land becoming steeper. The horses crossed over a trickling brook that tinkled and splashed over rocks. The air here was cool and crisp, hinting of spring with birds among willows that brushed the banks of the little brook. The woods' cool air gave off a dank smell from leaves that had lain on the woods' floor all winter. The earth was soon to send forth its surprises from beneath the soil below.

"I have been missing out on so much," Nat was thinking. "This is the life." He thought about how he wanted it to be his life from now on. His dad had said that the years begin to click off in a hurry after one passes the forty mark, so he'd better hurry up and settle down.

Chapter Thirty-Three

MONDAY MORNING, THE SKILLET WAS BUZZING WITH the news that had swept the whole town, but quietly, almost in whispers . . . reverently. What had happened was incredulous. How could such a thing as a kidnapping happen to two area men? Everyone was asking this question over and over. The small television up on a shelf behind the counter, with a chicken and rooster statue on top, was giving an update, which turned out to be no different than the last news. Both the Baptist preacher and the Presbyterian preacher were sitting in a booth watching while having their morning coffee and sausage biscuit. Mack was bent over the counter next to their booth talking with the two. Neither had any consoling words for him. Brother Jesse said he had been praying. In fact, he had gotten up a committee to telephone members and asked for a continuous prayer chain to go on around the clock, with each pledging a certain time to stop what they were doing and pray for Alyn Russell and Raymond O'Bryan.

Nat had not come in the cafe this morning, Mack told them. He saw him walking from his car toward his office, all bent over like a man with the weight of the world on his shoulders. John's secretary had stopped by for a take-out cup of coffee. She said that John had to go early to the hospital that morning. "It just don't seem right," Mack said with a sigh, "that ole Alyn won't be coming in with his morning paper and a whole lot of his foolish gab. And I s'pose Nat has told his workmen that they won't be doing anything up on the hill today at the inn. He hasn't been in here though," Mack repeated.

Brother Jesse said Teresa had called him with the news. "Said she'd stay by the TV today, and Miss Tis would have special prayer in the school chapel for anyone who wanted to join in."

"Ahhh," the Presbytertian preacher said, "the kidnappers will let them go when they get a safe distance away from Atlanta."

"Well, I sure hope so," Thelma said as she went by with a tray of food for a couple who were waiting in a booth. "But, they could have fooled the police about the direction they are heading in."

"Ah, they don't know any more than we do, but you'd better believe they have an all-points bulletin out all over th' place," Mack said. "Ole Percy was in here earlier with his fingers wrapped around 'is belt and a-struttin' like a' ole rooster. He was talking like he knowed just what they would be doin'. Yessir, I wish there wuz something we could do instead of standing around here talking about it," Mack said, walking over to the cash register where a customer was waiting with money in hand.

Chapter Thirty-Four

ON MONDAY AFTERNOON, THE LINCOLN PASSED CARS with unconcerned passengers, heading north and south, the occupants smug and secure, all knowing what their destinations would be. Alyn was thinking how his life had been lived in a cut and dried fashion. He knew what had to be done each day, when the work would be completed, what he would eat, and that he would go to bed in the same bed he had slept in for years. Every Sunday he would be going to church without fail and have a big dinner with his children and grandchildren. His days would start by going down to town, buying an Atlanta newspaper, going to the Skillet, picking up his mail, then going back home to attend to matters that needed to be seen after. Saturdays, he would go fishing or hunting with the boys and sometimes sit in the swing reading to his granddaughter. People get into a set pattern with their lives and this is the way it should be, he was thinking. "We never expect anything out of the ordinary to happen to ourselves. Reverend Atkins said recently that we are to thank God in all things, but it seems odd to thank God that Ray and myself have been kidnapped. It could be a wake up call that I should not live my life so complacently and take things for granted. Well, I do know that I will enjoy life to the fullest from now on."

Last night, Thatch decided they would sleep in an old barn he discovered behind a deserted farmhouse. He held the gun while Blade forced the rickety barn doors open and then pulled the car inside with the men in it. After the doors were closed, the men were ordered out and allowed to use a corner one at a time and then return to lie down on a stack of old hay. Alyn and Raymond both heard them quietly discussing what to do with their captives. Blade said it would be a good place to shoot them because no one would be coming in this old barn. Thatch contemplated the suggestion and decided that it wasn't yet their time. The men could be useful to them still. They may have to be used in a standoff as hostages.

A bright silvery moon that seemed to beam down directly over the old barn cast light that filtered through wide cracks between the antique boards and a small overhead window. It was decided that Blade would stand the first watch while Thatch caught some sleep since he had been driving all day. Blade sat on the floor and propped against a wall of the barn, the gun lying on his lap. Thatch said he would sleep between the two men so he could be ready for anything they might try to pull.

"I've certainly had a prettier bedfellow," Raymond mumbled and received a swift kick for the sarcasm. The spot smarted, leaving Raymond rubbing it.

Even with the discomfort of lying on the floor, the three slept for a little while. After nearly an hour, Alyn felt the urge to turn on his other side, meaning he would be facing the despicable Thatch with snoring breath of a hog. Disturbing Thatch, he turned back, causing a scream in the ear and a knife pointing against his neck. Blade had dozed off. Now he jumped to his feet with the gun dropping to the floor and going off. Falling to his feet, he crawled to where the gun had fallen and quickly grabbed it, then jumped up dashing over to where Thatch now stood over the dazed Raymond. He held an arm around Alyn with the knife still against his throat. "I orter kill you, right here, Mister! And I would, mind you! I would! But I need you just a little while longer. Okay! Now git over there and down again. Jest don't git anywhere near your friend! Blade, you can come git a hour, and we'll decide then what to do." So the two men exchanged places; Blade took the knife and Thatch the gun. One more watch was exchanged before they decided to move on.

Lying there hoping for sleep, Alyn was reliving the Sunday morning happenings. Thatch had stated they would stop at a station somewhere ahead to gas up. Blade held his gun steady, expecting the men to try some funny stuff. Neither man wanted to get shot and decided to wait for a better chance about doing something to escape. Everyone felt hunger pangs. Blade told Thatch that he would have to stop somewhere and get them something or he would not be able to hold that gun up any longer. "The station will have something," Thatch told him. "So quit your belly-aching."

True to his word, and probably the first time in his life that he'd been true to his word, Blade had pulled into a station where he saw only one car at the gas pump. "They'll be gone by the time I gas up," he thought and got out, took the cap off the tank, and stood there with the pump running. After the pump shut off, he screwed the cap on and walked to the station. A woman was inside talking with the clerk, so Thatch went around a counter looking at what they might eat. When the woman went out, the clerk went to a back room, telling Thatch that he would be right back.

Alyn tried winking furiously several times when the woman crossed in front of the Lincoln on her way back to her own car. Blade could not see his motions but the woman noticed and stuck her nose in the air, taking his winks as simple flirtation. With no other customer inside but himself, Thatch was left with a clear opportunity to help himself to the cash drawer. Passing up an opportunity like this was not in his personality, and neither would it be like him to pass up the counter where his favorite candy, Heath bars, stared him down. After grabbing all the bills in the drawer, he swiped as much candy as he could carry and fled the store. Alyn knew what he'd done when he saw him running from the station with the candy in his hand and not in a sack; that would not be all he'd taken, for his pockets were bulging!

Opening the door on the driver's side, he threw the candy inside to be grabbed by anyone who could grab it. "Hey, gimme one!" Blade demanded who could not hold the gun and grab a candy bar. Alyn tossed one over his head toward the thug with the gun, causing the gun to fall to the floor. Raymond did not miss the opportunity to swiftly kick his captor in the leg with all his might. In the melee, Thatch had started the motor, the wheels scratching off with the car swaying, as Alyn leaned over grabbing the wheel, sending the car into a spin. Things were happening so fast that no one had time to think but just to follow instincts. Raymond reached over putting Thatch into a choke hold, which was working . . . until . . . Blade retrieved the gun and Raymond felt it against the back of his head.

"Hold it right there, mister!" Then he saw the store clerk standing in the doorway waving his hands and yelling. Somehow, an elbow, a knee, whatever . . . somehow, the back passenger side window had been lowered. Raymond sat back when he felt the gun to his head, and watched Blade lower the gun from his head, point it back toward the clerk, and pull the trigger. The clerk fell to the concrete, dead.

The Lincoln sped away, nearly hitting a pickup truck that swerved and hit a telephone pole instead. Thatch screamed warnings to everyone in the car. He became violent, ranting and raving, swearing that he would get rid of all of them, including the insolent Blade, his eyes blaring as someone completely mad. It was evident that this person definitely had a mental problem, and it had now gone out of control. The car sped down the road, turning off onto the first side road, unpaved and rough, dust boiling up behind them.

"You have went and done it, Blade! Now they can get us for murder! Ain't you got a lick of sense?"

"None," Alyn was thinking. "I'd rather teach a polecat to purr that try to teach either of them a single thing."

"Well, I just thought he would be calling th' cops 'fore we could git away, Thatch," Blade told him in a voice like a child trying to explain to his mother why he had done a wrong thing. "Th' cops will be all over this neck of th' woods, Thatch. I hope you know where this here road goes to." They were bouncing around over potholes, the car now on the wrong side. When they topped a small hill, an old rattletrap truck hit a ditch to miss them and the driver crawled out shaking a fist in the air; but the Lincoln sped on.

Speaking very softly so as not to offend their chauffeur, Raymond said that Lincolns were gas eaters and he hoped Thatch had filled the tank to the top.

"I know what I'm doing!" Thatch exclaimed. "Everbody just settle down. My grandma used to live in these parts, and I know where th' road comes out. We'll be long gone 'fore they can gather their wits," he said speaking of the state patrol. Then, Thatch spied the run-down old house with a sagging barn out back and decided this would be a good place to spend Sunday night.

Now, on Monday morning while Teresa and Nat were riding up to the falls above Knollwood, Alyn Russell and Raymond O'Bryan were again hustled into the Lincoln at gun point to continue their journey into the unknown.

Chapter Thirty-Five

TISSY RUSSELL, A SMALL AGELESS WOMAN WITH NO lines to expose the hard life she had lived during her early years, sat supine in her chair behind the desk, incongruous of her usual Monday morning routine. From lack of sleep, she felt like a rag doll that had been tossed unwanted on a rubbish pile. Subconsciously, she began to name off a few epithets to describe Alyn; stable, dependable, trustworthy, her best friend from childhood. She never in her wildest dreams would have thought that something like this would have happened to him. And her new friend, Raymond O'Bryan . . . she knew little about the man except that he was very nice and likable. He and Alyn had become fast friends and they both were good for one another with matching personalities. Then, a soft smile touched her face as the thought came to her that Raymond's subtle advances had not gone unnoticed by her. "He was actually flirting with me! A woman of my age!" She was jerked back to reality by a soft knock on the door and answered with a, "Come in," all the time wishing whoever it was would simply go away.

Miss Sullivan, the school's secretary, cracked the door open and said in a whispery voice that Beth Russell wished to speak with her on the phone. "Of course, Elsie, thank you." Tissy's heart was in her throat. Maybe there was some news! "Dear God, please let it be good news," she breathed heavily, lifting the receiver. "Beth! Have you heard any news? Please tell me it's good news."

"No, Tiss, and I'm sorry if I startled you. There have been no new developments this morning. I just wanted to ask you to come up to the house this afternoon after you leave school. Maybe we could cry on each other's shoulders."

"Sure, if you'd like. I'd rather be with some of you than alone in my house. I can't seem to concentrate on anything I'm doing this morning. Everything is just a blur." And almost in the same breath, she asked how the children were.

"I think you can imagine that. They are moping around aimlessly. Al is glued to the TV, Penny is up in her room, and Susan is sitting in the tree house with her tablet. She said she is writing a poem about Papa, and I saw Peter walking around out in the yard holding the dog. John went on in to work; said he had patients that had to be seen after."

"It is a very sad time, Beth, for all of us. I've known Alyn since I was about six, possibly all my life. Alyn, Cynthee, and myself would sit for hours watching the men build the old school. He's as much a part of that school as his Aunt Joyce and Uncle Anson."

"Oh, Tiss . . . he'll be alright, I just know it in my heart." Then changing the subject, which no one seemed to want to do, Beth said, "I want you to see the paintings. They look pretty good to me, and I think I've done about all I can do with them."

"Marvelous! I'm anxious to see them, so I'll be up about four o'clock then." Tissy hung the phone up thinking to herself that she was glad this was one item that had been completed toward homecoming. Alyn had to be there! If he would not, then the well-laid plans would be cancelled.

Her rattletrap Ford pulled up into the driveway shortly after the four o'clock hour. Penny heard the car before she saw her getting out, and went out to meet her.

"Hello, Penny, my love," she said, slamming the car door, which would not catch if it was not slammed. She put her arms around the girl and squeezed her tight. "Are you being brave as can be, dear?"

"No, Aunt Tissy. I'm not brave in the least." Away from school, she had always been Aunt Tissy to the children. "Did many come to the prayer meeting at school today?"

"My, my, they certainly did. Even a lot of people from the Gap came up." She kissed the girl on the cheek and as they walked toward the house, she said that in honor of her grand-father and his friend, Raymond, she sang the song, "Sweet Hour of Prayer."

"Oh, I wish I had been there," Penny uttered softly.

"I know you would but it would have seemed like a funeral to you and it's best that you all stayed home." She gave the girl another hug. They had reached the steps, and Penny stood aside to let Tissy go first.

"Pete and Al are both glued to the TV, and Susan has been up in the tree house most of the day. I think she went to sleep up there on her blanket." Penny turned the knob and motioned for Aunt Tissy to go first. "Come. Look at the paint-ings my mom has done. She's in the den." The two of them went in to where Beth was putting away her painting supplies.

"Hi, Tissy. I thought I heard your voice and was just trying to tidy up a bit before you saw all the mess." She picked up a paper towel and wiped her hands. "I know I smell like turpentine. John simply hates the smell."

Tissy spied the paintings, both propped on easels. "Oh, my goodness gracious sakes alive, woman! They are utterly marvelous! Beth, you have outdone yourself with these two . . . one for the school and one for the inn. They are like carbon copies!" She turned to see the pleased look on Beth's face. "I don't see how you did them so quickly. If I had painted them, and, of course I couldn't paint a lick, well, anyway . . . it would have taken me a whole year at least."

"Oh, with the kids in school and John at the office or the hospital, I've had a lot of time on my hands. Penny has been a great help with the house work, too." They stood in silence for a minute or so still gazing at the paintings. "I'm glad they are finished now because my heart would not be in them at all," Beth said softly.

"I know, dear. I've had a hard time today keeping my mind on school affairs."

Beth turned to Penny asking her to go out and check on little Susan. "Tell her to come in now, please. She's been out there long enough for one day, and see if Sally is with her."

"Sally was with her the last time I looked in on her, and they both were asleep then," Penny answered as she went out the door.

"Come and sit awhile, Tissy. Let's have a cup of coffee or would you prefer tea? I've made a pitcher of iced tea . . . or there's softdrinks, too." Beth led the way through to the kitchen and motioned for Tissy to sit at the table. They both decided on iced tea. She took the pitcher out of the refrigerator, placed ice in two tall glasses, and then sat across the table from her visitor.

"I hope Susan doesn't spill iced tea in my lap," Tissy teased with a solemn face that brought on a light giggle from Beth. "That was the funniest thing I've encountered in quite a while, but of course, I would not say so in front of the child. I'm sure she apologized to what's-her-name."

Beth sat her glass down, looking at Tissy with a grin. "I'd say Miss Lila deserved every bit of what she got! Resa said her dress drew up to the indecency point." And to that statement, Tissy nearly got strangled over the tea she had in her mouth. They both laughed and then decided it was wrong for them to be joking when there was such sadness in the family.

The two girls burst into the room with little Sally clicking her feet across the kitchen floor. "Here she is," Penny said, adding that she probably would not sleep a wink that night.

"Look, Aunt Tissy," Susan said holding her tablet up and then placing it on the table in front of her. "I wrote a poem about Papa. I know some of the words may be spelled wrong, but I can erase them when Mama tells me how to spell them."

"Let me see, Sweetheart. Do you want me to read it or do you want to read it for me?"

"You can read it and I'll see if it sounds alright. I've read it a hundred times already." Tissy put an arm around the child who stood beside her as she read the poem out loud.

I love my Papa very much,
He meens a lot to me.
He reads me storis, tells me jokes
All funnie as can be.

Peter and me, we sit in the swing
With Papa in betwene
He tells us things that he did
When he was just a little kid.

Some bad, bad men came along,
And took him far awaye.
Why can't they see the hurt they kaused,
And send him home today?

Tissy wiped tears from her eyes and then hugged the child. "Susan! Do you mean to tell me that you wrote this poem all by yourself with no help at all?" The little girl nodded her head up and down.

"Yessum. I did," she said in a whisper. "If you will tell the television man to read my poem, then maybe the bad men will be watching and maybe they will let Papa and Mr. O'Bryan go. Do you think maybe they would?"

Beth also had tears in her eyes and dabbed at them with her shirttail. "This is the first time I've heard the poem. Pete came in and said she was up in the tree house writing one for Papa."

"I think we have quite a poet here!" Tissy exclaimed. "And it is a very good idea about showing it to the television men, Susan. I'm going right this minute to see what I can do about that. May I take the poem with me? And I'll make a copy of it."

This was the first time today Susan had smiled and shown any interest in anything. She went running through the door and into the living room to tell her brothers that her poem was going to be on television.

"Not another one!" Al said, and Pete said, "Yuck!"

Tissy rose from the chair with a thoughtful look on her face. "Beth, I'm so amazed at that child's writing abilities, and even before she can spell very well." Then she fanned a hand and said, "But you can work with her on that part. After all, she'll just be going into the third grade next time." She looked as though she wanted to say more but hesitated to go on.

"Okay, Tiss . . . out with it. I know there is something else you want to say. Are you not suppose to tell what it is?"

"Ah, I am a spoiler by telling you but I know you can keep a secret." She looked at Beth waiting for her vow not to tell what she was about to say.

"You know I will keep whatever it is to myself, so go on."

"Well, there is a publisher who is putting out a book on children's writings . . . short stories and poems, you know . . . and I submitted Susan's 'Springtime' poem to him and it was accepted! Isn't that simply wonderful?"

"Oh, Tissy, I am so grateful to you for doing that. Don't you know Susan will be so proud!"

"We all will be but that isn't quite all, my dear. You see, her poem will be the very first thing in the book, and she is the youngest writer to have her work in the book." She had lowered her voice to a whisper and was all smiles. "Now, here's what I have been thinking and I'm sure you will agree . . . I think this is just the neatest thing in the world." Beth could hardly wait to find out what she had in mind. "Now, the school can buy a bunch of the books, and at homecoming we can set Susan up at a table in the entrance way as people go out after the program and have people purchase her books and she can sign them." The two women hugged one another and agreed that this would be a wonderful thing to do.

Beth held her arms outstretched on Tissy's shoulders and said, "Tiss, Papa will be so proud."

"Yes, he will, and he will be back, so we'll just keep our little secret for a surprise announcement at the gathering." She picked up her purse as they went through the dining room where she'd left it on the corner of the table. "Oh," Beth said as an afterthought, "Don't stop by to see Resa; she called this morning and said Nat was coming up so they could be miserable together." Tissy only raised her eyebrows and said, "Mmm."

Chapter Thirty-Six

EARLIER THAT MORNING BEFORE THEY LEFT, TERESA
made some sandwiches and took a couple of canned drinks
for each of them. She hooked the little lunch carrier by its
straps around the saddle horn. Now, nearly the noon hour,
they were giving the horses the lead who knew where the
well-worn path would carry them. Over the years, the
Russells, the Harris family, and the Kelly couple had
frequented the falls for outings such as the one Teresa and
Nat now would enjoy and long remember. Teresa turned in
her saddle telling Nat that there were two or three other
favorite spots she felt sure he would enjoy and if he would
like, she'd take him there another time. She had in mind
Overlook Rock, where one could look down upon Union Gap
and Brasstown Bald in the distance, and see forever across the
Blue Ridge Mountains. Then there was the cave where Alyn
and Luther had found the hidden money, and where Chief
Little Bear had lived. One of her favorite spots was "The
Meadow," as they called it . . . not that cows grazed there, but
a beautiful clearing where as a child Papa had taken her and
her brothers to roll down the hill and scamper up again,
racing and laughing. One time, Papa had taken three card-
board boxes along, a great mystery to the children, until he
flattened them out to be used as sleds. Of course she had
already taken Nat to the lake for the disastrous fishing trip.
While they sat beside the pool where the falls pounded,
having their meager lunch, Teresa would tell Nat about all
these places; he could not help but be awed.

"Listen!" Teresa exclaimed, pulling the horse to a stop with Nat's horse coming up beside. "Hear that roaring?"

"Yes! The falls! It is certainly loud all right. But I thought it would be just a trickle over a few rocks."

"Not on your life. It's a jim-dandy. It's just around this curve on the path." She pulled on the reins and the horse carried on. As they rounded the bend, the falls was now in full view.

"Wow!" Nat exclaimed. "What a sight! This would make a wonderful picture post card." There was a family of deer drinking from the pond at the bottom of the falls. The buck lifted his head, spying the two, and made a dash out of sight followed by the rest of his family.

"Nope. Papa would never allow it, for then people would be coming from all over to see it." She paused and then added, "Actually, that's what my brother, Charles, wanted." Nat had a blank look on his face for he had not known she had another brother. With agility, she slid down off her horse and wrapped the reins around a bush; Nat followed suit, however, not so agilely. He followed Teresa over to some large boulders where she was carrying their lunch. He reached out to help her up on the rock, but she had already seated herself and was looking up at the pounding falls as though she had never seen it before in her life. Nat sat beside her, still awed at the sight, with spray lightly misting their faces. He took a deep breath and said, "Smell that fresh air! Are we dreaming, or have I died and gone to heaven?" Her only answer was a satisfied smile; satisfied that they had decided to come here today.

"This is one evidence of God's great power," she said, breaking the short silence while he sat there completely awed. "How could one gaze upon a sight like this and not believe that God is the Great Creator of everything?" It was a question that needed no answer.

Nat turned to her, knowing how he felt about her but not really knowing exactly how to put it into words or how she would take him. "You amaze me as much as the falls," he said simply and let it go at that. "If I'm not being too nosy, I'd like to ask about your brother, Charles. I didn't know there was another brother."

"Yes. He was younger than John but older than myself. He died on an airplane on the way back from New York only two years ago. He was married to Beth and was the father of my nieces and nephews."

Nat turned to her, wrinkling his brow. "You mean John . . ." he hesitated and Teresa finished his sentence. "Yes, he's their uncle but now known to them as 'Pop.'"

She continued the saga of John and Beth. "You see, they had been sweethearts in high school and we all thought they would marry but when he finished school and went on to university, Charles stepped in. Oh, it's too painful to talk about, but you get the picture, I'm sure." He did not answer; only nodded, silently. "But, what I was saying before, Charles wanted Papa to let him develop the land into a place for tourists and they butted heads over it often. Charles was a developer. He had a partner in the business, located in Atlanta." To drop the subject, she asked Nat to try the little radio he'd brought along. Nat turned it on, only to hear static. They would not be able to hear any news.

"Well, then," Teresa told him, "we'd best have our lunch and get on back so we can be near the television." She opened the lunch carrier, handing him one of the sandwiches and a cold drink. "I wonder if the cans are still cold," she said. He had popped his open, took a sip, and said it was cold enough. As they ate, between bites of the sandwich Nat told her about his Atlanta home and described his mother, a wonderful petite woman, who doted on her only child. "She would have loved this place up here . . . and she would have been so excited about the inn. I wish she could have seen it to completion." Suddenly, he thought about his missing father and commented that he hoped his father would see it to completion. Teresa took Nat's sandwich wrapper and put it into the lunch carrier, then he handed her the empty can. She was up on the horse's back before Nat got to her side to assist her. After several tries and several disgusted looks toward his riding partner, who sat laughing, Nat led the horse to stand beside a rock, where he stood and then succeeded in mounting. The horse turned his neck around as if to ask, "Are you sure you're ready now, buddy?"

Teresa started off again in the lead, chattering nonsensically. Nat was enjoying just being in the woods, away from the everyday humdrum of things. Alyn and Raymond's disappearance had now made everyone's day anything except humdrum. For a while, their son and daughter had relaxed and not talked about the terrible incident. As they rode in silence now, Nat looked up into the treetops. Thickly needled evergreens that usually meant a cold winter would be in store come December, now swayed in the light May breeze. Again, Nat was relishing the cleanness of the air. The shaded grassy area was cool and when they crossed a little brook trickling down from the waterfall pool, he noticed the dank, musty smell of moss beside the stream. Teresa broke the silence by saying that everything was so still, no birds or anything making their usual sounds. "Papa says that at this time of day everything is still, dogs asleep under the porch, cows laying on the ground chewing their cud. There's no use in trying to catch any fish at this time of day because they are not active either."

"Is that part about fishing your own wisdom or your dad's?" Nat questioned.

"With the kind of fishing we do, it wouldn't matter what time of day we go, would it?" she sighed.

They rode on in silence for a good distance, and then Nat pulled on his reins and said, "Woah, boy!"

Teresa stopped her horse and turned to see what was wrong. "Why have you stopped, Nat? What's up?"

"Uh, oh, Resa. I've left my billfold on the rock back at the falls. We'll have to go back."

"Well, why in the world did you even take it out in the first place?"

"I remember taking it out to show you a photo of my mom but it wasn't in there, and I must have not put it back in my pocket all the way and it fell out. That's got to be where it is."

"Then let's be off, you lead on." They both turned the horses back up the path. "What a waste of time," she was thinking to herself. "But time that would have been saved for what? Only, I'm so anxious to get back to the TV."

They rode on in silence other than the time Nat apologized for the inconvenience he had caused. Teresa said it was okay but he shouldn't talk quite so loudly or he may attract some bears.

"What! You didn't tell me about that hazard! Either it's water moccasins or bears. I can't seem to win. I don't think I want to go in that cave you were telling me about."

"I suppose the bears are all out of that cave for the summer months so we wouldn't have to worry about them there. Bats, maybe, but no bears." Nat turned toward her with a big shrug of his shoulders.

"I think I'd better head back to the big city," he mumbled.

"Sure, where you can get mugged and robbed. One or the other; it's a no-win situation."

They rode on and finally returned to the place where they had sat on the rocks. Nat slid down off the horse, looking all around for his billfold. "That's funny, I could have sworn it would be right here." Then he looked around on the ground. "Would you mind coming down here and see if I'm overlooking it, Resa?"

"Oh, for heaven's sake," she grumbled as she slid down. "If you don't see it anywhere why do you think I would?"

When she was beside him, he turned, grabbed her with his arms around her shoulders and said, "I lied to you, Resa. I didn't lose my billfold at all."

"Then wh . . ."

"Just hush for a minute, please. I did overlook something . . . that is, I didn't overlook it but, well, I . . ."

"Nat, please stop stammering and tell me what is going on!"

"I couldn't get up the nerve, Resa. There's something I want to tell you."

"I wish you'd just say it and let's get on back . . ."

He cut off her words by covering her lips with his and she responded. If she had thought the kiss in the living room was a humdinger, this would top them all. When they parted, he held her close to his chest, rubbing his hands over her soft hair and whispering, "Resa, Resa . . . I'm sure you know that I'm terribly . . . no . . . wonderfully in love with you and have been from the first moment I laid eyes on your beautiful face."

When she looked up into his eyes, he saw tears glistening in hers. She reached up to rub them away and softly asked, "Why were the words 'I love you' so hard to say?"

"It's just that I'm such a dumb cluck when it comes to showing my feelings. I was afraid you would slap my face or run away, or you would think that I was absolutely out of my mind." She was incapable of forming a reply for a short interval. He took the opportunity to kiss away a tear that escaped and rolled down her cheek.

She pushed back from him and said, "Nat, we've only known each other since March fourth at Papa's birthday party." He started to say something, but she put a hand over his mouth, and continued, "Now, here it is the middle of May, a little over two months . . . what I want to know is, what took you so long?" She smiled as she gazed into his handsome face, "I have felt the same way and when that Lila showed up, I thought I would die." Nat laughed, saying that she had put on a very convincing act, and she answered that she was a good actress, then they both laughed, remembering that disastrous Sunday dinner. After a few seconds, a more serious look touched her face and the soft pink lips turned up at the corners for a fleeting moment. "But, Nat . . . why did you go through all that fibbing about your wallet and want to come back up here? You could just as well have told me this there on the path, or waited until we got back to the house."

He kissed her lips lightly and answered that this was the most romantic place he'd ever been and wanted this in his memory of telling her of his love for her and the spot where he had asked her to marry him.

"What? You never even asked me to marry you!" She drew back at arms length, looking up into his face.

"I didn't? Oh, I knew there was something else I wanted to say and it completely slipped my mind," he teased, grinning. "I was getting to that but was delayed because I couldn't get enough of your sweet lips." He held both her hands together in his, kissed them and then said, "Teresa Russell, will you marry me and spend the rest of your life with me? I'll try the best I can to make you happy. We'll have a wonderful life together, I promise. I love you from the bottom of my heart and all my being."

Tears dominated her vision and her face radiated warmth. She felt so much love for this man and now knew what it felt like to be loved in return. "Yes, Nathaniel O'Bryan, I will be your wife for the rest of my life and I, too, love you with all my heart." They sealed their commitments with a kiss and with arms around each other, turned to go back down the path toward home, leading the horses by the reigns. "Why, Nat, did it take so long for you to come to Kendell Mountain and us to find each other?"

"Well, my dear, I would surmise that it was because God was working it all out, getting things all lined up and now . . . here we are . . . and nothing can ever dissolve what God has planned."

"Of course you are right about that. Shall we wait to announce our plans until our dads come back?"

"Yes. I think that would be best if we do wait, then they will not feel so left out in their absence." And she wholeheartedly agreed.

Returning back to Knollwood, they received no further news on the radio or the television. When Teresa turned the TV on, she made the statement, with disgust, that every time she turned it on there was a full ten or fifteen minutes of advertisements. Nat phoned the Atlanta Police for the second time that day and got only a slight piece of news. He was told that someone had reported seeing a black Lincoln Continental with four men in it traveling south on Highway 41 at a great rate of speed. The police were searching in that area, but as yet nothing had turned up.

"At least then we know they are still alive!" Nat exclaimed as he hung up the phone. "I wager they'll have them before the day's over," he told Teresa, putting his arms around her and hugging her close. "I'll never get enough of holding you in my arms," he told her as he planted a kiss on her forehead.

She smiled up into his face saying, "You're not about to leave now are you?"

"Yes, as much as I'd rather stay, I suppose I should go down and check on the carpenters, and I'd like to go by the grill also.

But . . . it will be the hardest thing I've ever done to go in there and not mention a word about my beautiful bride-to-be. They'll all wonder why I look so happy with our dads missing."

"And all you'd have to do is tell one person and in five minutes, the whole town would know," she giggled like a teenager. "Nat, if you don't mind, I must tell Tissy our news. She won't tell a soul and, you know, she's more like a mother to me and we don't keep a thing from one another."

"I understand, Sweetheart. Just explain to her why we want to keep it to ourselves."

They walked back through the door to the hallway, hand-in-hand, dreading being parted even for a short while.

Chapter Thirty-Seven

RYAN WAS SPRAWLED ACROSS THE COT IN HIS ROOM where he had been reading the book John had given him. Tired now from studying his school books before and now the large volume before him, he closed the book and laid it aside, thinking. School would soon be coming to an end, and it appeared that he would be graduating at last! He needed to get in touch with G. G. and Pappy, for they would be so happy to hear the good news. But it would be so hard to explain his disappearance without a single word to them. Now he was having regrets for having done them that way for it must have hurt the old couple. But at the time, he was afraid of what the police would do with him. Now that thought returned to haunt him and he felt afraid still. He needed to confide in someone. There were a number of people who had been so helpful to him here at school, but he couldn't decide who should be the one to whom he would confide.

Doctor John had been so nice to him and his family treated him like a family member. Then the principal, Mrs. Russell, was the one who gave him the chance to finish school, a job, and a place to live. And the assistant principal, Teresa Russell, had studied with him to make sure his grades were up to level. Even the Tyners in Tennessee had taken him in and offered a permanent job. So many people were willing to help!

The biggest problem now was contacting G. G. and Pappy, but it had to be done. Even his grandfather would be extremely worried and concerned, but he would be one who would rant and rave about the police situation. If only he had not picked up that bag of money! At least he had not kept it. Maybe someone found the bag where he'd tossed it. If so, and if they had spent the money, it would be impossible for him to prove that he had not used it himself. He could be in for a jail term. Oh! What should he do? Whom should he turn to?

It was now late Monday night and the lights-out bell had rung. This didn't concern him because his room was in the basement and not in the dormitory, but he usually obeyed the lights-out rule in order to get enough sleep and keep up with his work and studies. Tonight, he would get little sleep from worry. The problem had been upper-most in his mind all along; however, he had pushed it aside and tried not to worry about it until he finished school. He was leaning toward talking with Doctor John, whom he saw occasionally in the hallway on his way to the school clinic. He was always friendly to the young man and stopped to shake hands with him and ask about his schoolwork.

Maybe the answer will come to me in my dreams, Ryan thought as he tried to dose off to sleep.

Chapter Thirty-Eight

AROUND NOON, JOHN PHONED BETH, ASKING IF SHE would like to get away for a little while and come down to have lunch with him, just the two alone. Penny could watch after the children. She named over a dozen things that needed to be done and she would like to stay by the radio. The kids had a program going on television.

"Come on down, Sweetheart. We need the time to ourselves for just a short while. I have to go over to the hospital at two o'clock and then up to the school clinic after that."

"My dear husband, you are always working so hard, and you need a break, too. I'll be right down; give me a few minutes to get out of these sloppy clothes or folks will think you've picked up a bag-lady from the city."

He laughed into the phone. "They'd wonder where I found such a beautiful bag-lady. Okay then, I'll be waiting for you at the office."

They decided not to go to the Skillet but on down the highway a few miles to a little restaurant that attracted mainly travelers. Since they had missed the lunch crowd, they noticed few cars in the parking lot as they walked across the pavement. "We haven't been here in quite a while," Beth commented. "I always liked this place."

"Good food," John said, "but not very romantic to take my wife out for us to be alone."

"We don't need a gourmet restaurant, love. We're old married folks."

"Yep, but I can still be romantic if I want to," he said, holding her elbow up the steps and through the door.

There were two couples seated and already eating when they were seated at a table and handed menus. "I ate with the kids," Beth said, "so I am just going to have a dessert and coffee." She ordered a peach cobbler and coffee and John ordered a salad and chicken sandwich.

While they were waiting for their food, they talked unenthusiastically about Papa and Raymond's return. "I know they will be back, Beth. But I am concerned that they will be harmed. There's no telling what those characters will do to them . . . then, they may shove them out of the car somewhere."

"Ah, John, you are always the one to have faith. With all the groups praying for their safety, you've got to believe they'll be returned unharmed, and soon," Beth replied, trying with all her power to believe what she was saying. "For just these few minutes, let's try not to think about what has happened."

"I'll try, but it won't be easy," he answered.

"I was thinking about all that we have going for the next few weeks, and I will say that Papa has to be back for all that, for sure. He needs to be here for the cave trip. The school kids are all looking forward to this so much, but, you know, I'd really rather that Pete and Susan not be allowed to go until they are older. I'm afraid they may try to go up there again on their own and we can't have a repeat of the Thompson's bar-b-que outing."

John sat his coffee cup down and said that this thought had crossed his mind also. "Anyway, it is really for the older kids only. We'll just have to tell them that they can go when they get to be the age of this group and their class will go. It may get to be an annual affair."

"Homecoming and graduation are two events that Papa will be looking forward to by all means." They could not think of any coming plans without thinking about Papa Russell. His first grandchild to graduate from his old school would make him so very proud. Their food was brought out quickly, with no other diners to be served. Beth picked over the cobbler, not really wanting anything at all to eat.

"Tissy came up to see the paintings," she said. "Even if they looked terrible, she'd be very complimentary. You know, Tiss. She was very excited over them."

"But she couldn't not like them," John said feeling proud of his wife and her accomplishments. "After all, a professional could not have done a better job. I think they are great, too . . . and just think, when you have some paintings displayed for sale at the inn, then you will be a professional yourself, maybe even become a famous artist!" Beth smiled at the thought even though she was satisfied with things just as they were, being his wife and the mother of her children.

"Oh, there is another thing Tiss told me. She said it would be okay to tell you and asked that we keep it a secret until homecoming." He looked at her over his cup, wondering, "What now?"

"She said Susan's poem is going on the first page of the book of children's short stories that is to be out this week!" she said with great satisfaction. "Isn't that the nicest thing! Papa will be so proud of her."

"Quite young to be an author, isn't she! We'll all be very proud. But . . ."

"But, what?" Beth could not imagine what he had thought of. Surely, nothing could throw a damper on Susan's poem.

"I was just thinking that so much attention being given her could make Pete rather jealous. We'll have to be careful to find something to praise him for." Beth agreed, saying she had been so excited that she had not thought of how Pete would feel. "See if you can think of something to give him to do that might be rather special," Beth suggested.

Then John changed the subject by saying that he had an idea to put before her and would like her opinion. This was the reason he had brought her out alone today. They needed time alone together. They had not been out anywhere in ages. His time was not his own and he needed some relief from the nighttime phone calls, dragging him out of bed to go see after a patient in the hospital or a sick child in the clinic at school. "I've been thinking lately of taking a doctor in with me to ease my heavy load. The town is growing, and I can't keep up the pace like it is and give it my all. What do you think?"

It took his wife only a second to decide. "I think that would be a wonderful idea, John! I've been worried about your putting in such long hours. You can't wait on so many patients and keep up your own health. After all, you do have to look out for number one. Yes, by all means! Get right on it. Do you have anyone in mind?"

The waitress came over and replenished the coffee cups and laid down the ticket. When she went away, John told Beth about a doctor, Neal Swanson, whom he had talked with at the last medical conference he attended and whom he had attended medical school with. "He told me then that some day he may like to have an office in a smaller town, so I thought I'd get in touch with him and see if he would be interested now in coming in with me. He's located now up in Norfolk."

"That's the best news I've heard in a while," Beth told him. "Does he specialize in one particular thing?" she asked.

"Yes. Gynecology." They had finished with their coffee and refused another offer for refills, so they left, satisfied with the decision that John had made for a partner. He would go back to the office and place a phone call to Doctor Neal Swanson.

On the way home, Beth told John that Tissy had suggested that either she or Teresa start teaching Susan to sign her name in cursive so she could autograph books neatly. "They will be on sale in the lobby after the program in the auditorium and there is another child from our school, Timmy Stephens, who will have a short story in the book."

Beth moved over close to her husband and laid her head on his shoulder. "John, have I told you lately that I love you very much?"

"Let's see now. Let me think," he teased. "I do believe you haven't told me since I left this morning."

When John returned home later that evening, the younger children were in bed and the older two were in their rooms getting their homework done. He found Beth in the kitchen just hanging up from talking with Teresa on the phone. "Oh, hi, Babe, I didn't hear you come in. How was your day? You look tired."

John came to where she stood after hanging up the phone and gave her a kiss on the cheek. He sat his medical bag on the table and started undoing his tie, leaving it to hang around his neck, and removing his jacket. "Whew! I'll say; I am about beat. Got any coffee, love?" He pulled a chair from underneath the table and plopped down. Beth said she had kept the pot warm for him. He usually wanted a cup to help him unwind before supper. She took two mugs from the cabinet overhead and poured them full, then turned to get the creamer and spoons. Knowing he always wanted to have a shower and relax before eating, she sat down across the table from him.

"So, did you get Doctor Swanson on the phone? I've been anxious to hear what he had to say."

"Yep. Sure did, and he's very interested. Said he'd get back with me in a day or two."

"That sounds promising, Hon. I'm so happy for you; and for us, for it will be a big burden lifted."

"I've been thinking about old Doctor Harris lately and wondering just how he managed to care for everyone around these parts for so many years and all by himself. Of course there weren't as many folks then as there are now and the school has grown so much meaning the boarding students require a lot more attention. He used to tell me that he made his rounds of the mountain residents on horseback and Kate would go along with him."

"I'm anxious to meet them both and hope they will be able to come to homecoming."

"I know Papa will be back, and he has to be here for that. He will want Doc and Kate to stay at Knollwood but we'll have to have them up to visit us, maybe for dinner; after all, this used to be their home, you know."

"Yes, we will have them, of course, and you had told me that you bought the house from Doc." Then Beth changed the subject saying, "Oh, I think it is looking rather serious with Resa and Nat."

"Really, now? What makes you think this?" He drained his coffee mug and sat it down with hands still encircling it.

"I was just talking with her on the phone as you came in. She told me that they went up to the falls today. She was so love-struck sounding and giddy-like; not like she's been sounding since Papa and Raymond have been gone."

"Tell me. Just how does someone sound who is love-struck?" John asked, putting her on the spot.

"Oh, you know what I mean, John, for heaven's sake." She got up, saying, "Come on, let's go see if the news is on."

"Hold on a minute." Still sitting, he reached up and caught her by the hand. "It isn't exactly news time on the TV yet, but I have some more news for you, confidential news."

"Oh? What more can there be?" She expected something long and drawn out and sat back down with folded arms.

"I met Ryan in the hallway at school a while ago, and he asked if he could talk with me. He looked rather serious and worried, so I told him to come with me to the clinic office. We talked for a while and he told me quite a tale. He's been bottling all this inside him, and he really needs help."

"What kind of trouble is he in, Johnny? Nothing real serious, I hope?"

"It could be. You see, the police are looking for him. I know he has done nothing wrong, but he got himself mixed up with two hoodlums who robbed a bank and they have involved him."

"Oh, my goodness! This could be very serious indeed!"

John told his wife just how it all happened, as related to him by Ryan. "What can we do? If we contact the police they'll take him away, and he won't get to graduate. And to think of all his hard work!" Beth felt devastated. "I . . . I feel like bawling," she said softly. "John, have you told Tissy or Resa?"

"No. I've not told anyone except you. What do you think about waiting until after graduation and homecoming and then get it hashed out?"

"Would we be harboring a criminal? What's the penalty for that? Oh! I wish he hadn't told you yet."

John stood to his feet and pulled his wife into his arms. "Tell you what, I'll talk with him again in the morning and tell him not to tell anyone until later on, and then I'll help him, even if I fly up to Pennsylvania with him. We'll go to the police and get this straightened out. I just hope that bag of the bank's money will still be laying in those weeds."

Beth considered what he had said and worried as she was, finally agreed that this was all they could do. "Just ask Ryan not to say anything at all about this to either Penny or Al, or anyone else for that matter."

Down the hill at Knollwood, Teresa held the phone with Nat on the other end, as the news came on. They had to listen to what Teresa said must have been a jillion advertisements and then news of happenings around town before they gave an update on the kidnapping. Each newscast left only shattered hope, deepening her sense of desolation. It was as if their fathers had simply disappeared into thin air. "When the unimaginable happens, one is never ready," she sighed, when Nat cut in asking, "Just how does one get ready for something terrible as this?" Their talk was filled with, "Why don't they"—meaning the police—or, "What if," until Teresa said she was exhausted and was going to bed. She was exhausted from worry, but exhilarated at the same time because she was in love, and wanting more than anything to tell Papa that he would have a son-in-law.

Tissy came just as Teresa was about to have a shower. She knew who it was by the knock because Tiss always did a shave-and-a-haircut type of knock. "Coming," she called out as she went up the hallway toward the back door and flicked on the porch light.

"Hello, dear," Tiss said, giving Teresa a hug. "I just couldn't let you stay here alone, so whether you want me or not, here I am, after all . . . I need consoling, too."

"Come on in, Tiss, you know you're always welcome and frankly, I'm glad to see you. This old house feels spooky when I'm by myself." They were walking toward the kitchen. "Let's fix up some hot tea. Might help us to get some sleep."

"Ohhh, thank you, Resa. I could certainly use some," Tissy said as she took down the cups while Teresa put on the kettle. Tissy felt as much at home here as in her own little house; after all, she had been a member of the family since she'd married Alyn's Uncle Bob.

"How's Bess's family?" Teresa asked, mainly to dispel her gloomy feeling. "I haven't seen any of them in ages."

"Ah, they're fine. They just keep busy like all young families, you know," she said, expecting Teresa to know how young families felt and then quickly asked if Teresa had watched the news.

"What news? I watched but there still isn't any news of Papa and Raymond." She took out two tea bags and placed them in the cups. "The sweetener is in that container," she pointed. They both knew how each other liked their tea or coffee. Tissy reached for the packets of sweetener and sat down waiting for the water to boil. Teresa took spoons from a drawer. After the water was hot enough and had been poured into their cups, they sat facing each other.

"You can't fool me one bit, Patricia Russell."

"Now, just what do you mean by that?"

"I have been noticing the interested stares you and Raymond have been passing and how he has patted your hand, probably wanting to lay one on you instead, if you know what I mean?"

"What!" Tissy exclaimed with raised eyebrows, "I have not given him any interested stares; I've only been friendly, the same as with anyone else."

Teresa took the tea bag from her cup and stirred in sweetener, then took a sip and looked at Tissy over the rim of her cup, relishing that she had gotten a rise out of her. "Come on. Tell me. Really now, anyone could plainly see that you both are more than interested."

"Well, Miss Nosy, if you must know . . . yes, I am rather interested. He seems to be a very nice man."

Teresa slapped a hand on the table startling Tissy, causing her to jump. "See! I knew it! I can read people like a book." She lowered her eyes, smiling like a cat that had swallowed a mouse, with Tissy playfully saying that she did not have to go around spreading to everyone that she and Raymond had a thing going.

"Of course I wouldn't, only . . ."

"What do you mean, 'only?' Come on, I'm all ears!"

Teresa held a hand up. "Just wait a minute, now. I was only going to say, and this is a big secret until Papa comes home, except to you, that is . . ."

"For gosh sakes, Resa, can't you just tell me without all this long, drawn out business?"

Teresa smiled, greatly enjoying keeping Tiss in suspense. "Okay, then, I was only going to say that one of these days you could be my mother-in-law!"

Tissy nearly spilled her tea as she sat the cup down. "What! Do you mean to tell me that . . . that you and Nat . . . oh, Resa! I am absolutely thrilled." She reached across the table and took the young woman by the hands, squeezing them, her blue eyes bright as stars, yet a tear escaped and ran down a cheek.

"Yes, you are right, and I have not told a soul but you, and we plan on waiting until Papa and Raymond come home, so please keep it under your hat."

"What hat?" she teased. "But, of course, I'll keep your secret. I'll be about to pop to shout it out, but I won't tell it to a soul. And thank you for entrusting me with this wonderful news . . . the best news I've heard in a long time. Your dad has so much now to come home for. With homecoming, his granddaughter graduating, and now a wedding, he'd better be getting himself home and soon, too."

They waited up for the eleven o'clock news before retiring. They sat in front of the television in the living room just in time for the beginning of the news. "Oh!" Teresa exclaimed. "I don't believe it." They had missed all the advertisements. She backed up and sat down on the sofa, leaning forward so as not to miss a single word. The newscaster started out with an update of the murder-kidnapping, which had been reported earlier. The men were still missing, and the police and FBI were still asking for anyone who had seen the car to call in; they gave the phone number. Then the announcer said that he had a very heart-warming, touching plea from Alyn Russell's eight-year-old granddaughter, Susan Russell. Tissy drew in her breath, shoulders rising, as she sat on the edge of her chair. "Oh, they said they would do it."

Then Susan's poem about her grandfather was read, her plea going out over the airwaves.

Chapter Thirty-Nine

AGAIN, TERESA AWAKENED TO ANOTHER DAY OF emptiness. "Tuesday," she said to herself as she lay there watching the early morning sun seep long rays of bright gold through the curtained window beside her bed. Tissy would already be out and gone without disturbing her, but she had made up her mind that she must make herself get out of bed and face another morning without Papa. Poor, dear Papa, where was he? She wished he were there to share in her newfound joy of being in love. She got up to the sound of bird songs from the maple tree outside, and turned on the radio to get the six o'clock news. But, looking at the clock, she saw that it was seven and not six o'clock. She must make herself go in to work. It would help her face the day and help the time to pass.

Before she had gotten a shower, the phone rang. "That will be Nat," Teresa thought with a little shiver of delight. "Good morning," she said into the phone instead of the usual hello.

"Good morning, my beautiful love," he said, his voice sounding like music in her ear. "Did you get any sleep?"

"Well, better than the night before. What about you?"

"I did, and you were in my dreams, but when I awoke, I realized that it was true . . . you had said yes and that you love me."

"Oh, you are a romantic even in the early morning. When we have been married fifty years, will you still love me?"

"They tell me that it grows with each year, but I don't see how I could love you more than I do right now."

"Nat, you are a romantic idiot, but I love it."

"No new news this morning. Did you hear?"

"No, I just got up right before you called. Nat, you are going to call the police department, aren't you?"

"Yes, of course, and I'll call you back. I suppose John has already called there also."

"Well, I haven't talked with him either. Tissy stayed with me again last night, but she's already left. I'm going in to work today, so if you hear anything during the day, please call me at school. I could not take sitting here all day by myself and I may as well keep busy."

He did phone her back in just a few minutes, saying there was no further news, but he was assured that the police were working on it hot and heavy. It was a Federal case, since there was a kidnapping involved. The FBI wanted to talk with both John and him. Nat said he didn't know why, because they certainly could give them no leads at all.

"Nat, did you hear Susan's poem that was given on the news last night?" Teresa asked, since he had not mentioned it.

"Oh, yes. I did. Wasn't that the sweetest thing. That kid must have quite a talent. Maybe folks will take more notice of something that could turn out to be a clue just because of the little girl's plea."

Chapter Forty

ALYN WAS THINKING SILENTLY, HIS EYES CLOSED. HE sported an ugly bruise on one cheek that was beginning to turn brown and a crack across one eyeglass—the result of a temper tantrum by Thatch. Alyn had asked Blade his real name, surely his mama had not named a little baby "Blade," with the dummy obliging, giving his name as Shane Corbett. This brought on the fit by Thatch, that caused him to knock Blade to the ground and a scuffle ensued by all four men, until Thatch grabbed the gun that was dropped by Blade and Alyn received a blow to the jaw for asking Blade's real name.

For an instant, Alyn's fingers touched the dropped pistol that had fallen to the old rough board floor . . . until Thatch stomped on Alyn's fingers—which were still hurting, only slightly relieved by his rubbing. During the scuffle, Alyn's glasses got cracked. Raymond, too, had lunged for the Smith & Wesson just as Thatch grabbed it and stood up, pointing it at Alyn's head and yelling, "I orter just shoot you, mister! Right here and now!" Then he pointed the gun toward Raymond. "And you, too, Mister Fancy Pants, the both of you, then we'd be rid of you and some of our problems." Blade backed away from the group, for he had been the brunt of Thatch's rages before now. Always when it happened, Thatch's eyes became glassy, his forehead broke out with beads of sweat, and his body shook. Blade thought that he must look like Satan when he went into one of these fits. The man belonged in an asylum.

The old run-down house where they were had been lived in by Thatch's grandparents who had been hard-working, honest sharecroppers. Both Alyn and Raymond had thought he pulled into the barn after noticing it by pure chance, but he knew all along where he had been heading. The land behind the derelict barn and behind the long-abandoned house was now planted with corn, which was already waist high, blessed by rain and early warm weather.

"You!" Thatch's voice still loud as thunder, told Blade, "Go out yonder in th' barn and bring that rope I seen hanging on the wall," he ordered, pointing with the gun. Blade obeyed and returned promptly, panting from running with the coil of rope slung over a shoulder.

"Whatcha gonna do, Thatch?" he meekly asked.

"Whatcha think I'm gonna do, dummy, play jump rope? You're gonna tie 'em up, what else. Then we'll take off and leave 'em t' rot." He grinned with satisfaction as though he'd planned it all out in advance. "When we come in I seen some chairs in one of them rooms, so go get 'em and we'll tie these old geesers up to the chairs." Alyn and Raymond glanced at one another as if they could read each other's minds, both feeling thankful they would at least not be shot. Maybe they would have a chance this way. Blade went out to get the chairs and hurried back with them. "Place 'em facing each other. They can at least talk to each other or yell to their heart's content, 'cause nobody 'ill be around to hear 'em begging t' be cut loose. Ain't choo glad I was born so smart, boy? Stick by me and I'll teach you a thang 'er two." When he gave a smirky grin, Alyn noticed he had a tooth missing. Thatch handed the gun to Blade, asking for the knife at the same time in order to cut the rope in two lengths.

"What 'er we gonna gag 'em with, Thatch?" Blade questioned.

"Ain't got nuthin', 'sides, they won't need gagging. Ain't nobody 'round here t' hear 'em holler," he smirked, pleased at his wisdom. After Thatch had finished tying them, he stooped over into Alyn's face and said in a sing-song voice like his tongue dripped with honey, "Is dat too tight for mommy's wittle boy? Does it hurt your wrists too much?" Both criminals walked toward the door with Blade telling his partner, "Hey, Thatch, did ya know that this here gun ain't got a single bullet in it? The one that the store clerk got was the last 'un." They both laughed hardily as they walked out with Blade sliding the gun across the floor toward the men. Thatch threw a kiss, saying, "Adios, gentlemen," and they went out.

"Of all things!" Raymond exclaimed. "No stupid bullets!"

Alyn answered, "How 'bout that! I would have loved to have gotten my hands on those two! Think of all the chances we passed up because of that empty gun! And now we've got to get out of these ropes." He wiggled around trying to see how the knots were tied, but it was useless.

"Weel," Ray slowly said as though it took a good bit of effort, "I guess we just sit here and look at one another."

"Under the circumstances, my friend, we don't have much choice, and I'll have to be completely frank about it, you're sure not much to look at."

"Was that a put-down? I ought to punch you on the nose for that smart remark."

"Yeah, do it! Come on over, I'd like to see you do it." Both men tried to smile.

"What I'd give for a tall glass of well water or iced tea or lemonade."

"Yeah, me and you, and a toilet, too. Hummm. That rhymed. Did you know my little granddaughter is a poet? She takes after me, you know."

"I hope she doesn't have dark circles under her eyes like you. You know, this would be comical if it were not so scary." Cooped in the small, dark room with only one window was beginning to make him claustrophobic. He'd always shied away from elevators, taking the steps instead.

Feeling the urge to keep talking, Alyn said, "How can something that we used to think of as being so insignificant would now be so prevalent?"

"Man! You're getting philosophic on me now. So, what's insignificant?

"Oh, just going into th' kitchen, turning on the burner to heat water for coffee . . . just little things we've always taken for granted." Ray nodded his head in agreement, and Alyn continued. "But let me ask you a really philosophical question."

Raymond said he was getting too deep for him but guessed he'd get the question anyway. "Why does sour cream have an expiration date on it when it's sour already?"

"Beats the life out of me, but I suppose it's the same reason they always sing the song 'Take Me Out to the Ballgame' when they're already there."

"You are a very perceptive man, Ray."

"Yeah, I know."

"Conceited, too."

"I bet I smell worse than you do."

"No you don't, I do."

"Now that doesn't make a bit of sense, Al. How could you smell worse than you do?"

"Oh, just can it, Ray." Alyn's brow furrowed. "Do you suppose they're gonna come back?"

"Yeah and us with an unloaded gun. If that don't beat all."

"If we had a loaded one, what could we do with our hands tied behind us?"

"You know . . . I'm so hungry I'd settle for one of Mack's fatback biscuits right now."

"Yuck! I'd rather starve first."

"Actually, they're streak-o-lean, but we kid him about 'em being back fat."

Ray whispered loudly, emphasizing the 's' . . . "Listen! I hear something." He turned his head around as far as he could, straining to see the door, when a little hound dog came in wagging its tail and lifted its head in a loud wail. The dog sniffed around Alyn, stood on his hind legs, and put the front ones on Alyn's knees. "Hey, boy. I wish I could pet you but right now I'm sorta tied up."

The dog moved away and Ray could not pass up the dig by saying the hound didn't like his smell. "Hey, mutt . . . go get your master." Then he told Alyn that the dog must live around here close by. "Best thing I've thought of all day. Shoo, go on. In other words, git! Go get somebody pooch, anybody will do, that is except those villains." The dog must have understood Ray's words, for he trotted out.

"A lot of help he was," Alyn said. "What next?" Then Raymond asked Alyn if he could reach the rope's knot with his fingers.

"What do you think I've been doing, playing Tiddle-de-Winks? Of course I can't. There's no way."

Raymond thought for a few seconds and said he had an idea, and Alyn brightened at the prospect of his coming up with something feasible. "The screwballs didn't tie our feet so why can't one of us come behind the other like a turtle with a shell on its back and use our hands to untie the other's ropes?"

"Absolutely brilliant. Please allow me." Alyn rose slowly, carefully to a bent over but standing on his feet position with the chair on his back, the rope looped through the rails on the chair.

"Be careful now and whatever you do, don't lose your balance," Raymond warned. Ever so slowly, Alyn carefully shuffled his feet inch-by-inch toward where Raymond sat, five or six feet away. When he was half way over to Raymond, his bad knee popped, causing him to stumble and fall to the floor, yelling as he went from the pain the fall caused. "Oh, my!" Raymond exclaimed, "is anything broken, Al?"

"I don't think so, nothing but my spirit. Looks like we are sunk, Ray."

"I won't give up the ship! Wait a minute!"

"I'll have to wait, Ray."

"Hush," he whispered. "I hear voices!" And just then two faces appeared in the doorway before they had time to yell out for help. The inquisitive faces belonged to a boy of about fourteen or fifteen and a girl who could be no more than thirteen, followed by the dog. Both kids wore jeans and sloppy faded T-shirts. The girl's thick blonde hair hung down her back in a long plait.

"What's going on here?" the tall lanky boy questioned. The girl held back shyly.

"Hey, kids, are we ever happy to see you two. We're sorta tied up here and need some help getting loose from these ropes, and this other man lying sideways on the floor in his chair has fallen and can't get up. Could you please," he emphasized the word please, "untie us?" The boy made a move toward Raymond until he nodded his head toward Alyn and said, "Him first."

"Land sakes alive! Ya'll look a plumb fright," the girl said as she watched her brother struggling to get Alyn upright. "In fact, ya'll look like you've been plowing th' field all day in the hot sun." And in the same breath, she asked, "Who done this to you?" She got on one side and pulled with all her might to help her brother.

"Some bad men, Honey," Ray told her. "But they've gone away now. Have you seen the news on television by chance?"

"We ain't got one of them, mister. My name's Lucy, and this here's my brother Luke." The boy worked the ropes loose from Alyn's wrists after a lot of picking with his fingers and the aid of his small, dull pocket knife. Then the boy and girl on each side helped Alyn to his feet. He was stiff and every bone in his body ached, and he felt exhausted. He backed up and sat again in the chair, bent forward with his head in his hands. "You're not gonna cry, are you, mister?" the girl bent over and asked him softly.

"No child. But if you and Luke had not come along when you did, I might have." Luke was now working on loosening Ray's hands. After a second wind Alyn stood again, relishing the ability to do so and put his arms around the girl. "Lucy, you and Luke were sent from heaven."

"Really?" Lucy said with wide eyes, too wide for her features. "Mama says I'm her angel."

"You and Luke both are our angels. What is your last name and where do you live?"

"Our name's Sutton and we live on out th' road a ways. Ain't nobody home but us right now. Mama 'n Daddy have gone over to Ufallah fishing, and Granny will come this afternoon late to stay with us 'til they get home."

Raymond was now loose and standing. "Oh! How good it feels!" He said stretching his shoulders and moving them around in a circular motion. "We thank you kids so much." He hesitated and then said, "I tell you what . . . when we get back to where we live, you both can expect brand new bicycles to be delivered to your door. How about that?"

This time Lucy's eyes lit up like a Christmas tree. She clapped her hands together with glee and said, "Really? Brand new bicycles?" It was hard for her to comprehend. Not believing what they had just been offered, Luke asked, "With a horn on it?" And Raymond answered, "If that's what you want and perhaps a speedometer, too." Luke was standing there with hands in his pockets when he heard what Raymond had promised and with an unbelieving look, he said, "Goh-lee!"

"Did the hound come for you," Alyn inquired, patting the dog's head at last.

"No, sir," the boy answered, we was jest a-walkin' by and he come in here so we come in, too, to see if he smelled a rabbit or somethin'."

Raymond knew they needed further help. He told them that he and Alyn lived a long way away from here, in fact, it was way up at the very top of Georgia in the mountains and the bad men who tied them up had taken his car so they had no way to get home. "Do you suppose your daddy could get us to the nearest town, or could we use your telephone?" Raymond asked.

"Oh, mister, we ain't never had no telephone," Lucy told them wisfully and Luke added that their folks may not be home 'til tomorrow if the fish were bitin' real good.

"Okay then, but how's your granny going to get to your house?"

"She walks everwheres. I guess we are not much good to you with ya'll getting' on home a-way up yonder."

"That's alright, Sweet," Alyn told her, "You've already saved our lives. We'll get on to the main road and maybe get a ride. Just which way is th' nearest town?"

Luke walked to the door and pointed in the direction of the west. "That there a-ways, about ten miles and right chere our road is 'bout a mile to th' main road." No sooner than he got these words out of his mouth than his face brightened, and he said, "I know what I can do! I've got a rickety old rusty bicycle and one of you can ride on the seat while I do the peddling and after we get to th' road, th' first 'un can set on th' grass there and wait 'til I go back for th' other 'un. How's that sound?"

"Sure sounds feasible to me. Alyn, are you game?" Luke added that this time of week and particularly this time of day there just wasn't much traffic on the road, but further up on that main road was a little store and outside there was a telephone booth. If he could have mustered the strength, Alyn might have jumped up and down. "Well, let's do it, then. At least I won't have a gun pointing to the back of my head . . . loaded or unloaded." He grasped the boy's hand and gave him a powerful handshake. "It's a deal, Luke, my boy. Let's be off."

So they all went out into the sunshine away from the dark barn and gloomy old house. They looked a fright and smelled even worse. The short naps out in the barn and today's ordeal in the house had done little to eradicate the dark circles under their eyes. Beards now prevalent only tended to add to their disgusting appearance. Both men told the girl after Luke had taken off in a run to get the bike that they needed to make a trip out back. Alyn also asked Lucy if she'd run home and get them a jar of water to have before they left and maybe she could find them a cookie or two. So she, too, flew away like a bird on the wing. Luke returned before his sister returned with the water, so they waited, arguing who would be the first to go. The boy had pumped up the tires and hoped they would hold up the heavy men. It was decided that Alyn would be first since his name started with an "A" and the "A"s were always first. Lucy came hurrying back sloshing water from a plastic pitcher and she held a little brown sack with her mouth that contained a plentiful amount of her mama's fresh-baked cookies and one plastic McDonalds's drinking cup.

After much bouncing and jostling Alyn was delivered to the waiting place and Luke hurried away for his next passenger. When the bicycle rolled up with Raymond's feet nearly touching the ground, Alyn rose unsteadily on shaky legs. He had been waiting on a stump where evidently a road crew had come along chopping down trees that grew too close to the road. The men thanked the boy profusely for his help and repeated the promise that had been made already about the new bicycles. The tall, skinny boy's face beamed with joy as he took off throwing a hand up in a wave.

"You know, Ray," Alyn said with a deep sign while trying to stretch a kink out of his back, "I am weary of traveling." He stretched his shoulders and wound his arms around. "Drat the carnsarned keys anyway. I'd chop the trunks open with an axe if they were mine."

"I agree wholeheartedly, my friend. Come on," he said walking away. "Let's go home." The men started walking slowly, both feeling exhausted from the whole ordeal, with bodies aching and stomachs growling. They both had day-dreamed for three days of sitting down to a full meal with a nice nap afterwards.

"I can't understand why there's no traffic on this highway," Alyn stated extending an arm for emphasis. "All the time I've been sitting on that stump there's not been one single car come along."

"That's strange alright."

"Just look how flat this land is, not a hill in sight." Again, Alyn stretched out an arm with it making a circle to cover all the land that could be seen. "At least we won't be walking uphill. Man! That would be hard on these old leg muscles!"

"Well, there's no use in our standing around with our thumbs out, waiting for a car, but," he emphasized the word "but," "it does look like a bus would come along some time or other."

Alyn looked at Raymond over his broken glasses with his forehead wrinkled. "You got money for a bus?" he asked tonelessly.

Raymond looked at him with disgust. "Now you know if we told the driver our story he'd let us get on. Besides, I'll bet the news is full of our disappearance, wouldn't you say?"

"I s'pect so at that. Our kids are probably worried sick. Aww, somebody will happen by before long. We sure won't make much progress at the rate we're walking. If we make it to that store that Luke was talking about before we keel over, surely there will be some help there, don't cha think?"

Raymond figured his statement required no answer and did not reply. There were fields on each side of the road with corn waving in the slight breeze, evidence of someone's hard labor. Alyn commented that he was thankful for the breeze at least for a little while because after noon the sun would probably bear down. "Wish I had my old hat," he mumbled. They walked on in silence, each with their own private thoughts, looking at the weeds growing in ditches alongside the road and two buzzards in the middle of the road up ahead pecking at some road kill. "Looks like a car has come along here sometime this morning," Alyn commented. The buzzards saw the men coming and flew off complaining loudly. "I'm glad we're at least out of that place and those ropes. They cut into my wrists," Alyn said rubbing the wrist, "I already had enough aches and pains without having something else to contend with."

"Man, all you do is talk, talk, talk. Don't you ever get tired of listening to yourself?" Raymond was in no mood to be pleasant.

"Humph. If I could'a picked the one to be kidnapped with me, I would'o picked somebody who was a better conversationalist," Alyn answered.

In about an hour Raymond put a hand up to shade his eyes, squinted, and said, "Al, do you see something way up ahead?"

"With one eyeglass messed up, I sorta see something. What do you reckon it is?"

"It must be that store Luke was talking about. I don't see how they can stay in business way out here in the wilderness with no cars to stop there."

"I suppose they depend on just the local trade perhaps."

It was the little country store that sat right at a crossroad. They could soon catch a glimpse of it better and gave sighs of relief. They could get cold drinks, if the owner was benevolent enough after hearing their story that may seem far-fetched to him. "I hope that store owner has got a television or at least a radio. I'd certainly not like to stand around all day waiting for customers and have nothing to keep me company."

"Maybe he's got a wife that talks as much as you do," Raymond answered, and Alyn vacillated between being complimented or offended.

"Now, Ray, I was only thinking of you, ya know; I didn't want you to get bored." Alyn glanced at his watch that the kidnappers had not been smart enough to ask for. "A quarter past ten," he sighed. "How slowly time passes." His mind was filled with random images of home with his vacant look softening at just whispering the word home.

"Ray, did I ever tell you about old Adam and Lizzie Mae's granddaughter and what happened to her?"

"No, but I'm afraid I'm about to hear the story though."

"Well, anyway, she and old Indian Chief were taken away by a carnival that came to town and they wound up in south Mississippi. They were used to working with the carnival but after about a year they escaped in the night. I just couldn't help but think of their ordeal because they were doing just what we are doing . . . walking along hoping for help. But they had it worse than us because old Chief, he was real, real old and the girl then had a baby. So just thank the good Lord that we aren't in their fix."

"You may as well tell me if they made it back home okay." He had caught Raymond's attention, keeping his mind off their own plight, if only for just a few minutes.

"The girl and the baby did but pore old Chief, he died on a bus when a redneck jerk knocked him down and he hit his head in the fall. That little black girl went on to educate that kid and now he is running my deceased son's business in Atlanta, and she is a dean or something 'er other at Brown University."

"You don't say? I guess if folks set their mind to most any goal they want, they can make it with a lot of hard work."

In time, they reached the little grocery store with one pump out front. The building was small and looked like it had been there for years. There were metal Coca Cola and RC

Cola signs on the side and front; written on the screen of the double door was, "Colonial is Good Bread," and on the other door, "Tetley Tea." This was the most beautiful sight to them right now than anything they could imagine. They spied a telephone booth outside just as Luke had told them and hurried to it before entering the store. "Hey! Lookie here!" Alyn exclaimed, stooping over to pick up something off the ground. "Here's a quarter! Someone must have dropped it when they reached in their pocket . . . now we have something tangible," he added and grinned.

"Quick!" Raymond told him anxiously. "Put it in and dial the operator." Alyn quickly dropped the coin in and lifted the earpiece to his ear with his heart doing flip-flops. But the coin fell back to the slot. He picked it up and tried the dial again but the coin fell back again. "Oh, shucks! The blame thing is out of order!" Alyn exclaimed and Raymond grabbed the quarter and tried it himself, only to have it returned again. He hit the phone box with his fist. "Come on, Al, let's see if we have better luck inside." And they turned to go up the two steps to the door. The door was locked and lights off. Again, Raymond hit the door frame with his fist and uttered an oath. "Is the whole world against us?" he questioned, not looking for an answer from his partner, who was just as downhearted.

The two men sat down on the steps with elbows propped on their knees, dejected. "Well, Ray, it's not as bad as it has been. We don't have a gun to our heads or ropes on our wrists."

"Oh, you always think of something good, don't you? Then think of something to eat and maybe it will all of a sudden appear. And where are all of the darn cars?" Then he added that they must be the only ones left in the world.

"Nope. If folks start disappearing, I'm gonna be with 'em," Alyn answered. Then he brightened up by saying, "Maybe the kids' folks will come by soon on their way home."

They decided to just sit there and rest. Alyn spied a water spigot sticking out of the building above the foundation and his face brightened. Too low to drink from, he stooped down and cupped his hands, feeling satisfied for the water and splashed some on his face and head. Raymond admitted he felt better himself after doing the same. "Let's just sit here and wait for a vehicle of some kind," Alyn said. "Right now I'd be happy for a mangy old mule and wagon."

They sat down with stiff knees on the hard cement steps, both giving sighs. Alyn propped his elbows on knees and his chin resting in his hands. "I don't know about you," he said, looking straight ahead and not directly at Raymond, "but my cookies have evaporated. If you could wish right now for something to eat, and it would all of a sudden appear from out of the blue, what would you wish for?"

"I would wish for anything and be satisfied with anything," Raymond grumbled.

"If you could make something appear, then you'd better be careful of what you think about. Like, maybe a buzzard might land in front of you with a dead chicken in its beak."

"Oh, for heaven's sake, Al, can't you stop your foolishness for just a little while?" Raymond was in no mood for Alyn's glib words.

"Well, I've gotta do something to pass th' time. I sure can't catch a catnap in this uncomfortable position." Then he bounced into another subject. "We'll need to be home real quick-like so I can rest up for the school group's trip up to the cave next week. Right now I don't believe I could climb up there. Say, this would be a good time for you to go along with us. I tell you, man, you will not believe what you see. It's a sight for sore eyes."

This slightly caught Raymond's attention. "Why haven't you made some money off that place? Seems to me like it would be an interesting attraction for the public."

"Just didn't want folks traipsing around up there. That's what Charles wanted me to do, and we had some rounds about it." In his heart, Alyn had been wondering what he would do the rest of his life. He may have quit his apple orchard business and sold off his cattle, too, but he wasn't yet ready to take to a rocking chair and do nothing. It would be no fun to travel around alone. When he was young, there were dreams of taking Cynthee abroad to see famous places, which was not to be. He had lived his life for his children and grandchildren and now what? His health was good and his wheels were still spinning, and he was not ready to be idle and do nothing. John had told him one day recently that with all he had experienced in his early years he could write a good book, and it would be a treasure for his grandchildren. After all, John told him, kids today can't imagine what it was like to live with no air conditioning, no television or electric lights, and mules and buggies in place of automobiles. So much had happened there on Kendell Mountain that he could fill up more than one book if he set his mind to it. Maybe he should have let Charles build the resort up there at Knollwood. At least he would now be plenty busy with that. And look at Raymond. His son had given him plenty to do with the inn. "Ahhh," Alyn said to himself, "becoming old and retiring ain't what it's cracked up to be by a long shot."

But, Papa Russell argued, when confronted about writing a book, he didn't have a typewriter and could not use it if he did have one, and it would take too much writing to do it in long hand. No. That was not his bag, and there probably was not enough paper in the whole world to tell what all happened on Kendell Mountain. He would simply tell the kids, that is, if they were interested. And now, sitting on the store's steps, he was thinking of what he would tell the school kids on their trip up to the cave. At least that is something he could do.

"Ray, whatcha want to do? Just sit here the rest of the day?"

"Beats walking in the hot sun without a hat and water, and I know some cars have got to come by sometime today. I think we'd be better off to sit right here. And, too, what about the store's owner? You can look in the window and see it's well stocked, so it's still in business. Maybe the guy went home for lunch or something."

Alyn wrinkled his brow, dubious of what Ray suggested, and looked around noticing movement out of the corner of his eye. It was a puny cat that emerged from around the side of the building and eyed the two men warily. It walked closer to Alyn and peered cautiously at the hand held out for the creature to sniff, looked up into the strange human's face, meowed, and chanced to move closer. Alyn rubbed the yellow tabby that had now decided the man was friendly and had nothing to fear. With enough of the rubbing, it stiffened its long tail, prancing back and forth, purring with satisfaction, and then ambled off to sit in the sun and wash itself. Not in the least bit interested in a cat of any kind, Raymond leaned back against the door with his hands laced behind his head, ears alert for any sound.

"Yep," Alyn said with resignation long after Raymond had said they should sit and wait. "I s'pose there's no alternative but for us to sit here and wait, or rot . . . one or t'other." Raymond replied with a "humm," his eyes still closed.

In no less than fifteen minutes, Alyn subconsciously glanced at his watch at least twice, maybe more. Time was passing as slowly as it seemed to do when he was tied in the chair. He thought of this and began softly singing the words of a popular song: "Time goes by so slowly, and time can do so much, my darling, I hunger for your touch . . ." He sat with elbows on his knees and rubbed his hair. It needed washing, in fact, his whole body needed washing, which caused him to vow to himself that when he got back home he would soak in a tub of hot water for an hour. He looked over at Raymond and noticed that he was sleeping with his mouth open. "Not a pretty picture," he thought. Then forgetting his aches and pains, Alyn exploded to his feet, squinting his eyes to look underneath the crack in his glasses. Were the glasses playing tricks on him? "Yes!" he shouted loudly, causing his friend to jump up from a sound sleep to receive a great punch on the shoulder. "Look way down there, my pal. What do you see?" He pointed with one hand, the other around Raymond's shoulder.

"Well, I do believe it is a truck! Didn't I tell you that all we had to do was wait." The pickup truck was moving from the south toward where the men stood, slowly as though the driver had nowhere in particular to go. "At that speed, it may take him a while. I guess it's a man driving. Could be an old woman driving like that."

"Who cares? By jingo, Ray, we're gonna get help! Let's not stand here gawking, come on, let's go out in the road and wave our arms so whoever it is will not pass us by." The men hobbled on stiff joints out to the middle of the road waving their arms wildly to where no one could get by them without running over them, running completely off on the shoulder, or a third choice, running out into the corn field. The rattle-trap truck came closer. At one time it had been red, now mainly rusty. It was a man driving, and he must have been dubious about the two lunatics standing in the road waving their arms in the air. He must also be wondering where the men came from, since there was no car parked near the store. When the truck drew closer, it slowed, its horn sounding loudly. But the two crazies still waved their arms, determined that this vehicle would not get past them. Instead of stopping in front of the men, the driver turned and parked the truck on the left side of the store. The man, who climbed down from the truck, looked to be older than both Raymond and Alyn, dressed in a short-sleeved shirt tucked into bibb overalls, and on his head was an old straw hat. He slammed the door just as the men reached his side.

"Man! Are we glad to see you!" Alyn exclaimed, grabbing the old man's hand, pumping it up and down. When Alyn finally let go, the man reached in the overalls pocket retrieving a door key and walked toward the steps where the two men had been sitting.

"Wher's your car? How'd ya'll get here? You sure don't look too fit for walking. If you're aiming to hold me up, you're in for a big surprise." He flicked on the light and was talking as they all entered the store. "Ain't had no customers today. Cash drawer's empty," he announced in case that was what they wanted, and he went around the counter to the other side. The little country store could make anyone feel they had stepped back into time. It even had the proverbial iron stove with chairs around it and a checkerboard resting on top of a barrel. A jar of dill pickles sat on the counter beside a cash register and all sorts of candy in the glassed-in counter. Cans of food lined shelves along the wall; a long drink chest caught Alyn's eye right off. On toward the back of the store there were items that only a farmer would need: stacks of chicken feed, sacks of salt, and a number of antique items.

"We don't have a car, Mister . . . er, what's your name?"

"Just Leon will do," he answered, "but I asked you a question first. How'd you get here and what is it you want?"

"My name's Alyn Russell and this here is Raymond O'Bryan," he aimed a thumb toward Ray's chest. "It's like this, you see . . ."

Raymond broke in, "Do you have a radio, Leon? Have you heard any news lately?"

"Well, let's see . . . yes, I did. Last night the news was on when I crawled into bed but I was so sleepy that I didn't pay it much attention. But I tell you one thang, there's gonna really be some news tonight. Yes, sir!" He stopped talking and looked at first one and then the other to make sure he had their undivided attention, and since his mysterious visitors stood before him bug-eyed and waiting, he continued, relishing the opportunity to be the first to spread some astonishing news. "Well, this here chicken truck, loaded to the top with chickens . . . it collided with a great big hog truck and they said them pigs and chickens were squawking and squealing and running around everwhere! Whoowee! It was a big mess. I had went home to take Ma some groceries she said she needed 'cause she was s'pecting company today. Well, anyhow, like I was a-saying, th' police stopped traffic coming from up yonder at th' crossroads to down to where th' wreck was. So I found out why I hadn't had no customers in today, I did." Leon chuckled, commenting again about the terrible mess with some surviving hogs and chickens disappearing into a corn field. He wiped the smile off his face and asked, "What was it ya'll was wanting?"

Alyn leaned over the counter, softening his voice, trying to sound humble when he said they had no money and were very hungry and thirsty. They'd had nothing today other than a few cookies.

Leon looked from one man to the other with a blank face, not understanding why they were walking and had no money. But having a kind heart, he pointed to the cold drink chest and said to open it and help themselves to a softdrink, or whatever kind they preferred. They looked like bums but they didn't talk like bums.

One selected a Dr. Pepper and the other a Coke. Too busy opening his drink and pouring some of the refreshing liquid down, Alyn told Raymond to tell Leon what had happened to them. While Raymond was telling about the kidnapping, Alyn walked to the door and looked out when he noticed cars going by. The police had turned traffic loose. Raymond ended his tale by asking Leon if he had a telephone. "Sure, fellow. Be glad for you to use it and right here taped to the register is the police department's phone number. I got helt up one time and learnt me a lesson, it did, to have the phone number handy." He handed the phone over to Raymond. "You know," Leon said before Raymond got the phone in his hands, "I betcha that Lincoln ya'll was in was the one that crashed into those two trucks."

"What?" Alyn exclaimed, walking back to the counter.

"Yep. Sent them two men in it to th' hospital in an ambulance. That car was smashed up so bad they was bound to be hurt a whole heap. I heard one of them policemen say that one of 'em might not make it. That driver pulled right smack out in the road in front of one of them trucks and th'other'n swerved tuh miss 'em but he didn't miss 'em. It was a awful sight, it was."

The number Raymond dialed answered, "Police department. Sergeant Smith speaking." When he hung up he said, "Oh, that felt wonderful to speak with the police at last. And, you know I heard shouting in the background. Seems like some folks actually care about us." Leon saw a tear glisten on Raymond's face, then he reached over the counter and laid a hand on Raymond's shoulder, saying that since he heard their tale he cared very much about their plight. "But gentlemen, let me ask you just one question. Why were you two out at five o'clock on a Sunday morning at a filling station? That's an uncommon hour for folks your age to be out running

around, isn't it?" He looked from one man to the other, anticipating an answer.

It was Raymond who quickly answered Leon's question.
"We had planned on going to a town in North Carolina where
we were told there was an antique dealer who specialized in
very old keys along with his other antiques. You see, it's like
this: I have two old trunks that may hold a fortune in them, but
we don't have a key to fit the locks."

"Now, wait just a second," Leon said with his palms held up
in a pushing fashion. "You might not have to go to North
Carolina after all." The two men looked at one another with a
question plainly showing on their faces. Leon turned around
and extracted a large ring of keys hanging on the wall behind
him. "See this ri'chere?" Both Alyn and Raymond stood there
with mouths gaping open while Leon picked out a small key
from the ring, took it off, and handed it to Raymond. "You
know what this is?" And Raymond said it looked like a small
key. "Yep, sure is, only thing is this one here is a skeleton key
and will open any trunk anywheres. I've had this buncha keys
for years and years and never thought one of 'em would ever be
of any use 'cause they're all so old and there's not any locks
made now a-days for this kind of key."

"For crying out loud!" Alyn exclaimed when he realized the
man was actually handing the key to Ray that they had been
searching for.

"Oh, my! Leon, could I please buy the key from you?"

"Buy-smy. I wouldn't think of it." The two faces peering at
the man over the counter clearly showed great disappointment
and Leon could read their expressions. "But, I will gladly give
it to you, my man . . . here," he turned aside to get a small sack
that he used to bag candy purchases. "Best if you drop it in here,
roll it up, and I'll put tape around it so you won't lose the little
thing. What a pity that would be after all ya'll have been
through."

"Whoopee! Hey Al, our trip was not completely in vain after
all," Raymond exclaimed.

When the state patrol car came screeching its wheels in front
of the store, its blue light flashing, two officers and a TV camera

man got out, slamming doors in their haste to actually see the kidnapped men. They hastened inside with the bell on the screen door jangling. The first officer inside exclaimed with a broad grin, "All Georgia and the surrounding states have lookouts for you guys." He first grabbed Alyn's hand, giving a hearty handshake, and then Raymond's. "We've combed all of south Georgia, but I never dreamed we'd be the ones to bring you in!" Both officers were patting them on the back with the TV camera rolling all the time, filming the night's top news item that would go out over the airwaves. All the folks on Kendell Mountain and Union Gap would see them with beards, dirty clothes, and tired, haggard faces. No one would care how they looked, just that they were alive and safe at last.

"Okay, fellows, we're to take you to Macon and a patrol car from Atlanta will take over from there." The officer, who patted Alyn on the back as he said this, was a tall, stocky guy with a build that looked like he spent most of his time in a gym. Raymond was thinking at the moment that the officers both had faces of teenagers. "They get younger and younger, even the guys who are working on the inn, and they treat me like I'm an old man." The second officer spoke up, saying, "What do you fellows say about a nice hot meal? There's a great little restaurant up the road a piece." Alyn said it was the best idea he'd heard in a while and Raymond chimed in saying he hoped they would have a nice juicy steak. Leon shook hands with both men, feeling proud to have played a part in their being found. It was for certain that he would be watching the six o'clock news and possibly the late news, too. If he possibly could keep it to himself after he got home until the news came on, he'd make sure his wife was watching and wouldn't she get a grand surprise when she saw her husband on the news!

Meanwhile, in Union Gap, the news spread instantly after Percy dashed into the Skillet with the announcement. Nat was called at his office, John was reached at the hospital, and Teresa at school. People who were not within the sound of a radio or TV got it by word of mouth. It was the mayor's idea to put together a parade for the joyous return of the town's famous residents, and he immediately hopped into action arranging for the school band and anyone else who would walk along behind the band. He would have the Presbyterian pastor ring the bell in the church tower at the precise moment they got word by car radio that the patrol car was approaching. Everyone should be there, ready to march.

Early that morning, even before the news had broken, Nat went into Coble's Jewelry & Pawn shop and purchased a ring, planning on placing it on Teresa's ring finger that night. Later on, however, after getting the news, he made a dash up to the school, and being told that she had left already for home, he then went there completely surprising her. "I thought you would like to show this to your dad at once. But, I had planned to give it to you tonight. Mrs. Coble said she had a record of your ring size from when you purchased a birthstone ring not too long ago." Nat placed the diamond ring on her finger and sealed his love for her with a kiss.

Chapter Forty-One

IT WAS A BEAUTIFUL MAY AFTERNOON, BUT NEITHER of the men noticed whether it was or not. As the wheels of the patrol car whirled around, and sights he had seen for years but never really appreciated quite as much as he did today came into view, Alyn breathed a great sigh of relief. The beautiful day, a clear blue sky, cows in pastures, day lilies nodding along the roadside . . . all so familiar, and today in particular, were all so dear. Farmhouses and outbuildings were scattered along the land as though some great giant had randomly tossed them there. By every prospect, he was filled with pleasure.

They were traveling up Coleman Mountain where landmarks became very familiar. From the curvy road one could look over far below and see lush greenery everywhere. The patrol officer handled the car on the mountainous curves as though he had driven here many times before. Alyn Russell, in the front passenger seat, and Raymond O'Bryan, in the seat behind the driver, received stares from people in cars passing by, and Alyn laughed, commenting that they must be thinking, "Those poor devils are being taken to jail." "Well, Ray, a few days ago we were sitting in your automobile in this same position. Only thing was that gun pointed to the back of my head was rather bothersome."

"Yeah, but if we'd only known it wasn't loaded you could have reached over and jerked the steering wheel or something." Raymond answered and received a round of laughter from the two officers and the cameraman.

One of the officers said that this was a new one. "We think we've heard or seen it all, but then something new happens every day."

As they reached the top of Coleman Mountain, all of a sudden there it was in front of them looming in grandeur, tall and serene . . . Kendell Mountain, silhouetted against the blue sky, and not more than five miles ahead. "Home," Alyn said almost in a reverent tone. "Home at last." The driver reached for his mike and called in to report their location. The call, reported by the sheriff to Percy, who was on duty in his patrol car and now feeling of great importance, rolled to the spot he had designated for the parade to fall in behind the Georgia State Patrol car. He turned on the blue dome light and the siren; the band behind him was ready to strike up, with marchers following. Mack, Thelma, and the waitresses were standing out front of the Iron Skillet, and Lew Hendrix, hardware store-owner, was in front of his store, ready to flap his long white apron like a flag. All the workers up at the inn stopped work and came down, ready to tease their boss about setting off to find an antique shop with a trunk key. They would be in for a surprise. The seed and feed store people were there, and all the other businesses closed for the parade and mingled with the residents on the sidewalks. At the other end of the road, where the business area ended, the house where Nat and his father lived had been adorned with yellow ribbons by Penny and her friend, Gwen. Penny had done the same earlier at Knollwood as they had started down on the way to welcome home Papa and Mr. O'Bryan.

"It's coming! It's coming! The police car is coming!" someone yelled, and immediately Percy started blowing his whistle and turned on the blue light. The other town officer, Kenny Jones, stood waving people back on the sidewalks. He would motion for the car with the men to come on up in front of Percy's vehicle located behind the band.

Kendell Mountain had never seen such a parade. The television reporter got out just as they rolled to a stop before they joined in the parade, putting his camera into action. The band was loud, and people cheering drowned out the church bell.

When it was ended, Alyn's family and Tissy were all standing there on the sidewalk near the O'Bryan's residence with Nat and Raymond. No one could get enough hugging with tears running freely. The men's beards scratched faces and no one cared one bit. Penny commented that she liked her grandfather with a beard, and Al said it was cool. Alyn, who was holding his daughter's hand, felt the ring and holding the hand up, noticed the sparkling diamond. "What's this?" he questioned. Nat came and stood by Teresa, telling her father that he had asked his daughter to marry him.

"Well, since she has on an engagement ring, then her answer must have been yes," Alyn smiled and hugged his daughter, kissed her again and then shook hands with his future son-in-law. "But I hope this won't make me kin to my partner in crime," he teased, meaning Raymond of course.

The group stood talking and offering congratulations to the couple for a few minutes, and then John hustled his dad into his car to take him home for that long, hot bath, a shave, and plenty of rest. "I think I could sleep through the rest of the day and the night to come," Alyn said. Both John's and Beth's cars were there so John took his dad and Teresa home, with Beth and the children following. Tissy said she would see them all tomorrow after Alyn had rested.

What a wonderful day. Home at last!

Chapter Forty-Two

NAT AND RAYMOND DESCENDED THE STAIRS INTO THE basement with Nat in the lead. "I can't understand why this couldn't have waited until morning, Dad. It's been here all these years and one more day certainly wouldn't hurt anything, and besides, you need to be in bed." He knew these sagacious words would bounce off the walls and fall upon deaf ears.

Raymond, fingering the key in his pocket, felt like a small child on the night before Christmas; he couldn't wait until morning. He had waited long enough and surely would not sleep a wink because of anxiety. Besides, he had been through enough to get the dratted key in the first place.

Only the light from the open door upstairs filtered down into the dark basement until Nat reached up and turned on the light that one of the men had strung a drop cord for a temporary convenience. When the light touched Raymond's face, his expression showed pure anxiety that he said he would be saving himself from by coming here tonight. Raymond stooped to insert the key into the lock of the largest trunk with a hush of expectancy. In exasperation, he exclaimed, "Rats! It will not turn. We need some WD-40, Nat."

"Well, I don't happen to have any on me, Dad." He stooped, saying, "Here, let me give it a try."

"If it won't turn for me, it won't turn for you either," Raymond replied with disgust, reluctantly handing the key over. Nat joggled the key one way and the other and, as if by magic, the latch cover flew open; he looked up in his dad's surprised face. "Okay, Dad, it's all yours." He stood up, handing the key back, saying that he should immediately put it in his pocket. "Open it up. Let's have a look at what junk we have here."

Raymond stuck the key in a pocket and almost reverently opened the trunk's lid. "Would you look here, Son!" Side-by-side on their knees, both men stared into an assortment of items; a silver tureen, a silver water pitcher, serving platters, and, wrapped in a velvet cloth that had become stiff with age, silverware. Underneath this roll of velvet lay a set of Spode china. "Look at this here!" Raymond exclaimed with his excitement building, as he lifted out a bundle of Confederate money and gave a low whistle. "Man! If this stuff was any good today, we'd be filthy rich. The senator must have been sure the South would win the war and stashed this all down here to hide it from the Yankees."

"But," Nat said, "they never did come through here. Alyn told us at the Skillet one morning that they by-passed this little town . . . said it was only a crossroads and unimportant and saved them from coming down an unnecessary mountain."

"But, you know, this house was here and was the senator's home and it would have been feasible that they burn it down."

"I'm sure glad they didn't. Maybe they were in a hurry to get to Atlanta," Raymond mumbled as he scrambled further down in the trunk, moving articles aside to see what else had been hidden in the bottom. He lifted a small, flat box, removed the lid, and saw an envelope that was addressed to Senator Fullman in clear black ink and still visible after all these years. Taking the envelope carefully in his hands, sliding out the pages inside that were now brittle and yellowed with age, he drew in a deep breath and said in a whisper, "Son, this here is something to treasure. I wonder who it is from." He saw the seal on the upper left-hand corner, realizing that it was from someone of great importance.

"Hurry up, Dad. Read it, if you can make it out."

"Yes, it looks readable." Then Raymond exclaimed with eyes wide and heart beating fast. "Nat! This is signed by none other than President Abraham Lincoln!"

"My gosh! Read it . . . what does it say?"

They both stood up and Raymond held the letter under the overhead light bulb with Nat looking over his shoulder. "Dear Robert. . . . Get that, Nat. First name basis. They were friends!" Then he continued to read. "I write this letter to you, pleading that you understand my position in this heartbreaking situation that besets our nation. As president of this great country, I have a duty to fulfill and fill it I will. But it is my great sorrow that you have refused to agree with me on my stand. I was so hoping you and Mrs. Fullman would come to Washington and be one of us. I hold our friendship dear, and shall pray for you and your wife as the Federal troops move southward. I remain, yours truly, Abe Lincoln."

"Can you believe it, Dad! This is priceless! May I touch it, please?" He reached out to hold the letter than President Lincoln had once held in his own hands. "This letter will trump anything else that's in this trunk or the other one, too." Then he handed the treasure back to his father, who carefully replaced it inside the envelope and then in the little box.

Nat moved over in front of the smaller trunk. "Shall we?" he asked with his hand out for the key again. It unlocked with the first try. "We cannot expect to find such treasure also in this one."

"Bless ole Leon and his ring of keys," Raymond said under his breath. Inside this second trunk was an assortment of items; several paintings wrapped in clothing, English Spode, a Ming vase that was wrapped with a dress, and the rest of the contents were clothing, including what looked to be a wedding dress and some baby clothes.

"Humm, Alyn said Mrs. Fullman never had any children."

"Oh, you know how there were so many infant deaths back then. They could have had several," Raymond answered, closing the trunk and locking it.

Legally, the treasures were Nat's. His father had had a traumatic experience trying to obtain a key, and he had gone to bat for his son to finance and rebuild the old house, so the treasures would be his and his father's jointly, as would the inn, Nat quickly decided. As they turned out the light and went up the steps, they both had a feeling of having touched the past. They felt for Senator Fullman and the dilemma he had no doubt been in . . . as all the North and the South felt when families and friends were so cruelly torn apart.

Chapter Forty-Three

AFTER SEVERAL DAYS, THE TOWN'S TWO TELEVISION stars were all rested and back to as normal as could be, as Alyn put it. John told him that this experience would fill several chapters in his book. "I may get around to it in my old age," John was told. A spring rain, which had started during the night, slow and steady, by mid-morning had drenched planted fields and filled ditches along the roadsides. John rolled up in the driveway and getting out with an umbrella, scattered a flock of guineas that were portracking across the yard looking for shelter. Ole Charlie and his flock were nowhere to be seen. When John stomped his feet on a mat at the back door, Alyn heard him from the kitchen and came to let him in. "You're out fairly early this morning. I thought your office opened up at nine o'clock." He glanced at his watch and said, "You will be a little late, won't you?" He stepped aside for John to come in after he had laid the umbrella aside. "Come on in and have some coffee with me, son." Alyn had turned and headed back toward the kitchen. "Have you eaten anything?"

John answered that he had and sat down across from his father. "Beth has gone down to take the kids to school and after they left, her mother called."

"Pore ol' Miss Lilly," Alyn grinned. He had always referred to her this way, but not in front of Beth, of course.

"Old? I'm sure the two of you are about the same age. She may even be younger than you."

Alyn waved a conceding whatever sign and asked what she wanted so early in the morning as he walked over to the stove and brought back the coffee pot, for what the cup held had cooled down. "Seems like she's in trouble just south of Atlanta, down around the Farmer's Market," John answered.

"Trouble? But what's she doing there in the first place? That's a long way from where she lives."

"Just hold on, Papa, and don't laugh." But, of course, that was just asking for him to laugh, especially when John told him that she had been pulled over by the police for weaving and they took her to the station.

"What! You mean they put 'er in jail?" Alyn laughed and slapped his knee.

"Oh, no, at least the officer who called said someone would have to come get her."

"Uh oh," Alyn breathed, "do they think she was drinking?"

"Maybe, but the officer said they saw her turn up a bottle as she was driving. It turned out to be cough medicine with codeine in it, and they would not allow her to drive any further. He said someone would have to drive her car, so . . ."

"Oh, dear. I know what you are getting at. Here I go again! I swore I'd never ever go any further south than Blue Ridge!"

"Now, Papa, we can't let the poor old lady, as you put it, sit there in the police station all day, now can we?"

"Can't Beth go?"

"Ah, Papa, she has the kids to . . ."

"Okay, okay, but just under one condition. I drive your car back and you bring her in her car, and that's final."

"Agreed," John said feeling relieved, although reluctant to ask Papa so soon after his ordeal. "Are you sure you are up to it, Papa?" And, of course, he argued that there was nothing wrong with him at all and he couldn't let the old lady sit down there in jail suffering with only her cough medicine to soothe her nerves. John was supposed to make hospital rounds this morning and then start his office appointments at two o'clock. He said if they go now, he would possibly get back in time for the office patients. He said they would stop by the school to inform Beth about her mother or possibly would meet her on the road as she was going back home after leaving the children.

So, Alyn got his jacket and hat and went out the door into the rain saying, "Here we go again, but you'd better have a full tank of gas because I'm not stopping at a service station down there."

Two hours later, John drove into the parking lot of the Forest Park Police Station, thankful that he had not been pulled over for speeding and also thankful that the rain had stopped about ten miles back. Inside the station, he was taken to where Lilly was seated, watching the Andy Griffith program, drinking a softdrink, and eating some peanut butter crackers.

"Oh, John!" she exclaimed, happy to see someone had come for her, "and, Alyn . . . how good of you to come and so soon after all you've been through recently. My goodness! Everyone everywhere was sick with worry . . . and wasn't that the sweetest poem little Susan wrote! I about cried my eyes out."

Alyn rolled his eyes up toward the ceiling when Miss Lilly turned to John. "Please let her ride with John," he prayed.

"What's this about the cough medicine, Mama Lil?" John questioned. They were standing talking when an officer came in, but Lillian answered the question she had been asked.

"I've had a terrible cold, John, first in the head and then it went to the chest, you know, so the doctor gave me a prescription for some cough medicine. Well, in the car I had a coughing fit, so I just turned up the bottle and took a swig just as this state patrol officer came up behind me. And, would you believe it? He said I was in no shape to drive any further. Of all things, and he didn't look much older than Al. Can you believe it?"

When she paused for breath, John broke in. "Don't you worry about it, Mama Lil. We'll take care of everything." The officer took them to the desk and filled out some paperwork and let her go, handing John the keys, saying someone would bring the car around front.

Lillian, "Lilly" to her friends, was an attractive lady, dressed in an attractive tailored suit. When John first saw her sitting there waiting, he noticed how much Beth resembled her mother. But only her looks, as Beth was more reserved, and Lilly was a scatterbrain.

John got behind the wheel of Lilly's Ford. In the passenger seat, she complained that she was absolutely humiliated. "They made me feel like a dottering old fool." Then, correcting herself, said, "Fool, perhaps, but certainly not old." John smiled without a reply.

Alyn was following happily behind. Earlier, he had said that he hoped Raymond would come to Atlanta today like he said, because he promised to go to Sears and order the two bicycles and have them shipped to the kids. As they rode along, John was getting an ear full. He felt as though he knew everyone in Mobile, where Lilly lived, the name of her hairdresser, Randy Thomas, and how he had recently talked Lilly into dying her hair red, but she didn't like it because it made her look like a hussy. She had to watch her appearance carefully because she was supposed to look like a senior citizen since she was now modeling clothes. And she would have to be back in Mobile by the tenth of next month because she had a job to do in a swanky ladies clothing store. "But," she continued, as John was afraid she would do all the way home, "I just would not miss Penny's graduation for anything in the world. I have her a gift she will simply adore! It's a little diamond cross necklace. Just think, my first grandchild to graduate!"

John tuned her out and pictured in his mind how they would have to scrounge around to make room for Mama Lil. "Thank the good Lord above it will only be for two weeks," he thought and glanced in the rear view mirror noticing Papa happily engaged in a song that must be playing on the radio. At the rate his mouth was going, they could have heard him if the windows were down.

Chapter Forty-Four

THERE WAS NO SCHOOL ON FRIDAY BECAUSE IT HAD been declared a teacher's workday and also a day for pulling plans together for graduation. With no homework, Ryan got up the courage to go up to Knollwood and talk with Alyn. His work was completed at five o'clock and after supper, he took his dog and walked up the road. He felt like it could not be put off any longer. The problem must be resolved and, too, there was the secret that he wondered if Mr. Russell was aware of. If he was aware of it, then it would not be a secret to him. Ryan had talked with Doctor John about his own personal problem, but it was still gnawing at him.

Now standing at the front door, he knocked, and for a fleeting moment his courage faded, making him wish no one would be at home. Maybe he should not have come after all, he battled with himself. No one answered the knock so Ryan turned to leave, but just then the door opened and there he was, holding the screen door open. Ryan wished he could bolt suddenly back down the hill to his room at school. Collecting his wits, he greeted the man holding the door open. "Good evening, Mr. Russell," then nervously cleared his throat. "I was wondering if I could speak with you for a few minutes."

"Why certainly, Ryan. Come on in." The boy turned to his dog and ordered him to stay and he obeyed, watching his master disappear beyond the door as it closed. "You picked a good time. I'm alone and glad to have the company. Let's go into the living room." He led the way, and while behind him, Ryan's heart was beating fast. They entered the living room,

Alyn pointed toward the couch for Ryan, and then took his usual place in the recliner. The newspaper was scattered on the floor beside the chair where evidently Alyn had been when he heard the knock on the door.

Ryan leaned forward, feeling uneasy and awkward, with his hands resting on his knees, then changing positions, he rested an elbow on the arm of the couch. "I hope you have rested up after your ordeal. I probably should not come to you with my worries after what you have just been through."

"Oh, I'm fine, Ryan, but thank you for asking. I didn't realize so many people would care." Alyn saw that the boy was nervous. And even at eighteen, he considered him still a boy. Then he asked Ryan if he wanted anything in particular or was it just a friendly visit.

"Yes, sir. I sure do want some advice, and I thought you'd be the best person to talk with other than Doctor John." He cleared his throat again but before he could say more, Alyn decided he would try to put him at ease by asking about his schoolwork and the job. Maybe he should not have jumped suddenly into asking what it was he wanted.

"Oh, my school work is fine, and I love the school and my job. Everyone is so nice to me." He looked at Alyn searchingly, wanting to trust him, and then continued, "Not only the teachers but all the students as well."

"That's good, Ryan. I'm glad to hear you are pleased with the school. When I was a boy, I watched the school being built."

"It must be old then . . . I mean . . ."

"That's all right, son, no apologies necessary. Now, what was it you wanted to talk to me about?"

"Well, you see, I'm sort of in trouble back at home . . ."

"With your parents?"

"No. And frankly, they don't care one way or another, so I left home, or that is, they kicked me out."

"I can't imagine any parents doing that. Couldn't your problems be resolved?"

"No," he answered simply. "They wanted me to join the armed forces. My grades in school got bad, and I would not be able to graduate, but here, your daughter has helped me more than anyone. Since I've been here, it's like a light has turned on in my head."

Alyn smiled, pleased that Teresa had helped. "So, what is the problem then, other than your parents kicking you out?"

Ryan took a while to reply, and Alyn stared at him, waiting for a subsequent answer.

Searching anxiously for a way to start the tale about what had happened before he left Pennsylvania, it took a moment before he came out with it. "Well, you see, sir, I'm sorta in trouble back there with the law. No one has told me that they are looking for me, but I assume from what happened that they are. There were these two punks that I went to school with, real losers, you know the type," and Alyn nodded his head and flicked his fingers for the boy to continue. "I was just standing there propped up in front of a building, trying to decide where I could spend the night, and I saw this car coming down the street toward where I was standing. And I heard an alarm go off, like someone had broken into one of those buildings along there. I suppose they realized that a patrol car would be along before they could get far, because one of those punks rolled down the window and tossed out a money bag, yelling for me to grab it and meet them at a certain place, and they kept going. Well, I wasn't about to meet them anywhere, but I didn't want to be caught with all that money in my possession."

Alyn was thinking that this sounded like a movie and he leaned forward, anticipating the outcome. "So, I ran down behind the building . . . this was downtown, you know . . . and I pitched that bag over a fence in the alley. It landed in some tall weeds, and I disappeared in a hurry." He stopped talking, waiting to see what Mr. Russell's reaction would be.

"What you are saying, Ryan, is that you never reported the incident to the police, and now you are in trouble, and somebody is looking for a lot of money that was stolen."

"Yes, sir. That's it."

There was a short silence while Alyn digested Ryan's tale. Then, he asked Ryan how he got to Kendell Mountain and said that he had heard he was from somewhere up north.

"Pennsylvania . . . I walked most of the way and hitch-hiked. Found my dog. Saw some people put him out of their car. In Tennessee I got a job on a horse farm with a real great man and his wife. They wanted me to stay, and I would have except I wanted to come to Kendell Mountain before I decided to settle somewhere."

"That is quite a story, son." But Alyn was curious as to how Ryan knew about Kendell Mountain and just who had told him.

The boy took a deep breath and continued. "My grandfather used to tell me all kinds of things when I was little about all the things he and his twin brother did while they were growing up here, like going to school here and all, but I particularly wanted to see the cave. The cave is where I lived until the principal, Mrs. Russell, fixed me up in school and a job, too."

Alyn could not believe his ears. John might be right in suggesting that he write a book. "Tell me, Ryan, who is your grandfather?"

With trepidation, he hesitated and then answered. "His name is Matt Harris."

"What!" Alyn exclaimed. "Then you are David and Kate's great-grandson! Man alive! Matt had to marry awfully young for him to be a grandfather."

"Yes sir, they did, and my parents are hippies; they are on the wild side."

After a moment of silence, Ryan told Alyn that he was hesitant to go to his grandparents or his great-grandparents with his problem, but now he realized they would have helped. In haste, he just thought at the time it would be best for everyone if he simply disappeared. While he was waiting for Mr. Russell to say something, Ryan wondered if he had done the right thing in coming to him and spilling the beans.

"Ryan, this is a startling revelation. I know your grandparents and also your great-grandparents well. In fact, Kate is my adopted sister. Did you know that?"

"No, sir. She never told me about that."

Suddenly, Alyn was jolted by the revelation of the enormity of what the charges would be against Ryan if the moneybag was not where he said it could be found. Frowning, he sat back in the chair, rubbing his chin, which got to be a habit while he had the beard, and thought about what should be done. "Ryan, I believe it may be best to wait until after your graduation to reveal this to the police."

"Yes, sir . . . that's the same thing Doctor John said."

"Oh, then you talked with him about this also."

"Yes. I talked with him one day when he was leaving the clinic and I was out in the hall sweeping."

Alyn wondered why he also came to him, but answered, "Then you can rest assured that this is wise counsel." He did not tell the boy that David and Kate Harris were coming to homecoming. "We do not have any choice of who we are, Ryan, but we do have a choice of what we make of our lives. Sometimes patterns of who we are do not surface for a long time. I see a lot of your great-grandfather, David Harris, in you. He is a hearty soul, kind and caring. Walking in his shadow would take a person of truth and character. You are a special person, boy. Don't disappoint your family. They all care, at least your grandparents and great-grandparents do. Ryan, the lessons we learn in life are important, but what is more important is what we do with these lessons."

"Thank you so much for those words, Mr. Russell, they are comforting and that's what I needed most." Then with a relieved feeling of accomplishment and a wide smile, he rose to go. "Oh, and another thing, I wish you would go up to the cave with me Saturday morning. I found something in there of importance that you should see in case you don't know about it already."

Chapter Forty-Five

ALYN COULD NOT GET RYAN OFF HIS MIND. THE POOR kid had gone through so much and kept it all to himself. Keeping his problem to himself had no doubt upset Doc and Kate much more than knowing the situation. His disappearance must have been what the problem was when Alyn had phoned them about coming down for the school homecoming. Doc had mentioned that he wasn't sure they could come because there was a problem there, and Alyn, curious but trying not to be nosey, did not ask what the problem was. He had let the comment slide by and forgot about it until now after Ryan's visit. He would like to phone Doc and tell him that Ryan was there on Kendell Mountain and going to school. But he'd best talk with John about it first, since John already knew about Ryan's situation. John gave him good advice, Alyn thought. We think alike. "I wonder if it would be best for Doc and Kate to simply discover Ryan when they come down . . . but they may not come at all, thinking if they did come, they may miss Ryan returning home while they were away."

Alyn and Doc had not been close since Doc and Kate left Kendell Mountain, moving up to Pennsylvania to be near their sons. After Ryan left, Alyn sat in his recliner staring at the television, but not paying any attention to the program. He was thinking back to the olden days, as the kids called it . . . about when Kate, Anson Kelly's daughter, had come to teach at the school, and met Doc, who lived up in the house where John and Beth now lived. His thoughts rambled on until he dozed off and now in his dreams he was running through the woods as a kid, with his dog Beans, running ahead of him.

He was awakened by the back door closing and Teresa calling out to him, then he heard Nat saying something to her. He got up stretching and walked over to turn off the television. "I'm in the living room," he called out to them, knowing they would think he had gone to bed. Teresa had not wanted to go out at all, but her father insisted, saying he would enjoy watching a game on television and just being alone. He would be there when the couple returned. So they were sent out with his blessings.

"Oh, here you are," Teresa said as she walked to where he was and kissed him on the cheek. "It feels so good to do that, Papa, and to know that you will be here when I come in."

"We both know that feeling," Nat said. "After you two guys got settled in back at home, I've thought more and more that it could have turned out tragically."

"Ahhh, we shouldn't ever be pessimistic, but just thankful for the way it turned out. Now, tell me . . . I want to know when the big day is going to be." Alyn grinned, feeling that they had already set their wedding date.

Teresa backed away and looking at Nat, smiled and said, "Yes, we decided tonight. Now, tell us what you think of this, Papa. Graduation will be on a Friday and homecoming on Saturday. So we figured that Sunday afternoon would be a perfect time, and Doc and Kate would be here. I've thought about a lot of other people who would already be here so why not have the wedding that weekend when our friends are here?" She had stooped down in front of her father with her hands resting on his knees. He saw that her face radiated happiness, and he was happy for his daughter and very happy about her choice for a husband.

"Have a seat, Nat," he motioned and Nat backed up to the couch, anxious for his reply to Resa's question. "Well, I think you two have thought this through and know what you want to do, so it's your decision. I had thought you would wait until about June, but why should you wait? Yes, I think you have made a good choice. We'll have the whole she-bang over one weekend. Man, alive! That will be a blast."

Teresa reached her arms out to hug her father, then kissed him and stood up. "I just knew you'd agree, Papa. None of this excitement would have been worth a dime if you had not come home." This was the happiest time of her life and her face clearly showed it.

Chapter Forty-Six

ON SATURDAY MORNING, THERE WAS A SLOW STEADY rain, proving that this day would be dull and slow. Nat and Raymond were working at the inn, and around midmorning, Alyn decided to go down to get a morning paper and also drop by the inn. This left Teresa to make some necessary phone calls that would start her arrangements for the up-coming wedding. Since she now had this to arrange, she was overjoyed that Tissy was putting together the program for graduation and homecoming.

Laying the phone book aside, she decided that before making the phone calls she would do something else that had been on her mind lately and headed at once to the attic. She was glad Papa had gone down to town. She went up to the second floor and down the hallway to the door at the end where the stairs led on up to the attic. It was very dark and spooky up there, she thought, as she flicked on the light for the stairs. Ascending them, Teresa thought about the many times she went screaming down these very stairs with Charles hot on her heels, a sheet over his head and emitting ghostly sounds. As a child, she often had nightmares of something terrible lurking in the darkness of the attic. She would open the door at the top and Satan would be standing there, horrible, grotesque, with arms up over his head just waiting until she took the last step into the room where he would grab her. Then she would awaken and sit up in bed calling, "Papa! Papa!"

Teresa thought about this old dream now as she went up the stairs to the attic and even now felt shaky about going there.

There was another door at the top of the stairs, which she now opened and shined her flashlight around. Seeing no monsters, she came on in and flashed the light around looking at different items that had been stored there for years. The attic was stacked full of lovely old things. There were trunks holding old dresses that had been proudly worn by Cynthia Russell and reverently stored away after her death by her husband, Alyn. Someone had suggested that he give them to charity but he could not bring himself to do that.

Looking around, Teresa saw in a corner the old baby carriage that had held both the Russell brothers, now sitting where it was placed after Charles outgrew it, never being used for Teresa. Her mother died before knowing the joy of pushing it around town proudly showing off her darling little baby girl, and her daughter had no memory of her mother to rekindle scenes of years gone by.

She pulled the chain that turned on a dim light from a single bulb, which hung down from the rafters, and caused her hair to sparkle as though she had a halo. Her eyes fell on a trunk . . . the reason she had come up here this morning. "Thank heavens it isn't locked," she thought for there were no keys, and if she had had to go down to borrow Raymond's key, then Papa would know she had been prowling around up there. Bent over the old trunk, she reverently flipped the latches and slowly lifted its lid, while the slow rain made pattering sounds on the roof matching tears that now slid down her cheeks. She wiped them away with a shoulder and reached in to lift a lacy garment, holding it up under the dim light. A soft radiance on her face replaced the tears. She stood, longingly holding the garment to her body, brushing the folds from years of non-use. "This looks my size," she whispered. "I wonder . . . would Papa object if I . . ." Her words died away, replaced by a faint smile as she closed the lid, stood with the lacy off-white wedding dress across an arm, holding it up in front of her. "Yes, it will fit . . . but, the train . . ." She stooped back in front of the trunk rummaging through and found the net train with pearls across a crown for a headband. "Beautiful! Simply beautiful." Papa had caught her with the dress on when she was only ten years old and he went into a rage, peeling it off over her head. She had stood there in tears, with lips trembling, as he scolded the little girl and shook a finger in her face.

Again, she closed the lid and left the attic, the wedding dress and train draped over her arm.

Chapter Forty-Seven

ALYN WAS TIRED OF REHASHING THE ORDEAL HE AND Raymond had just been through, and knowing if he went in the Skillet, someone else he had not talked with would confront him to again go through the whole thing. So, he decided to go by the seed and feed mill to talk with the fellows with whom he had already relived the happenings. And then he'd go by the inn to check on the last day's progress there.

The columns on the veranda had been stripped and repainted since he had visited. He paused to glance around and saw Raymond coming from around the rear of the house. "Hey, Ray. Looks like you are back in the old grind again." He threw up a hand when Raymond noticed him standing there. Raymond came up the steps saying that he was glad to be back in the groove and now appreciated working much more. "Come on in, buddy-boy."

"I was just hanging out this morning," Alyn answered, "and thought I'd come by and take a look." He had been one time since their return to have a look at the treasure inside the trunks. The work there had come to the point where the house should be locked up and as a further precaution. Raymond attached a lock on the inside basement door, but he took the Lincoln letter home with him and hid it in a safe place until after the weekend; then he would place it in a bank safe deposit box. "I'm going to display it in a glassed-in counter at the inn for everyone to see," he proudly said. "To show my appreciation for the key, I'm going to write a letter to Leon and invite him and his wife to come up for our grand opening."

"That would be nice and they might like a nice trip to the mountains, that is . . . if he thinks he won't be losing too much business," Alyn grinned.

Raymond put an arm around Alyn's shoulders and said he didn't think he would miss being with him so much lately but he did miss the comradeship.

Alyn puttered through the house as though he had never been in it before, with Raymond right behind him, explaining what had been done and things yet to be done. Alyn shook his head in amazement, saying that he would never have dreamed this old place could be made to look like it now does and even before it was completed. He had thought for years that it should be torn down, and now it looked like new. Old Miss Ella Fullman would be proud as peas!

"Ray, let me ask you a question, ole buddy." They had completed the tour including the basement. Ray told him to shoot. "Are you going to have a few rooms with a bath that a fellow could rent?"

"I know I'm going to have one for myself. Who is it you are asking for?" he questioned.

"Oh, don't mention it to the kids. I was just thinking that I'd get out of their way and have a little place of my own somewhere."

"I guess that makes two of us then. That's what I had in mind also."

"You know, I have plenty of land where I could build myself a small place, but then there would be the upkeep, cleaning, and so on. I've just gotten to the point where I figure what's the use?" He shrugged his shoulders and his buddy agreed completely. "Well, you will have the inn to take care of. I'm just tired of farming and, too, I wouldn't want the kids moving away somewhere so I just thought I'd sorta give 'em some space, don't cha know?"

Raymond understood completely and commented that he was going to put his Atlanta house on the market in a few days. He said he had already called his agent friend down there and made an appointment to see him about doing this. "To answer your question, Al, we may have two or three little apartments fixed up, and I could keep you in mind for the first resident. I think you would make a grand greeter and historian for our guests."

"I'll give it some more thought," Alyn said as they went through the front door and onto the veranda.

"Oh, by the way, Nat says that Beth has invited us all up to their house for dinner tomorrow night. Sounds like a winner for me."

"And it will be a winner because she is a great cook."

The next evening after the good meal was finished and the women had gathered in the kitchen to clean up, John was showing Nat and Raymond around, and Alyn went to sit out on the porch with Miss Lilly. She was sitting on the glider and he kept a rocking chair going. They had been talking for a good while about various subjects, with questions being tossed at the lady to keep her talking. It seemed to Alyn that she enjoyed talking about herself and this latest craze she was in, which all seemed rather silly to him, but if that's what she liked, then he'd listen—everyone to their own desires. They had been discussing their lives from way back, which most older people are prone to do, and Alyn asked her if she ever got lonesome down there in Mobile, "Or was it Montgomery? Wherever it is," he thought.

"I've had a good life, Alyn," she said softly as if she saw it passing by in her mind's eye. "I don't regret anything. But, you know, now days it grows weary living alone. I try to keep busy with volunteer work along with the modeling job, which isn't full time."

"I thought you had a sister living with you, or wasn't it two sisters?"

"No. They don't live with me any more. One went to live with her daughter in Tallahassee and the other is now in a nursing home. She has Alzheimer's. It's so sad, but I just couldn't watch her as closely as she needed for twenty-four hours a day." She sighed deeply. Alyn looked at her keenly then turned his gaze out across the yard that was now lighted by the newly risen moon. A spring breeze whispered through the pines, sending chills down Lillian's spine and she pulled her sweater together.

"Would you like to go inside?" he asked her, leaning forward so that the strands of white in his brown hair caught the light and gleamed like silver. They had been sitting out there for a good while.

"No. I'm fine, thank you. It's very pleasant out here." Her voice was rich and deep, not high and shrill as most older women's voices usually become. "What do you think of our children, Alyn?"

"I think their marriage was meant to be. I'm as sure of it as knowing that the sun will rise each morning."

"The only thing is that it should have taken place years ago. I remember when they were in school here on the mountain and dating. They seemed like a perfect match, and I could not think of her marrying anyone but John. But, please don't get me wrong, I liked Charles, but . . ."

Alyn interrupted by saying somberly, "War changes a lot of things," and Lillian understood what he implied. He changed the subject by saying, "Well, I can say one thing, Lilly, you are a very attractive lady, and I commend you for keeping yourself so active. It agrees with you."

She accepted his kind words with gratitude and was annoyed with herself for having spoken of her sadness about her sister. After all, if she was to be a successful model, her face must radiate happiness and vivaciousness. She would need to conceal her personal feelings. She patted a strand of hair in place and was about to change the subject when Raymond and Tissy appeared.

"So, here you are. I was wondering where you two got off to," Tissy smiled and sat down in the glider next to Lillian. Raymond went down the steps to toss softball with Al, who was tossing it up in the air and catching it himself after Pete dropped the glove on the ground saying, "I quit." He missed too many throws and had to chase after the ball and now ran off with the little terrier at his heels. Around the house he heard Susan calling from the tree house, where Al had just that day installed a drop cord and a light bulb.

With the dining table all cleared and dishes washed, Beth called everyone to come in as the cool night air would get her mother to coughing again. Raymond pitched the ball to Al, saying that he'd go in with the rest of the old folks. They all went in to the living room where Teresa, Nat, and Penny were looking at a family picture album. John just hung up the phone from a hospital call and joined the group. Susan and Pete came down from the tree house and decided to go up in Al's room to watch a program with him as he had come in from the back and told them to come on inside. "If you two come in my room, I will not have any arguing from either of you and you'll have to be quiet," he bossed, leading the way upstairs.

The jovial banter with a lot of joking made Raymond feel that he had been completely accepted into this family. Lilly greatly amused him with her exaggerated, put-on airs. He liked the woman but could see right through her. She was trying extremely hard to pass for a woman twenty years younger than herself and doing a good job of it—more power to her! He wondered if she was still on the cough medicine Alyn had laughed to him about. No, surely John had warned her about that.

Snap shots were now being passed around with comments and laughing about how each other looked in years gone by. Lilly commented on the silly looking fashion and hairstyles of the fifties. Then a page was turned that showed the children's darling baby pictures that were admired by all until someone commented that the family had no little ones to cuddle now. Teresa felt her face go red, wondering if the comments were meant for her . . . that she would be next.

Beth and John had been standing, passing the photos from one to another when Beth casually said, "Oh don't give up, folks. I'd say in about seven months you will have another little one to cuddle and coo over." She looked up at John with a huge smile on her face and actually had not intended on telling anyone before he found out. His face, completely blank, held the surprise for a few moments and then grabbed his wife with a huge hug and kiss with their audience cheering and clapping . . . except for Penny. She stood up from the couch with the album sliding from her lap to the floor, and the color in her face drained and mouth open in unbelief. Gasping, she said,

"Mother! How could you? How terribly embarrassing, after all, I am nearly eighteen." Then the tears came as Penny turned, dashing upstairs to her room.

Beth felt crushed. "Oh, Beth," Tissy said, "She will be all right. Don't go after her." She caught her arm as Beth started to go. "Wait a little while until it sinks in. When it does, she'll soon be a proud, doting older sister. You'll see."

"Tissy's right, Sweetheart. We'll go up and talk with her later," John said. He kissed her on the forehead and told her how proud he was. In fact, he was more than proud, for this is what he had hoped for. The guests made their happy comments and began leaving, knowing Beth and John would prefer to be alone. Alyn, the last one out, whispered in John's ear, "Way to go, son!" and punched him on the shoulder.

Early the next morning, Alyn phoned John asking if he could leave a few minutes earlier than usual and stop by Knollwood for a few minutes. John knew that his father must have something on his mind and replied that he would be glad to stop by. Many times he did this but since Papa had called, he must have something he wanted to discuss and of course he would be down there shortly.

Teresa had left for school and Alyn was sitting at the kitchen table enjoying his second cup of coffee when he heard Ole Charlie and the hens fussing noisily and scattering with outstretched wings as John walked past and up the steps. "Come on in, son. The door's open," Alyn called out as he folded the newspaper and laid it aside. John wiped his feet on a mat, then entered, letting the screen door slam closed. "The hinges are gonna come off that door one of these day," Alyn mumbled, setting the coffee mug down. John, as well as his brother and sister, had heard that statement many times even though the hinges had never come off, and John answered that the spring was too tight. "All you hafta do is hold it." His dad got in the last word about the screen door. He pointed to the chair across from him. "Sit down a minute, son, if you aren't in a big rush." He took the last of his coffee and stood to pour the mug half full. "How 'bout you? Will you have some?" John pulled the chair out and sat down saying he had just finished his breakfast and declined more coffee, finishing his statement by asking, "What's up?"

"I had a visitor yesterday . . . said he'd already talked with you and . . ."

"Then it must have been Ryan," John interrupted and his father answered by simply nodding. "I figured he wouldn't mention the situation to anyone else until after his graduation," John said, surprised that Ryan had confided such information with someone else other than himself.

"Well, he actually came to discuss another matter, but then he also told me about the prevailing problem. The poor kid has a lot on his shoulders." Alyn was immediately on the defensive for Ryan. "He's wise to be so young. In fact, he seems much wiser than some grown men I've known." There was a short pause, then he went on. "You gave him the same counsel that I did, but this is what I feel one of us should do. It doesn't seem exactly right to keep his whereabouts from Doc and Kate, as well as Matt, but from all he told me about his parents, I'd leave that up to Doc." He waited a few seconds to read the reaction on John's face, then continued before John could reply. "It would be a shame for Doc and Kate to miss the reunion because of Ryan's disappearance when they could be assured of seeing him here. And wouldn't they be shocked to know that the guy is going to graduate? You know they wouldn't miss that for the world, unless they are not able to travel."

John nodded in complete agreement with his father. "Yes, Papa. You call them, but, well, what do you think about this?" Alyn leaned forward eager to have a suggestion from John, his arms resting on the table. John always knew the right thing to do when it came to decision-making. For instance, he purchased Doc and Kate's house, and then when the two little ones were lost on the mountain he took complete charge and had been the one who found little Peter. Susan had managed to find her way from the Thompson farm to her grandfather's house in the dark. And, by all means, his decision to marry Beth was the best thing that could happen to him and to Beth.

"Papa, tell Doc to have Matt go over to the location where Ryan said he tossed the bag of money in the grass and comb the area for it. If they do find it, then that will clear Ryan of the charges."

"By jingo, son, why didn't I think of this? But I want Ryan to be completely surprised to see Doc and Kate here at the homecoming. Let's not mention to him about my talking with them."

"Certainly not." John rose saying he had to get on down to the office. After he stood, fumbling with his car keys that he had laid on the table, he said as an afterthought, "What was the other matter you said the boy wanted to see you about?"

Alyn got up also, to walk to the door with him. "It's a puzzle to me. It's something about the cave, and I promised him I'd go up there with him tomorrow morning. Reckon you could go with us?"

"Sure, but I'll have to tell the family I have something to do and let them think I'm talking about something at the office, in order to not have some tag-alongs."

His father grinned as they walked toward the door, one hand on his son's shoulder. "Say, I'm thrilled that we may get a 'John Jr.'"

"You mean a 'John the Third,'" he corrected

Alyn held the door open when John stepped out on the porch. "How is it you were taken by surprise?" He was wondering why Beth had not told him ahead of announcing it to everyone at the dinner.

"Oh, she went to my new partner while I was making hospital calls yesterday, and I got home just a few minutes ahead of everyone arriving."

"Sneaky, huh?"

"Yeah, you could say that. I'll see you in the morning around ten o'clock." He threw up a hand and went down the steps.

Chapter Forty-Eight

AL WAS RIDING HIS BICYCLE DOWN THE ROAD ON Saturday morning; "just messin' around" is what he called it when he had nothing specific to do and was only killing time. He turned in at Knollwood to see what Papa Russell was doing this morning. Maybe they could hang around, he was thinking, noting that his aunt's car was gone. He propped the bicycle against the tree that held the swing and started toward the back steps with Ole Charlie and the hens scattering and Tad's flock of guineas fleeing, portracking as they went. Al bounced up the stairs two at a time, opened the door calling for Papa, and entered, leaving the screen door to bounce on it's hinges. When Alyn first heard the heavy footsteps on the porch, he thought it must be Ryan and got up from his chair in the living room and met his grandson in the hallway. "Oh, Al, it's you," he said with a blank face.

"Yeah, like . . . were you expecting Marilyn Monroe?" the boy said sarcastically.

"Don't get smart, boy. You're out early on a Saturday morning. I thought all guys liked to sleep in when there was no school."

"Ah, I guess it's just that I am used to getting up early and then when there is no school, well, I still wake up early. What's going on with you this morning, Papa? And, I see Resa has already left out."

"She and Tissy had a committee meeting at school about graduation, or homecoming, or something, you know."

"Yeah, I know. They're always busy. I don't see how she will have time to get married."

"I assure you, she will make time for that." Wondering if John had forgotten that he would join Ryan and himself to go up to the cave, Alyn casually asked, "What's John doing this morning?"

"Don't know. I heard his razor going when I passed by the bathroom. S'pose he's going over to the hospital or something."

Alyn looked at his watch. It was ten minutes before ten and just then he heard a knock at the front door. Al asked who in the world would be knocking on the front door and his grandfather knew it would be Ryan. "How about you going to the door, Al," he said as an order instead of a question, and while Al was gone, John's car turned in the driveway. Alyn heard the gravel crunching. Al came back in followed by Ryan and Jethro, the dog. The brown mutt immediately became friends with Papa Russell, standing with his paws up against him and tongue hanging out, looking for a head scratching.

Al was instructed to phone his mother and tell her that he was going somewhere with Papa. After he hung up, he asked where they were going and he pieced the puzzle together, saying that he also knew the secret of the cave. John had come back in and heard what was said. Both men looked at one another, showing amazement that the boy had kept the secret. Al had been faithful in keeping Ryan's secret to himself, and now the four mountain climbers set off.

Papa Russell said there was nothing about the cave that he didn't already know, as he and his old friend, Luther, and his dog, Beans, had been in there many times. His Aunt Joyce would have cringed if she had known they once even became lost in there and it was the heroic dog that had sniffed their way out. And she would have cringed if she had known about their trips to the top of the waterfall, too.

"Then you may know about this, also," Ryan told him, "and it may not be what I think it is." Alyn figured he had discovered the graves of the Indian family, but Ryan was determined to keep it a secret until they got there.

On this trip up to the cave, Alyn found himself being the tag-along, insisting that everyone should slow down; after all, they weren't being chased by a bear. John suggested that he needed more exercise than only picking up the newspaper. "When is it you are going up there with the school kids, Papa?"

"Supposed to be next Saturday, but after this climb I may not be able. Hope I have plenty of liniment in my medicine cabinet." Alyn told them that he knew this climb never used to be so steep. As a kid, he bounced up here like a mountain goat. "Of course there aren't any of those around here, but I've heard they can climb like a monkey and I do believe Jethro seems to be part goat." John said the dog knew where he was going because he had stayed in the cave with Ryan before they moved down to the school.

The two boys were way ahead and John would have been right behind them, except he felt he would go along at his dad's pace. "Whew! Whatever Ryan wants us to see had certainly better be worth all this," Alyn said to John's back and without stopping, John replied that this would be good practice for him for the school group's trip.

Ryan and Al were carrying the flashlights and had already reached the cave's entrance, sitting there waiting before the men arrived. The dog went happily to greet them, demanding to be petted. The boys handed over a flashlight to each and they went inside. Upon entering, Alyn immediately asked Ryan if Al had told him about the time when Alyn had found a satchel full of money right up there on that ledge. He pointed to where it had been found.

"Gollee! No, he didn't! When was that?" The boy's eyes grew wide.

"Oh, it was a long time ago when I was a kid. It turned out that some men had stolen it and hid it there. It was returned to the rightful owner and I got a reward. There was a friend with me so we both got a reward."

"Man alive!" Ryan exclaimed and then immediately thought about the bag of money he had tossed in the weeds. If he were to return it, he wondered if he would get a reward . . . or a jail term. But he said nothing about that.

"Okay, guys, where are you going to lead us now. Let's get on with it," John said. He'd heard his dad's tale many times before. Ryan led the way, or rather, Jethro led the way as he ran ahead and then came back, repeating the run over and over.

The group rounded several bends and then Ryan stopped, pointing the light toward the left where a small break was in the wall. "You have to turn sideways to go through this way. Did you ever go between here, Mr. Russell?"

"No. I have to admit that I never noticed this little squeeze-way. Do you mean we are going through there?" He held his light up to see how high it was to the ceiling in this area. Stalactites were hanging down from the ceiling about twenty feet up, he judged. Ryan turned sideways and easily went through the opening. No one in the group was overweight, so they all could do the same. "Have you been in here, Al?" his grandfather asked, and the amazed boy answered that he had not.

"And you are never to come up here alone, young man," John demanded as Al slid through the opening after Ryan. John saw that Papa could make the squeeze and then he followed.

"Is this what you wanted to show us, Ryan?" Alyn asked.

"No, sir. It's just around this bend, and I may have put you to a lot of trouble for nothing but I thought you'd like to see for yourself."

The group followed their leader as though he was a tour guide, waiting to see what it was Ryan was talking about. As they rounded the bend, Ryan told them all to flash their lights up along the left wall. They were quickly obedient and all gave out "oh's" when shining against the light were streaks of gold shone all along the wall. "Boy! Doesn't that about put your eyes out?" Ryan said. "Do you think it is gold, Mr. Russell?"

Alyn was speechless for a few minutes while he walked over and rubbed a hand over the substance. "What do you make of it, John?"

"I've never been in a gold mine, Papa. The only gold I've ever seen is the ring on my finger, but it certainly does look real."

"Ryan, I believe you really did have a secret." They each stood there in silence with their own private thoughts, wondering if this was a rich find, then Alyn turned to Ryan asking, "Were you ever a Boy Scout?"

"Yes, sir. I sure was. While I was in the sixth and seventh grades."

"You had to give a Boy Scout oath, didn't you?"

"Well, sure. We all had to. Why do you ask that?"

"I want you and Al, too, to take an oath to me that you will not tell a single soul about this. Scout's honor?"

"Yes, sir. Scout's honor," Ryan answered and Al agreed, but he asked why he did not want anyone to know about the gold.

"Because we aren't going into the gold mining business, and I don't want a lot of folks traipsing up here with their picks and digging in this cave. Understand?"

"Mr. Russell, I really didn't mean to be prying," Ryan said, and Alyn quickly told him that he was not prying and he was happy that he told him about this. He had lived here all his life and did not know this secret, "But let's just keep it a secret, okay?" He put an arm around Ryan's shoulder to reassure the boy that he had done nothing wrong in showing him. And turning to his grandson, he cautioned him about the seriousness of keeping the secret and never was he to bring his younger brother up here. "You remember that could have been a tragedy when he and Susan were lost, don't you?" Al agreed and held up his fingers in a scout's honor sign.

On the way back down the mountain, Alyn asked if Al had told Ryan about Chief Little Bear and to his surprise, he had not, other than his grandfather saying that an old Indian lived in the cave, but that was all he had said. So this was the subject for the rest of the way down.

That same afternoon, Alyn phoned Doc and Kate in Pennsylvania as he told John he would do. After breaking the shocking news to the old couple about their great-grandson, he asked Doc to have Matt phone him, since he felt the charges against Ryan would be dropped if the money bag was found and, too, he could direct Matt to where it should be. And he also asked Doc to keep quiet until after graduation if the bag was not found. Doc understood and completely agreed. He was so happy that Ryan was pursuing his education and still had the ambition to be a veterinarian. "He always had a compassion for animals and a talent for doctoring their ailments."

Kate, listening in on an extension, had been interjecting her comments. "Oh, Alyn, I'm so happy to know Ryan is safe and sound but at the same time, I feel hurt over what he had to go through, and not because of anything of his doing . . . just standing there all alone and wondering what he was going to do. I've about cried my eyes out, but outweighing my feelings of hurting for him, I feel happy and overjoyed . . ."

Alyn broke in. "Be thankful, Kate. He did what he thought was best at the time for himself and everyone concerned."

"I realize that, but all this time we could have rejoiced in knowing he was there and safe."

"I assure you both, Kate, if I had known who he was, I would have called you and Doc at once. You know that, don't you?"

"Yes, of course you would have," she answered simply and with a sigh. "We'll be there with bells on, little brother. You can bet on that. Frankly, I can't wait."

Alyn asked if Doc was still on the other line and when he spoke up, saying he was all ears, they received another shock with the news of Teresa's wedding, and on the same weekend as graduation and homecoming. He told them about Nat, their local dentist and the two of them seemed very well matched. Kate brightened, exclaiming that it would all be so wonderful. "I can't wait to meet the groom! He sounds just lovely."

Neither Doc nor Kate had mentioned the kidnapping, evidently not having been on the news up north, but Alyn decided he would save that tale until they arrived. "I'm sure Matt and Rebecca will accompany us on the plane, and frankly, Doc may have to sedate me even before we board," Kate laughed.

"Ah, you'll be here before you have time to notice you are afraid," Alyn told her. "Just pretend you are a big bird floating on the currents."

"Oh, Alyn, you make it sound so nice. I'll do my best to relax and enjoy it."

"Before I hang up, I want you both to know that you are expected to stay here at Knollwood with me, and also Matt and his wife. Teresa and Nat will be leaving on their honeymoon after the wedding, so you can have her room, and Matt and his wife can use an upstairs bedroom."

"Wonderful," Doc said. "You know, after all my years there on the mountain, I never spent a night at Knollwood, that is, except for the night I spent in a chair beside your bed after I found you knocked out on the trail. You do remember that, don't you?"

"How could I ever forget that! Well, your old house is full with John's family, plus his mother-in-law, but I certainly have room here at Knollwood, so let us know your flight arrangements and some of us will meet you at the plane in Atlanta."

"Great. Then it's all settled; I can't wait to get in touch with Matt and Rebecca and tell them the wonderful news about our little boy."

"He isn't so little any more, and frankly, he is years ahead of his age. We've all come to love him, so don't go planning on trying to take him away."

Doc spoke up saying, "Ryan probably wouldn't leave if we asked him to come back home . . . and, oh, before we hang up, Alyn, I'll tell you that his parents have taken off to Arizona to live in a commune." Alyn told them he would not let on to Ryan that he had talked with them, and if they wanted to tell him about his parents, then it was up to them.

Chapter Forty-Nine

ANOTHER SCHOOL YEAR WAS WINDING DOWN. IT would be joyful for some, sad for others who would be leaving to be scattered to the four winds, some never to see their friends again. The younger children were anxious to be free and fly like birds on the wings of summer and play in fields and paddle in streams with no cares to mar their summer months. The graduates were wondering, "Is this all there is?" And some, like Penny Russell, were wondering, "Where do I go from here?" What a blank feeling it was, and always would be, to leave school and all the years of childhood and be pushed all at once into making adult decisions. Some were now wondering if they could have done better and realized they now had no opportunity to go back.

Penny had been thinking on these things lately. Her mother had the younger children to think of and the coming of the new little one. The sale of her father's business had left funds for their college education and she would take advantage of it now. Yes, she would go to the University of Georgia. That's where Ryan intended on going; Tissy had gotten him some scholarship funds that were made available by different organizations. Being Anson Kelly's great-great-grandson, he was due it if anyone was. So Penny decided she would not be completely alone for Ryan would be there, and being the outgoing person she was, it would not take long for her to make new friends.

At present, everyone was busy with preparations for the graduation and homecoming events. Each year, the festivities were over after graduation but the school board decided there needed to be something more because of Mrs. Patricia Russell's retirement. They also wanted to recognize those who had played a big part in the founding of the school, so a home-coming was decided. This next year would be the first time that there would not be a member of the Russell family on the board of directors of the Kendell Mountain School. Alyn Russell had taken over after the death of his Aunt Joyce Abernathy Kelly and Uncle Anson Kelly, his legal parents by adoption.

Added to the flurry of activities, Teresa was planning her wedding, which she and Nat decided would be a simple affair on Sunday afternoon. She chose her sister-in-law, Beth, to be her matron of honor, Penny was a bride's maid, Susan was the flower girl, Pete was the ring-bearer, John and Al were to be ushers, and Tissy was to sing the beautiful song "Because." Of course, her father, Alyn, would walk her down the aisle, and Raymond would be Nat's best man.

Teresa hired a caterer to prepare refreshments for the reception to be in the church's dining hall and a florist to do bouquets and simple floral arrangements. She did not want anything elaborate. Alyn agreed on it being simple because he said he would not put on one of those monkey suits. The bride and groom decided to go on a cruise to the Bahamas for their honeymoon. "Wait until Lila sees that announcement in the newspaper!" Teresa thought.

Chapter Fifty

ALYN WAS STANDING IN THE PARLOR OF THE KENDELL Mountain Inn, which would be the registration office upon completion, talking with Raymond on Thursday, the day before graduation. "It's looking good, Ray. Every time I come in it's looking nearly ready. It won't be long until you'll be hiring your employees. Have you thought of that?"

"Yep. Sure have. In fact, I've already had some inquiries. You want to hire on as janitor?"

"Ha! That would be the day. You'd fire me on the first day. I can't wait to see that first bus load of folks to come up that drive and park out front. You'd better have some real good cooks, my man, but let me give you a word of advice."

"Yeah? Well, shoot. I need plenty of that."

"Don't go hiring any of those fancy-pants gourmet cooks who stir up all that stuff that folks don't know what they're eating. There're lots of good cooks right here in Union Gap that could cook rings around them. All that good down-home type of stuff you know. That's what folks want when they come to a place like this. Just sit 'em down to long tables and let 'em pass th' food down to their neighbors and keep it coming. Man! That will bring in bus loads!"

"You don't say?" Raymond answered scratching his head and thinking about what his friend had suggested. "I hadn't even thought about the food part of this business."

"Believe me, son, it will be the biggest part of the drawing card. Hey, come on down with me to the Skillet for a while. Speaking of food, isn't it about time for you to knock off for a bite to eat?"

He agreed, saying his stomach was beginning to growl, so together they walked down the hill and across the road to the Skillet where they saw Preacher Jesse Adair sitting in a booth by himself.

"Mack," Alyn said upon entering.

He greeted Alyn courteously, inclined his head and said, "How you doin', Alyn?"

"Can't complain, Mack, can't complain. I see Brother Jesse back there," he nodded, "so we'll just go sit with him."

"Okay, gents . . . how's it going? You fellows all ready for the big wedding?"

"Oh, we may show up," Alyn joked. "How's Thelma?" He didn't see her anywhere.

"Like everybody else, she's all hyped up for homecoming and she's at home cooking for that now. Ya'll go on back."

They walked back to the booth where Brother Jesse sat and slid in the bench across from him. "Hi, Brother Jesse, you all ready to tie 'em all up in knots?" Alyn asked, grinning.

"Got my speech all ready, and it will tie them up for life."

"Ole Ray here hadn't never been a father-in-law before, and he will probably need a special speech for him, too," Alyn teased.

"That's fine. I can fix him up real good, too." He reached across and shook hands with both men. They took up menus and scanned them just to be doing something, for they already knew them by heart. The waitress came over to take their orders, and Alyn said he'd just have his usual; she knew what he meant—a sausage cat head biscuit with coffee. Raymond told her what he wanted and then Mack came and pulled up a chair in front of the table with them.

"Well, Alyn, how did the cave trip with th' kids go?" Mack inquired.

"Cherokee history lesson. In fact, I think even ole Raymond was enlightened." He reached over and gave his friend a punch.

"Yesiree! I had no idea there was anything like that around here, and you know, the thought just came to me that when the inn is finished, you could sell tickets there and take groups up on a tour. Why, you'd make a fortune, man!"

Alyn only answered, "Humm," which sounded like a "Maybe, we'll see."

"Boy! Things are sure changing around here. First thing you know we won't know what town we are in. Have you been up to see th' inn lately, Preacher?" Mack asked.

Brother Jesse wadded up his napkin and put it on his plate. "Well, no. Not lately, I haven't. Things progressing along nicely, Raymond?"

"Yes. Suppose they're going along right well. Come on up when you leave here and I'll give you a grand tour."

"Just may do that, thanks. The wife and I are looking forward to the Sunday meals after church. I assume the restaurant will be open to the public and not only for guests," he said in way of a question.

"Of course, the more the merrier. Alyn and I were just a while ago talking about serving the family-style method. What do you think?"

"Oh, by all means. That's the only way to go. Have you ever eaten at the one down in Dahlonega? It's really good."

"Yes, I have been there several times, and I did enjoy it. We might just do that."

Mack said they thought they were going to close up his business but folks would soon get tired of all that good eating and want a hamburger and fries and all that good greasy food. "When you get that inn in operation we probably won't ever have our nice chats here again. See, we're already missing John and Nat."

"You all heard about our new little one on the way?" Alyn asked. And Mack said "Yeah, several times." Alyn said he was just checking but knew he had told them.

"You guys are going to be at the rehearsal tonight, I assume? But, of course, that was a silly question. We'll expect you by seven. I'm going to go do a couple of errands and then will drop by the inn, that is, if you are planning on going back up there?" he asked Raymond.

"Sure thing, Preacher. I'll be back there shortly." Brother Jesse got up to leave and Mack went with him to the front.

"Looks like our meeting today is rather boring, Ray, so I guess I'll be going. The women have got things all bustling around the house and John has asked me to go with him to get Doc and Kate at the airport. He said he'd meet me at his office at ten-thirty so I'd better be off."

Chapter Fifty-One

ON FRIDAY AFTERNOON, TERESA GLADLY MOVED THE things she would be needing until the wedding to an upstairs bedroom in order to give her room up for Doc and Kate's use. At their age, they would not be asked to attempt the stairs. There was another bedroom and a den that could be used for Matt and Rebecca. Beulah Mae was happy to help with the house cleaning and do some cooking. She went about her work joyfully, knowing she would be well paid, and by the time the guests arrived, the house was spotless, flowers were on the table, and wonderful aromas came from the kitchen.

Teresa thought about how tired the old couple would be after arriving at three o'clock and being hustled to north Georgia in time for the graduation at seven-thirty that night. They would scarcely be able to catch their breath after freshening up and having some supper. They would have a lot of fast talking to do over the meal. Teresa was nervous just thinking of it. She had asked Nat to come up for supper and meet their life-long friends whom they had not seen for years.

It was now time for her to get dressed and ready before Nat came in. She opened her closet and took down the first dress that caught her attention, a feminine soft pink dress with a flowing skirt. Each time she wore it she felt eighteen. "It suits you," Papa had told her the last time she wore it. "Makes you look like my little girl again." Today she felt like his little girl, and she had only two more days to feel this way. She slipped the dress over her head, twisting and turning before the mirror and figured she had put on a pound or two since last wearing this outfit, but it would have to do. Evidently she and Nat had dined out a little too much lately. She gave her hair a few strokes with the brush, patted it in place, and looked at her watch. "Goodness! It is five o'clock and I need to be at school by six-thirty."

About that time she heard Nat calling as he opened the back door and entered. She went to meet him in the hallway, saying that she had hoped John and Papa would be back by now with their guests. She held her hands out to him. "Ah, look at you, my beautiful bride!" He held her at arms length admiring the dress and telling her how gorgeous she looked, and they embraced in a long kiss. "I can never get enough of holding you in my arms." She smiled, gave him another peck on the lips, and removed his arms saying, "Well, right now, you can help me set the table." They went to the dining room where she took out china and silverware from the buffet. "Oh, Nat, would you please reach up high in the cabinet over the kitchen sink and get some coffee cups, the nice ones, not our usual mugs."

Teresa had placed bowls of food in the oven warmer and some pans on the stove with lids and the burners turned on low. The coffee had perked and the warming light was on. Everything was ready, and at five-thirty they heard John's car turn into the driveway.

Papa led the way, opening the door and calling out, "Teresa, look who we have here," as they came through the door. She heard them talking and someone exclaiming about the wonderful aroma of food and coffee, and she went to fall into the arms of her friends, who were more like family. To her surprise, not only were Matt and Rebecca with them but also Matt's twin brother, Dan. As they entered, each gave a great big bear hug, all exclaiming about the beautiful bride-to-be, and they met the groom standing behind her.

"Come on in, folks, it is so good to see you all again after so many years. Please come in and make yourselves at home," Teresa said with her arm still around Kate. She spoke to Rebecca and Matt, followed by Dan, she assumed, since the other one had his hands on Rebecca's shoulders, and she thought that one must be Matt. "I can't understand how you still look so young,

Kate. My . . . you haven't aged a bit since the last time I saw you!" And she meant it for Kate was still tall and erect, not thin, but not fat either. "You're just the right hugging size." She turned loose of Kate and put an arm around Doc, saying, "And you are still the handsome fellow who brought me into this world."

"Honey, you were squalling so loud you couldn't have cared whether the one who delivered you was ugly as sin or the handsome devil I was." He laughed, as did everyone else. Then Nat was introduced while they walked toward Teresa's room. John placed their luggage down and left while Teresa showed them the bathroom and told them to feel at home. They could freshen up while she put dinner on the table and was sorry to hurry them, tired as they must be, but they would be pushed to get down to the school. Then John went to show the others to their rooms upstairs.

While everyone was in the rooms they were shown, Alyn took his son aside and asked him to go and do something and hurry right back. He agreed, thinking it was a great idea. Then Alyn phoned Beth, informing her that John would be home shortly and they would all meet up again at school.

They were sitting at the dinner table eating and renewing old friendships when they heard the car returning. "I hear some more company coming in," Doc said. "There always was something going on around here." Teresa answered that it was probably John's crew dropping by on their way to school and saying they could let themselves in, so she did not get up. The dining room door opened and it was John again, followed by none other than the long-lost grandson and great-grandson, Ryan Ratcliffe. Ryan had not been told who was there and why he was brought up to Knollwood right before the graduates would be given their last minute instructions. He was still worried with the thought that at this very last few minutes, something may have happened to prevent his graduating. He felt shaky inside.

They entered the back door and he immediately heard voices and then laughter coming from the dining room. John walked beside Ryan down the hall, with an arm around the boy's shoulder. "Don't look so worried, Ryan. It's just a big surprise that we knew you would love." Ryan did not smile until he walked into the room and there was his family, all jumping to their feet when they saw him and each trying to hug him at one time. Ryan had tears of joy that made him feel like a child again.

Before the graduation service began, Principal Patricia Russell asked Ryan to come to her office for a few minutes. With his heart in his mouth from fear that he might be told there would be no graduation for him, he followed her, thinking it was all over for him and he would end up doing menial jobs for the rest of his life. She flicked on the light in her office, then went behind her desk to retrieve some papers from a drawer. They would not have time to sit, so he stood facing her on the other side, his legs feeling like they were made of rubber. She looked into his eyes as though she could read his future there, and for a brief moment, Ryan just knew his heart would beat out of his chest.

Pausing, Mrs. Russell chose her words carefully and smiling secretly to herself said with the utmost sincerity, "Ryan, I want you to know how proud you have made me. I took a chance on placing my faith in you to do what I hoped you would do. From the first time I laid eyes on you I felt that you were a person with great potential and good character that only needed to be honed. I knew that with a little help, you would be set for a good life." Then she went around the desk with the paper she had taken from the drawer and handed it to him with one hand, resting the other on his shoulder. "This will see you through college, Ryan. Make me proud again. It's a full scholarship to the University of Georgia."

He accepted the paper she handed him with tears streaming down his face unabashedly. Since he had the graduation gown already on, there were no pockets to retrieve a handkerchief so Mrs. Russell handed him a tissue from the box on her desk.

"Mrs. Russell, I . . ."

She placed fingers over his lips. "No time for words. Graduation has got to go on, you know, and everyone is all lined up. I asked them to halt the march until we returned. You can thank me by getting good grades and sending me an occasional letter . . . oh, and I suppose I will take that scholarship paper back until after the ceremony as we will be handing out the scholarships to the students who earned them. I just wanted to tell you about it in advance. You'll get it back shortly," she assured him with her arm again around his shoulder as two happy people returned to the group waiting to go through the auditorium doors for the last time as students and as principal.

Graduation, an exciting time for everyone, was carried out without a flaw. Dr. David Harris and Kate could not have been prouder, as well as Ryan's grandparents, Matt and Rebecca. After it was over, Penny put her arms around her mother, and with tears of happiness but also of remorse, apologized for being such a brat. "I'm really happy for you and Pop, Mother." Penny had grown up. Beth kissed her beautiful daughter, telling her that she was her first baby, and she would always be her little girl.

All the family was invited up to Knollwood for refreshments and to enjoy being with their visitors. There would be a lot of rehashing old memories, fond memories that never die. And, of course, there would be gifts for the graduates, but the best gift Ryan would receive was the knowledge that Grandpa Matt had recovered the moneybag that was now in the hands of the police. A relief of mind is the best gift anyone could receive, especially Ryan, who now felt like a new person . . . a man.

The next day dawned bright and sunny for homecoming, a brilliant morning for such a momentous occasion. The occasion would begin with the meal in the cafeteria at one o'clock. Local residents were bringing additional plates of food, supplementing the school's meat and drinks. Before the noon hour, tables were laden with bowls of steaming food and cakes and pies that had been delegated by the food committee. Each participant brought her special recipe that had been secretly guarded over the years.

Teresa, Tissy, and the other teachers had been there all morning making ready for their guests who would visit the classrooms after the lunch hour before the afternoon program at two o'clock. Most of the Bible college students had already left to be scattered to the four winds, most living too far away for parents to attend.

Alyn Russell came in at twelve-thirty with his guests, seating Doc and Kate, their sons and daughter-in-law where they could survey the early arrivals and would, no doubt, soon be surrounded by older residents, eager to shake their hands and discuss old times.

Kate, a neat and good humored lady with beautiful white hair, sat with reticent eyes, viewing those who entered and enjoying the pleasant blur of happy voices. Mainly, she was looking for Ryan's entrance. From the first time they sat down, someone was waiting in line to speak with Doctor Harris and Kate. He commented to someone that it was a tonic for the spirit to be here today. Kate kept reverting her eyes toward the door until she spied the boy, who was all smiles and coming straight to his family when he noticed where they were sitting. They hugged as if they had not seen one another at all last night. Matt stood and playfully roughed Ryan's head with his hand and commented about his becoming a man now, a graduate, and out on his own. Last night after the graduation ceremony, Ryan held out his scholarship paper to show them. They were all so proud! Doctor Harris had then presented him with his gold pocket watch, which had been his treasure for seventy years. A farm couple there in the area gave the watch to the good doctor for payment when he delivered their child, and he tried for years after that to give it back. They would not hear of it, saying it was found on the barn dirt floor after they bought the property and said they had no use for the watch. The farmer said he started working at sunup and quit at sundown and the sun was all the timepiece he needed.

While standing there talking, Ryan noticed Mr. and Mrs. Tyner coming in, threw up his hand to them, and immediately made his way to meet them. The couple told him they were sorry they could not make it in time for his graduation last night, but in the hug and handshake he was handed an envelope containing a nice check and they were led over to meet his family. After learning who they were and how they had helped Ryan, they were invited to come up to Knollwood after the day's activities were over. The Tyners were seated and immediately blended in with the group.

While they were all enjoying their food, Ryan said to Alyn, who was sitting across from him, "Mr. Russell, I think maybe I could safely call you 'Uncle Alyn.'" Of course, Alyn looked at him blankly, waiting for an explanation. "I understand you and my great-grandmother Kate are legally brother and sister, so that also makes me your great nephew, I believe."

Everyone was quiet for a few seconds to figure this out in their heads and then laughed and agreed with Ryan. So, "Uncle Alyn" it was and would be from there on.

The meal was a fantastic time of reminiscing. Matt, Dan, and Rebecca became the brunt of jokes when someone came up to them talking about the time Becky Stephens had nearly drowned in the creek on a school picnic, and the twins had saved her. She could never determine which one had pumped the water out of her and thought she loved them both. At that time she was a little redheaded girl with freckles, horn-rimmed glasses, and buckteeth, and neither twin would claim the fame of being her lifesaver. Now, Becky had no horn-rimmed glasses, her teeth were straight, and she was an attractive lady with streaks of gray through her red hair. The incident made joyful conversation. Dan admitted that he had never found the right woman for himself. Still, no one could tell the twins apart, except for a few who knew about the small brown mole on Dan's ear. One lady who came over to talk told them that she remembered them as boys who were always in a scrap, with skinned knees, and at least one of them had a black eye—they surely must have kept their doctor father busy. She said their faces today were still just alike and all the time she was talking, Dan was thinking she had the fade of an old reliable mule.

John told Doc that sometime today or tomorrow he wanted the couple to come up and see the old house where they used to live, and how they had added on to it. About the time he said this, he called attention to Beth, the children, and her mother walking in the door. He said he would pull another table up at the end for them.

The afternoon program was being emceed by Patricia Russell, assisted by Teresa Russell, with some words to be given later on by the president of the board of directors, banker Nolan Roberts. With an auditorium filled to capacity, the program began with a presentation by the glee club, after the invocation by Chaplain Alfred McGee.

After the Glee Club's two songs, announcements were made by Patricia Russell, and she gave her personal congratulations to the graduates. Then she made recognition of the first board members of the school after it was constructed in 1913. "They are Doctor David Harris and his wife, Kate Harris. The residents and students who were here before they left the area will all remember 'Doc' as we called him, and Kate, who also worked in the office. Will you both please stand." The audience not only clapped loudly, but stood in honor of the old couple. When they sat back down, the principal said, "I would like for those of you who were brought into this world by Doctor Harris to stand." They were scattered over the auditorium and if anyone had counted, there would surely have been fifty people standing. Doc looked around at them and felt proud for having been a part of their lives.

"And you will remember the others on the first board of directors by having been told who they were but I would like to repeat their names. Of course, there were the founders of the school on the board, Joyce Abernathy Kelly, and her husband, Anson Kelly, who were Alyn Russell's adoptive parents and Anson being Kate Harris's father. Then, there was my deceased husband, Reverend Robert Russell, and of course, Mrs. Ella Fullman, who donated our first clinic. I want everyone to see our paintings in the entrance of Joyce and Anson Kelly, which were painted by Beth Russell, and also the painting of Mrs. Ella Fullman on the wall in the clinic. You all have seen the work being done on the old Fullman mansion by Doctor Nathaniel O'Bryan and his father Raymond O'Bryan. Would you two gentlemen please stand." This took the two men by surprise as they stood to be recognized for their restoring some of Union Gap's history. "You will also see some of Beth Russell's art work that will be hung there upon completion of the project." She paused there and then continued. "I do not want to leave out an important board member who took over as president after the death of Joyce Aberthany Kelly." She stretched out her hand toward where Alyn was sitting and said, "You all know our beloved Alyn Russell of Knollwood Orchards." Completely embarrassed at being surprised, he stood while Patricia added, "And our school has always been indebted to him for all the apples he has donated to our school for not only eating, but for home economic projects." Patricia looked around to where Teresa was sitting on the stage and said that the assistant principal has something to say now about two outstanding young students. She backed up to take a seat as Teresa came toward the microphone.

"It gives me great pleasure to tell you that there are two little students who are to receive awards for winning a writing contest. And I take pleasure also in announcing that their writings have been included in a published book of children's writings and the books are available here today for you to purchase autographed copies in the lobby for five dollars each after this program is over today." She turned to glance to the side of the stage to see the children who were waiting there to come out. "I'd like to call to the stage Miss Susan Russell and Mr. Timothy Silvers." The two children were waiting nervously with their mothers, both dressed in new outfits and looking like little movie stars. Timothy was asked to give the title of his story and tell what page it was on in the book. After congratulations and a handshake from Teresa, she handed him a wooden plaque; he said thank you, and then stood aside like a little gentleman. Susan was asked to recite her poem. She had practiced the poem so much that the family knew it by heart and was sick of hearing it. Susan could say it in her sleep. She stepped up to the mike like a professional, all her nervousness now gone, and recited her poem, "Springtime," without a hitch, smiled sweetly, gave a curtsy, and walked off to a thunderous applause and was called back to receive her plaque. Her grandfather stood up, placed his fingers between his lips, and let out a loud whistle. Beside him, Pete slid down in his seat, saying simply, "Yuck!"

The only boring part of the program was a speech by the board of directors president until the very end, when he dropped the bombshell about Principal Patricia Russell's retirement and the promotion of Teresa Russell to principal. Sad murmurs could be heard throughout about Mrs. Russell's retirement until the announcer added to his sentence, "Except I understand that Miss Russell will be returning as Mrs. Nathaniel O'Bryan," and then there was a loud round of applause.

The program went on for a while with more singing by students and a short final speech by Patricia Russell about the school's accomplishments and bright future. Kendell Mountain had come a long way over the years and would have, no doubt, exceeded all expectations of the founders, Joyce and Anson Kelly.

Chapter Fifty-Two

SUNDAY'S CHURCH SERVICE AT UNION GAP BAPTIST was so crowded that additional chairs had to be placed down the aisles alongside the pews. The preacher made a witty comment that they needed to have a wedding after service more often. Teresa wanted a simple service with the only decoration in the sanctuary being a beautiful flower arrangement in the baptistery and a tall basket arrangement in front of the choir rail. She relented when it came to decorating the Family Life Center for the reception and allowed the florist and caterer their freedom.

During the church service, the wedding party assembled in some basement rooms to dress; however, Alyn said he would show up from home in plenty of time, that is if his truck would start. He loved to tease his daughter and this day was no exception. The groom and his father lived nearby. They would appear in the church office before the service was over, which seemed to be long and drawn out to both the bride and the groom. Actually, Reverend Atkins cut his sermon short and at the sound of singing above their heads, the florist lined up the party in the basement. She assured the nervous bride that she had seen her father upstairs in the vestibule, and the groom and his dad were in the room behind the baptistery. She breathed a sigh of relief that all was going well and in order as they all went up the steps leading to where Alyn was waiting . . . with red eyes. When she appeared, wearing her mother's wedding gown and veil, he held out his arms, enfolding his baby girl to his chest, thinking that she was the image of the lovely bride that he had held in this very same dress. He unabashedly wiped away more tears, reached into a pocket and drew out a little velvet box, placing it in her hands. She opened the lid and lifted out a lovely string of pearls that he had given her mother on their wedding day. Her sparkling eyes revealed the joy she felt as her father fastened them around her neck.

Standing at the double doors ready to enter, they heard Tissy Russell singing the tender love song, "Because." When the last notes died away, the doors were opened and Nat turned, his glance drinking in his beautiful bride, holding her father's arm, with a soft sweet glow on her lovely face. Was this for real or was he dreaming?

The ushers entered and took their place at the altar, then the matron of honor, wearing a soft pink calf-length dress and a bouquet to match, followed by the bride's maid, dressed in the same style and color. Next was little Peter, dressed in a new suit and carefully carrying a pillow that had a ring attached.

As the bridal march intensified, Susan came in looking like she just stepped out of a Shirley Temple movie, scattering rose petals from a little basket. Then the bride came in on the arm of her father, her eyes sparkling, and looking straight ahead to where Nat O'Bryan was waiting at the altar.

Chapter Fifty-Three

PAPA RUSSELL HAD SOME SERIOUS THINKING TO DO. All his life, when he was feeling nostalgic or when he needed to sort something out, he went to his place of solitude, the overlook, where he could look out and see forever . . . or down upon the town . . . or up into a delphinium blue sky, dotted with fluffy white clouds.

The house was too quiet and he did not feel like rambling around in it alone, so shooing Ole Charlie out of his path, he took his truck out of the shed and started down the road with a sudden compulsion to go down to the overlook. John was working, Raymond was working, and Beth had taken all four kids—if he could still call Penny a kid . . . but not to her face—and the kids' grandmother to Atlanta to see the Ice Follies. They invited him to go along but that did not interest him in the least.

The truck chugged past the school grounds, now empty of teachers' parked cars, and the school empty of students. "It was a nice weekend," he thought, "a full weekend, too, but I'm glad it's all over." John had taken their guests to the airport after the wedding the previous day and, instead of taking two vehicles, Alyn elected to remain at home.

Further down the road, he rounded the bend and pulled off to the side, discovering Tissy's Chevy parked there where the beaten path led out to the overlook. He had been along this path so many times over the years that he was certain he had been the one to make the path in the first place. He remembered the time back when he first returned to Kendell Mountain after World War I, and he had rented a horse from old Lemmy

What's-'is-Name, at the livery stable, and rode up the mountain from the other side. He had gone to the Turner cabin, Tissy's family's place, to see if Deputy Turner could give him some information about Jim Abernathy, Aunt Joyce's brother. The deputy was not at home but this was the first time he encountered Tissy as a grown woman. When he was kidnapped from Kendell Mountain at age thirteen, Tissy was then only seven.

Now, as Alyn walked along the path, a covey of quail darted across in front of him into the brush, dispelling his thoughts. He had seen her car, so he knew she would be here, and obviously she was doing the same thing he had come here to do—think. Retiring after so many years of teaching surely must be traumatic for her. Or he could be intruding, for she may have brought Raymond up here to the huge boulder where so many lovers had sat over the years. Nothing was further from his mind than finding someone here. He brushed aside a vine hanging down from a tree limb and rounding a bend in the path, came to a clearing where he saw her sitting alone on the boulder, her arms folded across her lap. "Ahh, she is alone." Not wanting to frighten her, he coughed and she turned to see him.

"Well, I thought this was my private sanctuary," he grinned, as he climbed up and sat beside her.

"Yours? I was thinking it was only mine."

"After all, it is my property, you know."

"So . . . would you have me leave?"

"Don't be silly. You know I was only teasing. Wow! What a bang-up weekend we had, and you did a grand job, ma'm! It was all because of your hard work."

"Oh, you know that isn't so. It took a lot of hard work by a lot of dedicated people."

"Yeah, but I know who put it all together, and Teresa is going to have a long row to plough in order to fill your shoes."

"I don't have any qualms about her being a good leader," she answered, and changed the subject by adding that he really looked nice at the wedding. "In fact," she told him, "you were downright handsome."

"Flattery will get you anything, ma'm," he answered with a gleam of amusement. "But, maybe you are right, 'cause ole

Raymond said I clean up pretty good." Then he added that her song was great, as usual.

They were two friends sitting here in a dazzle of warm sunshine, looking down upon jade green pastures under an incredibly blue sky. The scene below them was a charming panorama of the town, ploughed fields on its outskirts, scattered lines of washing with white sheets waving a greeting to the two people high above on the boulder.

"It's breath-taking," Tissy said, drawing in a deep breath. "But I say that every time I come here."

"It was right here at this spot that Bob Russell proposed to me."

"And probably a lot of other couples made their great decision here, too," Alyn truthfully answered.

"Resa told me that Nat proposed to her at the falls," Tissy replied matter-of-factly.

"I asked Cynthee to marry me out of the blue while riding along in the truck." He was silent for a few moments as the statement he had just now said brought on another memory. "After I left her at the school that night, I smelled smoke . . ."

"Alyn, please don't rehash the fire again. We've had a wonderful weekend and this is not a time to be sad." Then she added, "Although I am rather sad because of the ending of an era."

"Well, I know you wouldn't be here yourself, Miss Smartie, if you weren't sad about that. We're just two old has-beens, aren't we?" Her quick smile altered the sad expression on his face.

"Yep. I suppose there always comes a time like this in everyone's life at some point." He reached out and picked up a little stone beside him on the boulder and tossed it over the cliff.

"You probably just hit somebody on the head down there," she said and made a face. They both grinned and then broke out into gales of laughter. He reached over and put an arm around her shoulder as friends are prone to do.

"Alyn, tell me, if you had your druthers, where would you like to go right now?"

"Oh, let me see. If you mean just for a nice vacation, I believe I would like to go to that far-away place where my aunt and uncle took me to when they whisked me away from Kendell Mountain on my thirteenth birthday. You know, when they kidnapped me and took me by force." She nodded that she understood and he continued, "We went down in the South Pacific to New Zealand. I'd really like to go there again. I remember what a beautiful place it was . . . all the sailboats and the parks with all sorts of strange trees and gorgeous flowers in every yard. And, I saw a lake full of black swans, snow-capped mountains and, ahhh, so much I couldn't do it justice by only telling you about it."

Both of them became silent, picturing the scenes that he had depicted in their own private thoughts. The group of buzzards they had been watching—Alyn called them country airplanes—riding air currents, now amassed together until they became as one and disappeared from sight. Impulsively, she broke the silence by saying, "Do any of us actually know what we really want?"

"Not really. Some people search their whole life and never find it."

"I think I'd like to get lost for a while myself and forget it all," she said casually.

His face broke into a smile, then he turned to Tissy and impulsively said, "Then, let's go together, Tis! Let's run away and get married and get on a plane and fly away to New Zealand!"

"Alyn Russell! Of all things! Why, I'm your aunt!"

"No, you're not! You never were. You were my uncle's wife, and you're not even that anymore. And, besides, I'm a lot older than you. Come on . . . what do you say? Let's shock the whole town! We'll be lovers who've run away!" They both laughed so loudly that the sound echoed down through the valley.

"Well, I'll have to go home and get my purse," Tissy laughed again, her assurance of a brighter future rising like her laughter.

Alyn took her hand and helped her down off he boulder. They stood there hugging one another, rocking and acting like young lovers. "You won't need your purse. I'll buy you another one in the city."

"But . . . my makeup and my toothbrush . . ."

"We'll buy that, too. Leave the old things behind."

They were walking hand-in-hand back toward the road. "We can't do that."

She looked up into his face and he saw stars in her eyes. "Why can't we?"

"Because we both are old."

"We are not."

"Are, too."

When they came to the hanging vine, Alyn stopped, put a finger under her chin tilting it upward and kissed her for the first time flat on the lips. "You know something? I've loved you for years. Never could get up the nerve to tell you."

"The feeling is mutual. I was afraid to admit it to myself."

"Want to know something else?"

"What now?"

"You'll still be Mrs. Russell, you know."

"Yes, I know."

"You hadn't rather be Mrs. O'Bryan?"

"Never," she answered, "I like being Mrs. Russell."

He kissed her again, then she said, "I do know one thing. You are either a romantic or a complete maniac!"

"Both of the above. Let's be irresponsible like young folks and live only for today, for who knows what tomorrow may bring? And who cares! Let's laugh and dance and feel free as those stupid buzzards flying on the currents."

"Yes, Alyn, let's, but . . . what about passports?"

"We'll see the justice of the peace in Atlanta first and then see about the passports."

"We'll have to leave John and Beth a note."

"Of course we will, and your daughter, too."

The gold of his youth had gone, but the twinkle in his brown eyes remained. They were drawn to her's, and he felt wonderful.

Yes! They would make that trip to New Zealand! He would cash in some of his savings bonds that he'd saved for his old age. After all, was this old age, or what?